Praise for *American Rust*

As featured in Patricia Cornwell's *Scarpetta*

'In Philipp Meyer a new American master is born. A tender chronicle of a civilisation's corrosion. yet always watchful for something in the human soul that remains untarnished, *American Rust* is a beautiful, bleak and ultimately redemptive masterpiece. The best book to come out of America since *The Road*' Chris Cleave, author of *The Other Hand*

'I look through his book even now because I admire his writing so much. The same way, frankly, that I do Hemingway' Patricia Cornwell, *New York Times*

'An elegiac portrait of a disintegrating society' *Financial Times*

'Meyer visits the North America immortalised by Steinbeck in this excellent Depression-era debut' *Metro*

'*American Rust* is so timely that it makes painful as well as enjoyable reading. The novel is a paean to the end of empire . . . Meyer's voice is assured, and the story crackles with narrative tension. He develops his characters with impressive psychological and sociological insight . . . masterfully painted' *Economist*

'This first novel surprises you with its sureness of tone, its narrative propulsion and the singular and perceptive way in which it steers clear of all the usual redneck clichés . . . More than anything, *American Rust* impresses because it reminds us that even the most archetypal of situations can be given an intriguing remake in the right hands. Meyer never wears his social conscience on his sleeve and he never tries to pander to the reader's metropolitan guilt. And, simultaneously, he does make you want to turn the page. This is a new writer who clearly knows what he's doing' Douglas Kennedy, *The Times*

D0376245

'Meyer has a thrilling eye for failed dreams and writes uncommonly tense scenes of violence ... Fans of Cormac McCarthy and Dennis Lehane will find in Meyer an author worth watching' *Publishers Weekly*

'With its strong narrative engine and understated social insight, *American Rust* is reminiscent of the best of Robert Stone and Russell Banks. Author Philipp Meyer locates the heart of his working class characters without false sentiment or condescension, and their world is artfully described. An extraordinary, compelling novel from a major talent' George Pelecanos

'[Meyer] has a documentarist's eye for an uncertain, self-destructing world, the lyrical style to nail a friendship in a sentence and an almost effortless devotion to a page-turning story. Debut novelists are often adept at one or two of those ingredients but Meyer's triumph with *American Rust* is to excel in all three' Book of the Week, 5 stars, *Metro*

'Meyer has created a desperate, tragic narrative, depicting with poetic economy the beauty of hills and rivers; a lush landscape underwritten by desolation. His writing glints with sharp dialogue, and he displays an almost virtuosic ability to change mode, from thought to voice, from colloquialism to lyrical description. But Meyer's triumph isn't simply that of a story teller, although he is masterful, driving through the narrative at an addictive pace. It is primarily the ability to occupy minds, twisting from character to character, allowing their thoughts to animate action and bring it dazzlingly to life' *New Statesman*

'Meyer creates a jigsaw of characters that click together into a vivid portrait that expertly shakes the blue collar of small-town America in an assured debut' 5 stars, *RTE Guide*

'With its lush, rustic hinterland populated, "like Indian times", by bears, coyotes, and deer, which surrounds a decaying industrial base, where all the town's steel mills have shut down, it is hugely evocative of Michael Cimino's movie, *The Deer Hunter*' *Irish Examiner*

'Honour, loyalty, love and belonging are the grand themes of this power-ful American novel, which owes as much to Steinbeck as Kerouac' Summer Reads, *Sunday Telegraph*

'The American dream dies and is reborn yet again. Set in a beautiful but bleak post-industrial landscape with characters who are compellingly engaging, *American Rust* is a startlingly mature and impressive debut' Kate Atkinson

'Philipp Meyer's *American Rust* is written with considerable dramatic intensity and pace. It manages an emotional accuracy, a deep and detailed conviction, in its depiction of characters. It also captures a sense of a menacing society, a wider world in the throes of decay and self-destruction' Colm Tóibín

Philipp Meyer grew up in Baltimore, dropped out of high school and got his GED when he was sixteen. After several years volunteering at a trauma centre in downtown Baltimore, he eventually got into Cornell University, where he studied English. Since graduating from Cornell, Meyer has worked as a derivatives trader at UBS, a construction worker, and an EMT, among other jobs. Meyer's writing has been published in *McSweeney's*, *The Iowa Review*, Salon.com, and *New Stories from the South*. From 2005–2008 he was a fellow at the Michener Center for Writers in Austin, Texas. Philipp has already won worldwide acclaim for *American Rust*, his first novel.

Visit www.philippmeyer.net

American Rust

Philipp Meyer

POCKET
BOOKS

LONDON · SYDNEY · NEW YORK · TORONTO

First published in Great Britain by Simon & Schuster UK Ltd, 2009
This edition published by Pocket Books, 2010
An imprint of Simon & Schuster UK Ltd
A CBS COMPANY

1 3 5 7 9 10 8 6 4 2

Simon & Schuster UK Ltd
1st Floor
222 Gray's Inn Road
London WC1X 8HB

Simon & Schuster Australia
Sydney

www.simonandschuster.co.uk

A CIP catalogue record for this book is available from the British Library

ISBN 978-1-84739-412-5

Printed by CPI Cox & Wyman, Reading, Berkshire RG1 8EX

For my family

"If there were no eternal consciousness in a man . . . if an un-
fathomable, insatiable emptiness lay hid beneath everything,
what would life be but despair?"

—SØREN KIERKEGAARD

". . . what we learn in time of pestilence: that there are more
things to admire in men than to despise."

—ALBERT CAMUS

Book
One

Book
One

1.

Isaac's mother was dead five years but he hadn't stopped thinking about her. He lived alone in the house with the old man, twenty, small for his age, easily mistaken for a boy. Late morning and he walked quickly through the woods toward town—a small thin figure with a backpack, trying hard to keep out of sight. He'd taken four thousand dollars from the old man's desk; *Stolen,* he corrected himself. The nuthouse prison-break. Anyone sees you and it's Silas get the dogs.

Soon he reached the overlook: green rolling hills, a muddy winding river, an expanse of forest unbroken except for the town of Buell and its steelmill. The mill itself had been like a small city, but they had closed it in 1987, partially dismantled it ten years later; it now stood like an ancient ruin, its buildings grown over with bittersweet vine, devil's tear thumb, and tree of heaven. The footprints of deer and coyotes criss-crossed the grounds; there was only the occasional human squatter.

Still, it was a quaint town: neat rows of white houses wrapping the hillside, church steeples and cobblestone streets, the tall silver domes of an Orthodox cathedral. A place that had recently been well-off, its down-town full of historic stone buildings, mostly boarded now. On certain blocks there was still a pretense of keeping the trash picked up, but others had been abandoned completely. Buell, Fayette County, Pennsylvania. Fayette-nam, as it was often called.

Isaac walked the railroad tracks to avoid being seen, though there weren't many people out anyway. He could remember the streets at shiftchange, the traffic stopped, the flood of men emerging from the billet mill coated with steeldust and flickering in the sunlight; his father, tall and shimmering, reaching down to lift him. That was before the accident. Before he became the old man.

It was forty miles to Pittsburgh and the best way was to follow the tracks along the river—it was easy to jump a coal train and ride as long as you wanted. Once he made the city, he'd jump another train to California. He'd been planning this for a month. A long time overdue. Think Poe will come along? Probably not.

On the river he watched barges and a towboat pass, engines droning. It was pushing coal. Once the boat was gone the air got quiet and the water was slow and muddy and the forests ran down to the edge and it could have been anywhere, the Amazon, a picture from *National Geographic*. A bluegill jumped in the shallows—you weren't supposed to eat the fish but everyone did. Mercury and PCB. He couldn't remember what the letters stood for but it was poison.

In school he'd tutored Poe in math, though even now he wasn't sure why Poe was friends with him—Isaac English and his older sister were the two smartest kids in town, the whole Valley, probably; the sister had gone to Yale. A rising tide, Isaac had hoped, that might lift him as well. He'd looked up to his sister most of his life, but she had found a new place, had a husband in Connecticut that neither Isaac nor his father had met. You're doing fine alone, he thought. The kid needs to be less bitter. Soon he'll hit California—easy winters and the warmth of his own desert. A year to get residency and apply to school: astrophysics. Lawrence Livermore. Keck Observatory and the Very Large Array. Listen to yourself—does any of that still make sense?

Outside the town it got rural again and he decided to walk the trails to Poe's house instead of taking the road. He climbed steadily along. He knew the woods as well as an old poacher, kept notebooks of drawings he'd made of birds and other animals, though mostly it was birds. Half the weight of his pack was notebooks. He liked being outside. He wondered if that was because there were no people, but he hoped not. It was lucky growing up in a place like this because in a city, he didn't know, his mind was like a train where you couldn't control the speed. Give it a track and direction or it cracks up. The human condition put names to everything: bloodroot rockflower whip-poor-will, tulip bitternut hackberry. Shagbark and pin oak. Locust and kingnut. Plenty to keep your mind busy.

Meanwhile, right over your head, a thin blue sky, see clear to outer space: the last great mystery. Same distance to Pittsburgh—couple miles of air and then four hundred below zero, a fragile blanket. Pure luck. Odds are you shouldn't be alive—think about that, Watson. Can't say it in public or they'll put you in a straitjacket.

Except eventually the luck runs out—your sun turns into a red giant and the earth is burned whole. Giveth and taketh away. The entire human race would have to move before that happened and only the physicists could figure out how, they were the ones who would save people. Of course by then he'd be long dead. But at least he'd have made his contribution. Being dead didn't excuse your responsibility to the ones still alive. If there was anything he was sure of, it was that.

* * *

Poe lived at the top of a dirt road in a doublewide trailer that sat, like many houses outside town, on a large tract of woodland. Eighty acres, in this case, a frontier sort of feeling, a feeling of being the last man on earth, protected by all the green hills and hollows.

There was a muddy four-wheeler sitting in the yard near Poe's old Camaro, its three-thousand-dollar paintjob and blown transmission. Metal sheds in various states of collapse, a Number 3 Dale Earnhardt flag pinned across one of them, a wooden game pole for hanging deer. Poe was sitting at the top of the hill, looking out toward the river from his folding chair. If you could find a way to pay your mortgage, people always said, it was like living on God's back acre.

The whole town thought Poe would go to college to keep playing ball, not exactly Big Ten material but good enough for somewhere, only two years later here he was, living in his mother's trailer, sitting in the yard and looking like he intended to cut firewood. This week or maybe next. A year older than Isaac, his glory days already past, a dozen empty beer cans at his feet. He was tall and broad and squareheaded and at two hundred forty pounds, more than twice the size of Isaac. When he saw him, Poe said:

"Getting rid of you for good, huh?"

"Hide your tears," Isaac told him. He looked around. "Where's your bag?" It was a relief to see Poe, a distraction from the stolen money in his pocket.

Poe grinned and sipped his beer. He hadn't showered in days—he'd been laid off when the town hardware store cut its hours and was putting off applying to Wal-Mart as long as possible.

"As far as coming along, you know I've got all this stuff to take care of." He waved his arm generally at the rolling hills and woods in the distance. "No time for your little caper."

"You really are a coward, aren't you?"

"Christ, Mental, you can't seriously want me to come with you."

"I don't care either way," Isaac told him.

"Looking at it from my own selfish point of view, I'm still on goddamn probation. I'm better off robbing gas stations."

"Sure you are."

"You ain't gonna make me feel guilty. Drink a beer and sit down a minute."

"I don't have time," said Isaac.

Poe glanced around the yard in exasperation, but finally he stood up. He finished the rest of his drink and crumpled the can. "Alright," he said. "I'll ride with you up to the Conrail yard in the city. But after that, you're on your own."

★   ★   ★

From a distance, from the size of them, they might have been father and son. Poe with his big jaw and his small eyes and even now, two years out of school, a nylon football jacket, his name and player number on the front and BUELL EAGLES on the back. Isaac short and skinny, his eyes too large for his face, his clothes too large for him as well, his old backpack stuffed with his sleeping bag, a change of clothes, his notebooks. They went down the narrow dirt road toward the river, mostly it was woods and meadows, green and beautiful in the first weeks of spring. They passed an old house that had tipped face-first into a sinkhole—the ground in the Mid-Mon Valley was riddled with old coal mines, some properly stabilized, others not. Isaac winged a rock and knocked a ventstack off the roof. He'd always had a good arm, better than Poe's even, though of course Poe would never admit it.

Just before the river they came to the Cultrap farm with its cows sitting in the sun, heard a pig squeal for a long time in one of the outbuildings.

"Wish I hadn't heard that."

"Shit," said Poe. "Cultrap makes the best bacon around."

"It's still something dying."

"Maybe you should stop analyzing it."

"You know they use pig hearts to fix human hearts. The valves are basically the same."

"I'm gonna miss your factoids."

"Sure you will."

"I was exaggerating," said Poe. "I was being ironic."

They continued to walk.

"You know I would seriously owe you if you came with."

"Me and Jack Kerouac Junior. Who stole four grand from his old man and doesn't even know where the money came from."

"He's a cheap bastard with a steelworker's pension. He's got plenty of money now that he's not sending it all to my sister."

"Who probably needed it."

"Who graduated from Yale with about ten scholarships while I stayed back and looked after Little Hitler."

Poe sighed. "Poor angry Isaac."

"Who wouldn't be?"

"Well to share some wisdom from my own father, wherever you go, you still wake up and see the same face in the mirror."

"Words to live by."

"The old man's been around some."

"You're right about that."

"Come on now, Mental."

They turned north along the river, toward Pittsburgh; to the south it was state forest and coal mines. The coal was the reason for steel. They passed another old plant and its smokestack, it wasn't just steel, there were dozens of smaller industries that supported the mills and were supported by them: tool and die, specialty coating, mining equipment, the list went on. It had been an intricate system and when the mills shut down, the entire Valley had collapsed. Steel had been the heart. He wondered how long it would be before it all rusted away to nothing and the Valley returned to a primitive state. Only the stone would last.

For a hundred years the Valley had been the center of steel production in the country, in the entire world, technically, but in the time since Poe and Isaac were born, the area had lost 150,000 jobs—most of the towns could no longer afford basic services; many no longer had any police. As Isaac had overheard his sister tell someone from college: *half the people went on welfare and the other half went back to hunting and gathering.* Which was an exaggeration, but not by much.

There was no sign of any train and Poe was walking a step ahead, there was only the sound of the wind coming off the river and the gravel crunching under their feet. Isaac hoped for a long one, which all the bends in the river would keep slow. The shorter trains ran a lot faster; it was dangerous to try to catch them.

He looked out over the river, the muddiness of it, the things buried underneath. Different layers and all kinds of old crap buried in the muck, tractor parts and dinosaur bones. You aren't at the bottom but you aren't exactly at the surface, either. You are having a hard time seeing things. Hence the February swim. Hence the ripping off the old man. Feels like days since you've been home but it has probably only been two or three hours; you can still go back. No. Plenty of things worse than stealing, lying to yourself for example, your sister and the old man being champions in that. Acting like the last living souls.

Whereas you yourself take after your mother. Stick around and you're bound for the nuthouse. Embalming table. Stroll on the ice in February, the cold like being shocked. So cold you could barely breathe but you stayed until it stopped hurting, that was how she slipped in. Take it for a minute and you start to go warm. A life lesson. You would not

have risen until now—April—the river gets warmer and the things that
live inside you, quietly without you knowing it, it is them that make you
rise. The teacher taught you that. Dead deer in winter look like bones,
though in summer they swell their skins. Bacteria. Cold keeps them down
but they get you in the end.

You're doing fine, he thought. Snap out of it.

But of course he could remember Poe dragging him out of the water, telling Poe *I wanted to see what it felt like is all.* Simple experiment.
Then he was under the trees, it was dark and he was running, mud-
covered, crashing through deadfall and fernbeds, there was a rushing in
his ears and he came out in someone's field. Dead leaves crackling; he'd
been cold so long he no longer felt cold at all. He knew he was at the end.
But Poe had caught up to him again.

"Sorry what I said about your dad," he told Poe now.

"I don't give a shit," said Poe.

"We gonna keep walking like this?"

"Like what?"

"Not talking."

"Maybe I'm just being sad."

"Maybe you need to man up a little." Isaac grinned but Poe stayed serious.

"Some of us have their whole lives ahead of them. Others—"

"You can do whatever you want."

"Lay off it," said Poe.

Isaac let him walk ahead. The wind was picking up and snapping
their clothes.

"You good to keep going if this storm comes in?"

"Not really," said Poe.

"There's an old plant up there once we get out of these woods. We
can find a place to wait it out in there."

The river was a dozen or so yards to their left and farther ahead the
tracks bordered a long floodplain with the grass bright green against the
black of oncoming clouds. In the middle of the field, a string of boxcars
swallowed by a thicket of wild rose. At one end of the floodplain was the
Standard Steel Car factory, he'd been inside it before, the plant was half-
collapsed, bricks and wood beams piled on top of the old forges and hy-

draulic presses, moss and vines growing everywhere. Despite the rubble, it was vast and open inside. Plenty of souvenirs. That old nameplate you gave to Lee, pried it off that big hammer forge, polished the tarnish off and oiled it. A minor vandalism. No, think of all the people who were proud of those machines, to rescue a few pieces of them—little bit of life after death. Lee put it over her desk, saw it when you went to New Haven. Meanwhile this rain is coming in. About to be cold and wet. Bad way to start your trip.

"Christ," said Poe, as the rain started to fall. "That plant doesn't even have a roof. Course with your luck I should have figured."

Isaac pointed: "There's another building back there that's in better shape."

"I can't wait."

Isaac walked ahead; Poe was in a foul mood and he wasn't sure what to do about it.

They followed a deer path that led through the meadow. They could see the smaller building beyond the main factory; half-hidden in the trees, it was dark and shaded. Or sheltered, he thought. A brick building, much smaller than the main plant, the size of a large garage, maybe, the windows boarded but the roof was intact. It was mostly grown over with vines though there was a clear path leading to it through the grass. The rain swept over them and they began to run and when they reached the building Poe shouldered the door. It swung open without any trouble.

It was dark inside but they could make out it had been a machine shop, maybe a dozen lathes and milling machines. A gantry and series of grinder stands for cutting tool bits, though the grinders themselves were missing and the lathes were missing their chucks and cross-feeds, anything a person could carry. There were empty bottles of fortified wine scattered everywhere, more beer cans. An old woodstove and signs of recent fires.

"Jesus H. Christ. Smells like about ten bums are taking a dirtnap under this floor."

"It'll be alright," said Isaac. "I'll get a fire going so we can dry off."

"Look at this place, it's like Howard Johnson's for bums; stacks of wood and everything."

"Welcome to my world."

"Please," Poe snorted, "you're a fuckin tourist, is all."

Isaac ignored him. He knelt in front of the stove and began to build a careful fire structure, tinder and then kindling and then stopping to look for the right-sized sticks. Not the best place but it'll do. Better than spending the rest of the day in wet clothes. This is what it'll be like being on the road, prioritizing the small comforts—simple life. Back to nature. You get tired of it you can always buy a bus ticket. Except then it won't mean anything—you could just buy another ticket and come back. The kid is not afraid. More to see this way—detour to Texas, the McDonald Observatory. Davis Mountains, nine-meter telescope, Hobby-Eberly. Try to imagine the stars through that—no different than being up there. Next best thing to astronauts. Very Large Array, New Mexico or Arizona, can't remember. See it all. No hurries, no worries.

"Don't look so happy," said Poe.

"I can't help it." He found some more small pieces and went back to building his fire, using his jackknife to shave splinters for tinder.

"You take for goddamn ever to do anything, you know that?"

"I like a one-match fire."

"Which, by the time you get it lit, it'll be dark and time to go, because I ain't spending the night here."

"I'll give you my sleeping bag."

"Fuck that," said Poe. "We've probably already caught tuberculosis just from being in here."

"We'll be fine."

"You're useless," Poe told him.

"What do you think you'll do when I'm gone?"

"I imagine I'll be extremely happy."

"Seriously."

"Quit it. I want someone to nag me, I'll talk to my mother."

"I'll talk to your mother."

"Yeah, yeah. You bring anything to eat?"

"Some nuts."

"You would."

"Hand over your lighter."

"What would be perfect right now is a pie from Vincent's. Christ I was up there the other day, the house special—"

"Lighter."

"I'd order us one but Nextel turned my phone off."

"Uh-huh."

"That was a joke," said Poe.

"Extremely funny. Give me your lighter."

Poe sighed and handed it over. Isaac got the fire going. It grew quickly. It was a good fire. He kicked the door of the stove all the way open and then sat back and looked at his work with satisfaction.

"You'll still be smiling when this place burns down on top of us."

"For someone who put two guys in the hospital—"

"Don't go there," said Poe.

"I wouldn't."

"You know I think you're an alright guy, Mental. Just wanted to throw that out, in case you could consider my opinion."

"You could probably walk onto any football team out there. They've got lots of colleges, it's like *Baywatch*."

"Except everyone I know lives here."

"Call that coach from the New York school."

Poe shrugged. "I'm happy for you," he said. "You're gonna make it, just like your sister. Right down to the rich guy you'll end up marrying. Some sweet old man, you'll do the circuit in San Francisco . . ."

There was a pause as they looked around the hideout. Poe got up and found a piece of cardboard and set it down again to lie on. "I'm still drunk," he said. "Thank God." He lay back on the cardboard and closed his eyes. "Ah Christ, my life. I can't believe you're doing this."

"Boxcar Isaac, that's my new name."

"Loved by sailors."

"Duke of all hoboes."

Poe grinned. "If that's your way of apologizing, I accept." He rolled onto his side and wrapped his football jacket around him. "Might rest my eyes a minute. Make sure you wake me up the second it stops raining."

Isaac kicked him: "Get up."

"Just let me be happy."

Isaac went back to watching the fire. Seems to be drawing—won't die of carbon monoxide. Kick him again. No. Let him be. Probably pass out. Anytime he sits still. Not like you—barely fall asleep in your own bed. Wouldn't even close your eyes in a place like this. Wish he was coming with. He looked around at the old machines, old rafters, cracks of gray light through the boarded-up windows. Poe is not afraid of people, that's the difference. Except he is in his way. Not physically afraid, is all. Meanwhile, look at you, already worrying, wondering if the old man's alright. When you know he'll be fine. Lee has a rich husband—they can get a nurse whenever they want. No reason as long as you lived there, but now that you're gone, a nurse will be found. Lee will buy her way out again. You put in five years and she puts in a couple of days every Christmas, her and the old man acting like it was fate. But still—look at it—somehow you're ending up the bad guy. The kid turns thief, abandons his father, his sister remains the hero and the favorite.

He tried to make himself relax but couldn't. The kid would like a triple dose of Prozac. Or something stronger. He took the money out and counted it again, it was not quite four thousand dollars, it felt like an enormous sum, though he knew it wasn't. Things will only get harder, you've got Poe right here and you're still in familiar territory. Thought you'd planned for everything, your notebooks and school transcripts, everything you need to start over in California. Made perfect sense on paper, but of course now it's ridiculous. Even if the old man doesn't call the cops. Just pride keeping you out here.

There was a noise at the other end of the building and Poe sat up groggily and looked around. There was a door they hadn't noticed. Three men appeared, stomping their feet and dripping, wearing backpacks. They were standing in the shadows, two tall men and one short one.

"Y'all are in our spot," said the biggest of them. He was substantially taller than Poe, thick blond hair and a thick beard. The three of them made their way around the machines and stood a few feet from the fire.

Isaac stood up but Poe didn't move. "This ain't anyone's spot," Poe said.

"No," said the man. "This one is ours."

"Dunno if you've been outside recently," said Poe, looking at the puddles the men were making on the floor, "but we ain't moving."

"We can go," said Isaac. He was thinking about the money in his pocket and he looked away from the newcomers. He thought the big blond lumberjack one might say something more but he didn't.

"Who gives a shit," said another of the men. "Least they got the fire going." He took off his pack. He was the smallest and also the oldest, somewhere in his forties, a week's stubble, a thin nose that was very crooked, it had been broken and never reset. Isaac remembered that Poe had been messing around at practice once without his helmet, taken a hard hit that broke his nose, but he'd just grabbed it and straightened it himself, right there on the field.

The three men looked like they'd been on the road a long time. The older one wrung out his watch cap and set it near the fire and his wet pants clung to his thin legs. He told them his name was Murray and they could smell him.

"Do I know you?" he said to Poe.

"Probably not."

"How would I know you?"

Poe shrugged.

"He used to play ball," said Isaac. "He was tight end for the Buell Eagles."

Poe gave Isaac a look.

The man noticed Poe's football jacket draped near the stove. He said: "I remember that. I used to change oil at Jones Chevy and we'd watch the games after work. Thought you'd be outta here. College ball or somethin."

"Nah," Poe said.

"You were good," Murray said. "That wasn't that long ago."

Poe didn't say anything.

"It's alright. Otto over there was Golden Gloves in his younger days. Coulda gone pro but—"

"I was in the army," said Otto. He was the tall Swede. Most of the people in the Valley were ethnic in some way or other: Poles, Swedes, Serbs, Germans, Irish. Except for Isaac's people, who were Scottish, and Poe's, who had been here so long no one knew what they were.

"Otto is on leave from the VA." Murray tapped his head.

"Fuckin Murray," Otto said.

Isaac glanced over but Otto had gone quiet and was staring at the ground. As for the other man, he was dark and Hispanic-looking and a little smaller than Poe, he had a tattoo on his neck that said JESÚS in bubble letters. All three of the men were much larger than Isaac; the Swede, it now appeared, was close to seven feet.

"You're lucky it was us come in," said the Hispanic one. "They got some real lunatics around here."

"Jesús," said Murray. "Stop being such a fuckin Mexican."

"Murray might want to shut his mouth," said Jesús.

Otto, the Swede, added: "Pretty soon it's a fuckin convention in here."

"These two ain't like that, they're locals."

The room seemed dark and small and the Swede picked up a long piece of lumber and rammed the end noisily into the stove. Isaac wondered how he'd get Poe to leave. The embers popped and shot across the floor and by the shadows on the wall all five men looked like sitting apes. This won't get any better, Isaac thought. Jesús jerked something from his pocket and Isaac flinched and Jesús burst out laughing. It was just a bottle of whiskey.

"I gotta take a piss," Isaac said. He didn't have to piss; he wanted to leave and he looked at Poe but Poe didn't get it.

"Go on," Poe said.

"Those two usually piss together," said Jesús.

Isaac waited but Poe stayed where he was, staring at both Jesús and the Swede, he noticed Poe's jacket sitting there on the floor along with his backpack. Poe was in a definite mood, thinking he was indestructible. Isaac picked up the backpack, he could not afford to lose anything inside it, he held it by a strap and felt everyone watching him. He didn't know how to tell Poe to bring his coat. Finally he went out alone.

It was nearly dark and the storm had broken temporarily, though more clouds were coming in—across the meadow he could see the trees swaying by the river. He wondered again how he'd get Poe to come out. Thinks it's still school. No consequences. As for the field, it was full of scrap metal, tall grass grown up around piles of train parts, huge engine blocks, wheels, driveshafts and gears. A handful of bats were cutting and darting over the piles of rusted steel.

There was a patch of high clouds in the bloodorange light and he watched until the sun faded completely. He didn't know whether to go back and get Poe or if Poe would come out on his own. Poe was always doing these things. He'd nearly gone to jail for beating up a kid from Donora, he was still on probation for it. He can't resist a fight, not something you understand. Probably it's not his fault. Probably you can't be as big as him without having some kind of robot mentality.

Suddenly there were raised voices from inside the building, then shouting and banging around. Isaac tightened the straps on his pack and picked an escape route across the field and waited for Poe to come running. But Poe did not appear. Keep waiting, he told himself, just sit tight. The shouting and noises stopped. Isaac waited a while longer. Maybe it's okay. No, something is wrong. You have to go back in.

His hands were shaking but he took the money from his pocket and stuffed it deep inside his backpack and then quickly hid the pack under a piece of sheet metal. This is fine. The kid's got this under control. Don't go in empty-handed. He saw a short length of iron pipe but it would just get taken away from him. Underneath the other scrap—he reached his hand carefully through the stack of rusted metal to where a dozen or so industrial ball bearings were scattered in the dirt. He picked one up. It was the size of a baseball, or larger, cold and very heavy. Maybe too heavy. He wondered if there was something else. No, there's no time. Get in there. Don't use that same door.

After coming quietly through the back door he could see what was happening. Murray was laid out on the ground. The Mexican was standing behind Poe holding something to Poe's neck; his other hand was down Poe's crotch. Poe had both hands in the air like he was telling the man to calm down. They were standing in the light from the fire with their backs to him. Isaac was in the dark, invisible to others.

"Otto," the Mexican shouted. "I ain't got all fuckin day."

"Your little buddy ain't outside," said a voice. "He must of already took off."

The Swede came back from the other side of the building with his face shining in the firelight, grinning at Poe like he was happy to see him.

Isaac found his grip on the bearing, felt how heavy it was, five pounds, six pounds, he rocked to his back leg and threw as hard as he could; he threw so hard he felt the muscles in his shoulder tear. The bearing disappeared in the darkness and there was a loud crack as it hit the Swede in the center of the head, just at the top of his nose. The Swede seemed frozen in place and then his knees went loose and he seemed to fall straight down, a building collapsing on itself.

Poe broke loose and went running out the door; Isaac stood frozen for a second, watching the man he'd hit, the hands and feet were twitching slightly. Go, he thought. Murray was still lying on the ground but Jesús was now kneeling over the Swede, talking to him, touching his face, though Isaac already knew—knew from how heavy the bearing was, knew from how hard he'd thrown it.

*   *   *

They could barely make out the train tracks in the darkness. It was raining again. Isaac's hands and face were slick with mud and his shoes were heavy with it and he was soaked through but from sweat or rain he didn't know.

You need your pack, he thought. No, you can't go back there. How bad is that guy hurt? That thing was really heavy, your arm hurts just from throwing it. You shouldn't have hit him in the face.

Up ahead, they could see the lights from Buell; they were getting close. Poe turned suddenly and began to make his way through the brush toward the river.

"I need to wash myself," he told Isaac.

"Wait till you get home."

"He touched me right on the skin."

"Wait till you're home," Isaac repeated. His voice sounded like it was coming from somewhere else. "That water won't clean it anyway."

The rain was turning into sleet and Poe was wearing only his T-shirt. Soon he'll be hypothermic, Isaac thought. Neither of you are thinking straight, but he's in worse shape—give him your coat.

He took off his coat and handed it over to Poe. After hesitating, Poe tried to put it on, though it was too small. He handed it back.

Isaac heard himself say: "We should run so you can get warm."

They jogged for a while but it was too slippery. Poe went down twice in the mud, he was in bad shape, and they decided to walk again. Isaac could not stop thinking about the man lying there, it had looked like blood coming down his face but it could have been the light, or anything. All I did was knock him out, he told himself, but he was pretty sure that wasn't true.

"We need to get to a phone so we can call 911 for that guy. There's one at the Sheetz station."

Poe didn't say anything.

"It's a payphone," said Isaac. "They won't know it was us."

"That's not a good idea," said Poe.

"We can't just leave him."

"Isaac, there was blood coming out of his eyes and the way he was moving around it was just reflexes. If you hit a deer in the spine it does the same thing."

"We're talking about a person, though."

"We call an ambulance, the cops will be right behind them."

Isaac could feel his throat get tight. He thought again about how the Swede had gone over. He'd made no effort to stop his fall, and then the way his arms and legs kept moving afterward. A person knocked out didn't move at all.

"We should have gotten out of there when those guys showed up."

"I know that," said Poe.

"Your mom is friends with Bud Harris."

"Except technically the guy you hit wasn't doing anything. It was the guy holding me."

"It's a little more complicated than that," said Isaac.

"I dunno," Poe told him. "I can't really think right now."

Isaac began to walk faster.

"Isaac," Poe called. "Don't do anything stupid."

"I won't tell anyone. You don't have to worry."

"Hold up a second." Poe grabbed him by the shoulder. "You did the right thing, we both know that."

Isaac was quiet.

Poe nodded up the road. "Anyway, I need to cut off here to take the back way to the house."

"I'll walk you."

"We need to split up."

Isaac must have had a look on his face, because then Poe said: "You can go back to the old man's for one night; it won't kill you."

"That's not the point."

"You did the right thing," Poe repeated. "In the morning when our heads are straight we can figure this all out."

"We need to be figuring it out right now."

Poe shook his head. "I'll meet you at your place in the morning."

Isaac watched as he turned away and made his way up the dark road toward his mother's house. He paused once and waved. Once Poe was out of sight, Isaac continued down the tracks in the darkness, alone.

2. Poe

He went up the muddy road toward his mother's trailer. He'd tried to keep his head on in front of Isaac, the last thing Isaac needed to see was Poe going batshit. But it was a definite possibility. At least it was dark, it was comforting, there was no one to see him like this, he thought about the way the knife had felt to his neck and the man's hand on him. The rain had picked up again, back into sleet and then flurries. He was extremely cold, he'd left his jacket at the machine shop where the big one named Otto was lying dead. He was so cold he would have given anything for a jacket or even the shittiest hat you could even imagine, he would give a gallon of blood for just a shit wool hat and good Christ anything for a coat, a plastic garbage bag, even. He thought he ought to run to get warm but he could barely manage a walk. He thought he would make it to the house. It occurred to him he had not split any of the wood for the stoves, as always he'd left it to the last minute then gone off with Isaac and the house would be freezing, out of wood and the electric heaters costing thirty a day, his mother would never turn them on and with her hands all rheumatoid she couldn't swing the axe.

He hoped his mother wasn't too cold for having a shit son like him. Sitting in that doublewide with her hands all clawed up from the arthritis you are a shit a genuine shit who cannot even keep your own mother

warm, a fucking chickenshit punk can't even keep his hours at a goddamn hardware store. He wondered what Isaac had thrown at that prick,
something heavy, a big rock, it had smashed his face in he'd seen it.
Pushed his forehead back into his skull. Puke if you remember it too
much. Big fucking rock it must have been. Isaac and Otto, a match from
heaven. Thanking Christ for his arm like that. Saving my life. Getting
cockhandled by those bums and pissing your pants the cherry on top.

Now the one night he needed the house to be warm it would be
freezing, needed that heat for being an accessory to murder, really self-
defense only it was murder now, walked away from the body but good
Christ if anyone thought he would call the cops on those fucks with that
dead one Otto a smile on his face wide as a goddamn stadium walking
toward me, walking toward me while I had a knife to my neck and someone's hand crushing my nuts, not much question on what he was thinking about. Yes he thought this is what girls must feel like when a stranger
puts hands on them. Not a feeling that goes away in a hurry.

The thought of Otto lying there rotting a goddamn coyote eating his
face it made Poe feel almost warmer, if you'd asked him that morning
he'd never hated anyone but now by Jesus he hated the dead one Otto
the way he smiled seeing Poe getting held literally by his balls and even
more he hated the one with the beard who'd cut his neck and held him
like that and as for the third one, the older one, he had not meant to kick
him so hard. He couldn't remember his name, the older one who had
tried to keep the fight from starting, the older one who smelled so bad.
He wished he hadn't kicked him so hard. Yeah he was the good one. The
one you hit hardest.

It was not murder but what they were doing it did not look good. He
knew he had started it. He knew when Isaac went out to piss he wasn't
really pissing. It was the old Billy Poe fire going and it was not the first
time it had caused a predicament. He'd wanted to lay hands on those
fucks. Thought I'll take all three of them, thought that will be fucking
something I'll take all three, only they'd nearly killed him and it was little
Isaac English who ended up on top, literally killing and not even just
hurting that big Swede. With the stone and not the sword, as they said.
Christ he thought they will give you the goddamn chair. Don't give a

shit, wish it was both of those fucks dead, the one Otto and the bearded Mexican who cut my neck and goddamn cockhandled me, felt his fingers on my penis. He touched himself between his legs, it was very tender and even jostling it sent waves up into his stomach and he had to stand still a second. He would clean himself with soap. Soap and hot water. Hot bath and soap. It was a big fucking knife but Jesus it was a serious knife. You're alright now. He saw the lights of the trailer up ahead. He thought he would make it.

He got closer and saw his mother's shape watching for him in the window and he realized he would have to tell her what happened, how his pants got reeking like piss and his neck cut and his walking in a snow-storm nearly frozen to death in a T-shirt. He moved slowly off the road into the trees at the edge of the yard, he would wait until she went to bed, can't tell her those things. She'd tell his father though Christ this town he'll hear anyhow. He thought his mother might be letting that old bastard move back in. Seeing him out with that fucking math teacher, twenty-four fucking years old. He winks at me. Didn't tell Mom about it only I should have because now she is letting him back. Only she is in a bad state and maybe it is what she needs, the other assholes she's bring-ing home aren't any better, that older guy was fine but the rest of them sitting on the goddamn couch watching TV while she cooks their din-ners, acting like king of the castle, couple of those I should have beat with the axe handle for treating her like that. Look on their faces like they thought they could do better. Told that fat one with his Honda mo-torcycle *this ain't your fuckin house* and he stopped smiling when he real-ized I'd break his jaw. Should have done it but Jesus the look on her face when she heard me say that. Didn't speak to me for days. Mental note if you make it to forty remember on how all those fucks treated her. Stop being an asshole while you're still young.

He sat down under a tree. He watched the flurries land on the grass, had a faint awareness that time was passing and he began to feel warmer, sitting there under the hemlock. The miracle being it was Isaac who'd saved him. He didn't look like much, his wrists and hands were so thin. Delicate, that was the word you would use for Isaac, his face as well, he was light-boned, it was not a man's face. It was the face of a boy, bug-eyed, people teased him about his eyes. He was an easy target but Poe had always defended him, he had a much easier time because of Poe. Poe was king back then, glory days. Two years gone by since. Now Isaac was the only one who didn't look down on him. The others were all happy to see the king come back to earth, he had been someone and now he was not—that was a story everyone liked to hear. The human race—they despised anyone they thought was better than them. The sad thing being it was all in their own minds, he didn't think he was better than anyone. He had no such illusions. He had always known it wouldn't last. He had made friends with Isaac, who had no other friends—and why? Because he liked him. Because Isaac was the smartest person in the Valley, maybe the entire state, Pennsylvania—it was not a small place. Though possibly, he could admit it, he'd known that hanging out with Isaac would get him points with Lee.

The wind, he thought. Getting out of that wind was all it took. He kept sitting and felt warmer. He felt better and he thought it must really be warming up now, it was definitely warming up, so why could he still see the flakes swirling in the porchlight. He had not always defended Isaac, that was the truth of it. Isaac did not know about those moments but they had occurred and there was no undoing them.

Except that things equaled out. Two months back the river had been frozen over, skim ice, Isaac had looked at him and said you dare me and then stepped off the rocks and only made it a few steps before he broke right through and disappeared. Poe had stood panicked for a minute and then jumped in after him, crashing through the junk ice, he'd dragged Isaac out of the water, both of them soaking wet and nearly frozen to death, Isaac who had gone swimming in the river like his mother. If that wasn't a sign, he didn't know—he had saved Isaac and now Isaac saved him. It showed you there was a reason for all of it.

He looked at their trailer, his mother had not wanted to buy it but there was a lot of land and his father had wanted the land. Somehow he won that one, but then they split up and his mother was stuck with the trailer in the boonies. His mother, who talked about moving to Philadelphia, who'd done several semesters at college. Who used to roll out of bed looking good but now goes shopping in dirty old sweatpants and her hair tangled up. That and her husband leaving her. Your own situation not doing much to ease her mind, either, should have gone off to college if only for her. He decided to think about something else: all this wetness and sun the grass will be fresh tomorrow and the rabbits will be out. Wild meat heals you. Stew and a beer for lunch. He thought maybe there was some of last year's venison in the freezer but nothing was as good as a fresh rabbit, stew it a couple three hours falling off the bone. Or pound it flat and dip it in Bisquick and fry it. Yes it was the wild meat, before the games he ate it and now it would sort him out as well. So get up. He watched himself from a great distance. English won't tell anyone they grabbed you like that but so what, saved you—owe him now. Whatever he says you have to do. Probably tell his sister about it. She won't care, though. He didn't want to think about Lee. He had trouble thinking about Lee anyway but especially right now, not to mention she'd gotten married, she hadn't told him, she hadn't told him a goddamn thing about that, even though he'd always known it was just fun and games between them. He watched the flurries in the light, it was warm under the tree watching the snow come down, something is wrong, he thought, he couldn't quite put his finger on it, everything was quiet.

*   *   *

Grace Poe was sitting in the trailer in the shapeless gray sweatsuit she wore nearly every day now, even when going to town. She didn't know how long she'd been sitting there, staring at the brown panel walls inside the trailer. She'd turned the TV off to let herself think, it might have been nearly an hour, recently she'd come to prefer it to the television, just sitting and thinking, crazy thoughts, she was imagining herself on a trip to the Holy City, a trip she knew she would never take. She imagined herself on a steep rocky coast in Italy, all the old castles and the hot sun, hot and dry. Easy on the bones. Lots of wine and everyone suntanned.

Outside it was not quite as dark as normal, the storm clouds carried light from the town. She thought she'd seen her son coming up the road. Maybe she'd just imagined it. You're turning into an old lady, she thought, you're going a little bit crazy. It was either tragic or funny. She decided it was funny. She was annoyed at her son—they were out of firewood and she was wrapped under two blankets and it wasn't so much to ask, keep the wood split and the house warm. It was okay to be angry about that. It wasn't as if they were going to freeze, there were electric baseboard heaters but they cost a fortune, it was out of the question to run them. The best thing would be installing propane or oil heat, but she hated living in a trailer and for years she'd been hoping to move out of it. Buying a real furnace, sinking money into the trailer, was like giving up. It was better to be cold. She got up and went to the window, looking through her reflection, but nothing was moving in the road or the field, just the quiet emptiness that was always there. She had never expected she would live in a trailer, never expected she would live in the country.

She looked back at her reflection. Forty-one and her hair had gone mostly gray, she'd stopped dying it when her husband moved out, to spite him or herself, she didn't know, but she'd put on weight, too, it was bunching up under her chin. She'd always been a little heavy but it had never showed in the face. It seemed to her that even her eyes were going dull, burning down like old headlights. Soon enough she would have the kind of face you saw and could not imagine as anything but old. Cut the pity party, she told herself. You could take care of yourself a little better. She was right to let Virgil come back. Virgil would not have let the stoves sit empty.

As for Virgil, she had her hopes but it was getting not to matter—the ones her age, if they had jobs, would stay around a few weeks, months at most. Each time she'd gotten her hopes up and each time it'd spoiled, they all wanted to be taken care of, for dinner to appear in front of them, it should have been a joke but it wasn't. Half of them didn't even put any effort into sex, you would have thought there'd at least be the dignity of that, but not even. At the library she'd signed up for an Internet dating service, but all the men her age were looking for women much younger, and even in the bars it seemed there was nothing for her but the fifty- and sixty-somethings, men expecting to screw women they could be the fathers of. So at least Virgil was coming back. Yes, she thought, now that it's convenient for him, quiet little mouse that you are.

The snow was beginning to fall harder and she saw someone moving at the edge of the yard, drunk, she thought, playing around, pissing his name in the snow while the stoves are out of wood. Years earlier, just after Virgil left, she'd gotten a job offer in Philadelphia and she'd nearly taken it but Billy was doing so well in school, playing football, and she'd still had hopes that Virgil would come back to her quickly. She knew what that life would have looked like—thirty-five, apartment in the city, night school, single mom—like a movie. She would have married a lawyer. Finished her own degree. Instead she was living in Buell in a trailer with her spoiled child, man, whatever he was now, her son who had nearly had everything, a football scholarship, but had decided to stay home with his mother, going hungry if she didn't cook his dinner. She wondered why she was in such a bad mood. Maybe something was happening.

She decided to go out to the porch. Her feet got cold and wet but it was beautiful outside, it was all white, the trees, grass, the neighbor's empty house, it was like a painting, really, a spring snowfall, a month out of season, you could see the green underneath, it was very peaceful. "Billy," she said quietly, as if her voice might disturb the scene. He was sitting under a tree at the edge of the yard. Something was wrong. There was snow in his hair and he didn't have a coat. She leaned over the porch railing. He didn't look up.

"Billy," she called. "Come inside."

He didn't move.

She ran out into the yard in her bare feet. When she reached him his eyes moved slowly, focused on her, then looked at something else. His face was white and there was a gash on his neck and blood had come down onto his shirt and stained it. She shook him. "Get up," she said.

She tried to pull him up but he was dead weight, no, she thought, this is not fair, she got an arm under him but he still wasn't helping her, he was so heavy, she wouldn't be able to lift him, he barely seemed to know she was there. He was so cold he could have been a log or a rock. "Get up," she shouted at him, her voice muted by the snow. He pushed weakly with his legs and then they were standing and she told him we are going to walk now, we are going to walk to the house.

She got him to the bathroom, set him in the bathtub in his clothes. She ran hot water into the tub and took his shoes off.

"What happened," she said, but his eyes were somewhere else. The hot water was pouring into the tub but he stared numbly ahead. He didn't know her. The water turned the color of mud. There was a strong odor; she wondered distantly when he had washed himself last, he had not been taking care of himself, she knew that, getting laid off from the hardware store had sent him into a tailspin, she should have done more. She had decided to let him find his own way. She had made the wrong decision. His skin was white and icy to the touch and she pushed his shoulders deeper under the water.

The steam filled the room and the scab on his neck loosened and his cuts were running and the water nearly black from dirt and blood. She was kneeling and splashing the warm dirty water on his face. His body had cooled it and she drained it partially and ran more hot in. After a few minutes he began to shiver as he warmed up. She couldn't remember if you were supposed to warm a person this fast. She knew there was something you were not supposed to do, you warm them too fast and they die. She sat him up and wiped the scratch on his neck with iodine, the brown stain ran down into his shirt.

"Let's get these clothes off," she said, the soft mothering voice she hadn't used in years. He let her take his shirt off. She undid his belt, undid the button on his filthy jeans, tried to get them off but he was holding them up with both hands—he would not let her take his pants down.

"Billy."

He didn't say anything.

"Let go," she said.

He did and she took the pants off with some difficulty, careful to leave his underwear in place. The cut on his neck was bleeding again, it was straight and deep, done with a knife, she realized, like a piece of cut meat, she saw a hint of whiteness, unnatural-looking, she knew it must be the tendon or some other kind of tissue. She tried to remember if she had locked the door. Virgil had left a shotgun but she didn't know where the shells were.

"Is someone coming after you?" she said. She shook him. "Billy. Billy, is someone going to be coming here?"

"No," he said. He was waking up.

"Look at me."

"No one is coming," he said.

She saw spots in front of her. It is too hot in this room, she told herself. Her head was getting light. Next time you see him like this won't be in this house, he'll be laid out on a table in a hospital basement. She picked up his wet pants and began folding them, he had pissed his pants when they cut him. Now he was lying there flushed and awake and looking at his pants in her hand.

He sat up and reached and she leaned over the tub to hold him. He took the pants from her hand.

"I can wash them myself," he said.

*   *   *

When she left, Poe stripped his shorts off and scrubbed himself where the bum had grabbed him. The cut on his neck stung and he remembered knowing Isaac had left him, for a second all he'd thought was fucking Isaac he left you here and then he'd felt the cutting burning on his neck. He'd felt the cutting and he'd gone loose, done what was expected of him. Would have cut me all the way, Jesús his name was, Jesús the cocksucking Mexican who is still alive now somewhere, he was not a cruel person but help me Father I'll find him I'll put a stick through his ankles and hoist him up and skin him. Poe could imagine him screaming and the thought of that, of old Jesús screaming as Poe skinned him alive it nearly gave Poe a hard-on or maybe he would gut him first, field-dress him, as it were, leave his guts all hanging out so old Jesús could get a long look. Christ, he thought, listen to yourself. Your fucking brain is out of adjustment. He splashed water on his face. The Mexican had squeezed on his balls so hard he'd tasted the puke come up. That was when he pissed himself. *I ain't kiddin,* said Jesús. *I'll cut these off you don't settle down quick.* He'd felt the air going in and out of him and the man's heart beating against his back the way you feel a girl's heart beating when you're on top of her it was fucking disgusting and he'd let it happen, he wanted to sink back under the water and never come up.

He remembered that enormous fucking crack, though, it sounded like a pistol and the Mexican let go and Poe took off toward the door. He saw Otto, the eyes all bulged out Otto was crying blood and it was swelling from his mouth and ears. Isaac was waiting for him by the door, he was a good man Isaac no doubt about that, a fucking standup human man. Though he might say otherwise he was not sure, when the moment of truth came, that he himself could have done that for someone. He was not that kind of person, that was the truth of it. That was a thing he knew about himself. Whereas Isaac—Poe would have wanted to but he might not have been able. Might not have been capable of making his feet take him in the direction. He had always suspected that but now he was sure. Except I would have gone back for Isaac, he thought. Maybe not for someone else but definitely for him.

He knew Otto must still be right where he fell. They wouldn't try to bury him—burying a dead body, you're fucked if you get caught doing that. He wondered if they would go to Harris, everyone knew Harris hated bums but maybe these guys didn't know. Maybe they would tell him and Harris would have no choice but to check it out. Went with Mom for a while. He wondered if his mother had done it with Chief Harris. There was no question about it. Bud Harris had gotten Poe out of an assault charge. Everyone knew about that—that Poe had gotten a free ride for what he'd done to the kid from Donora. This time Harris would not be able to help him.

After a time he got out and dressed and went into the living room. He was so exhausted he could barely keep his head up. The house was dark, she'd turned nearly all the lights off, but it was warm and he could tell by the singed dusty smell that she'd turned the baseboard heaters on. He felt guilty but also relieved.

She said: "Was anyone else with you?"

"Isaac English."

"Is he okay?"

"Better than me."

"Your father is coming over."

"Did you tell him?"

"No. I just thought I should warn you."

"Does that mean he's back for good?"

"I don't know yet." she said. "We'll see."

He sat on the opposite side of the couch from her and then she pulled him over and he laid his head in her lap. His head was against her belly. He let his eyes close and he stopped thinking about the Mexican, he could hear her breathing in her belly and everything was going to be fine and he fell asleep immediately.

He slept like that for half an hour and then they heard his father's truck in the driveway. Poe got up and his mother gave him a hurt look and he tried to smile at her but he didn't think he could stand taking any shit from Virgil right now. He went to his room.

He could hear Virgil and his mother talking. Soon they would either be yelling or screwing. He figured the yelling would come soon enough—he'd seen enough of his father to know where this would go. But the next sound Poe heard was the maul ringing against the wedges, the sound of Virgil splitting the wood that Poe himself was supposed to split. Shit he thought shit shit shit, it should have been him going out there and doing it but it was too late, he'd fucked it up and now the old man would get the credit.

He thought about Otto again, thought you should call Chief Harris, he got you out of the last scrape, only it was too late for that, too—now they would look guilty. It was not that simple anyway. Technically, the big Swede hadn't been doing anything. He was about to, that was for goddamn sure, but really all he'd done was toss a couple of punches. He thought about him there on the floor of the machine shop with his head all bashed in and he felt guilty. He was supposed to be in college right now, going to class, his coach at Buell High, Dick Cannedy, old Dick had gotten Poe into three colleges, that one Colgate in upstate New York looked good but he wasn't ready. No, the truth was he'd been plenty ready, if they'd left him alone he would have gone. But when everyone is shouting at you to do something . . . He'd flipped them all off, given the entire town the middle finger, turned down college for a job at Turner's Ace Hardware. And he'd flip them off again when he disappeared suddenly and went away to college. The coach at Colgate had told him to call anytime, anytime you change your mind, Mr. Poe. Well, he thought, I have changed my mind. I am going to call him.

It seemed his head was getting clear, things would be alright. Then he thought: my coat. My letter jacket is sitting in that machine shop with my name and player number on it, right next to a dead man and probably covered in blood. They would find the body, it was only a matter of time and it would not be Isaac English they'd come after. It would be him, Billy Poe, the one who had a reputation, he'd nearly killed that boy from Donora, it was self-defense but that was not how anyone else saw it.

They would get his jacket and the body as well. We will drag it to the river, he thought. How many deer had he dragged out of the woods—it would be no different. Only he knew it would be. But there was no choice about it. They would have to go back.

3. Isaac

Isaac didn't sleep and in the morning he could hear the old man moving around downstairs. When he'd come in the previous night, he and the old man had looked at each other and nodded and the old man hadn't said anything about the stolen money.

From the window of his second-floor room he could see that the snow had already melted on all the hills. He remembered looking out this same window in the dark when the mill still ran and the night sky was enormous with fire. It was a faint memory from youth. It was not the first dead bum that year. The other they found in that old house, January. Froze to death. Except this one didn't die—was killed. That was the difference. This is the one they won't let go.

It was a strange time of year, not quite spring and not quite winter—certain trees were already leafed in while others were still bare. It would be a warm day. All the hills and hollows and nooks—it felt comforting. There wasn't a flat piece of land for a hundred miles. Hidden away wherever you were. That will not help you with the Swede, he thought. They will find the Swede eventually and they will not be on your side—see a dead man, think mother father brother sister man. Think I am a man like him. Don't let dead men lie without asking why. Dog left to rot—man is different. Do dogs look at dead dogs and wonder? No, you've seen it, they walk by without looking. Nature of a dog to accept a dead dog.

He could feel things were changing. This is your room but soon it won't be. A picture of his mother over his desk, smiling, young and pretty and bashful. A few awards from the science fair, first prize in seventh, eighth, ninth grade. No more after that—they didn't understand your projects. You knew they wouldn't but you went ahead anyway. Quarks and leptons, string theory, and then you learned your lesson. Half of them think the earth is four thousand years old. The others aren't much better—Colonel Boyd telling the class that humans had once had gills but the gills disappeared when we stopped using them. *Actually, you tried to suggest, that's classic Lamarck. I'm not sure people believe that anymore.* Gave you a C for making him look stupid. Only C you ever got. Naturally Colonel Boyd loved your sister. Why? Because she tells people what they want to hear. Didn't care if all her classmates were being taught things that weren't true.

He went back to looking out the window. He had always admired his sister for her easy way with people, tried to learn from her. Only now you see the cost—she lies more easily than you do. Same as the old man. No, he thought, the old man is different. Doesn't understand or have interest in anyone but himself. Meanwhile ask yourself if you'd act any better in his shoes—spine broken at L1, progressive neuropathy. Or take Stephen Hawking—your favorite crippled genius abandons his wife. Twenty-six years of changing his bedpan and then—sorry, honey, I think it's time for a newer model. He and the old man would understand each other well.

He looked at the clock and tried to remember when Poe was coming. Did we set a time? He couldn't remember. That was unusual. He made a note of it.

There was the sound of a car turning up the driveway and he jumped up and ran to the window to see a white sedan—cop? No. A Mercedes. Lee's car. She must have left Connecticut in the middle of the night to be getting in now. He watched her park next to the house. Knows you stole the money, is why. Christ. He began to feel even worse. I don't care, he said out loud. She's done a lot worse herself. But had she? It was hard to explain exactly what she'd done. Left you here, he thought. Promised she'd come back for you but she didn't. Meanwhile that car she's driving is worth more than this house.

He heard her come into the house and greet their father downstairs and a few minutes later he heard her on the stairs, coming up to see him. He slipped quietly under the covers and pretended to be asleep.

She hesitated outside the door, listening for a long time before opening it silently, just slightly. He felt the air coming in. She stood there, she must have been looking at him, he didn't open his eyes. He felt himself choke up but he kept his breathing even. He could imagine her face, nearly the same as their mother's, the same dark skin and short hair and high cheekbones. She was a very pretty girl.

"Isaac?" she whispered, but he didn't answer her.

She stood a minute or two longer and then finally she closed the door and went downstairs.

Was that right? he thought. I don't know. How many promises can someone break before you stop forgiving them? There had been a time, most of his life, really, when it had been very different. When he and his sister could finish each other's thoughts, when at any given time each would know exactly what the other was doing, whether at school or just in a different part of the sprawling brick house. If he had a bad day, he would go to his sister's room and sit on the foot of her bed while she read or did homework. He went to her before he went to his mother. The three of them, Isaac, Lee, and their mother, had been like a family within the family. Then their mother had killed herself. Then Lee went off to Yale. His one visit, she'd taken him around the campus, all the tall stone ivy-covered buildings, and he knew it was where she belonged, and where he would someday follow her, but here he was, twenty years old and still living in Buell. And now, he thought.

None of it was permanent. The Swede will go back to the soil, blood goes from sticky thick to dust, animals eat you back to the earth. Nice black dirt means something died here. The things you could trace—blood, hair, fingerprints, bootprints—he didn't see how they would get away with it and there was a picture fixed in his mind of the Swede with his face shining and the bloody color of the light on him. He had never stopped looking at the spot between the Swede's eyes, even after the shot was gone from his hand. Made it go into him. With my mind I made it hit him there. He tried to call back the Swede's hands to see a weapon but he couldn't. His hands had been empty. Unarmed man, worst words there are. Why did you throw that thing at him? Because he had a look on his face. Because I couldn't get at the Mexican—might have hit Poe. The Mexican had a knife to Poe's neck but that was not the one you killed. The dead man was the one standing there doing nothing.

Basis of everything, he thought. Pick your own over a stranger. Dead Swede for living Poe. Ten dead Swedes or a hundred. Long as it's the enemy. Ask any general. Ask any priest—millions die in the Bible, no problem if God says thumbs-up. Babies, even—dash em on the rocks say Jesus made me do it. The Word of God and the hand of man. Done the deed now wash your hands.

*   *   *

In the early afternoon he saw Poe come up to the edge of the field, two hundred yards away, and he dressed quickly and put on his shoes and coat and went out the window, hanging by his fingertips before dropping the rest of the way to the ground. His sister had come up to check on him but he'd locked the door.

As he looked back at the house, a big Georgian Revival originally built for one of the steelmill's managers, he saw the old man sitting on the back porch in his wheelchair, his broad back and thin arms and white hair, looking out over the rolling hills, forest interspersed with pastures, the deep brown of the just-tilled fields, the wandering treelines marking distant streams. It was a peaceful scene and he wasn't sure if the old man was sleeping or awake. Like an old planter looking over his plantation—how much overtime he worked to buy this house. How proud he was of the house, and look at it now. No wonder you're always feeling guilty.

High-stepping through the tall grass he made for the stand of trees at the bottom of the property where the spring came out, he knew them all—silver maple and white oak and shellbark hickory, ash and larch. There was the redbud he and his father had planted, in full bloom now, pink against the green of the other trees. Judas tree. Fitting name. Poe was sitting there, waiting for him in the shadows.

"You get any strange knocks on the door?" he said.

"No," said Isaac.

"Whose car is that?"

"Lee's. The new husband's, maybe."

"Oh," said Poe. For a second he looked stunned. Then he said: "E320—goddamn." He was looking at the house.

They made their way through the woods toward the road, kicking up last fall's moldering leaves, the sweet smell from them.

"This is stupid," Poe said. He looked at Isaac. "I mean, I don't see a way around it, but that doesn't mean it's not stupid."

Isaac didn't say anything.

"Christ," Poe said. "Thanks."

They crossed the road and picked their way down to the stream through the alder. Except for a slight coolness there was no hint it had snowed the previous night and they walked along the gravel banks or over the dark mossy rocks, the sky blue and narrow above them, vegetation spilling into the gulch, honeysuckle and chokecherry, an old rock maple tilted overhead, the ground eroding beneath it.

They passed an old flatbed truck, doorless and half-sunk in the sand. It occurred to Isaac that there might be blood on him, he hadn't taken a shower or washed or anything. It wouldn't spray that far, twenty or thirty feet. Still, he thought. That was extremely stupid.

They took the long way around town, through the woods where they wouldn't be seen. It was late afternoon when they could just make out the shell of the Standard plant through the trees.

"Let's just go in and get it over with." Poe found his cigarettes but took a long time to fumble one out of the pack, and though it wasn't hot, patches of sweat were showing through his shirt.

"We need to wait till it's almost dark. It'll probably take us half an hour to get him to the river."

"This is insane," said Poe.

"It was insane staying in there yesterday."

"You know we're half a mile from the nearest road. It'll be months before anyone else stumbles in there, maybe years."

"Your coat will still be there."

"Guess I should have remembered to grab it on the way out. It was probably the guy with the knife to my neck that distracted me."

"I know that."

"It's freakin me out goin in there again."

"The great hunter. He shoots the guts out of a deer but when it comes to a guy who was actually trying to kill him—"

"It's a lot fuckin different," Poe said.

"Well, you should have maybe worried about that yesterday."

"The only reason I was anywhere near this shithole was you," Poe told him.

Isaac turned away and walked off into the trees along the river. He found a rock by the water and sat down. It was average for a river, a few hundred yards across and in most places only nine or ten feet deep. Nine feet under. Good as five fathoms. Good enough for your mother and the Swede both. Drained of heart and freed of flesh. Listen to you, he thought, just turn yourself in. Thought you'd be the one saving people.

Sometime later Poe came and found him and they watched the water in silence, there was the sound of leaves shushing, the squawk of a heron, a distant motorboat.

"You know he isn't just gonna disappear. Some fuckin Jet Skier'll run him over by lunchtime tomorrow, guaranteed. Shit doesn't just magically evaporate because you stick it in a river."

"It doesn't take much to sink a body," said Isaac.

"Jesus, Mental. Listen to us."

"It's already done," said Isaac. "Pretending we can walk away is just going to make it worse."

Poe shook his head and sat down a good distance away.

The sun was getting lower over the hills on the other side of the river, it was a pleasant quiet scene, sitting there looking over the water, but that was not how it felt. You're just a visitor here, he thought. Look at the sun and feel like you own it but it's been setting behind those hills for fifteen thousand years—since the last ice age. Glacial period, he corrected himself, not ice age. When those hills were formed. This area was the edge of the Wisconsin glaciation. Meanwhile here you are. Temporary visitor on the sun's earth. Think your mother will be here forever and then she's gone. Still sinking in five years later. Disappeared in a day. Same as you will. Nothing you can see that won't outlast you—rocks sky sun. Watch a sunset and feel like you own it but it's been rising without you for a thousand years. No, he thought, more like several billion. Can't even get your head around the real number. You're the only one who even knows you exist. Born and die between the earth's heartbeats. Which is why people believe in God—you're not alone. Used to, he thought. It was my mother that made me believe. And it was her that made you not believe. Stop it. You're lucky to be here at all. Don't be a weak thinker.

They're simple facts is all. Your only power is choosing what to make of them. She stayed under two weeks with a few pounds of rocks in her pockets. There is your lesson from that. No different this time. They'll find him at the lock, hook him out with a pole. Or he'll slip by them— Old Man River, a long journey drifting. Catfish doing their work. Victim none the wiser. Roof of water, bones beneath. Judgment day he'll rise. No such thing, he thought. And not possible even if there was. Once you lost your water, most of your weight was carbon. Your molecules scattered, were used again, became atoms and particles, quarks and leptons. You borrowed from the planet which borrowed it from the universe. A short-term loan at best. In the eyeblink of a planet you were born, died, and your bones disintegrated.

They waited until the sun went down before getting up from the rocks. Everywhere there was a bruised purple light. They heard the clicking of bats and looked up and the sky was full of them. They were several weeks early.

"Global warming," said Isaac.

"You know I'm sorry, don't you?" said Poe.

"Don't worry about it." He began to walk through the grass and Poe followed reluctantly behind. They crossed from the darkness of the river trees to the clearing along the train tracks and back into the trees again. In the meadow they stayed hidden behind the old boxcars and the long thicket of wild rose; they were well concealed but Isaac felt his legs getting shaky. One in front of the other. Close your mind for a while. He won't smell yet. But don't look at his face. Except you'll have to—won't be able to move him without looking at his face.

He checked back on Poe, who was grinning nervously, his skin pale and his hair flattened and damp with sweat, his hands shoved in his pockets as if trying to make himself smaller. When they came to the edge of the thicket and stopped to survey the open ground ahead, there was a smell like cat piss in the air. The smell didn't change and Isaac realized it was him. Smell of your own fear. Adrenaline. Hope Poe doesn't notice.

Around the machine shop everything looked different. The grass was crushed and beaten, the ground rutted with tire tracks. Leading up the hillside was an overgrown fireroad they hadn't noticed the previous day, but had since been churned into mud by heavy traffic. At the top of the hill they saw Harris's black-and-white Ford truck. Harris was inside, watching them.

4. Grace

The main road south of Buell angled away from the river to cut through a steep sunless valley, it was a narrow fast road with the trees tight along both sides. She passed vacant hamlets, abandoned service stations, an exhausted coal mine with a vast field of tailings that stretched on forever like sand dunes, gray and dry and not even the weeds would grow on them. Her old Plymouth wallowed and clattered over the potholes, she thought about Bud Harris but she didn't know if calling him would make things better or worse for Billy. She wondered if Billy had killed someone.

In recent years she'd developed her grandmother's arthritis and nearly any change in the weather hurt her hands; she could only manage five or six hours a day sewing before they fixed themselves shut into claws. Once, a union organizer had come poking around the shop, waiting outside the front door at closing time, he was the one who'd suggested that her condition might have been a repetitive stress injury—not arthritis. That's common, he said. Arthritis at your age isn't. Unfortunately the organizer had given up on their shop, as none of the other women would talk to him—they all knew they'd lose their jobs immediately. And the truth was Steiner wasn't so bad to work for. She knew that with her strange hours she would have been fired from a bigger company, but Steiner, the shop owner, let her do whatever she wanted. Flex-time, he called it. As long as she kept making him money. He paid Brownsville wages but sold his wedding dresses in Philadelphia, got city prices for them, was expanding to New York. Grace's only question was could she afford to keep living that way—everything kept getting more expensive and the only part-time jobs were fast food, Wal-Mart, or the Lowe's supercenter—all of which required her to use her hands and only paid minimum wage. Not to mention you had to wait awhile to get one. Once people got jobs, even crappy ones, they tended to stay in them. Just to try it, the year earlier she'd taken a second job at Wendy's, but she'd only lasted a week.

She would take things as they came—her mother had worked three jobs before getting an aneurysm at fifty-six and Grace, unlike her mother, was determined to live with a little dignity. That did not include coming home soaked in rancid grease, getting bossed around by teenagers for five-fifteen an hour. It was a reasonable thing to ask—a life with a little bit of dignity. She didn't take up much space otherwise.

She came into Brownsville along the river and the road climbed up past the bridges and then she was downtown. It was easy to find parking. The city had once been promising but now it was mostly abandoned, ten-story office buildings and hotels, all empty, brick and stone stained dark by soot. The downtown had a European feel, at least from what she'd seen on the Travel Channel—narrow cobblestone streets winding and dipping, disappearing quickly among the buildings. She liked that. Continuing down the steep hill toward the old warehouse, she passed the Flatiron Building, there was a historical marker on it and she knew there was another one like it in New York City, though she guessed that one wasn't empty.

By one o'clock her hands ached so much she knew she had to stop. Christ, she thought, it's Saturday. We shouldn't be here anyway. But as always she felt guilty and worked slightly longer, more than she should have, waiting until she'd finished both long seams of the dress she was constructing for a bride in Philadelphia. The dress would sell for about four thousand dollars the mortgage on Grace's trailer for an entire year. Nervous, she walked across the shop floor to tell Steiner, having the feeling, as she occasionally did, that he might tell her to not come back. But Steiner, thin and unseasonably tan in his golf shirt, his few remaining white hairs combed across the top of his head—he looked up from his desk and smiled and said: "Get better soon, Gracie. Thanks for coming in." He wasn't angry. He was happy they'd all come in on a weekend to get rid of the backlog. Keep making him money, she thought.

Walking back across the shop floor she was already thinking about the hot towel she would wrap around her hands when she got home, how good it would feel, her body began to relax just in anticipation of it and a thought occurred to her: this is what it means to get old, you don't look forward to pleasure so much as easing pain. She said good-bye to the dozen or so women at their workbenches, the old wide-open factory floor with its brick walls painted white for cleanliness, it was a space much larger than they needed, cold, they all ran space heaters under their benches. The material they worked with was expensive, it wasn't like they were sewing blue jeans; only Jenna Herrin and Viola Graff looked up to say good-bye, the others nodded or raised a pinkie. They all knew what the dresses sold for but it didn't do any good to talk about it; most of the work they did could be done for a few dollars a day in South America. Not the same quality, but close enough. It was only that Steiner was too old and lazy to go down there and set up shop.

After taking the freight elevator downstairs, she walked up the narrow street that was permanently in the shadow of the tall empty buildings, finally emerging into the sunlight. By the time she reached the top of the cobblestone hill where she'd parked her car, she was out of breath. At the top of the hill was a big vista, the whole valley was green and full-looking, the gorge, the river cutting between sheer cliffs. She stood a while longer and watched a long tow of barges, a dozen or fourteen of them, pass under the two tall bridges that spanned the gorge. It was a beautiful place to live. But that did not put any more money into her pocket, and besides, Steiner could wake up tomorrow and move his operation somewhere else.

The year previous she'd visited the university across the river at California, talked to a counselor who had figured it would take her four years to get a bachelor's if she went to school at night, that was taking two classes a semester, a load she was not sure she could manage. And how to pay the tuition? You only got loans if you went full-time, and she was falling behind on bills as it was. Snap out of it, she thought. Choose to be happy.

She got into her car and was quickly out of Brownsville, onto the winding road through the woods that separated Brownsville from Buell. She passed a big black bear standing on the ridge overlooking the road, its spring coat full and glossy. It watched lazily as she passed. The bears were definitely coming back, as were the coyotes and deer. They were about the only ones that seemed to be doing well.

As she came into Buell and the wide riverflat, the few old mill buildings still standing, she passed the house she'd grown up in, now abandoned, the windows broken and the shingles blown off the roof. She tried not to look at it. She remembered when the whistle blew and shiftchange clogged the streets with men, their wives, other workers, even twenty years earlier there had been so much life in Buell it was inconceivable, it was impossible to wrap your head around the idea that a place could be destroyed so quickly. She remembered being a teenager and being sure she would leave the Valley, she had not wanted to end up a steelworker's wife—she would move to Pittsburgh or even farther. As a kid, she would get out of school and some days the air was so heavy with soot the streetlights would be on, the middle of the day and all the cars driving around with their headlights. Certain days you couldn't hang your laundry outside for how dirty it would be when it came off the line.

She had planned to leave, that was always the case. But at eighteen she'd come home from her high school graduation and found a new Pinto in the driveway and a book of pay stubs. Whose car is that, she asked her father. Yours, he said. You start at Penn Steel on Monday. Bring your diploma.

Both then and now, she thought, it's some man making half of your decisions. She'd done a year on the rolling line, which was where she met Virgil. Then she was pregnant and they got married. She half-wondered if she'd done it to get out of the mill. Nothing to wonder about, she thought. She'd started going to school right away, first pregnant, then dragging a baby around with her, was nearly through her AA when the layoffs came. Virgil had made it through six rounds but then his number was up. You had to have whiskers to keep a job in those days—at first ten years' seniority, then fifteen. Virgil had five. He had been so proud of that job—doing better than the rest of his family, they were hill people, coal-patch people, their father had never worked a day in his life.

Things had been lean. They had waited and waited for the mills to re-open. But the mills just kept laying people off, all up and down the Valley, and then they were closing, and Grace had a young child and that was the end of school for her. There was not a single job to be had. Not two nickels to rub together. Meanwhile Virgil's cousin, who had nine and a half years in the mill and big payments, a nice house with an inground swimming pool, he'd lost his house, his wife, and his daughter on the same day. The bank changed the locks and his wife took the daughter to Houston and Virgil's cousin broke into his own house and shot himself in the kitchen. Everyone in the Valley had a story like that—it was a horror show. It was when Virgil started talking to his family again. Which was when he began to change, she thought. When he started thinking he wasn't any better than what he came from.

Dark days. Things had not been that bad for a long time now. The trailer had gone into foreclosure but gradually people started picketing the sheriff's sales, deer rifles in the trunks of their cars, and when one of the bankers had come down to insist the sheriff take action, they had turned his Cadillac over and burned it. To keep people from getting shot, the judge put a moratorium on the foreclosures. Eventually it had become the law. So they had managed to keep the trailer, living on what they could get from the food bank and the deer Virgil poached. That was why she couldn't stand the taste of venison. For two years it had been all they ate.

Virgil had done two years of job training to learn robotics but that hadn't gone anywhere—those jobs had never materialized. Then he'd done the stint at the barge-making plant but that had closed as well—most ships and barges were now made in Korea, where the government owned all the industry.

Keeping that trailer might have been a curse, she thought. At least we might have moved somewhere else and started over. But it was hard to make those calculations, figure out where to go. Men went to Houston, New Jersey, Virginia, lived six to a motel room and sent money back to their families, but plenty of them came back in the end. It was better to be poor and broke around your own people.

A hundred fifty thousand unemployed men didn't leave room for the good life but neither she nor Virgil had relatives anyplace else. You needed money if you wanted to move; you had to move if you wanted money. The mill had stayed closed, and then it had stayed closed longer, and eventually most of it was demolished. She remembered when everyone came out to watch the two-hundred-foot-tall and almost brand-new blast furnaces called Dorothy Five and Six get toppled with dynamite charges. It was not long after that that terrorists blew up the World Trade Center. It wasn't logical. but the one reminded her of the other. There were certain places and certain people who mattered a lot more than others. Not a single dime was being spent to rebuild Buell.

At the end of the dirt road she turned in next to their trailer. Virgil had promised he'd be home by two but it was nearly four. He was breaking his promises already. You knew this would happen, she thought. She called the women's shelter in Charleroi to tell them she wouldn't be coming in to volunteer the rest of the week, had a pang of sadness, it was her lifeline to the rest of the world, all sorts of people worked there, a teacher, a pair of lawyers from Pittsburgh, a financial adviser, all women, they would sit around listening to the public radio stations you couldn't get in Buell. That was what she planned to do, if she could ever afford to finish her degree—become a counselor.

Why not, she thought. Even if it takes six or seven years, you could just start now. She went into the kitchen to prepare her heating pad, put the pad into the microwave oven and turned it on. While she waited, she took a pile of newspaper and started a fire in the woodstove, piled kindling on top and one thicker piece. The timer beeped and she went and got her towel from the microwave, scorching hot, she let it cool for half a minute and sat down on the couch and wrapped her hands. It burned at first but a few seconds later the relief came. She leaned her head back and focused on the feeling. It was almost like sex. She felt good all over. She felt herself get sleepy. She knew if she drifted off she would wake up with the towel cold and damp but it was worth it. She thought about Buddy Harris, a strange and guilty thought now that Virgil was back. The K-Y stayed under the bed with Bud, they'd been on and off for years, two different times she had nearly left Virgil for Bud Harris, but in the end she hadn't been able to do it, he was too awkward and quiet and she hadn't been able to imagine a life with him. She wondered if she had used him, poor Bud, though she didn't think so. Ten years ago he'd become chief of police, though, as he was always pointing out, it wasn't like being chief in a real city, there were only six full-time officers, and with all the financial crises, half of them were due to be laid off. At any rate here she was, still thinking about him, she and Virgil had broken up so many times that she'd dated a dozen other men, only somehow she was still thinking about skinny old Bud Harris.

She heard a truck come up the road and pull into the driveway. Virgil came inside. He was drunk, maybe stoned, she could see that. That would suit her purposes. She kissed him on the neck, took his hand and put it between her legs.

"What a good day," he said.

"What'd you do?"

"Went fishing with Pete McCallister."

She put the towel aside and laid against him. She rubbed his leg.

"I thought you said you'd be out looking for something," she said.

"It's a goddamn Saturday," he said.

"Well, that's what you told me."

"I forgot what day it was when I said that."

She shrugged. "I heard U.S. Steel is doing aptitude testing next month. You could put in a call up there."

"Goddamn hour and a half in traffic each way."

She could smell the booze on him. "We could move closer in to the city, live in an actual house."

"We ought to be moving further away. Live a real country life instead of trying to pretend we're gonna move up in the world."

He looked at her. "What are you laughing about," he said.

She shook her head and stopped smiling. They looked at each other awhile longer and there was something about his face. She was looking at him and he had a strange look and then she knew.

"What," he said.

"Virgil," she said.

"What?"

"The mortgage is due this week, plus it's April and we still owe taxes from two years ago. I'm on a payment plan with the IRS."

"Danny Hobbes owes me three hundred bucks. We can always make more money."

It was quiet and she kept rubbing his leg. "Remind me again why you came back," she said.

"You know I've got money."

"What about your disability this month?"

"That's what I lent to Danny."

She nodded.

"What about getting other money from the government."

"We ain't gonna pass the asset test for welfare. Plus they sign you up for some shit job now so you're fucked if you think you're gonna have time to look for a real job. There's no goddamn point if it don't lead to actual wage-paying employment."

"You should apply for it anyway," she said. "Your son isn't working, either."

"I already looked into it," he said. "Between the house and my truck we're not even close to qualifying. It's the asset test."

"Your truck is six years old and I make nine-fifty an hour."

"Well it's too much," he said. "You still giving away your time at that shelter thing?"

She looked at him.

"Maybe for a little while you could do something else that paid instead, I mean if you're so worried about all this."

She closed her eyes and took a deep breath.

"I was just thinking out loud," he said. "Don't get all mad, now."

"We'll get by," she said. She still had her eyes closed.

He leaned over and kissed her.

"Let's have a drink to get this out of our heads." He grinned and went out to the truck.

Give him some time, she thought. Be a little more generous. He came back inside brandishing a half-empty bottle of Kentucky Deluxe and, after finding clean glasses, poured one for her and one for him. She wanted to tell him about Billy coming home hurt last night but something stopped her. She took down her shot of whiskey and so did he and then he started kissing her.

Then he unbuckled her jeans and slid them down.

"You don't want to go to the bed?" she said.

He shook his head. He slipped inside her and she lifted her legs around him. Soon she could feel it building and then she forgot where she was, she was pulling him in and in and trying to get closer, they could not be close enough. He was still going and she hoped the feeling wouldn't end. She felt him get very hard and his whole body went rigid and it started to build up in her again but then he stopped moving. She rubbed his back and he was not looking at her, or at anything, he was just still. She found a comfortable position for her legs and they were like that for a long time. She dozed awhile, had strange thoughts, if Virgil was able to take home some money she'd be able to go back to school, here he was, then she thought you could probably plant the tomatoes soon, take them off the windowsill and get them into the garden, the peppers as well. She decided she could spare a few dollars and plant more herbs this year. Virgil began to move again inside her.

"Let's go to the bed," she said. "I don't want Billy coming home and seeing us like this."

She got up and walked to the bedroom; Virgil followed after her carrying the whiskey bottle. Worry about tomorrow's problems tomorrow, she reminded herself. They sat in bed and Virgil took a long pull from the bottle and then another, and then passed it to her.

"Drinking that whiskey like you stole it."

He mumbled something in response—there was something going on. He didn't look at her; when she reached between his legs again he wasn't interested and then she didn't think she was, either.

"What's going on with you?"

"I've just been thinking."

"I'm sure you have."

"Maybe we should take it slow," he said.

She thought about that. In the old days she wouldn't have dared say it, but now she told him: "You just want to fuck, in other words."

"We don't have to put it like that."

"Except that's how you'd put it to someone else, right? What you told Pete when you went fishing today."

"Nothing's changed with you, has it?"

She wiped between her legs with the sheet and pushed it away, her stomach got tight but then she didn't feel anything, she was just looking out the window. The day was nearly over. She could have been lying next to anyone. There was still time to get the tomatoes in the ground. She felt herself choke up.

"You leaving?" she said.

"I wasn't planning on it."

"Maybe you better."

"This is still my house."

"I've made every payment on my own since you left, and a couple hundred dollars here and there doesn't make a dent."

"Come on." He rolled toward her and she felt the frame give under his weight. They had never been able to afford a proper bed. Then there was the trailer with its fake wood paneling. She had never wanted to live here—she'd let herself be talked into it.

"I talked to a lawyer from the shelter."

He looked at her, half-grinning.

"She said the house is legally mine until you pay your share."

"That's a bunch of bullshit," he told her.

He was right—she hadn't talked to any lawyer. But she was surprised how angry her own lie made her feel. She believed those words. They might not have been the truth but they should have been.

"Go talk to someone," she said. "See for yourself."

"You're a fucking nightmare, Grace."

"Get out. Bud Harris said it's a felony, you still owing so much on child support."

"Our kid isn't a child anymore."

"It doesn't change what you owe. The court still ordered it."

"You would bring a cop into it, wouldn't you?"

"I would. I will."

"Well, that figures."

She was quiet.

"Petey's wife said your cop boyfriend takes enough pills to kill a steer—Xanax, Zoloft, the whole routine. Biggest prescription in Fayette County."

"Maybe CVS ought to know their employee is going around talking about people's business."

"Most people think that Barney Fife motherfucker is queer."

She thought, he's got a bigger pecker than you do, but she kept her mouth shut. She suppressed a giggle.

"What," he said.

"Go on and take everything you brought last night." She watched him dress and walk out, he was shaking his head the whole time. When his truck pulled out she thought she might cry but she didn't. She forced herself to get out of bed, knowing that if she didn't she might end up stuck there, wallowing. She wondered who she could call to find out for sure but it didn't matter, she knew, knew he'd run out of money, maybe gotten dumped by one of his girlfriends so he'd looked her up. It was what the girls at work had told her was happening, they'd been watching it go on forever, but she hadn't wanted to believe them. That was when she started crying. Not too much, though. She picked up the bottle of whiskey he'd left, undid the cap but it seemed distasteful that his mouth had touched it. Into the trashcan.

The sun was getting lower. She hoped Billy would come home soon but what if he didn't? She should get a dog, maybe. It wasn't too late to go to the shelter, they could always use extra help. She could call Harris.

It hit her suddenly how cruel Virgil was, he was an empty shell, he'd gotten by his whole life on his looks, but that would change for him as it was changing for her, and what would be left—just the mean streak. The parts of Billy she worried about, the quick temper, it all came right from Virgil. She wondered how she'd never seen it before, but then she knew she'd always seen it, she'd chosen to ignore it. She was making another decision now, or it felt like it had been made for her, it felt impossible at that moment that she'd ever loved him. You're probably just in shock, she thought, but then no, it was like a switch had been turned off.

The tomatoes were there in the window, she carried them out and got a shovel from the shed, out behind Billy's half-done projects, a parts car he'd bought to keep his other car running, riding lawn mowers, the four-wheeler. Worrying about him again, coming home last night with the cut on his neck. But things like that had happened many times before, never that bad but still, he was a magnet for trouble. She should have taken him out of this place a long time ago.

Kicking the shovel hard into the dirt, she planted all six tomatoes and the peppers as well, setting the trellises and stepping on them to set them firmly. It was nice standing in the breeze, her hands dirty, looking at the plants and the freshly turned soil, looking out over the rolling hills, it was a good view. Forty-one was not so old. It was almost too young to be president. She would call Harris. He was a good man, she'd always known that.

Of course she could just keep going like this, being alone, but there was no point to it. You felt strong for about a week and then you were just alone. And Bud Harris, he was a good man, uncomfortable but what did it matter, the ones that had the easiest time talking also had the easiest time screwing around behind your back. That was a lesson you didn't learn until it was too late. But it was not too late. Harris, he was respected, there was a reason she'd nearly left Virgil for him, two different times she had thought seriously about it, and Virgil, Virgil was not respected by anyone and there was a reason for that as well. I will sleep with Buddy tonight, she thought, it will clean me out, it was a giddy notion. Virgil had done worse, he'd come to her smelling directly of other women. She wondered if he'd given her any diseases. She had been checked, though most of the time she'd made him use condoms, that was the one smart thing she'd done in her life.

She walked around the inside of the trailer. When they bought it Virgil swore it was temporary, that they would build a house soon enough. She wondered why she'd listened. It was an old trailer, at least it was a doublewide but it leaked air everywhere, fake paneling from the 1970s, she'd splurged to replace the carpets but with the boy in and out of the field so often they were quickly ruined again. Virgil had wanted to put plastic covers on the couch but she hadn't permitted it. She sat on the couch and could feel herself drifting away, thinking about things, but there was no point in it, she needed to get a handle on life instead of spending her time daydreaming. At least the garden was done. That was an accomplishment, it would pay off the rest of the year.

She nearly called Harris's cell phone but then she thought about how he would feel if he found out that Virgil had just been over. It wasn't fair to him. Not to mention Harris probably had other girls himself. Not to mention she had burned him twice, now. She would have to ask him gently. She would have to allow him his dignity. He wouldn't just come at her beck and call. She could wait, collect herself, have some dignity of her own. She went to the mirror, pulled her hair back in a tight ponytail. That was the way she should wear it, tight and away from her face. She would get a haircut, no one wore their hair long anymore, it was stringy. She still had her cheekbones, she'd always had good bone structure. Half of it was the way you carried yourself, she had been depressed, there wasn't any question about that. She would take baby steps. With a little mascara things would be fine, she'd run out months ago, she would get more tomorrow. She fixed herself a small dinner and watched the sun go down from the porch, there was no moon and the stars came out very bright. She went back inside and watched an old scratchy yoga tape the director of the shelter had given her, she liked all the stretching, it felt as if the poisons were coming out. After that she fell easily into sleep.

5. Harris

Harris and Steve Ho had been sitting in the black-and-white Ford Explorer about three hours. It was Harris's idea—he just had a feeling. The state cops, the county coroner, the DA, everyone else was long gone. From the top of the ridge they could see over the meadow, the half-collapsed remnants of the main Standard Steel Car factory, grown over with vines, the small machine shop where they'd found the body. There were old boxcars in the field and a peaceful, pleasant air about the place. Nature assimilating man's work. In his much younger years, he had seen things like it in Vietnam, abandoned temples in the jungle.

Harris glanced at Steve Ho. Steve Ho was off duty; he was not being paid to be there, which was not unusual. Ho looked comfortable, young and comfortable, a short stout man, a full head of black hair, resting his hands on his big belly. An M4 carbine across his lap—like many other younger cops, Ho had an inclination for things like that, body armor and such. Ho was only three years out of the academy, but Harris was overjoyed to have him on the force. Steve Ho was easy to work with and left his radio turned on even when he was off the clock.

By comparison, Harris felt old and bald. He reminded himself that he was not—not that old, anyway. Fifty-four. Anyway this feeling had nothing to do with being old, it was just that this was turning into a very bad day. He wanted to be at home, sitting in front of a fire with his dog and a glass of scotch, maybe watching the sun go down from his back deck. He lived by himself in a small cabin, *the compound* was how he referred to it, a high place overlooking two valleys. The sort of place a boy would dream of living, but then reality, in the form of a wife and kids, would set in. Harris had talked himself into buying it a few years back. Though well built, the cabin was remote and depended on a pair of woodstoves for heat, had little radio or television reception, was accessible only by four-wheel drive. Not a place any woman would ever want to live. It was another excuse. Another way to keep an even keel, cowardice pretending to be independence. Though Fur, his malamute, loved it.

He'd been first to arrive at the crime scene—there'd been an anonymous tip—and he'd felt relief when he saw the body. Clearly a transient. No painful phone calls, no horrible visits to people he liked. Those things got worse with age, not better.

He was still standing near the body, absorbing things, when he saw a familiar jacket. Then heard another vehicle—the state trooper—bouncing down the old access road. He scooped up the jacket and stuffed it behind a workbench. The young state trooper walked in just after and Harris had tried to conjure his name. Clancy. Delancey. He couldn't think straight—he knew this man. But Delancey was oblivious to what Harris had just done. He nodded his greeting, then looked at the body. *He's a big one, huh?*

People came and went all day but the jacket had remained, unnoticed, where Harris hid it. Now, sitting here with Steve Ho, he was extremely nervous, not so much that he'd hidden the jacket as much as that the jacket belonged to Billy Poe. He rubbed his temples; he'd gone off Zoloft a few weeks earlier, which was not helping things now. He tried to separate the things in his mind. Hiding the jacket was probably not bothering him. You didn't arrest every kid you caught breaking windows. Or every citizen who drove home after a few too many Budweisers at happy hour. Good people got one free pass. Kids got two, though the second one might be a handcuffed ride in the Explorer. There was a role everyone played in the community, an unspoken agreement. Which was basically to do right. Sometimes that meant stopping people for a dirty license plate, other times it meant letting people go who were committing felonies. Which is what anyone did when they consumed three beers and put their keys in the ignition. You couldn't say it but that was the truth—it was not the law so much as doing right. The trick being to figure out exactly what that was.

Listen to you, he thought. Trying to distract from the question. Which is whether you ought to be defending Billy Poe. Get out of this truck and go down there and discover that jacket. You should have already arrested him. At least that was one take on it—Even Keel's. Even Keel had also made him buy a cabin on top of a mountain that no woman in her right mind would ever consider living in. Even Keel was a coward. Harris decided he would sit there. He would watch and see what happened. He would see which part of him turned out to be right.

★   ★   ★

Near sundown, they spotted movement at the far edge of the meadow near the train tracks.

"Now there's two people who don't want to get seen," said Ho.

Harris got an even worse feeling. He lifted his binoculars. He couldn't make out the faces on either of the two people in the meadow but he could guess from the size and the strange bouncing walk. Coming back to get his jacket. A tightness was growing in his chest. As the two got closer, he could see clearly that it was Billy Poe and one of his friends, the short kid whose sister had gotten all those scholarships. He thought about Grace. He felt sick to his stomach.

"You okay?" said Ho.

Harris nodded.

Ho was looking through his own binoculars, an expensive Zeiss model.

"That who I think it is?"

"Believe so."

"You want me to go down there?"

"Just hold on."

It was quiet for a few seconds, then Ho said: "You better make sure this doesn't burn you, Chief. The whole town knows you put in a good word for him last time. You've said yourself—"

"Do me the favor."

"You know all I'm saying, Chief. This ain't the old days."

Harris turned on the light bar for a few seconds to let the two in the field know they should come up. They both froze.

"They're gonna run for it."

"That kid's sister is at Harvard. He isn't running anywhere."

As predicted, the two began to walk glumly up the hill toward the Explorer.

"You ought to take a look through these glasses, Chief. I can see every last goddamn zit on their faces."

"Later," said Harris.

But it was a clear enough picture. Billy Poe and some friends had come out here to drink, maybe score some meth, and things had gone bad. Meaning Billy Poe had beaten one of them to death, then panicked and took off, and was now coming back to clean up his mess. The saddest part being he'd gotten this other kid mixed up in it. Harris wondered if there was a way to keep that one in the clear. People like him still had a chance.

It was not Billy Poe he really worried about. He'd known for years where the boy would end up. He'd bent over backwards, he had put his own name on the line, knowing the entire time what would happen. By a certain age, people had their own trajectory. The best you could do was try to nudge them into a different course, though for the most part, it was like trying to catch a body falling from a skyscraper. Billy Poe's trajectory had been clear very early; it wasn't Billy Poe he was worried about. It was Grace and what this would do to her.

Ho said: "You know I always hated that prick Cecil Small, but it's bad timing with the new DA. Cecil Small might have been willing to float a break."

"I never said a thing about it."

"I know you're worried about your nephew there."

"He ain't my nephew."

Ho shrugged. They watched the boys walk up the hill. *Young men,* Harris corrected himself. Billy Poe was twenty-one. Somehow that seemed impossible. When he'd first met Grace, her son was five years old.

"Here they come," said Ho. "I'll put on my mean face."

6. Isaac

Looking up from where he and Poe had just emerged from the brush at the edge of the field, he saw Harris's truck. But the same instant he wondered if they might be able to make it back into the trees, the lights at the top of the truck came on. Poe began walking through the waist-high grass, toward Harris and toward the machine shop. Isaac followed in a daze.

They were across the field and near the muddy torn-up ground by the machine shop when Poe slowed to let him catch up. "We're good," he said quietly. "He knows where I live and if he found my jacket he wouldn't still be here."

"You think he'll see us being here as just a big coincidence," said Isaac.

Poe nodded.

Isaac was about to discuss it further but then he wondered if Harris could somehow hear them, even from up there. Poe began to walk more quickly as they passed the building where the Swede was lying. Not any-more, he thought. The Swede is already gone. The coroner's probably al-ready been here, the DA, everyone. Half the town, judging by the tire tracks. What's-her-name, coroner's daughter, Dawn Wodzinski. Due to inherit the family business. Her father being both county coroner and funeral home director. No, knowing her is not going to help you. The DA is that new guy. What's-his-name.

Meanwhile see how fast Poe is walking. Relieved he doesn't have to look at what he did. Because of him a person is dead but he'll forget that detail soon enough. He'll remember he's innocent. He'll remember it was your choice to do what you did. Meanwhile it was him who wanted that fight, didn't care what the cost was because the cost was not to him—it was to you and the Swede and he will not take any of that off you. Know him well enough for that.

They made their way up the fireroad through the trees, climbing the hill under a dark gray sky. Their pants legs were soaked and stuck with burrs and grass seed and Poe climbed with long strides, staring only at the ground in front of his feet. Isaac nearly had to jog to keep pace, it was humiliating and he was angry at Poe for that as well. There was the sharp odor of crushed weeds and skunk sumac, a more pleasant smell of damp soil. They passed a dug-out mudhole where a vehicle had gotten stuck, clods of dirt sprayed up the sides of the trees. He could feel his face getting hotter and he tried to calm down. Sacrificed on the altar to others, presenting Isaac English. His own fault. Not the Swede you traded for Poe—traded yourself. You aren't going to California. Aren't going anywhere.

They reached the top of the hill and Harris stepped down nimbly to meet them. He didn't look particularly threatening—around fifty, skinny legs and nearly bald, hair close-cropped around the sides and back of his head. Then a much younger cop got out of the truck, a barrel-chested Asian man only five or six years older than Isaac. He was wearing sunglasses despite the encroaching darkness, holding an M4 carbine at low ready. Isaac only vaguely recognized him. He was not one of the cops everyone knew.

"Y'all stay cool," said the second officer.

Harris appeared to grin despite himself. He gave a signal and the man lowered his rifle.

"That Billy Poe?" said Harris.

"Yessir."

"Come here a lot, do you?"

"No sir," said Poe. "First time."

Harris looked at Poe for a long time, then at Isaac.

"Alright," he said. "First time y'all have been here."

The other cop smirked and shook his head. In addition to his assault rifle, which had such a short barrel it might have been a submachine gun, he had a load-bearing vest with several extra magazines for the rifle, a baton, some other equipment Isaac didn't recognize. He could have been a military contractor just out of Iraq. Harris, by comparison, had only his pistol, handcuffs, and a small police flashlight.

"Interesting place to spend the night," the officer said.

"Sure is. Now Billy, you don't have any strange proclivities, do you, coming out here at dark with another young man?"

"No sir. Not at all sir."

"Well, I guess in that case I won't arrest you."

The two looked at him.

"That was a joke."

"You want me to check them out?" said the other cop.

"They look fine from here," said Harris. "I don't think we need to lay hands on them. Maybe if they promise to stay out of trouble we can give them a ride home."

"We can walk," said Isaac.

"You ought to take the ride."

"What are y'all doing out here, anyway?" Poe said.

"Let's go," said Isaac.

"You two are good boys," said Harris. "Officer Ho, why don't you take your fancy night goggles and go sit in those bushes. See who else comes onto the premises."

"It's still soaking wet down there, boss."

"I apologize," Harris told him. "Go ahead and wait till it's to your liking."

Ho scowled and collected his things and made his way down the fireroad cradling his assault rifle. The other three watched him go, looking down over the meadow and the river. In the distance most of the hillsides were nearly black but there were a few patches of errant light where the land shone a bright green. They stood quietly watching the colors change until the light was gone completely.

Harris said: "Like an advertisement for church, isn't it? You wonder why people don't notice what a beautiful place this is."

"They're all a bunch of freakin complainers," said Poe.

Because none of them have jobs, thought Isaac, but when he glanced at Harris the police chief seemed thoughtful. It seemed likely he had already taken that view into consideration.

After a minute Harris motioned them toward the backseat of the Explorer and started it and, after flipping a switch to lock the differential, pulled a wide U-turn through the forest. This truck would not have gotten stuck in that mudhole, Isaac noted. There were plenty of other cars here besides this one. At the top of the fireroad Harris got out to open a gate and they turned south on the main road.

"You two stay out of that area," he said. "I don't want to see you there again."

There was a Plexiglas divider between them and his voice came through muffled. He slid the panel open.

"Did you hear me," he said.

"Yessir," said Isaac.

It was dark in the back and Isaac couldn't see much, just the back of Harris's bald head and the glow from the computer between the front seats. They were driving very fast down the curving river road. Your money and notebooks are still down in the meadow. Unless someone already found them. Not likely. That place is covered with junk and what they wanted was in plain sight in the machine shop.

"Son, I can't remember your name but I know your daddy. He was the one working in Indiana when that Steelcor mill caught fire."

"Isaac English. My dad is Henry."

Harris nodded. "I was sad when that happened," he said. "Your sister is the one that went to Harvard, isn't she?"

"That's her," said Isaac.

"It was Yale," Poe said. "Not Harvard."

Harris made a modest hand gesture. "Excuse me," he said.

"No problem," said Isaac.

"You all still live in that big brick house?"

"What's left of it."

It was quiet after that. Ahead of them, where the river bent, Isaac could see the lights scattered along the hillside that was Buell. He closed his eyes, heard the tires whirring against the road in the darkness, thought you can't really be sure what you were thinking. How pure was that decision. What thoughts you were having without being aware of them, you can barely see the surface of your own mind, there's lower layers running all the time. I just want to sleep, he thought. But you won't. Meanwhile big Otto he's sleeping all the time. What made you throw that bearing? He couldn't remember. He couldn't remember what thoughts he'd had, or if he'd thought anything at all. It will be first degree—you picked up that chunk of metal for a reason and took it inside. Premeditation. Lethal injection. They said it didn't hurt but he doubted that. Knowing what it meant for you, that shot would hurt.

He pushed his fingers to his temples. Keep this to yourself, he thought. Need to convince yourself you didn't do this. Except that is hopeless. That is not the kind of person I am.

Poe nudged him and Isaac opened his eyes. He saw they were passing the new police station, heading on toward the center of town. He craned his neck slightly as the police station disappeared into the darkness behind them. They passed Frank's Automotive Supermarket, a new spinal rehab place, Valley Dialysis, Valley Pain and Wellness, Rothco Medical Supply. A barbershop for rent, a tanning salon in a dingy storefront that had once sold model trains. Then Black's Gun and Outdoor, the closed Montgomery Ward, the closed pharmacy, the closed Supper Club, the closed McDonald's, a Slovak Lodge, the Masonic Hall.

Then, more stores, their windows boarded, he would have to think hard to remember what had once been there. Stone buildings with their elaborate cornices and ornate iron windows, all covered with plywood, the walls plastered with posters for the Cash Five lottery. An unusual number of people stood on the sidewalks; it was Saturday night.

"If the welfare office ever saw where their money went," said Harris. He stopped the Explorer in front of the first bar they came to; people were already walking away.

"I'm gonna give you two the option here—you can catch a ride home with me or you can get out and call for one yourselves."

Isaac wasn't sure but Poe quickly answered: "We'll call."

"Alrighty then." He shrugged. "Go ahead and get out. Tell whoever's workin there I said let you use the phone."

"We can walk it from here," said Poe.

"You get a ride," said Harris. "Make your phone call. Don't let me catch you around later."

The two nodded.

"By the way," said Harris. "How'd you get that cut on your neck?"

"What's that?"

"Don't play with me, Billy."

"Fell on some barbed wire, sir."

Harris shook his head. "Billy," he said. "Oh, Billy." He turned all the way around in his seat. "Keep this up and it won't end good for you. You hear me?"

"Yes, sir."

"You too," he said to Isaac. "Both of you stay inside the next couple days. Stick around where I can find you."

They went into the bar. The walls were wood panel with initials carved everywhere, the bar was dimly lit and much bigger than it needed to be; the only light came from neon beer signs. A keno game played on two of the televisions, a recap of a stock car race ran on the third. Outside in the hall there was plywood nailed in front of an elevator.

"This is all old-timers," Isaac said quietly.

"You wanna go to Howie's and have everyone in there see us?"

"We shouldn't be out here at all."

"Try explaining to my mother why I got a ride home from Harris."

"That's the least of our fuckin worries," said Isaac.

The bartender made her way slowly over to them. She smoked her cigarette. She was a young, pretty girl that Isaac recognized as being a few years ahead of them in school.

Finally she said: "Just so you don't waste your time, I just saw you both get out of that cop's truck."

"Emily Simmons," said Poe. "I remember you."

"Well, I don't," she said.

That was unlikely, Isaac knew, but there was no point in saying anything. "Harris said you'd let us use your phone," he told her.

"Anything for Mr. Harris." She set the phone in front of Isaac and stood watching as he called his sister.

Poe said: "Lemme get an Iron City while we wait for our ride."

"You left your ID home, didn't you?"

"I'm twenty-one."

"Got us confused with someplace else."

"You know I remember you from playing pool in Dave Watson's basement. I'm Billy Poe. I was two years behind you."

"I already said I don't know you."

She poured them both sodas. Poe took the cherry from his drink and threw it on the floor. The people in the bar watched with amusement. They were mostly older men in satin union jackets or hunting coats, faces thick from working too close to the blast furnaces or working outside or not working at all. Some of them went back to talking, a few had nothing better but to watch Poe and Isaac.

Isaac saw one of his father's friends from the mill sitting by himself, D. P. Whitehouse, he used to hang out Monday nights watching football, took Dad bird hunting after Dad moved back from Indiana, after the accident. But that had been a long time ago—D.P. hadn't come around for years. Now D.P. didn't recognize him, or didn't want to.

"Maybe we should wait outside," said Isaac.

"No shit. Least go where we can get a fuckin beer." He gave the bartender a hostile look but she ignored him.

Outside, there were too many people milling around so they decided to go into the alley to wait for Lee. When their eyes adjusted they saw two men sitting in a dark pickup truck, waiting for something. The driver motioned for them to leave the alley and they did, returning to the street to stand awkwardly.

"Were those cops?" said Isaac.

"Fuck no. Don't get paranoid now."

"Harris knows. Not to mention you aren't the one in trouble."

"Come on," said Poe.

"You're right, this isn't really a big deal."

"If he knew, we'd be getting beat with a rubber hose right now. He thinks we're just a couple of kids and plus they found that lady in a dumpster last week—they've got bigger things to worry about."

They watched cars drive slowly up the street; then come back a minute later, going the other direction.

"He found your jacket," said Isaac. "Not to mention if he did any real investigating he's got our fingerprints and shoeprints and your blood all over the place."

"You've seen too much TV," said Poe.

"Dunno if you noticed how torn up that ground was, because that wasn't just from his truck."

"Mr. MacGyver."

"Why are you acting like this?"

"Harris's probably knocked off a few bums himself, and as far as we know he'll be braggin on this one and takin credit for it. Plus either of those other ones probably ran off with my coat to wear, it ain't like they were dressed exactly warm."

"The witnesses, you're talking about."

"The two bums."

"The older one who lives around here, who already recognized you."

"Go ahead and think yourself to death, Isaac."

A few minutes later, Lee's Mercedes came slowly down the street. She was looking for parking. They watched her stop and back the car easily into a small space.

"She'll be lucky if someone doesn't key that thing," said Isaac.

"It'll be alright."

They walked toward the car and waited. When she got out, Isaac said: "You're late."

"Sorry," she said. She smiled guiltily. "I had to get ready."

She had gotten dressed up—a long fitted skirt and an open-necked white blouse and when she hugged Isaac he could smell perfume on her neck. She did not look like someone from the Valley. Isaac noticed she was wearing makeup—unlike her. Then he saw how she hugged Poe, the light touch at Poe's waist. He felt a surge of confusion and wasn't sure what to make of it.

"What's our plan," she said.

"I think a drink wouldn't kill us," said Poe. He was standing at his full height now, grinning self-consciously, blushing, he couldn't take his eyes off Lee. Nothing good is going to come of this, Isaac thought. He regretted not asking Harris to take them home.

"We really have to go," he said quietly.

"We can get one drink," Poe insisted. "We can all just visit a minute."

"What's wrong?" said Lee.

"Your brother's just tired."

Poe nodded to Lee and started ahead of them down the street, then stopped to smoke a cigarette while they talked.

"Well," she said to Isaac.

"I'm fine," he said. He wouldn't look at her.

"You wanna talk?"

He didn't answer.

"Buddy," she said.

"Since when do you call me 'buddy'?"

After standing there a minute Lee seemed to make a decision. She turned and began walking quickly to catch up to Poe. Isaac followed slowly after them.

7. Poe

L ee was walking ahead and he caught up and stayed close to her, he didn't care if Isaac followed them or not, he accidentally brushed against her and she let him and, as for Isaac, he'd always been like this, he was afraid of everything. Small wonder how they'd treated him in school, he was Ralph Nader Junior, an old fucking man. Harris could have locked them up but he hadn't, he'd taken care of things, old Harris had definitely taken care of it. Everyone knew Harris didn't give two shits about dead bums he'd burned all those old houses down hadn't he, he'd burned down an entire block of houses where the bums were living, Serbiantown it was called and Harris he had burned the entire thing, it had gone all night, eight-alarmer. He did not give two shits about a dead bum in a factory. Anyone could tell you that much.

Lee had gotten all fixed up to meet him. Eight months now she hadn't called, it had never been anything but fun and games to her and now she was married. He had heard it from Isaac, she had not even bothered to tell him. Only—here she was looking her very best, she didn't wear much makeup but she was wearing it all tonight, she had taken care to look her best for him. Turning heads walking down the street like this, they know she's in a different league, they would never recognize her. A giddy feeling overwhelmed him, he wanted to grab her up and hold her, hold some part of her in his mouth. Even being this close to her, if he could keep this feeling it would be enough.

They passed Howie's, there was no way they were going in there, Christ knew the things his friends would say in front of Lee. He decided on Frank's Tavern instead. A slightly older crowd, usually, though not by too much. Inside it was dark and humid and people were dancing. Empty drink glasses everywhere. Isaac sulking back behind them. Go on, Poe thought. Lee brushed his hand it was not accidental, he took her hand and squeezed it, in the crowd no one could see him, he looked at her she was blushing, she had that crooked smile, she only smiled that way when she couldn't help it. He would ignore Isaac, he decided, for the entire night. For his entire life. Inside the bar it was the aftermath of a wedding, a young couple, he recognized a bunch of people, spotted James Byrne across the room and turned quickly the other way. Jimmy Byrne who used to bring his girlfriend to the games only she started coming by herself, she used to give Poe rides home, they would park in the bushes. Did Jimmy know? Poe wasn't sure. Jimmy was one of those types who got his permit to carry a handgun as soon as he turned twenty-one, he used to pass the permit around at parties so everyone could look at it.

Everyone was dressed up, all the girls in church clothes and their boyfriends in new shirts. Getting a thrill rubbing on each other. Someone left their baby in the stroller, it was sitting there by itself, watching things.

"It's like old times," Lee said, but Poe wasn't sure if she meant good or bad. They decided she would have a better chance of getting a drink and he watched her make her way to the bar, they were all jostling, she crossed her arms she was very small, a few dark hairs coming out of her ponytail, she looked, he didn't know, she looked like she was from someplace else, from Spain, she looked like a girl in a bar in Spain, a girl from a picture. He almost went in after her but he made himself stand there. He leaned against the wall, hands in pockets, took them out, crossed his arms, finally he put his hands behind him. She brushed her hair behind her ear and turned back and smiled at him. He smiled back at her and they looked at each other for a long time, across the room. He felt as if he could breathe and breathe and still never get enough air. His neck was tingling and he didn't want the feeling to go away, and then there was a commotion, the bride and groom came downstairs from some secret place, the bride's dress no longer on quite right and a cheer went up and the bride looked down and the groom raised his hand in the air like some kind of general, big deal Poe thought we all know you fucked her. But when he looked at Lee, he got a sick feeling—she had just been a bride herself. He was sick, literally sick for a second, he could feel things rushing up from his stomach and he took a swallow of someone's beer, someone's half-finished beer just sitting there, to push it back down. Look at you he thought you are not thinking right you should not even be here with her. She'd gotten sidetracked in the people dancing and she caught his eye and waved for him to come out and dance but he wasn't sure now, he didn't know what to do he just stood there. She was only doing it to be nice.

Isaac was standing in the corner with his arms still crossed. Poe went over and clapped him on the shoulder. "Relax," Poe told him, but even to him his voice sounded strained and uneven and Isaac wouldn't look at him. "You want a beer?" Isaac still wouldn't look at him. He turned back to Lee. She was dancing. She danced with a fat older man in his baggy church suit, sweat pouring down his face, it was Frankie Norton's dad, Frankie who was still away at Lehigh. Then she danced with a freckled kid who looked about fifteen and then a guy in Marine Corps dress blues who was taking it a little easier. Lee and the marine danced for a while, it seemed like a long time, he twirled her around slowly. Poe hated this song it was Faith Hill, he hated new country. The marine tried to put his white hat on Lee, being playful. Then Frankie Norton's dad came back and handed her two beers and Lee stopped dancing and pushed her way back to Poe. He could see the marine sizing him up from across the room and then the marine turned away, Poe saw he had a scar across the back of his head where the hair didn't grow, a surgery scar. They had done something inside his head. After graduation a lot of people had signed up and three kids from the Valley had been killed in the last month alone. One of them was a girl he'd fooled around with, she was a little weird, everyone thought she was a dyke. He'd fooled around with her a few times but he hadn't defended her. She was driving a truck and an IED got her, it was what got all of them over there. All she'd done was join the Reserve. He hoped the Arabs that did it were dead, hoped they'd been gutshot by some hucklebuck sniper who'd grown up with a deer rifle in his hand, hoped those Arabs thought they were safe and meanwhile that sniper was judging his windage and boom—they were holding in their guts. Christ, he thought, what happened, a second ago you were happy.

Lee handed his beer over and said: "They wouldn't let me pay for drinks."

"You got that on someone's SSI," Isaac told her. "Or their welfare."

Lee got a look on her face. Poe wanted to throw Isaac through the window. She opened her mouth to say something but the marine had come over next to her. He didn't look more than twenty or twenty-one, short brown hair that looked as soft as a boy's, acne on his neck and temples.

He said: "You ain't gonna sit out long, are you."

"I'm finished dancing," Lee told him.

"Come on."

"I came to see my friends here."

He looked over Poe. Then he took her hand up lightly.

"No, thank you," she said.

Poe stepped in front of her, squaring himself to the marine.

"Husband to the rescue, huh?"

"That's right," said Poe.

"Except you ain't her husband."

"Yes he is," Lee said.

"Bullshit he is."

"Go back to your friends," said Poe.

"We're leaving," Lee said.

The marine took a step forward but Poe was already backing away. Then the marine kept walking after him but he stumbled on something and went over hard. He was drunk. He began to shout something from the floor, just lying there shouting. Poe kept backing up. Lee and Isaac were already out the door.

Poe backed away without taking his eye off the marine, people were starting to notice, the kid's medals were flopped awkwardly on his pressed blue coat. Poe felt bad for him, *stand up,* he thought, just stand up. Then he noticed something strange, one of the kid's legs was twisted and longer than his other leg, Poe saw something shiny underneath and he felt all the heat go out of him, and kept looking at the leg, where the sock didn't cover it, it was pale brown plastic with a steel bolt for the ankle and Poe couldn't stop looking at it, his head felt light, *you might have hit that kid,* he realized, *in the old days you might have hit him* and for a second he thought he'd pass out, there was a slight space in the crowd and Poe shoved people aside and pushed through to the door.

Outside a state trooper was parked and Poe steadied himself against the wall but someone was already in the back of the car in handcuffs and the cop was writing. Christ he thought something is happening to your life, your mistakes are piling up. He wondered how he'd never seen it before. And now the thing in the factory with those bums. He had to get out of this place, away from this town. He had thought he would be okay staying here but it was the opposite, people had tried to tell him but he hadn't listened. He couldn't remember where Lee had parked, he'd only had two beers but his head was spinning. There was an ambulance at the other end of the street, its back doors wide open, bright inside, two people being treated. He saw Lee and Isaac waiting. They had Lee's car idling in the street when he got there and Poe checked as he got into the car, a half dozen men had come out of the bar looking for him.

"Took your sweet time," said Isaac.

"That guy had a fake leg."

"You didn't punch him," Lee asked.

"I didn't touch him," Poe said. "Jesus Christ."

"Good thing we had that drink," said Isaac.

"I'm sorry," Lee said. "I shouldn't have talked to him for so long."

"It's not your fault."

"The fuck it's not," Isaac said.

Isaac was quiet the rest of the way home. When Lee parked he got out and went inside without looking at either of them. Poe and Lee watched Isaac go and then looked at each other and he braced himself for her to say good night. He would walk home. He needed to get his head clear.

"Do you want to come in for a drink or something," she said.

He hesitated for a long time. "Alright."

She squeezed his arm gently. "You can't stay over, though."

"I won't."

They sat on the back porch on the couch with a blanket over them, faces cold but the rest of them warm, they could hear a stream running down to the ravine where it met the other stream and then the river. And from there, he thought. From there it met the Ohio and the Ohio met the Mississippi and then down to the Gulf of Mexico and the Atlantic, it was all connected. It's all connected, he thought. It all meant something. He drank more wine. He was just drunk.

It was warm under the blanket, they were holding hands and he closed his eyes and let the feeling sink in. There was a dark patch where the neighbor's yard began, it was a thicket now, the empty house obscured by brush.

"When I left, someone still lived there," said Lee. "Pappy Cross."

Poe finished the bottle of wine, held it above his lips for the last drops. It was a new moon, a dark night, it seemed like anything could happen, it felt like the old days, he wondered if he was just kidding himself.

"We might as well talk about it."

"I'm sorry I didn't tell you," she said.

"It's fine."

She laid her head against his shoulder.

"It's the same one from before, isn't it?"

"Simon."

"The one who was with all those other girls?"

"I'm sorry. I'll say it as many times as you need to hear it."

"He changes his mind so everything's different. That's pretty much the story." He didn't know why he was saying these things, they were having a good time, from the way it was going he guessed there was a good chance she'd sleep with him if he would just pretend it was like the old days, like he forgave her.

She tensed and it was quiet for a while but then she said: "There's a reason I was with him in the first place, you know, he wasn't all bad. Anyway, now that we're married, they feel better about helping to take care of my father. Things are about to get easier for all of us."

"Hope you got that in writing."

"Poe." She shook her head. "Poe, you have no idea how easy it is for you to say that."

"I was defending you to your brother but now I think I shouldn't have."

Still he didn't know why he was pushing but it seemed like she'd been prepared for it, for him to act like this, she'd always been fine with having different sorts of feelings.

"I hope you didn't tell him about us," she said.

"No, but I'm sure he knows now. After tonight."

She was shaking her head some more. She was not happy about it.

"It's kind of his own fault."

She took her hand back.

"I found out from your brother," he said. "You could have called and told me and it would have been okay. You could have told me yourself but instead I find out from him and I'm guessing you would have split town again without calling me if we hadn't needed a ride tonight."

"Because I'm married."

"Well I'm glad you're happy."

"If it makes you feel better there are days when he and I don't even talk. I can't even remember the last time we had sex."

He wondered if she was making that up but he didn't care. He needed to hear it. Of course it made him feel better, and it seemed to make her feel better also, and after a minute they were holding each other again. He heard her swallow and he could feel her heart going and he thought go on and do it. She let him kiss her. She let herself be pulled into him and he smelled her warm breath and they held their heads together and he took in her smell, some girls smelled like their perfumes or the soaps they used but her it was just her skin. He would know it anywhere. In the mornings when she'd been sleeping all night he would just smell her, smell her chest, smell where the hair began at the top of her neck. They were like that for a long time, breathing in each other's hair, and then he started rubbing her back and her leg.

"You're not being fair," she said.

"I love you," he told her.

She sighed and burrowed into him.

"You don't have to say it. I don't care."

"I love you, too," she said.

Soon she was touching the bare skin on his stomach. He put his hand up her skirt and she pushed against it and he undid his pants and slid them down and reached for her. She let him. She rolled on top of him and he pulled her underwear over and got partway inside, it was as quick as that. She raised herself up to get it in smoothly. They were still for a minute. She grabbed his shirt and squeezed it hard and then quickly rolled to one side and took her underwear off.

They started again and after a minute or two there was a look on her face like she was concerned with something and he pulled her mouth to his neck so she wouldn't make noise. Eventually the tension went out of her and they were going slower.

"Do you want to be on top," she said.

"I think I'm done."

"Me too," she said.

After lying like that for a while they took all their clothes off, just to be touching, and she lay with her back to him, his arms around her. She had a raised mole on her back, on the one shoulderblade, and he leaned and kissed it. He knew the other one wouldn't, is why. He knew she meant something different to the other one, she did not mean as much to the other one. It didn't matter. She was not the same for him but that didn't matter, he was going to write it down, a life lesson. Shut the fuck up, he told himself.

Then he thought she was just doing this as a favor. It was just her doing a favor for you, old times' sake, next time she will be gone to you. He felt cold. He was considering all the possibilities but then he decided no, it wasn't from pity, it was from several different things, he was fine with it. But it was time to get going, in an hour he might be nervous or angry, he didn't want her to see that. He slipped out from behind her and began to look for where his clothes had fallen, then stood up and began dressing.

The coldness woke her and she opened her eyes.

"Where are you going?" she said.

"I dunno," he said. "I guess home."

"I'll drive you." She stood up, naked. She was so small. "Jesus, I'm shitfaced," she said. "No wonder I wanted to seduce you." She smiled at him.

He was slightly hurt by the implication but he smiled anyway and his head began to feel straight again, this was as good as it would get, two old friends, occasional benefits, any more and she'd take him under and then leave him there. He was glad it had happened, a good reminder of how it was supposed to be. It was supposed to mean something, it was more than just body parts. Life was long and he would feel this way again only not with her. He couldn't figure out why he was feeling so natural about it, he hoped the feeling would last, he knew this was how he should close it. The end of one book of his life. He did not want to think about it.

"I'm glad I got to see you again," he said. He cleared his throat and made himself lean forward to kiss her forehead. She tried to pull him back to the couch.

"You might as well stay a while longer," she said. "We might as well do it all night."

"I should get home."

"I meant what I said."

"I know," he said. "I know you did."

As he was leaving, he turned to wave and saw something move in Isaac's window. He kept walking. Soon he was in the dark under the trees.

8. Lee

She was lying on the couch, looking around at the home she'd grown up in but had put from her mind five years now, water-stained ceilings, patches of wallpaper curled from dry plaster, Isaac's books flung everywhere. Since she'd left, the books had filled the house. Old science textbooks he'd picked up at thrift stores, copies of *National Geographic, Nature, Popular Science*, piles of them on every shelf, on her mother's upright piano, the stacks of books and magazines spread across the living room in unruly masses. It was a large room but still there seemed barely enough space for her father's wheelchair to pass. Obviously, Henry had decided to tolerate it. But maybe he no longer cared. A person looking in the window would have thought the house belonged to some crazy old lady and about twenty cats.

On one hand she loved her brother for it, his curiosity, he was always teaching himself things, but she was beginning to worry about him. He was getting more isolated and eccentric. Right, she thought. You're the one who stuck him here. It didn't seem like she'd had a choice about it. She'd always thought she had escaped just in time, outrun the sense she'd had her entire childhood that with the exception of her even-stranger younger brother, she was fundamentally alone. It was not a good way to think. It had changed completely when she got to Yale, not right away, but quickly enough, her sense of aloneness, of what she would now describe as an existential isolation, had disappeared. Her entire childhood in the Valley now seemed like a past so distant it might have been another person's life. She'd found a place she belonged. It seemed impossible she'd have to give that up and come back here.

There was a creaking from upstairs—her brother was still awake. She felt guilty. I'm working on it, she told herself. Simon's family had agreed to pay for a nurse, she'd made some phone calls, tomorrow she would start the interviews. It could not have gone any faster. Same as what they taught you as a lifeguard—you have to save yourself before you can save anyone else. That's what she was doing. She had gotten herself to solid ground and now she was coming back for her family. You sure took your time about it, she thought, but that probably wasn't true, she was just being hard on herself. She hadn't been a particularly good lifeguard, either—her body wasn't big or buoyant enough and technique only went so far. A heavy enough person would drag her under every time.

She got up and walked around the stairs, through the small dining room, and into the kitchen. Off the kitchen, in the den which had been converted to a bedroom, she heard her father snoring, the long pauses when his breathing seemed to stop. It is him, she thought. He is the problem. Her ears and neck got very hot and she had to wash her face in the sink, it was the old feeling that there were terrible things in motion and she would only understand when it was too late, it was the feeling she associated with this house, with the entire town. She felt it every time she came home. Soon they would all be gone from it. It was a conversation she'd been planning for years, telling her father it was time for both of his kids to leave. That he could stay in the house with a nurse or move to a home, but that the time for Isaac to stay had passed.

She had always been the favorite. Their father treated Isaac like a foster child, because he, Henry English, was a big man from a line of big men, because Isaac had a curious mind and Henry English did not, and while those same faults, smallness and fine-mindedness, were acceptable in his wife and daughter, when they appeared in his son it was as if everything he had to offer, everything he had valued in himself, it had all been submerged under the character of his wife. Including her Mexican coloring, which both children had inherited. Their skin wasn't that dark, really, they just looked slightly tan, Isaac could have passed for someone from the hills. Not so much her, though. A little more foreign. Dark eyebrows, she thought. Meanwhile Henry English was pale and red-haired. Or had been, anyway.

Their mother had come to the U.S. to study at Carnegie Mellon, and as far as Lee knew, she had never gone back. By the time her kids were born she had no trace of an accent and neither Lee nor Isaac had ever heard her speak Spanish. Right, she thought. As if Henry would have allowed that anyway. He wouldn't have been happy either if he knew you checked the box, called yourself Latina, on your college and law school applications. She'd thought it over many times, but when the time came she hadn't hesitated to do it. It was true and not true. She could look the part if she wanted, but she didn't know the language, not even a nursery rhyme—she was the daughter of a steelworker, it was a union family. At Yale she'd learned French. As far as college and graduate school went, she probably would have gotten in anyway, she had perfect SATs and nearly perfect LSATs but there were times she wished she could know for sure. Obviously it was a luxury to even wonder about it.

She took a handful of vitamins for all the wine she'd had, drank a glass of water, and went back to the living room. She couldn't get over the house—it was bigger and grander than some of the houses of her professors. Built for some businessman in 1901, the date in stone over the front door. A little ostentatious, but that was the style then. Her father loved the house more than he would ever admit. They had bought it in 1980, when things were beginning to slow, when people in the Valley were much less sure about buying big houses. Later, it had been the reason he had to take the job in Indiana, after the mill downtown had closed, living in a shack while he sent back money. In hindsight it seemed stupid. But of course that was the American Dream. You weren't supposed to get laid off if you were good at your job.

She wasn't ready to go upstairs and face her brother and decided she would sleep on the couch. Cheating had always seemed a male thing to do. She wondered why she'd slept with Poe. Maybe because she owed him, she'd made him some silent promise, the sort of promise you made with your body and she had broken it. Not so much by getting married as by not telling him. Or maybe she wanted this marriage to be over sooner rather than later, and was trying to speed up the process. No, that was not what she wanted but still, married at twenty-three, it was a little ridiculous. She had done it to show Simon she forgave him, it seemed as good a reason as any. Still there were days when he wouldn't get out of bed, barely acknowledged her existence. He was going through a hard time but maybe he had always been like that. He was going through a hard time but he'd grown up on an estate in Darien, Connecticut. He was a little bit spoiled.

Also, she still loved Poe, in a hopeless sort of way, in a way she would never love anyone else because she knew it could never go anywhere— Poe was a boy from the Valley, Poe loved the Valley, Poe had not read a book since graduating from high school.

She didn't feel sorry yet but that was probably still the endorphins. Or maybe not—Simon he'd cheated how many times, three girls she knew about and then how many others she didn't? She wondered if the statute of limitations had expired on those things. She wondered what she would do about Simon. He was already getting testy, she'd only been away two days but he wasn't doing well on his own, he'd gone to stay with his parents in Darien. From Darien it was only an hour train ride into New York, he had maybe fifty friends in the city but he didn't feel like leaving the house. It was depression but it was also a habit. It was his habit of acting helpless. To say he was a little spoiled—it was a gross understatement. If his supply of money were to somehow run out . . . he wouldn't make it. Maybe half of her Yale friends would make it. Most of them worked very hard, but none had any idea what it was to want something they wouldn't get. A specific lover, maybe. You're being defensive, she thought. This is better than you ever thought it could be. You are happier than anyone you know.

She still had principles—there was no longer any real reason to go to law school but she was still going. Simon was trying to talk her out of it, he wanted to do some extended traveling—there was a family house in Provence that was barely used. Only it was too cliché, blue-collar girl marries into rich family, benefits accrue. When she thought about that it made her sick. She would not take their money. Except they're happy to have you, you'll be the most well-adjusted person in their family—a scary thought. Obviously they had more money than she could reasonably expect to make in her entire life, even if she got a job at a Big Firm, which she would not do, she'd end up doing something for humanity, work for the Department of Justice or something, civil rights law. That is what everyone tells herself, she thought: I'm going to Harvard Law so I can be a public defender. Was it Harvard? She had gotten into Stanford and Columbia as well, all she had to do was pick. Actually she knew. Harvard, obviously. She couldn't help smiling. Christ you're a snobby bitch. That was alright. As long as you don't let anyone know. You just tell them you're going to school in Boston, and then if they ask further . . . but under no circumstances offer the information otherwise. It just sounded too snotty—Harvard. It was the same as Yale but worse. What about your brother, she thought. What is your brother going to do?

She wondered if she and Poe had been loud, she wondered if Isaac was a virgin and he'd heard her having sex with Poe. It would be horrible. She was not sure how much she knew him anymore. Part of her worried he was headed for serious trouble. She couldn't sleep. She opened her eyes and sat up.

She made a mental inventory of all that was wrong with the house— roof, paint and plaster on the inside, the trim around the windows was rotted, the bricks needed repointing—those were just the things her father had told her. It was a gorgeous house but it would likely cost more to fix those things than they'd get out of selling the place as is.

Because that was what was going to happen. Isaac was not going to stay here any longer, and she was not coming back, and Henry would have to accept that. He was willing to sacrifice Isaac, but she was not. Except you did, she thought. You let this go on way too long.

She wondered what they'd get for the house. In Boston or Greenwich it would sell for two million, but in the southern Mon Valley it might go for forty thousand. The neighbor's house had been empty twelve years, even the For Sale sign had faded and rotted away. The state had built a brand-new highway running north to Pittsburgh but there were never any cars on it, it was hard to imagine that in any other place, an enormous highway that no one used, the central artery, empty. Driving around New York or Philadelphia, the entire I-95 corridor, you wouldn't believe a place like this existed, and only a few hours away.

To help her get to sleep she decided to read in front of a fire. She opened the flue and piled some logs on the grate and put newspaper under them and lit the paper but after the paper burned out the logs were just smoldering, no real heat or flame. The smell of smoke filled the house and she opened the windows so the smoke detectors wouldn't go off. She was an idiot, really, how she'd managed to grow up in a town like this and still be such a girl. She did not know how to start a fire, shoot a gun, anything like that, she'd never had any interest though she'd grown up in Pennsyltucky, for Christ's sake, it was embarrassing. Maybe before she left she would ask her father to do that, teach her how to shoot one of his handguns, tin cans in the backyard or something. That was something he'd be happy to do.

Looking through the books she'd brought, she picked up *Ulysses,* but couldn't figure out where she'd stopped. She wondered if it was really such a great book if you could never remember what you'd just read. She liked Bloom but Stephen Dedalus bored the crap out of her. And Molly, she'd skipped ahead to read that part. Racy for then, pages and pages of masturbating. At least she would not have to do that tonight. That was a relief. It had gotten to be a chore, really. Here she was, a young hot piece of ass and no one to give her what for, only her own hand to depend on. She shouldn't be so hard on Simon, really. It was only because she worried about him. He had hurt that girl, it had not even been his car, it was John Bolton's car, it was John Bolton that should have been driving. John Bolton had been nearly sober but he liked to encourage Simon, the bad part of Simon. John Bolton was one friend she wished Simon didn't have. Actually, there were several others. Anyway there was the black ice on the road. That was what the investigators had determined. There was no point in even thinking about it. She had forgiven him. You did not forgive people and then change your mind later. Simon hadn't forgiven himself and that seemed like enough punishment. She wanted them to have a normal life again, it didn't have to be crazy googly eyes or anything, just back to the way it was. Except there was Poe who is so warm you want to wrap yourself around him, you see him and you cannot stop touching him. You would not be happy with Poe, she reminded herself. Poe who gets in bar fights. Poe will never leave the Valley no matter how all the blood rushes down there and everything so sensitive and wanting pressure even thinking about it now she closed her legs together very hard Poe Poe Poe she squeezed her legs harder she thought about his flat stomach and the muscles on his chest she listened her father was still asleep she slipped her hand under her skirt, no she thought, there's no need for that. She took her hand back.

She picked up *Ulysses*. Hands are for turning pages, she decided. Leopold Bloom was having lunch. She wanted to fall asleep. She wondered if she had any Henry James. Except right there on the side table was her old copy of *Being and Nothingness*. Sartre—that was an equally good choice, good as Ambien. What should she pick? It was a very tough decision her life was full of them. She decided to stick with Joyce, she would get as far as she could. After a few more pages she was dozing happily.

9. Isaac

There was a noise and he woke up; he hoped it was morning but there was just the blue black of night, bright stars. The TV is on, he thought, but it was not the TV. It was from the porch. Poe and Lee talking. You know why. After a time he heard Poe say he loved her and she repeated it back to him and then it got quiet, he could feel the skin on his neck tingle like he was drunk. It's all of them, he thought. Lying right to your face.

They were on the porch, where his father had hung his workclothes so as not to get the dust in the house. He remembered grabbing his father's legs but his father, wearing dirty long johns, pushing him away until he dressed. Is that a real memory, he wondered. Or just something you think might have happened.

He listened a while longer, heard his sister suddenly whimper. All of them, their human condition. Even your own mother waded out to sink. Pocketful of rocks. Final eyeblink, saw her whole life in it. Wonder did it make her feel good or bad.

He needed something to rinse his throat. Keep this up, he thought. Keep this up and it's back to the river in no time. He got up and stood near the open window in the cold breeze his head was swimming, he had a feeling his room was enormous, looking around in the dark it seemed the walls stretched on forever like a fever dream, he remembered his mother holding iced towels to his neck. Taught fourth and fifth grade because she couldn't handle the older ones. Old man tells everyone she was pushed. Coverup, he says, uninvestigated murder. Can't go to heaven if you kill yourself.

Even her—she lived only for herself. Got tired and checked out. Easy to be generous when it doesn't matter but when the hard decisions come you see what they all choose. It doesn't matter doing right when it's easy. Her, Poe, Lee, the old man. As if they're the only ones alive on earth. Meanwhile you're always expecting different. It is your own fault expecting things.

You are the one who let her go—watched her walking down the driveway, last you saw of her. Maybe the last anyone saw of her. Maybe she saw someone along the way. Wish she did and wish she didn't. That was the happiest you'd seen her in a while. Went up to your room and then saw her walking. Seemed out of place but didn't know what. A nice day, she was going for a walk. Back to your reading. *Time* magazine. I was reading *Time* magazine when my mother died. If I had chased her down, he thought. Why would you have—there was no reason. Nice day for a walk. What no one knows about you. I didn't know, he thought. Alright alright alright. Put it out of your mind.

He stood in the dark listening. The voices started again, giggling, then the porch door opened and closed. He watched them walk out into the driveway holding hands, kissing their good-byes. Maybe you only care because they're happy, he thought. But he didn't think that was true. Poe was walking alone across the dark lawn, down the hill toward the road, Isaac watched him and the strange way he had of bouncing on his toes. Poe turned again and waved to Lee. That's all, you're being petty. Angry because they are happy. Then he thought no, it has nothing to do with that. It's because of what they have inside. But somehow you've turned out worst of all of them.

He reached for the light but it was too late, there was a loose fluttery feeling in his chest, his heart was beating faster than it ever had and his legs went loose and he sat down. There was a warm feeling like he was pissing himself. Faulty wiring. He took deep breaths but it was beating

too fast, fluttering too fast to pump blood. Like the kid who died at soc-
cer. Didn't confess. Please God, he thought. He sat against the wall and
he couldn't get enough air and he was distantly aware of being cold again
and wet everywhere. He tried to call out for his sister but he couldn't and
then the feeling began to pass. He felt embarrassed.

You need to get out of here, he felt more than thought. On shaky legs
he got himself up and turned on the light, examined himself, his thin
naked body, there was almost no substance to it. He was still shaking and
wanted to sit back down but he made himself stand until his legs felt
strong again. He was clammy with sweat but that was all. Get up and get
moving. Get. Out. Of here. He wiped himself off with a shirt and grimaced. Look at you—when it comes down to it you think Lord God
come and save me. Confession get my pardons. Christ, he thought. He
felt embarrassed though of course there was no one to be embarrassed
in front of. Go on and pay a visit to St. James. Dear old Father Anthony,
moral guide and choirboy fondler. Ten Hail Marys and a blowjob. Jerry
what's-his-name, the kid from Lee's year, had a breakdown. Meanwhile
half the town still goes—easier to believe that young Jerry was a liar. Did-
dle our sons but you can't shake our faith.

He knew it wasn't true about his sister. She was not a bad person.
Their mother dying, it had driven Lee away, she'd gone off to college
right after. He didn't think she'd chosen another life, not exactly, but a different path had been offered and eventually she'd decided to take it. How
can you blame her? You made one visit to New Haven and knew it was
right for her. Probably right for you, too, but too late for that. No, he
thought, that's just your pride.

Most of what he needed was in the backpack he'd left by the machine
shop. That was the first order of business. It was a crime scene but so
what. He couldn't believe they'd been so stupid today, just walked
through the field. It would have been easy to stake the place out and
make sure no one was watching. Lessons of hindsight. You are not playing by the same rules as last week, even. No more stupid mistakes. He
found a spare set of thermals and began dressing, his heavy cargo pants,
a heavy flannel shirt, wool sweater. Get your fishing knife, you might
need it.

He bent the sheath loop backwards so it would sit inside his waist-band and still clip to his belt. He looked at himself in the mirror, a knife in his belt, and felt ridiculous. Go down and talk to your sister. No, it's too late for that. It was stupid but there seemed to be no way around it. You're going to die alone, he thought. This isn't kid's stuff anymore.

You didn't have to leave this way. Only now you do. Took the car the other day up to Charleroi and then you were on 70 West and you kept going, just to see what it felt like, nearly ran out of gas and got home after dark, he was waiting for you. Sitting on the porch, just waiting for you in the dark. Meanwhile you are twenty years old.

I had an appointment with Terry Hart that I missed.

Why didn't you ask him to pick you up?

You know I don't like to do that.

Alright, you told him. *I'm sorry.*

It's my car, he told you. *Don't borrow it again unless you tell me where you're going and when you'll be back.*

Knew he was pushing you—the car was your only freedom. But that is his way. Could have lent you the money to buy a car but didn't. When you got that job in the Carnegie Library—two hours each way on the bus—he got sick all of a sudden. Four visits to the doctor in a week. Wanted you home but wouldn't say it. That was his way of telling you. And you gave in. Some part of you was happy to give in. The same part of you that has kept you here waiting two years now.

The air in his room suddenly felt thin and he had an urge to get outside as quickly as possible but he took a final look around and made himself think. There was the ceramic bank his mother had given him, he hadn't wanted to break it before, it was in the shape of a schoolhouse and it had been full for years but now he cracked it on the edge of the dresser, took the dollars and the quarters, counted it, thirty-two fifty, left the rest of the change on the bed. Rifling his desk for anything else he needed to bring, Social Security card, anything, but he'd packed so carefully the last time that there was nothing. Everything—the money, his journals, everything else—was in his surplus Alice pack sitting under that pile of scrap metal in the field. Unless someone found it. Unlikely, he decided. They had no reason to search the field, everything they needed was in that building. He glanced briefly at the picture of his mother over his desk but it didn't inspire any sort of feeling. It is because of her checking out that you lost Lee and now you've lost Poe as well. Or maybe that happened a long time ago. Either way it's better that you know it.

He got his spare schoolbag and put a blanket and extra socks in it just in case. In case nothing. You need to get the other pack. After a final inventory he went softly down the stairs, found his sister asleep on the couch, her foot tucked in a hole in the torn plaid cover. He watched her as he laced up his boots. Cheats on her husband, falls fast asleep. Miraculous conscience. Deleted at birth. These are just things you are saying to yourself, he thought.

She opened her eyes, groggy, not sure who was there. He walked past her toward the door.

"Isaac?" she said. "Where are you going?"

"Nowhere."

"Wait a second, then."

"I heard you and Poe."

She looked confused and then she was more awake, she looked again at his backpack, his coat and hat and hiking boots. She untangled herself and stood up quickly. "Hold on," she said. "It isn't how it sounded. It isn't anything. It's an old thing but now it's over."

"You told him you loved him, Lee."

"Isaac."

"I believe you. I know that somehow in your mind, both of those things can be true."

"Just hear me out."

She took another step toward him and bumped a pile of ancient books, which fell heavily to the floor, startling her. For a second he seemed to see her clearly, her hair disheveled, hollows under her eyes, the grand old living room now filled with junk, so different from the way their mother had kept things. The house literally falling apart around her. She didn't know how to handle any of it. The only thing she knew how to do was leave.

"Soon we'll both be out of here," she said. "We're really close."

"It doesn't matter anymore."

She looked confused and then the old man began calling out from his bedroom. Isaac ignored it.

"Should we check on him?"

"He does that in his sleep every night."

She nodded. Because nothing is required of her, he thought. Then he was angry again.

"I swear this is all about to get fixed."

"You were a day too late," he told her. Before he could hear her reply he was out the front door, making his way toward the road in the dark.

Book
Two

1. Poe

It took him, he didn't know, half an hour to walk home from Lee's house. Two miles, give or take. He passed through town, the long main drag, it was even darker than normal, no lights on anywhere except for Frank's Tavern. It seemed like forever since they'd been there but it had only been a few hours. It was long after closing time now, but the lights were still on. Everyone knew why that was. Poe was careful to not look in the windows as he passed, you didn't know who might be in there. The bar had nearly gone out of business for back taxes but somehow Frank Meltzer came up with a bunch of money, claimed it was some aunt that gave it to him but most people said he'd flown down to Florida and driven back in a minivan full of dope. Ten-thousand-dollar paycheck, if you had a clean record you just had to call the right people, but only if your record was clean. Being a mule, they called it. But it was just like the movie said: once you were in, they didn't just let you out. He wondered if Frank Meltzer was sorry he'd done it. There was another place like that, Little Poland, supposedly the Russian mob had bought it but meanwhile the food was still good, people would drive all the way down from the city to eat there, pierogies and kielbasa.

He was making good time. He had long legs—a fast walker. He was thinking a lot. He thought you'll follow her. You'll follow her to Connecticut. Plenty of schools up there you'll get a scholarship. Except Christ what was wrong with him. She had moved in with her boyfriend, husband now. It was all a fantasy, what he'd just had, it was not the last time they'd sleep together it didn't have that feel, it didn't have that tragic, sitting around crying feeling. But it was close. They would do it one more time and it would be horrible, sex followed by five or six hours of intense bawling and holding each other and complete and utter misery. And then he would never see her again. She would not come back to the Valley he could be sure of that. Four years gone, down the tubes. Only Christ it wasn't four years, it had never been four years, it had only been fun and games that had gone on four years, it was not the same as being together. They had never been together properly except the one Christmas break three years back when she came home the whole week. One week of walking down the street and holding hands and all, kissing games, all your standard boyfriend-girlfriend activities. The rest of the time it was just sex. That had seemed good at first, a pretty girl who just wanted sex and not much else. You did not think those girls really existed. But now it didn't seem good at all. She would go back permanently to her other life, because that's what it was, she had two lives and this one, the one here in her hometown, this was the life she was trying to get rid of. It was another world entirely she had out there, he had not seen it but from the way she talked he could imagine it, that new world, mansions, educated people, a butler involved. It was not even doctors and lawyers, it was another level entirely. It was the level of having butlers. Only maybe those were only from movies. Butlers were outmoded, probably. He guessed it was all robotics now.

And look at him here now, walking down a dirt road, an actual dirt road, he imagined her new husband driving his BMW or whatever it was down the road, look honey, we are driving on an actual dirt road. How quaint. Well yes. He had seen a picture of the new husband once, back when he was still just a boyfriend. He looked queer. That boyfriend of hers looked like an actual homosexual. Wearing a pink oxford. Maybe that wasn't queer in Connecticut but still, that pink shirt, it had given Poe a good deal of satisfaction to see it in that picture. Though here he himself was on his dirt road, walking home as he had no functioning vehicle, his own home, not mansion but a doublewide trailer, just ahead of him. He could see the porch light just ahead. It was nearly five in the morning. Before going inside he took a leak in the bushes so as not to wake his mother with the bathroom noises. He was careful to be quiet—his mother she wasn't a good sleeper and if there was anyone who needed it, about three years of good sleep, it was her.

He made it into the house quietly and into his bed. Falling asleep he had to remind himself that bad things were happening to him, but that wasn't how it felt. This will all blow over, he decided.

It was late in the morning when he woke up, clearheaded, the best he'd felt in weeks, he checked the clock and knew his mother had already gone to work. He was thinking about Lee again, lying there in his bed in his room with the sun shining on him. The south-facing window, he hated it, you didn't get good sleep once the sun came up. He needed to fix the curtain rod, it'd been broken for weeks now. And the tape was coming off his old posters, Kiss, why had he ever liked them anyway, plus Rage Against the Machine, someone said they were communists. The good thing was that with no curtain over the window he could see a long way, almost to the river, and on account of the sun it was already hot in the room. It felt good though he hadn't slept well. The warmth.

He would go to the library and fill out the applications for schools, April 10th now, another day advancing, it would not stop until he died. Only even then it would not stop, the day he died would be like any other day. He hoped that was a long way off. He got up and went outside in his boxer shorts, it was another beautiful day the kind that reminds you how good it is to just be breathing, no matter if nothing else is going right. You are breathing, he thought, more than many can say. He looked at his car, his 1973 Camaro, last of the small-bumper models, before the government came in with its five-mile-per-hour bumpers that ruined the lines of the car. He would never own one newer than 1973. You would have to be an idiot. The Camaro was sitting where the tow truck had left it a month earlier, off to the side of the driveway. Leaves and dirt on top of the new paintjob he'd paid for. He'd dropped the transmission racing Dustin McGreevy in his new WRX Subaru, Dustin going on and on about pop-off valves and turbos and then Poe had smoked him the first time but the second time Poe'd dropped the tranny, the original Turbo-matic, torn the inside of it all to pieces and they'd had to leave the Camaro in the ditch and Dustin had given him a ride home. So much for American steel, said Dustin. Least it isn't my mom's car, Poe told him, flicking the Jesus air freshener.

That was a lesson, he decided, McGreevy's Japanese car, it had only won because it hadn't destroyed itself. They knew what they were doing, the Japanese—plenty of steel still got made there. Special alloys. You wanted to believe in America, but anyone could tell you that the Germans and Japs made the same amount of steel America did these days, and both those countries were about the size of Pennsylvania. He wasn't sure about that last fact, but he guessed it was true. Pennsylvania was a big state. Not to mention all the expensive cars were made there—overseas—Lexus, Mercedes, the list went on. Happening to the whole country, he thought, glory days are over.

Anyway he'd put almost eight grand into the Camaro, punched-out 350, Weld rims, new paint, much of it on a credit card he'd stopped making payments on. He'd probably get three or four grand all told. Maybe thirty-five hundred. Speaking realistically. It had rust. It was not a good investment. It was not like putting your money with Charles Schwab. Get something cheap, good on gas. Toyota or something. He tried to think but no, the car, that old Camaro, it hadn't gotten him any pussy he wouldn't have gotten otherwise. *Pussy magnet* is what the guys at the hotrod shop called that car of his, but that was a bunch of bullshit. You could not trust people who told you things like that. The car was a loser, through and through. As his mother had said it would be.

He would put an ad up on the Internet to sell it, do it at the library when he went to do his college applications. Some stupid kid would buy it same as he had. He'd pick up an old Civic or Tercel, good on gas. Listen to yourself, he thought. Buying an actual little car like that. Unthinkable even a month ago, you are changing. You are changing in front of your own eyes. He got a hose and bucket and sprayed the leaves and dirt off and got his special car soap from the house and sudsed the Camaro so it wouldn't look so bad for a buyer. He was still wearing his boxer shorts. It felt good being out there in the sun like that, practically naked, he could feel the heat all over him.

Then he heard someone coming up the road. It sounded like his mother's Plymouth. He didn't think his mother would be back that early, but maybe so—her hands were getting worse every day. That was another thing he hadn't considered—that soon his mother would not be able to work, at least not much. Winters were hell on her. She pulled in next to the trailer and there she was, his mother, dressed for church and him standing in his underpants in the driveway, nearly one o'clock in the afternoon. She shook her head, but not in a friendly way. She was not happy to see it.

"I'm selling it," he said, by way of making up for being caught like that.

She just looked at him.

"The car. I'm getting something that runs. I'm going to college. In September, if I can."

She didn't say anything.

"I'm gonna call that coach at Colgate College," he continued. "He said I could check in with him anytime. And there'll be other places. Either way I'll be in school by this September. And not any California University of Pennsylvania, either."

"Okay," she said. She went up onto the porch. She didn't believe him.

"I'm serious," he said.

She went inside.

He followed her in. He looked around for a pair of pants to put on, as if it would make him seem more serious.

"Are you really going," she said. "Or are you just saying that so I don't start charging you rent."

"I'm going," he said. "I'm going to the library to get the applications. Get them in the mail soon as possible."

"What about letters from your teachers and copies of your transcript?"

"Right," he said. "I'll do that, too." He had forgotten that part.

"Billy?"

"Yeah."

"You're a good boy." She hugged him but still, he could tell, she didn't believe him. Who could blame her? He was hungry and he went to the fridge, there was nothing he wanted. He checked the chest freezer on the porch, but it was nearly empty as well. Some venison wouldn't hurt anything. He would go and get a deer—poaching—it ran in the family. There were too many deer now, they kept on extending the hunting season but never enough to catch up with the deer population, a little poaching it was no big deal. Fifty pounds of venison, it was free money. Though his mother wouldn't touch it.

After getting dressed he took his .30-30 off its rack, his Winchester 94 from before Winchester went to shit, the gun was fifty years old. Top-eject the way God wanted and no scope—that was for people who couldn't shoot. An original Lyman peep. Someone might have guessed it was his father's or grandfather's rifle but neither one of them knew or cared to take care of anything this nice. He'd saved and bought it himself, passing up the clunky newer models, mostly plastic, that cost half as much.

He dropped a few cartridges in his pocket, three was the right number, then walked down into the field, it was definitely spring now, that rich green smell was everywhere, he wondered where it came from. After slipping into the small blind he'd built, he drew in the air, even the damp soil in the blind smelled rich, it was just the smell of things growing. Smell of life, really. He pushed a pair of blunt-nosed rounds into the magazine. It was all a cycle. It would continue long after he was gone. It was turning out to be a good day. Though already he'd nearly pissed it away, he wouldn't get to the library before it closed. It's Sunday, he thought. Probably closed anyway. He would get it done tonight and still mail the apps tomorrow. But for now it was a nice day and you did not piss away days like this in the library.

The field had not been mowed in a year and the grass was high and the goldenrod was taking over. He would have to mow it soon. He would do that tomorrow as well, a field unmowed did not stay a field very long. He would stop being the kind of punk that put everything off till tomorrow. No excuses it was time to grow up. In his way he was still a momma's boy. He admitted that now. He was good at some things but not at others. He looked out over the land, rolling off in all different directions as far as the eye could see, it was all ridges and hollows, deep wrinkles in the earth as if God had taken a great armful and squeezed it in on itself. Like when you play with the skin on a dog's face, it all wrinkles up. He had not even bothered to get another dog, he thought about that. He was still mourning Bear. But Bear had been dead two years. Was that mourning or being lazy? He went back to the rolling terrain. Of course God was not the explanation. Isaac would know why it did that. Underground plates, probably.

The field descended gradually to a stream and then the land went uphill again, a hundred different types of green, the pale new grass and new buds on the oaks and darkness of the pine tree needles, the hemlocks. Spring—Christ even the animals loved springtime. You called it all green but that was not correct, there should have been different words, hundreds of them. One day he would invent his own. The air was cool and the sky was very blue. Christ it was a nice day. It could have been back in Indian times, a day like this, with the land all greening up and beautiful. He did not see why people would ever want to leave here. It was a beautiful place and it was no exaggeration to say it. It was because of the job situation. But that was changing as well. The Valley was recovering. Only it would never be what it had been and that was the trouble. People couldn't adjust to that—it had been a wealthy place once, or not wealthy but doing well, all those steelworkers making thirty dollars an hour there had been plenty of money. It would never be like that again. It had fallen a long ways. No one blinked at taking a minimum-wage job now. He had not been old enough to see it fall is why it didn't bother him. He just saw the good parts of it. That is a gift, he decided, to only see the good parts. Because we're the first ones to grow up with it like this. The new generation. All we know. But things are improving in different ways. Right now, right from where he was sitting, there were patches of woods that he remembered being overgrown fields when he was younger. Oak, cherry, birch, the land going back to its natural state.

He looked at the area he was hunting, the strip of woods at the edge of their property, a long thin funnel of trees that ran along the edge of the field down to the creek. There were creeks everywhere, that was the other thing about this land. It was rich with life only most people went by it without noticing, as he often did himself. The deer would break from the end of the treeline into the small opening before the creek. He would take the smallest one. He sat and let his mind empty out.

Time passed, he was just watching, he was in his trance, his body was all numbed out he couldn't even feel it, he hadn't even twitched in an hour at least, just his eyes. That was the trick, disconnect your mind from your body. It felt very natural, his father had taught him, you watch any nature show and you know all animals do it, it was not possible to sit still for any length of time otherwise, to just completely blend in. You put every part of you to sleep except your eyes. But people didn't have to do that anymore. You did not have to be a part of your surroundings. You just went to the drive-through. He decided there was something wrong with that. He himself couldn't eat a McDonald's hamburger, he could taste the chemicals in it, he had a delicate stomach. He could eat a pile of vension, or rabbit or quail or anything that lived in the woods, just anything where he knew where it came from. Any wild meat you could tell, it gave something back to you. But Christ, McDonald's. Not to single them out. It was not that their product was inferior. Burger King, Wendy's they were all just as bad. They gave him diarrhea. It was most likely the chemicals. He checked his watch again and only a minute had passed. That's what you get for thinking, he thought. Time won't move if you think. He let himself focus again. He thought about the deer. Taking a nap under those trees where you'll hear anyone coming in after you. But soon you'll want to eat and maybe take a sip from that cool stream and you'll have to cross that little opening. He sniffed and turned his head slowly and sniffed again to check the wind. It was still favorable, coming from the direction of the treeline, blowing toward him. The deer couldn't smell him.

Wait for them to come get a nice cool drink from this stream. He thought about Lee. That will be fine, he thought. Even if she's married she still loves me. He wondered if he would see her that night. It didn't have to be so tragic, their ending. They loved each other but the stars were not in favor of it, so to speak. She was doing what was best. He thought about Isaac then, and the dead man in the factory. He shivered, it was not a good thought and he put it out of his mind. Harris had taken care of it anyway. It was a big fuckup and he'd caused it but Harris had taken care of it.

He heard another car come up the road and then pull into their driveway. One of Mom's friends. He wondered if he should go check. And waste all your two hours sitting and letting the woods forget you're here. All the squirrels and birds are feeding again like you don't even exist. Little Mrs. Whitetail's guard will be down. Sit like an Indian, wait them out. They're probably bedded down a hundred yards from here.

Twenty or so minutes later there was movement at the top of the field. He moved his body slowly in that direction but didn't raise his rifle. Then he saw it was not a deer. A person—Harris—appeared at the top of the hill next to the trailer. Poe could see the sunlight on his bald head. Harris was looking all around the field. Christ he'd get busted for poaching. First he catches me yesterday and now again today. He felt sweat run down his armpits all of a sudden, he could see Harris scanning the field, he could practically watch the man's mind working; Harris saw where the treeline funneled to the stream and then spotted the small thicket and the brush pile that gave good vantage on the opening. It was the best place to hunt that funnel and Harris began walking down the hill toward it, right toward him. Poe knew he couldn't see into the thicket, the sun was in Harris's face but still Harris was coming right for him. It was not for poaching. He would not have come all this way for poaching. He couldn't have known besides. It was that Isaac had been right—Harris was only biding his time and Christ he didn't know, he'd barely slept he couldn't think straight. Harris knew, you were not going to pull the wool over on Harris. Lee she would never talk to him again, getting her brother in trouble like that, the last one who needed trouble was Isaac English, tried to kill himself in the river like his mother did. He felt the weight of the rifle. It was two hundred yards to Harris, maybe one eighty, it was all he could think about, there were plenty of places to brace it was maybe a six-inch holdover at that distance. Only chance you'll ever have. You or anyone else Harris he was a fucking machine everyone knew it. He looked at Harris and thought that way for a long time. He had a strange feeling in his bowels, it was fear, he thought let this be over quickly. By the time he set down the .30-30, Harris was only seventy paces away. Christ. Christ you're a fucking lunatic an actual insane lunatic thinking about shooting a law enforcement officer you've known since you were a kid. As if that will make your problems go away.

He slid the gun under the brush pile and crawled for a while behind the brush so that when Harris saw him come out, he would not be near the gun.

Harris waited for him to stand up.

"Billy," said Harris.

"Afternoon, Chief Harris."

"Go on and fetch your rifle back up to the house so it doesn't rust."

Poe looked at him.

"Go on," said Harris. "We've got bigger things to worry about."

2. Isaac

He picked his way along the creek, the new moon, he thought, the night was very dark. Soon enough the ravine had shrunk to a flat streambed and he was on the grounds of the steelmill just south of town. He made his way north, past the long empty buildings, each a quarter of a mile long and twenty stories tall. He passed the four remaining blast furnaces and their powerhouses, the furnaces were rusted black but still rose high above even the buildings, hundreds of enormous pipes snaking over and around each other, intricate windings. There were dozens of slag cars still on their tracks. He passed under the ore crane and then passed stacks upon stacks of I-beams and T-beams, other structural members. They'd run out of money during the dismantlement. No one wanted to buy an old steelmill. Too much liability.

It was dark and he was comfortable. He followed the train tracks out of the mill, past the town and his old school, past the road to Poe's. All of it went quickly out of sight. The railbed was dark and narrow and winding, cut into the side of the hill, the woods dense on either side, the sound of his footsteps seemed to carry a long way. The kid begins his journey for real. As alone now as when he came into the world. Deadest time of night—the day creatures still asleep and night creatures bedded down. A kid afoot. Bound for California. Warmth of his own desert.

There were a few hobo camps in the woods along the tracks and he kept his eyes out for fires. The kid will be fine, he thought. King of the snakes and duke of all hoboes. He watched a light move quickly across the sky, high above him. A satellite. Comrade to Arab traders and astronauts. All wanderers.

Gradually the sky began to expand with a pale gray light and the few minutes before the sun rose properly he thought: *right about now,* and shortly after he heard a single chirp and then another, and within a few seconds the bushes and woods were rustling with movement, the sound of birdsong and fluttering wings, tanagers, grosbeaks, orioles. All on the same clock. Live by the same rules, never changing. Not like the kid. He makes his own sun. Decides he prefers the night.

On the opposite side of the river the sun was hitting brightly and the shadows on his side seemed to get darker. Ahead of him he could make out the tall smokestack and rotting water tower of the traincar plant. He began to feel nervous. No, he thought, the kid relishes any test. Pits his wit against any who tell him *thou shalt not.* Decides to retrieve his backpack and belongings just for the sake of doing so. Only this time he will approach the plant from the rear.

Leaving the tracks, Isaac followed a small stream up the hillside, a canopy of alder, the bark white against the green of everything else, moss dragging in the clear fast water. Flowering plants. White ones bloodroot, purple ones don't know. Mayflowers, too—nearly extinct—too pretty for their own good. At the top of the hill the stream came out of a hole in the ground and he lay in the damp moss and splashed the cold water into his mouth until his stomach was full. After that he moved slowly through the woods, slipping from tree to tree until he could see the clearing where Harris's truck had been parked the previous night. The clearing was empty. He stayed in the woods anyway, walking parallel to the fireroad until he reached the meadow and the machine shop. It had taken a long time and the sun was well up now. He looked into the open dark doorway of the shop. Guilt and another feeling. Place of victory. Shouldn't be proud but I am. Thinking that he had an even stronger guilty feeling and went to look for his backpack in the field.

This calls for further reflection, he decided. How many people do you know who have never struck a person in anger? Only you. Which includes what happened the other night.

Meanwhile here's your pack, just where you left it . . . money and notebooks still inside. Though slightly damp. A sandwich bag of raisins and peanuts. A nice breakfast. It occurs to the kid that he has not eaten in two days. No worries—food can be found anywhere. After consolidating the things he needed into the larger army surplus pack, he left his smaller schoolbag in the field and made his way back toward the train tracks, finishing off the raisins and peanuts.

*   *   *

Two hours later a short train passed him in the middle of a long straightaway and all he could do was watch in frustration as the cars sped by, too fast to grab hold. Tired and hungry anyway. Might have gone under the wheels if you even tried. What would it matter? Speeding up the natural process. Beings in time, moving toward our expiration. It's cowardly, he thought. That's why it matters. Of all the sperm and eggs that ever existed, here you are, moving under your own power. Odds of you existing—one in ten trillion, no, smaller. One to Avogadro's number: 6.022 times 10^{23}. Meanwhile people throw it away.

He decided not to think about it—sadness too much for him. He calculated where he was, and his speed. On flat ground he makes 3.5 miles per hour. Slightly slower on this gravel. Tires the ankles. Plus the tracks follow every curve in the river—the roads would be shorter. Except the land here is flat and the river will take him where he wants to go. The kid knows that the roads will just get him lost. He tunes himself to the rhythms of the cosmos. Slow and steady.

Belle Vernon was the next major town downriver. There'd been development there recently, a shopping mall, a Lowe's home improvement, a Starbucks, places like that. Traveling properly on foot, the kid is now beyond the places he knows anyone. His material comforts falling away, no place will be foreign. The world is his home. He teaches these lessons and sends them through the ether for others to soak through their skins. A child speaks his first words, a mother conceives a daughter. An old man in India and his deathbed realization—that's the kid.

He came around a sharp bend in the river, a retaining wall to keep the hill from sliding down over the train tracks, and surprised two men standing at the wall with their shirts off. It was an isolated spot, and the two men had cans of spraypaint in their hands. One had a shaved head and a tattoo of an eagle that spread across his entire chest. Isaac wasn't sure whether to turn around and go back the way he came or to keep going. Then he recognized one of them—Daryl Foster. He'd been a year behind Isaac but he'd dropped out. He worked at the Dollar Store in Charleroi. Isaac relaxed some.

"Isaac English?"

"Nice to see you, Daryl."

"Yeah," said Daryl, "been a while now, hasn't it?" He was smiling; he seemed genuinely happy to see Isaac.

"How you doing?" said Daryl's friend with the shaved head.

"Good," said Isaac.

"It's Nietzsche," said Daryl, pointing at what they were spraying.

Isaac nodded. They'd written, in tall neat block letters: OUT OF LIFE'S SCHOOL OF WAR, WHAT DOESN'T KILL and there he'd interrupted them.

"Alright then, brother," said his friend, giving Isaac a nod.

"Take it easy," said Isaac. He took the signal and began to walk again.

"Hey," called Daryl. "You still taking care of your dad? Shit I thought you'd be long gone, doing science experiments or something."

"Making my escape," Isaac called back. "If anyone asks about me . . ."

"Won't say a goddamn word, brother."

Isaac waved and kept going. That was the good thing about the Valley. There was a serious anti-authoritarian bent. Being a rat was lower than being a murderer. Even two like this are the kid's allies, he thought. He chooses equally among heroes and murderers. Among the rich and the helpless.

He continued walking. As for Daryl hanging around the white supremacists, it was not unusual. Stormfront, they called themselves. They'd come in when the mills went under and Pennsylvania was now full of them. More than any other state, he'd read. All the hills—they can meet without anyone knowing. Still, no one took them seriously. Never heard of them hurting anyone. Of course it's easy to say that when you're white.

Shortly after, he passed Allenport on the opposite side of the river, the Wheeling Pittsburgh steelmill still running there, though everyone knew it was bound to close soon—they were down to one shift, only a few hundred people. There was a long train pulling out of the yard carrying sheetmetal rolls.

Next he passed through a long section of forest and then a few miles later he saw the towboat station across from Fayette City, the piers and enormous white storage tanks, a handful of towboats tied up, smokestacks and pilothouses and stubby square bows, empty barges moored along the opposite bank. The trees and brush, the green was pushing out everywhere, it was an uprising it was above him and around him and over the water, there was not a single bare spot except for the trackbed gravel. Patch of white in the brush. Styrofoam? Legbone. Stripped and bleached, stray or suicide train jumper. Phosphorus donor. Old bones make new blooms. Regeneration. The kid has been here before. The kid has ridden Viking prows, hunted polar bear. Attempting to save his comrades, he is among the Fallen at Omaha Beach. Struck down, he rises again. Lives with honor—one of the few. The people retreat shamefaced from him and the kid stands alone. Accepts the company of the best and the worst. Accepts the company of himself.

The kid will rest a minute, he thought. The kid has not slept in seventy-two hours. He found a place along the riverbank in the heavy brush, lay out on top of his sleeping bag, and passed out quickly. It was near dark when he woke up and started walking again. You slept eight hours. Recharge. It was completely dark when he came into Fayette City, the low square houses and empty shops, the train tracks ran right at the river's edge, a woman's dress in the gravel. The tracks passed small white houses with manicured lawns. He was hungry again, he figured he'd come about ten miles, and he left the tracks and walked over to the main drag in search of food. There was nothing. All the stores had moved to the strip malls outside town. It's fine, he thought. Go thirty days without eating. Long way from today. He made his way back to the tracks.

The river was black and the stars were very clear. Feels like a long time since you've talked to anyone. Ignore that feeling in your stomach. Sharp pain then dull pain back to sharp again. Think about something else. Closest star is twenty-five trillion miles. Proxima something. Burning before the dinosaurs. Burning still when there isn't any human left on earth. Different galaxies, a trillion stars. However small you feel you're nowhere close to the truth, atoms and dust-specks.

Weak thinking, he thought. Of course it's true. Like getting depressed about your own death. Your only duty—make the best of it. The only true sin—not appreciating life. Meanwhile there's Charleroi on the other side, making good progress. Those cranes must be Lock Four. Wake up. He slapped his face. Felt that. On the other side of the river he could see the lights of Charleroi blanketing the hillside. He got closer to the cranes—it was the spot they had found her. In the actual lock channel they spotted her, it was only because of the contrast against the light cement walls. Lee told you that. How did she know? No one knew where she went in, only where she came out. Was taken out. Missing two weeks. Old man sure she was murdered, must have been skinheads, but then the autopsy: lungs full of water. I thirst. Found drowned, woundless otherwise—miracle she was noticed at all. River stones in her coat pockets, eleven pounds. Your educated guess. Filling your pockets with rocks from the field and checking the scale. Eleven pounds take anyone under, even Poe—precious balance keeps you afloat. The old man caught you doing it, weighing yourself. Imagining your mother walking along the river, collecting those rocks, humming. Had her own pain. Worst kind internal. Eternal. Let her off.

He began to walk faster, looking straight ahead, walk all night, put some miles between us. Sleep in the day. He was going past an old building, maybe a warehouse, when a car turned onto the small road alongside the tracks. He stepped into the bushes without knowing why and then saw a searchlight shine from the car—a cop. He squatted in the weeds until the cruiser went past, the light shone in the branches just overhead. People in the houses must have called. Hate just the sight of you. Then he thought you could just go ask him for a drink of water, but he didn't get up until the car was long gone.

He pushed through the brush making his way toward the old building. Mouth very dry now—fixating. Mental game and you're losing. Find a stream again. But there would be no streams—it was an industrial zone. Several minutes later he was walking down the gravel road toward the warehouse; off to one side there was an old front-end loader, abandoned and grown over with devil's tear thumb. He picked his way through the thorns and went to the bucket and it was full of rainwater. Brushing the leaves aside, he cupped his hand into it, it tasted tannic and like metal but he swallowed it anyway just to wet his throat, then took another palmful. Might be sorry about this later, he thought.

He was nearly to the building when he had a sudden urge to use the bathroom, he barely had time to squat in the ditch by the road. Nothing to wipe. Good-bye Mr. Clean. Something in that water? Too soon for that, just shock of something in the stomach. Can't remember the last time you felt this dirty.

He went around the warehouse, trying the doors, they were all locked but one. Shining his penlight around, the floor of the warehouse was filthy, piled with debris, people had been scavenging the copper wire and pipes. Right next to the door he'd come in through was another door that led to a small room, it looked like the office, it was cleaner and less dusty than the rest of the building. There were old file cabinets and desks. This is the spot, he thought. Smell of old piss. He took his sleeping bag out and spread it on a desk, it might have been a workbench, he couldn't tell.

It was hard but he kept getting warmer and then he was actually comfortable and warm but he lay there and couldn't fall asleep. Can't stop the mind from going, try the old trick. He put his hand down his pants and pulled for a while but nothing happened. Too tired. He thought about Poe and his sister he had heard her cry out once, a stifled muffled holding your breath noise, and after a minute of thinking about it he was hard, it was a disgusting thought, his own sister, but fine he'd take it, it was the closest he'd been to actual sex in two years, not since he and Autumn Dodson had done it after her graduation party, he still was not sure why she had done it, she'd gone off to Penn State after that. Because you were the only one with a brain in the entire school. That was not the only reason—the kid took over that time, too. The kid made it happen, saying things old Isaac English never would have had the balls to say. Then you're down on the couch in her den, she lifts up that cute little rear of hers to let you get her pants off. Then, look at you, a naked girl in front of you with her legs spread. Put your finger in her and watched it go in and out for a long time, seemed a miracle the way it was slippery like that. Lying there in the dark with his hand down his pants he thought about that, it was old material but good enough, he finished and fell asleep right after.

Sometime later he was dreaming, there was a car and then he heard voices and he was wondering if he could wedge the door closed when the voices got much louder and he realized he wasn't dreaming. There were people in the factory with flashlights.

"Someone cracked that door. It wasn't like that before."

"Come on, Hicks."

"You gotta look. You don't look from over there."

The next voice was loud: "If there's any piece-of-shit bums down there you might as well come out now and save us some work." People were laughing. Someone said: "You're a goddamn dumb-ass, Hicks."

Isaac began to disentangle himself from the sleeping bag; the room he was in was small, the office maybe, there was only one way out of it and he was only partially out of the sleeping bag when the door swung open and light swept around the room. He put his hand on his knife but he saw them and they were young people, high schoolers. He let go of the knife.

"Hold up," he said, but he'd barely gotten off the workbench when one of them walked directly up to him, looked back briefly at his friends as if to make sure they were paying attention, and punched Isaac in the face.

"I went to Buell Memorial," he said, but the others were on top of him and he was knocked to the ground. He tried to protect his head but something caught him on the jaw anyway and then in the stomach and then his ribs and back and he tried to protect his sides and got kicked in the mouth again. He covered his head and they kept kicking. His wind was knocked out and he couldn't breathe, he was choking. Then the light was in his face and the kicking abruptly stopped.

"Christ, Hicks. It's a fucking kid."

Isaac stayed where he was, covering himself.

"Shut the fuck up," said Hicks. "All of you."

One of the others said: "Fuck yourself, Hicks. The car is leaving, you can walk home if you want."

The person he knew was Hicks squatted down next to him and said: "You'll be alright, buddy. We got you confused with someone else. You want a beer or anything?"

"Don't touch me," said Isaac.

Hicks knelt there a few more seconds, unsure of himself, and then Isaac heard him stand and walk quickly outside. He heard car doors slam and then heard the car pull away. He was afraid to touch himself for what he might find. He stood up and walked outside to the dirt lot. It was empty. It hadn't taken more than a minute. Most of his face was still numb and he went back inside and repacked his things and finally he stopped heaving. He found a rubber welcome mat and carried it outside to sleep on. The kids had been sixteen, seventeen, maybe younger. Good, he said out loud. Now you know. He walked through the tall brush toward the river until it seemed no one would find him. When he crouched down there was no wind. His heart was still racing and his mouth tasted like blood. You could have stopped that, he thought. If you'd cut even one of them, the rest would have taken off. He decided it was fine. Fool me once. He took out the knife and set it next to his head. It took a long time before his heart slowed down enough for him to fall asleep.

3. Poe

He was in the back of Harris's truck and they pulled into the police station. It was not the first time he'd been there, it wasn't even properly the police station, in fact, it was called the Buell Municipal Building on account of there were other offices, the mayor's and the city council's. According to the newspaper, the mayor now slept in his office because his wife had kicked him out. It had been a minor scandal, the mayor living out of his office. The municipal building was white cinderblock, three stories with a flat roof, it looked like a big repair shop of some kind, not the headquarters of a town. The inside was painted yellow. It was not old but it looked that way. The original city hall had been condemned years ago and several times Poe had broken in and walked around inside; it was a large red brick building that looked like a castle, iron windows, wood paneling inside and dentil molding, it looked like the home of a rich person, a place you could respect yourself. But the city did not have the money to maintain it.

Inside the new building Poe saw the pudgy Chinese officer, he was watching Fox News, it looked like he was having a conversation with the television. Harris took Poe downstairs to the holding cells, Poe had been there before, a long hallway with what looked like big steel firedoors every ten feet or so. The cell had a butcher block for a bed and no mattress. The light fixture outside flickered like it would give him a seizure. There was one window that looked up from the ground toward the parking lot, but the plastic was hazed over.

"I'll be back for you in a bit," said Harris. When he wasn't busting heads he had an open, easygoing face, eyes that forgave you, like he was meant to be something else, maybe a schoolteacher. Which was probably the reason he had to bust so many heads, to make up for the way he looked.

"How long do you think—" Poe said, but Harris closed the door on him.

"Make yourself comfortable," he heard Harris tell him. He heard other doors slamming after that.

He had no coat and there seemed to be a vent blowing cold air directly onto him, not to mention there was a puddle from the leaking toilet; water covered most of the floor. Here he was, you didn't think they could do this to you—put you in a locked room—but they could. There was no way around it. It was a tragedy of life. In fact that was how he'd felt the first time they'd locked him up, that there had been no way around it, but in hindsight that hadn't been true. It wasn't true now, either. It was his own choices. They never felt like choices while he was making them, but nonetheless they were. It was nice to think it was a vast conspiracy of others but the truth was something different.

The last time he was locked up it was the boy from Donora. Big, though not quite as big as Poe, and aside from the pimples all over his face and neck there had been nothing wrong with him. A B student, people said. But when Poe got through with him it was different. He remembered holding the boy down, they were both bleeding some, girls watching. They were in a dirt parking lot at night and it was very quiet, everyone had stopped talking to watch them, there was no one even cheering them on, just the sound of their heavy breathing and grunting. The boy was pinned and Poe knew he should not let the boy up. Stay down, he whispered, but he knew the boy wouldn't, he could tell the boy did not want to lose, the boy did not have it in him to lose. It would be the downfall of both of them. Stay down, he said again, quietly into the boy's ear, but he had to let him up, they couldn't lie there all night. He should have choked him out, it would have been for the boy's own good, but others would have gotten involved if he'd done that. It was no win either way, and finally he had to let the boy up, though he knew what would happen. Obviously he did not know *exactly* what would happen, he only knew the situation would not improve.

The boy went to his car and came back and everyone stepped away. He had a knife, a military bayonet you might buy at a gun show, and the crowd made way for Poe to retreat but Poe had stood his ground, it would have been easy to walk away, the kid was insane at losing the fight, he was not really going to use the bayonet, he was the type who would go off to college, he was embarrassed, was all.

But Poe had stood his ground. Because his fire was going. Because he'd won and now he didn't want to lose. He had stood there and no one knew what to do, not him, not the boy, and then Vincent Lewis had put a bat in Poe's hand, a child's bat from Little League it was light and short, a good weapon. It was something out of gladiator times, knife versus club. Neither of them really wanting to do it, it was only because of all the people. The older you got the more serious things became. Your margins for fuckup disappeared. First there was the boy from Donora and now the Swede. It was getting worse. He wondered what would come next. Both times he should have known better but he hadn't. The next time Christ it would be someone he loved, his mother, or Lee, it would be something unthinkable.

As for the boy from Donora, Poe had asked after him several times but he was not okay. He couldn't even work a cash register, couldn't keep the numbers straight on account of Poe hitting him with the bat. He hit him and the boy went down in the dirt and then he didn't know, he'd hit him once more in the head. Because he was still holding on to that bayonet. And yet that was why the assault charge—the second hit, they were teaching him a lesson. But you didn't learn it, he thought. You did not learn that lesson.

He was always trying to see what he could get away with—that was why a man was dead. He was always trying to game it. See how far he could push. That was in the bloodstream and why he ever thought he'd escape it, who the fuck knew? Hiram Poe, his grandfather, the Valley's biggest poacher, had shot himself, no one knew why, because he was a crazy old fuck is how Poe's father put it. Don't worry, you ain't like him, is what his father told him, but Poe hadn't even been wondering. It hadn't even occurred to him that he was anything like batshit old Grandpa. Now, though. Now things were going downhill.

His father had a talent for making things go his way, he'd worked on the towboats when Poe was younger, then gotten fired because he hadn't lashed the barges right and a storm came up and a fucking barge full of coal went floating off down the Mon, nearly causing a wreck. But still that weaselly old fucker, weaselly Virgil had managed to come out on top, something had happened to him on the boats, he jammed his back somehow, so he managed to collect a little disability from it, claimed he had something permanently wrong with his back when really it was fine. He still lost his job but now he got a permanent paycheck from it. He was always moving around, he'd come into town once in a while for a piece of pussy, mostly from young girls, but occasionally from Poe's mother. It was not something Poe liked to think about, his mom in that position, but it was true, you did not have the luxury of thinking otherwise when you lived in a trailer. As for Virgil, he worked odd jobs once in a while, sat in the bars reading books so the girls would believe he was a great thinker, a rebel, when really he was just a lazy bastard who didn't give two shits for anyone. Probably holding the books upside down. Put his mind up against someone like Lee or Isaac, they'd crush him.

He looked around—outside, it had already gotten dark. His cell was big for a jail cell, maybe ten by twenty feet, but the floor was soaking wet. And now that no light was coming in from the outside, it was even darker—the light fixture in the hallway did a poor job—you would have gotten eyestrain if you'd tried to read. He had nothing to read anyway. He tried to keep his mind moving so the boredom wouldn't set in, the death spiral. What got old Hiram—sit around long enough with nothing to think about eventually your mind locks into it—fact that this here, your breathing, is a temporary situation, and why bother pretending otherwise.

Hiram had got what was coming and he was not sorry Hiram was gone. When Poe was seven, he and his father and old Hiram had been sitting in a deer blind, and Poe had fallen asleep, and when he woke up there were deer in front of the blind, and he'd said look, a deer, and spooked them all, including a big twelve-pointer, and Hiram had missed his shot. Later he'd heard his father saying *you ain't mad, are ya? He's just a kid.* But Hiram was mad—at a small boy on his first hunting trip. Virgil had knocked Poe around plenty, but once, when Virgil wasn't around, Hiram had done it too. The thing is it was not Hiram's fault, or Virgil's, it was in the blood and it was the fault of someone way back before either of them. God, maybe.

He stood up and banged on the cell door until his hand hurt, knowing the whole time no one would come. When he got bored with that he stood looking out the window, there were things moving but he couldn't tell what, a bird, a truck, a person walking. He himself was not going anywhere and he never had been. As for college the whole idea was a joke, if there was one thing he was bad at, one thing he'd never been good at in his life it was book learning. Let him do it with his hands no problem, rejet a carburetor, gut a deer, he was good at those things but stick him in a room with chairs and desks and he blanked out. He couldn't see the importance. He couldn't distinguish between what was important to know and what wasn't, he remembered the wrong things. It had always been that way.

It was only when he was playing ball, competing against others and living outside himself, something happened then, it was like information coming through a firehose but he took it all in, he would literally float above the others, he knew more about people than they knew about themselves, the exact patch of grass where their foot would land, the holes opening and closing between the bodies, the ball hovering in the air. It was like seeing the future. That was the only way to describe it, a movie where he moved in real time and everyone else moved in slow motion. Those were the times he liked himself best—when he was not really himself. When it was some part of him in control that he didn't understand, when others couldn't see him.

That was the truth—he was fucked. When it came down to it, when it came down to making life decisions, either his fire got going or he froze. He either went ballistic or came to a full stop, dead in the water, he needed to think about things too long, examine them from every angle. Like going to Colgate, it seemed they had not given him enough time to think, and then everyone telling him to go for it just go for it. And he froze—two years later he was still thinking. He should have just gone, then none of it—the boy from Donora losing his mind or the Swede being dead—none of that would have happened. If he had gone off to Colgate, it would not have been physically possible for any of that to have happened. It was a mistake and he had made it, only it had not really been. It was inevitable. There were men who would die heroes but he was not one of them. He had always known it.

4. Harris

He chose the worst cell for Billy Poe and decided to leave him overnight so the boy would figure out what was in store for him. Lying on that piece of butcher block. Which, when you thought about it, was fitting. Something big was going on at the DA's office, it wasn't clear exactly what, but Harris had a suspicion that however it turned out, it was not going to benefit Billy Poe. He locked his office and went to say good-bye to the night guy. It was Steve Ho.

"You again?"

"Miller called in."

Harris made a mental note to check how many times Ron Miller had called in.

"You look like you ought to call in yourself, boss."

"I'm just tired."

Ho nodded and Harris walked out of the station and got into his old Silverado. It was a nice evening and there would be several hours of daylight left still, even by the time he got home. That was something to be thankful for. Another advantage of being chief—you worked the day shift.

As he made his way south and west, eventually the paved road gave way to a rutted paved road and then a gravel road and then it was just dirt. His cabin was perched on top of a ridge, a thirty-acre inholding surrounded by state forest.

Getting out of the truck and looking at his house, it never failed to make him happy. A squat log cabin, stone chimneys, a forty-mile view. You could see three states from the deck. No one had ever accidentally come up the road, not once in the four years he'd lived there.

Fur, his big malamute, was waiting for him inside; Harris stepped aside to let the dog run but Fur just stood there, waiting to be petted. Fur's hips were getting stiff, his back sagging a little, the dog was shameless for attention, a prince. In the wild, Harris told him, affectionately shaking his neck, you'd be bear meat. Fur was too big for his own bones and there were nights Harris would sit in front of the TV, drinking whiskey and massaging the dog's hips. He gave him a final pat on the head and the dog leapt off the side of the deck, a five-foot drop, and took off full speed into the woods. Maybe he wasn't that old after all. Maybe he just has your number.

After pouring himself a club soda he went back out onto the deck and leaned against the railing, just looking. Nothing but mountains and woods—Mount Davis, Packhorse Mountain, Winding Ridge. The land dropped steeply away from the house and continued descending to the valley floor, fourteen hundred feet below. It was a good place. His Waldo Pond. His Even Keel. Walden, he thought. Not Waldo. He grinned at himself. There were plenty of other squares he could have landed on, such as his brother's, a computer programmer in Florida, four children and a Disney subdevelopment. Harris had one word for that: hellhole. Got into computers early, mainframes, the old UNIVACs, made six times what Harris did. Still down on himself—might be that runs in the family. He was no Bill Gates. Those were his own words: *Bud, I am exactly the same age as Bill Gates.* You're doing pretty good, Harris had told him. Neither one of them had any college but every two years his brother got a new Mercedes. I do alright, said his brother, but it's good to be able to admit that—I am the same age as Bill Gates. Harris wasn't sure. You could make anything up you wanted, there were always stories to justify your choices. This house in the woods, for instance. Which both keeps you sane and guarantees you'll be alone the rest of your life. Those things should not be equivalent, he thought.

He turned on the grill and took a steak from the refrigerator, though he knew what he had to do first. There were two messages on his machine, both from her. It was not a conversation he wanted to have. Well, he thought. You're the one who chose this.

Grace answered on the first ring.

"It's me," he said.

"I'm nervous," she said. "Can we skip the hey how's it goings?"

"Fine with me. I got my Netflix to watch same as you."

There was silence.

"That was a joke," he said.

"What's happening with my son, Bud?"

He wondered how he ought to answer that. After thinking a few seconds, he said: "Billy was hanging out in places that he would have done better to have stayed away from." He almost added, *as usual,* but didn't. Then there was something about the way she breathed into the phone— he didn't know how, but he got a feeling she knew exactly what her son had done. Probably she knew more than Harris. Harris felt himself get annoyed.

"He hasn't been charged yet," he continued, "but I have a feeling he might be."

"What about your friend Patacki?"

"Grace," he said.

"I'm sorry," she said. "He's my kid."

He felt himself pass from annoyance into anger and then Even Keel took over and he was just bored. It had never been any different from this, she was always asking for things.

"It looks like Billy might be tied up with this dead man they found in that old plant," he said. "How tied up, I don't know, because he's not talking."

"Should we be getting a lawyer?"

"Yes," he said. "Knowing Billy, you ought to be getting a lawyer."

"Buddy—"

"I'm trying to help you," he said. "I'll do all I can."

He got off the phone quickly. Why was he trying to help her? He didn't know. Resisting the urge to pour a tall drink, he glanced out over the deck, the colors were getting nice, it would be a fine sunset. Put a potato in the nuker. Cook your steak. Make a salad. He carried the steak out to the grill and felt himself getting into his routine again. Fur had come back from his adventuring, impeccable timing as always.

"Not for you," he told the dog. He closed the grill on the steak and went back in to fix the rest of his meal.

There was plenty else to worry about besides Billy Poe. The state's attorney was investigating Don Cunko, Harris's good buddy on the city council, and soon enough they'd discover that the club basement and wet bar installed in Don's house had been paid for by Steelville Excavation, the same folks who'd won the bid to replace Buell's sewer system. Harris liked Cunko. Maybe he had bad taste in friends. No, he thought, Cunko had crossed the line, first by taking the money, then by having parties in the new basement. But it was not a good idea to get self-righteous—there was plenty they could get him on as well. He'd never taken any money, but he'd always taken other liberties, especially when encouraging certain townspeople to move to greener pastures. It was the reason Buell had half the crime rate of Monessen and Brownsville. There were a lot of people who could talk. None of them were particularly credible, but there were enough of them. The Cunko investigation brought that fresh to mind.

There were some pressing decisions as well. The city council had just come out with the new budget, the infrastructure was crumbling, and the EPA had ordered the city to repair the sewer system, which had been spilling sewage into the Mon during heavy storms. The Buell PD's share of the budget had gone from $785,000 to $541,000—the biggest cut in the department's history. In addition to cutting back training and keeping the department's already clapped-out vehicles in service indefinitely, he would have to lay off three of his full-time guys. Which was nearly everyone.

He looked at his six-by-six elk and wondered when he'd be able to get to Wyoming again. Not till after retirement. As of next month, the department would consist of him, Steve Ho, Dick Nance, and twelve part-timers. Bert Haggerton was gone for sure. No one would miss him. But Harris would also have to get rid of Ron Miller, who had kids in college. Miller, who he'd known twenty years. But Miller was lazy, a clock-watcher, if Miller got a call in the middle of lunch, he would order dessert. Jerzy Borkowski, who was also going to get cut, was no better. They were small-town cops but things were changing, you needed a different attitude, the Mayberry days were over. He felt another surge of relief at keeping Steve Ho—he'd thought the council would make him keep Miller, who was the most senior officer. He could probably lie to Borkowski and Miller—tell them the council had made the decision on who to fire and who to keep—but in a town this size they would hear the truth soon enough. Neither one of those men would ever speak to him again. He would have to accept that. Haggerton wouldn't, either, though he didn't care about Haggerton.

The steak, he thought. He went out and flipped it. All was not lost.

"Beat it," he told Fur, who was inching closer to the grill.

Eventually, everyone knew, the department's budget would be cut again and the Buell police would cease to exist—they would have to merge with the Southwest Regional out of Belle Vernon. Three years before there had been another budget crisis; the city ran out of money in late November and for the last four weeks of the year all the city employees went to the Mon Valley Bank and took out loans in lieu of paychecks. On the first of the New Year everyone took their loan slips to the city cashier's office and the city paid them off. Harris was pretty sure those things did not happen in other places.

The Valley's population was growing again but incomes were still going down, budgets still getting smaller, and no money had been put into infrastructure for decades. They had small-town budgets and big-city problems. As Ho said, they were approaching the tipping point. Most of the other Valley towns, with the exception of maybe Charleroi and Mon City, were over the edge and would never come back. The week before, a man had been shot in the face in broad daylight in Monessen. It was like this all up and down the river and many of the young people, the way they accepted their lack of prospects, it was like watching sparks die in the night. Just to get an office job you had to go to college and there were not enough of those jobs to go around—there could only be so many computer programmers, only so many management consultants. And of course those jobs were moving overseas now at the same rate they'd once shipped the steel jobs.

He didn't see how the country could survive like this in the long run; a stable society required stable jobs, there wasn't anything more to it than that. The police could not fix those problems. Citizens with pensions and health insurance rarely robbed their neighbors, beat their wives, or cooked up methamphetamine in their back sheds. And yet, everyone wanted to blame the cops—as if the department could somehow stop a society from collapsing. The police need to be more aggressive, they would say, until you caught their kid stealing a car and twisted his arm a little hard—then you were a monster. Civil rights violator. They wanted easy answers, but there weren't any. Keep your kids in school. Hope those biomed companies move down here.

In the meantime, enjoy what you can. He fixed his plate and gave Fur his two cups of kibble. The dog looked longingly at Harris sitting there with his plate in his lap, his steak and his chive potato. Harris shrugged and went on eating.

There would be time later for a nice fire, maybe he would finish that book. James Patterson. He would forget about Billy Poe.

"Get over here, meathead."

Fur came and sat down next to Harris, knowing he was about to get some steak.

*   *   *

When he went into the office the next morning there were already messages. The important one being from the DA—they'd found a witness in the case who claimed to have been present at the time of the murder. The witness was fingering a football player whose name he couldn't remember, but he was positive he'd know him in a lineup. Did that ring any bells?

Harris returned the call but the DA was out somewhere. He sat at his desk and rubbed his temples. His little stunt with the jacket had not mattered one bit. It was still there, for all he knew, but it was no longer relevant. Murray Clark—the name of the witness—Harris ran him in the computer. DUI in '81, another one in '83, an arrest in '87 for disorderly conduct. Nothing since. He rubbed the stiff muscles on his neck. A man who had, most likely, turned himself around. Not enough to discredit him on a witness stand. He switched off the computer monitor. He couldn't let himself think about this anymore—it would turn him inside out.

The office felt hot; he opened all the windows and sat down in his big leather chair, looking over the river, leg bouncing. He deserved a cigar. It would clear his mind. The humidor was right there. The air currents were good—the smoke wouldn't bother anyone. After finding the one he wanted and lighting it he eased farther into the chair, savoring. A glass of whiskey would top it off. You're going a little far now, he told himself.

It was a good place, his office. More of a clubroom, really. Everyone hated the new building and he didn't blame them, cinderblock and fluorescent lights, but it was all what you made of it. The old building had cost a hundred grand a year to keep in operation. Of course, it had also been a piece of artwork—towers and gables and wood panels inside, high ceilings, open spaces. You felt like someone working in a place like that. The new place, everyone rightfully said, looked like a garage.

He turned the smoke around in his mouth. He thought about Grace, looked at his own skinny legs and scuffed ropers on the desk, then around the office again. He'd salvaged a few things from the old building, this big oak desk, table lamps, leather furniture, a few impressionist paintings of the Valley as it had been in the old days, men poling flatbottom boats up the Mon, the night sky glowing orange above a steelmill. There were deer heads, another elk, a moose he'd shot in Maine. One of the deer was a little spike that the taxidermist had been embarrassed to mount. But Harris had carried that deer from deep in the woods, it was the last day of the season and he'd walked in four miles and got his deer and then carried it out, four miles, the others on the wall had similar stories, none of them were trophies but they all reminded him of times he liked to think about, times that had turned out better than they should have.

As for Billy Poe he'd dealt with this a million times—it was the downside of working in a small town, knowing who you arrested, knowing their mothers. In this case, sleeping with their mother, though obviously it was more than that. There was a mountain of paperwork as always but he decided to let himself watch the river for a while, twenty minutes to

sit and watch the sky change, the river just flowing, it had been there before man laid eyes on it and it would be there long after everyone was
gone. It was a good way to clear his head. Nothing mankind was capable
of, the worst of human nature, it would never linger long enough to
matter, any river or mountain could show you that—filthy them up, cut
down all the trees, still they healed themselves, even trees outlived us,
stones would survive the end of the earth. You forgot that sometimes—
you begin to take the human ugliness personally. But it was as temporary
as anything else.

Only a few minutes had passed since he'd started the cigar but he
went down his to-do list anyway, both the one on his notepad and the
real one he kept in his head. He banished Billy Poe from his mind for
good—the boy had built up a good head of steam but he was about to
run out of track. He felt bad for Grace but that was all.

So why was his headache coming back? In eighteen months he could
retire, had always presumed he would, though the closer it got the less
sure he was about how he really felt about it, he liked coming in to work
every day, liked his job. An extra day or two off a week would be nice, but
seven days off might kill him—he couldn't spend the whole time hunting. It suddenly struck him what an enormous mistake it had been to
move into the cabin: once he retired, he'd be completely alone. Steve Ho
and Dick Nance, Dolly Wagner and Sue Pearson who worked in the city
council's office, Don Cunko, even Miller and Borkowski—those people
were the closest thing he had to a family. Everything, all of it, seemed
like a mistake. He had done it to himself.

He stood up quickly and went to his bag to get a Xanax, shook one
into his hand but didn't take it. He put the pill back and did three sets of
situps and pushups. If you took care of your body, your mind would follow. So they said. He was not doing badly. Well, in fact—enough money
had been put away, he wouldn't end up like Joe Lewis, the Monessen
chief who'd had to work as a school security guard when he retired. And,
as he reminded himself constantly, he did good work, he could be proud
of what he'd done. Despite being one of the poorest, Buell was still one
of the better towns in the Valley to live in, the kids didn't spraypaint so
much, the dope dealing was not public. But it was only a delaying tactic.

A young woman's body had been found a few weeks back, she lived in Greene County and her system was full of methamphetamines, no one knew what she was doing in Buell. There had been six other bodies in Fayette County this year as well, half of them gave up no leads at all. The newspapers were onto this and the new DA was on the defensive. And the last two are in your jurisdiction, thought Harris. He's gonna need to bang this one out of the park.

There was a knock and Harris unlocked the door to see Ho, carrying his big belly in front of him. He had strangely small hands and feet. His parents were from Hong Kong and they owned the Chinese Buffet in North Belle Vernon. He came into the office, pushing past Harris and sniffing the air, and, upon finding the cigar in the ashtray, picked it up and pitched it out the open window.

Harris grimaced. It was a seven-dollar cigar.

"It's ten in the goddamn morning," said Ho.

"I'm a grown man," said Harris.

Ho shrugged. "We might be getting a complaint," he said. "Last night I got a noise violation at the Sparrows Point Apartments and ended up deploying my carbine. Twelve rounds."

Harris blinked and then he thought no, if it was bad I would have heard about it already. Either way he was glad for the distraction. A good number of their problems came from Sparrows Point, a block of HUD apartments at the edge of town.

"It was just a pit bull," Ho continued. "You know that little bald-headed dude, the one with all the tattoos on his face? He let the dog go on purpose to come after me, like I'd jump on the roof of the car or something, act like a funny Chinaman."

"Did anything get hit besides the dog?"

"Hell no. But you should have seen all those motherfuckers, diving behind cars and shit. Wish I had it on tape."

"What were you doing with the rifle for a noise violation?"

"There was like seven or eight of them. What the fuck was I supposed to do?"

"Do you know what our insurance costs," he said to Ho.

"Fuck the insurance," said Ho. "What about shock and awe? Those fuckers are cooking up crystal in the units back there. It's a fuckin environmental hazard."

"They don't bother the citizens," said Harris. "People will get it somewhere."

"That's just your liberal politics talking," said Ho.

"Libertarian."

"Whatever." Ho grinned.

"You better watch your mouth if you want to keep that rifle."

"Yessir."

"You do the paperwork yet?"

"I wanted to ask you first."

Harris rubbed his temples. All in all, it was better if there was no record of Ho shooting a dog with an automatic rifle. But if a complaint was ever filed . . . "Lemme think about it. In the meantime, around eleven o'clock why don't you get some Dairy Queen for Billy Poe."

"That boy's fucked, ain t he? Heard about Carzano's witness."

"We'll see."

"Sorry, Chief. Like I said before, looks like it'd be better if that prick Cecil Small was still the DA."

"Alright," said Harris. "I got work to do." He gave a little wave and Ho left him alone in the office.

Ho was right. Cecil Small, who'd been DA of Fayette County longer than Harris had been a cop, had come looking for Harris's help in the election last year. Harris had demurred and Cecil Small had lost by fourteen votes. Cecil Small could have made something like this go away—in fact, he'd already allowed Billy Poe to plea down an assault charge. But Harris had never liked Cecil Small—he enjoyed playing God a little too much. It was undignified, a seventy-year-old man still getting high off locking people up. Expecting people to buy him drinks every time he won a trial. Like he was a key player in the battle between good and evil. For thirty years he'd been the emperor of Fayette County, though finally it had caught up to him—the voters got sick of it. The new DA, who was only twenty-eight years old, and who Harris had both voted for and essentially put in office by not making the requisite phone calls for Cecil Small, needed to prove himself and was now tripping over his own feet to be getting a case like this. There were consequences to voting your conscience.

He wondered what Ho thought about all this, about his protecting Grace's son. Most likely he just accepted it as natural behavior. Ho was very realistic. He did not think he could change things. He was part of the new generation, his stubby assault rifle went with him everywhere, he dressed like he was walking into a war zone, whereas Harris rarely even bothered to wear his bulletproof vest, his "duty boots" being these cowboy ropers he'd bought on a Wyoming trip—not a good choice if he had to run someone down. But Ho was right. If something went wrong, backup in the form of the state police was at least half an hour away, things were changing, the kids were all on speed now, they were cooking it up themselves and you didn't know what they might do. No, he thought, even thinking that way is a problem. Puts you and them on opposite sides before the word go. He shook his head at himself. There's probably never been an old man who didn't think that all the young people were degenerate. Nature of youth and age. Painful to see the world changing without you.

Still, he couldn't blame Ho for not wanting to walk into those situations with only a sidearm. Not to mention Ho was still here because Harris made the job fun, gave him carte blanche. The feds were getting rid of all their old M16s, giving them away to police departments, and Harris had ten of them, free except for shipping costs. They'd also gotten binoculars, night vision, riot shields, old ballistic vests, all free. They had more weapons and gear now than they had cops, they had more gear than Harris had had when he'd gone to Vietnam with the marines. It was all because of Ho, who had spent weeks of his own time filling out the paperwork, then thousands of dollars of his own money to customize his rifle, a ten-inch barrel and holographic sight. At the moment, Ho was happy living in his parents' basement, doing gunsmithing on the side, but someday he would decide to move on. Sooner than later if Harris made the job boring. He would miss Ho. But he was getting ahead of himself again. Ho wasn't gone yet.

He tried to remember what he was supposed to be doing but then Billy Poe was on his mind again, and what this would do to Grace. He vaguely remembered the man Ho said was the owner of the dead dog, he'd just moved to town from West Virginia, typical toothless speed freak, had relatives here. He wondered if the man deserved a special visit. But probably watching his dog get machine-gunned was enough.

After an hour more of catching up on paperwork, he decided he couldn't stand it. He went and got Billy Poe from the cell. Billy looked depressed. That was a good sign.

"Let's talk in the office," said Harris.

Billy Poe followed him into the office and stood politely until Harris motioned him to a chair It occurred to him that the kid had been through this plenty of times before, called to the principal's office and lectured. Called to this very office and lectured. He tried to recollect what he'd said last time. He hoped he didn't repeat himself—they all remembered.

"I watched you play ball," he said.

Billy Poe didn't say anything. He was looking at the floor.

"You should have gone to college with it."

"I was sick of school."

"Won't tell you that's smart. I know other people did, or just didn't say anything. But I won't. That was one of the dumbest moves you ever made."

Poe shook his head. "You ought to be able to grow up in a place and not have to get the hell out of it when you turn eighteen."

Harris was slightly taken aback. "I might agree with you and I might not," he said, "but either way it doesn't change a goddamn thing."

"I'm gonna call up the coach at Colgate."

Ho knocked and Harris told him to come in. He was carrying a box from Dairy Queen and Harris went through it and set a hamburger and French fries and a milkshake in front of Poe. They could all see the steam coming off the food.

"Vanilla shake?" said Harris.

"No, thank you."

"Go on and eat."

"I can't," said Poe. "That stuff gives me problems with my stomach."

Harris and Ho looked at each other, then at Billy Poe.

"He didn't eat what I brought him last night, either," said Ho.

"It's the chemicals," Poe said. "That stuff isn't fresh."

"What do you think prison food is gonna be like?" said Ho. "You think they offer organic?"

Harris grinned but waved him out of the room, and then faced Billy Poe across the desk again. He decided to push the boy a little. "No job," he said. "No skills to speak of, no car, if you're counting ones that actually run. Mostly likely headed to get some girl in trouble, if you haven't already. And now you're a cunt hair away from a murder conviction and I do mean a cunt hair, too." Harris held up his fingers. "So whether some college football coach remembers you or not, that's pretty much the least of your worries."

Poe didn't say anything. He began to pick at the fries.

"Tell me about this man," said Harris.

"Don't know anything about it."

"I saw you there, William. Returning to the scene of the crime to . . ." He nearly mentioned the jacket but stopped himself. "The only reason I didn't take you in right then was because of your mother. Plenty of kids like you get out but the ones that stay, I've seen what becomes of them."

"You're here, if it's so good to leave."

"I'm an old man. I've got a boat and slip and a cabin on top of a mountain."

"Big deal."

Harris rummaged in the broad oak desk and came out with a manila folder, from which he took several printouts of digital photos. He passed them to Poe. From the way Poe dropped the papers, he recognized the scene pictured.

"Otto Carson, if you want to know the guy's name. The DA over in Uniontown is a brand-new guy as you may or may not know, he's got a dead woman in a dumpster with no clues and here you are dropping this in his lap. The staties want me to confiscate your goddamn shoes."

Poe looked at his sneakers.

"Thing is, Billy, the now-deceased Mr. Carson was a piece of shit. Been locked up for all kinds of crap, some stays in mental wards, two outstanding warrants for assault, one from Baltimore and the other from Philadelphia. Sooner or later he was going to kill somebody. Most likely he already had."

"What's your point," Poe said.

"If it were up to me, if you'd come to me right away, this would have been an easy self-defense plea. Or it might have just gone away on its own. But that's not what you did. You ran. Now you got a guy who was there with you in that machine shop claiming you killed his buddy."

Harris leaned back in his chair, into the sunlight. Usually he liked to watch people in these situations, every tic on their guilty faces. But he did not want to look at Billy Poe. "You need any coffee?" he said.

Poe shook his head.

He waited for Poe to comment, or make a gesture, but he didn't. Harris got up and walked to the window and looked out over the Valley. "I'm guessing there were five of you in the machine shop. You, someone else who was probably Isaac English, Mr. Carson, and two of his friends—"

"Then why haven't you picked up Isaac?"

"Isaac English is not a suspect," Harris said, "because the DA doesn't know who he is, and the more the DA knows, the worse off you are going to be."

"Like I said," Poe told him, "I don't know anything about it."

Harris nodded. He decided to try nice cop. "You did the right thing, Billy. You need to tell me what happened, and who else was in that plant with you, so we can make sure this goes to trial as self-defense. Because if all the jury sees is that you killed a man and fled the scene, even a bunch of good ole boys are gonna vote to hang you."

"His buddy had a knife to my neck and the dead guy was coming at me to finish the job," said Poe.

"Good."

Poe looked at him.

"Don't stop now."

"It was dark," Poe said. "I couldn't see the rest of their faces."

"No."

"I didn't kill him."

"Billy, I goddamn caught you going back to the crime scene." Again he resisted mentioning the jacket he'd found. "I got your footprints everywhere. Size fourteen Adidas—know how many people wear those?" He looked under the desk at Poe's feet. "Most likely blue in color, right?"

Poe shrugged.

"If you're lucky this is going to put you in jail until you're fifty. If you catch a bad break it'll send you to the injection booth."

"Whatever."

"Billy, you and I know that the truth, the one that matters, is that this man was killed by his own choices in life. That for all practical purposes, you had such a small part of it as to mean nothing. But you need to help me now."

"I couldn't see their faces."

Harris shook his head. He motioned Poe to stand up.

"Am I gonna be booked now?"

"For your mother's sake I'm letting you go home tonight to get yourself in order. Tomorrow I'm going to come by your house and pick you up before the staties do. Make sure those shoes don't exist anymore, and if you still got the box, or any kind of receipts, burn them, too. And don't get any ideas in you. They'll send you up for sure if you run."

"Fine," said Poe. "I'll be there."

"This witness," said Harris. "Claims he saw the whole thing. Tell me about him."

"I need to go home," said Poe. "Give me a day to think about it."

"You gonna run if I let you go?"

"I ain't goin anywhere."

What does it matter, he thought. Then he thought: don't be stupid about this. But they had nothing to hold Billy Poe on anyway. Or at least nothing the DA knew about.

"I'm guessing you got a day, maybe two, before they put a warrant out for you, so I'm gonna come by your mother's house tomorrow morning. Make sure you're there."

Billy Poe nodded.

Well, thought Harris, as he walked Billy Poe to the station's front door. You might have just made your life a lot more interesting.

5. Lee

Isaac had been gone almost two days and she'd been calling Poe's cell-phone ever since but all she got was a message saying the number was out of service. He'd been late again paying his bill. The sorts of things Poe did—not paying his bills on time, driving an old car that was always breaking down—she'd always found them rebellious and somehow ad-mirable but now they seemed immature and frustrating. She needed to find her brother. What kind of person doesn't pay their phone bill? Then she thought: a person who can't afford to. She was angry at him anyway. She was angry at herself. She put her head down on the table and counted slowly to ten. Then she got up to find her father: he had an ap-pointment at the hospital in Charleroi and they needed to get moving.

From Buell they headed north along the river and her father, piloting the Ford Tempo he'd outfitted with hand controls, drove too fast for the narrow road. But soon enough she was distracted by the beauty of the Valley: the opposite riverbank rising steeply from the water, thick with trees and vines and sheer outcroppings of red-brown rock, the untamed greenness cascading over everything, tree limbs stretching for light over the water, a small white rowboat tied in their shadows.

Farther along she couldn't help noticing the old coal chute stretching the length of the hillside, passing high over the road on its steel supports,

the sky visible through its rusted floor; the iron suspension bridge crossing the river. It was sealed at both ends, its entire structure similarly
penetrated and pocked by rust. Then it seemed there was a rash of abandoned structures, an enormous steel-sided factory painted powder blue,
its smokestacks stained with the ubiquitous red-brown streaks, its gate
chained shut for how many years, it had never been open in her lifetime.
In the end it was rust. That was what defined this place. A brilliant ob-
servation. She was probably about the ten millionth person to think it.

As for her father Henry in the seat next to her, he was more content
than she ever remembered, he was happy she'd gotten married, it
soothed him, it made her less like her mother, who had not married until she was over thirty, who had been engaged to another man before she
met Henry. Henry would never get along with Simon, she knew that. It
was not possible for him to even comprehend someone like Simon. They
had never met, she had always made up excuses, they had gotten married
on the spur of the moment at a city office. She wondered if Simon understood why. Certainly he hadn't complained about it. And yet Henry,
knowing they were excuses, knowing the reason she must have had for
making them, he had gone along, saying only: *I suppose I'll meet him someday.* He had always held her in a certain awe, same as he had held her
mother. It was a feeling he'd always needed to balance with a disdain for
Isaac. There was only so much a man like Henry could give up.

The money Isaac had stolen had not been mentioned in several days
and regarding Isaac's second disappearance, all her father would say
about it was *he'll be back soon enough.* Somehow this made her certain that
Isaac was not coming back, now or ever.

*   *   *

Outside the Charleroi hospital she waited in the sun, high up on the hill,
looking out over the town, the immense cemetery across the river that
occupied the entire hillside, stretching on as far as she could see. The
cemetery seemed bigger than the town. She felt a surge of guilt.

But Isaac had stayed here of his own volition. That was the only explanation she could think of—he'd visited her in New Haven once, it
seemed to have gone well, he'd even gotten a sort of patron there, her

ex-boyfriend Todd Hughes, who had offered to help Isaac with his application and asked after him a half dozen times afterward. But Isaac had never taken her up on her offers of further visits, and finally she had stopped offering. Maybe it had put a certain pressure on him, visiting like that. She had not visited a single college, not trusting her own judgment at the time, which she guessed was provincial. And it was, she thought now. It really was better to not visit, to go by reputation. At seventeen, you'd pick a school based on the nice architecture, or that a professor had smiled at you, or that your best friend was going there—you made choices based on feelings, which were bound, especially at that age, to be arbitrary and ill-informed and rooted mostly in insecurity.

Still, she couldn't make sense of Isaac's choice to remain in Buell. He didn't respect their father; his disdain for Henry precisely mirrored Henry's disdain for him. But there seemed to be some contract between them that she did not understand, one Isaac seemed unwilling to break. Henry, though weakening could shop for himself, drive the car with the hand controls, cook, clean, and bathe himself. Of course it was not safe for him to live alone—if there had been a fire or something. But the Mon Valley had an aging population and finding an inexpensive caregiver would have been easy—it seemed to her that if Isaac had gotten into a good college, Henry, out of pride, would have been forced to let him go. But Isaac had not done that. Maybe he had wanted to be released, instead of having to bully his way out. Or he had wanted to leave with Henry's respect, and thought that looking after him all these years would earn him that. Not knowing that it would more likely have the opposite effect—that it would be difficult for a man, especially a man like Henry English, to respect anyone who amplified his feeling of helplessness. And eventually Isaac had figured this out, had been so desperate that he'd stolen the money from Henry, *the rainy-day fund,* Henry called it, the cash he kept hidden away to soothe his worry that his bank might fail, or that the country itself might fail. And now . . .

She sat down on the curb and smoothed her skirt and looked out over the Valley again: though she was sitting in an asphalt parking lot, around her the trees were all popping with spring and it was a pleasant view. In fact there were very few places in the Valley that did not offer a pleasant view; this had always been true, even when the mills ran. The terrain was interesting and it was very green, everywhere it was just little houses terraced up and down the hillsides, the mills and factories in the few flat areas along the river, like the pictures of medieval towns from schoolbooks—*this is where the people lived, and this is where they worked.* Entire lives visible in the landscape.

She got up again. Really, her capacity for self-deception was enormous. Isaac's decision to stay here did not require so much analysis. He had a stricter sense of right and wrong than she did. Than anyone else she knew, really. He'd stayed because he thought it wrong to leave their father alone, and it had taken five years to convince him otherwise. Five years— when you said it like that, it didn't seem so long. But years were lived in days, and hours, and sometimes even a few minutes with Henry could be excruciating, at least for Isaac. Lee herself had felt very little guilt about leaving, you have to save yourself before you can save the world. And Isaac was only fifteen then. And to live your life in a way that you were not buried by guilt . . . Please, she thought. There has to be a balance.

She needed to call Simon. Naturally, her phone had no reception. She would call him tonight from the house, get Simon to call her back so her father wouldn't complain about the long-distance. Boredom setting in— searching through Henry's car she found there weren't any books or reading material of any kind, maybe that was normal, though it seemed that she always had a few books or magazines under the seat, there were advantages to keeping a car messy. Since there was no way she was going back into the hospital to read *Us Weekly*, she sat listening to the Pittsburgh NPR station, then got a mischievous feeling and turned all the radio presets to it; her father had them all set for AM talk radio. For some reason that gave her a great deal of satisfaction.

When Henry was finished with his appointment, they made their way south again. In Buell they parked the car and ran a few errands; both the bank teller and the supermarket cashier recognized Lee, the cashier remembered that Lee had given the graduation speech both in middle school and in high school, she remembered that Lee had gone to Yale and graduated; she also remembered that Lee had been a National Merit scholar. Lee felt guilty—she didn't recognize the woman at all, though she smiled and pretended to. She instinctively handed over her credit card to pay for the groceries but Henry, clearly embarrassed, reached up from his wheelchair and took Lee's card from the cashier. "I'll be paying by check," he said. Lee didn't know whether to apologize or not. As they left the store it occurred to her that there were probably only a handful of people in New Haven who knew as much about her as the cashier did.

In the parking lot, a few people stopped to talk to Henry, though she could tell many of them simply wanted to say hi to her. She noticed how many retirees there were. More and more the population of the Valley seemed split between the very old and the very young, it was either retirees or fifteen-year-old girls with baby carriages, there was no one left in the middle. As she folded the wheelchair to put it into the trunk there was a deafening noise and a train carrying coal rumbled slowly down the tracks past the supermarket, then past the half-demolished steelmill that still towered over the downtown, the place her father had worked twenty-odd years. She remembered going with her mother to meet him at shiftchange, the whistle blowing and the streets packed with clean-looking men in overalls and heavy wool shirts carrying their lunchboxes in to work, another group of men, most of them filthy, walking out, their lunchboxes empty, the awe her mother commanded in the crowd despite being so small and quiet, the pride Lee had felt at looking just like her, she had never gone through an awkward stage, she had always looked just like her mother. Her father never touched her mother in public as the other men pawed at women, he kissed her respectfully and took up her small hand, he was a tall, fair-skinned man with a heavy nose and brow, not handsome but imposing, in a group of other men he stood out the way the steelmill itself stood out among the smaller buildings of downtown.

When they got home, Lee helped her father get out of the car but as he was lifting himself from the seat to the wheelchair he fell and she was unable to catch him—even old and shrinking, he was still twice as heavy as she was. It was not a bad fall but as she helped push his chair up the ramp to the house she was angry at herself for doing that with Poe, it had not been fair to anyone.

* * *

That night there was a strange noise outside and then she heard it again and a third time before she realized that someone was knocking on the front door. Henry was watching TV in his room. For a moment she thought it was Isaac but as she hurried to answer the door she realized Isaac would not have knocked. It was dark and she peered out. Poe was standing on the front porch.

He smiled but she only half-smiled back and he saw something had changed in her.

She opened the door and the first thing he said was: "I need to talk to your brother."

"Let me get my coat," she told him.

They didn't say anything further until she'd come outside and they'd walked far enough down the driveway to be out of earshot of her father.

"Isaac left yesterday morning," she said. "A few hours after you did. He had a bag packed."

She watched his face go from confusion to fear and then to a face she hadn't seen before, it wasn't showing anything.

"Poe?"

"We need to talk," he said quietly. "We shouldn't do it here."

She went and checked on her father. The TV was blaring.

"Pirates versus the Padres," he said. "If you're interested."

"I think Poe and I are going out for a drive," she told him.

He looked at her suspiciously, then nodded.

They drove to a park by the river, just at the edge of town. It was dark and everything looked overgrown and there were large patches of mud, she seemed to remember it being grass but it was hard to trust her memory. She had begun forgetting about this place, forgetting details about the town, the moment she'd left for college. There was one bench, lumpy with years of repainting, that looked out over the river and they sat down.

"He heard us the other night," she told him.

"What did he hear?"

"Everything."

Poe didn't say anything and she looked out over the water. She'd been to this place many times. She remembered it being nicer, it was one of the standard make-out spots for kids in school. With her first boyfriend, Bobby Oates, she had come out here skinny-dipping, she'd been floating on her back looking up at the sky and then she'd looked around and he was gone, she'd turned around frantically looking but he had disappeared. Everyone knew there were undertows and she dove under looking but it was hopeless, it was too dark, she'd begun shouting for him, not caring if anyone heard her, she had been crying and was swimming back to the bank to get help when he popped up. He'd been holding his breath. Later that night she had slept with him, he was eighteen and she was sixteen, her first time. Yes, she thought, but then I broke up with him. At least I had some dignity about it.

"Are you there," Poe was saying.

"Sorry."

"Me and him are in some trouble. I got questioned today and tomorrow they're going to arrest me."

She looked at him—it didn't make sense.

"We're in some trouble." he repeated. "Me and Isaac."

"What happened," she said. Her own voice sounded to her as if it were coming from someone else.

"That guy they found near the old traincar plant. It was in the paper, they found a dead bum."

She could feel something tighten in her stomach, she closed her eyes and a numbness came over her.

"It wasn't me."

"Where's my brother," she said.

"I don't know. I know he's not a suspect."

"He's involved, though."

"Yeah," Poe said. "You could say that."

She wanted to press him but she was afraid. Then she was thinking of the four home health care services in the Buell directory, she could call one and be back in Darien tomorrow afternoon, she felt herself closing off to everything here, to Poe, to her father, she imagined sitting in Simon's backyard, looking at the fireflies over the pond, Simon's parents somewhere in the background, entertaining guests. A place where nothing weighed her down. "I think I should take you home now," she told Poe.

"I didn't do it."

"This isn't something I can get involved in."

"Lee, I swear I didn't even touch that guy."

"Let's go," she said. "I'm sorry."

"It was Isaac."

She looked at him for a long time.

"It was Isaac," he repeated.

"You're lying," she said, though there was something about Poe's face. She believed him. It was quiet for a long time. Her scalp was tingling and she began to feel very cold, she was shivering, it might have been from the temperature, she didn't know, it felt like all the blood had run out of her.

Poe leaned forward onto his elbows and didn't look at her, he began to talk as if he were only telling himself what happened, or speaking to the river, he didn't leave any of the details out and after a time she leaned into him, half because she wanted comfort, half because she was so cold. It seemed she should be crying but she wasn't—the sensation of surprise had already passed.

He was telling her how he'd nearly frozen to death sitting in his yard because he couldn't face his mother after what had happened. Lee was still listening but the doors were opening in her mind, she was thinking they will both need lawyers but they are not on the same side anymore. You will have to pick a side it is simple. It is Isaac against Poe, it is Isaac and your father against Poe. Prisoner's Dilemma, Econ 102. If everyone cooperates, keeps their mouth shut, it turns out okay—Nash Equilibrium. Or was Nash Equilibrium when both sides didn't cooperate? That was the point of the exercise—people rarely cooperated. Poe was still talking but she could no longer pay attention. The checkbook was there in her purse, hers and Simon's names at the top, she had brought it home because she knew she would need it for the nurse, to fix things in the house, she could write a check just like that and get Poe a good lawyer, give him a chance to get out of this.

Except Poe having a good lawyer was not going to help Isaac. If anything it would be the opposite. He was still talking, telling her about his meeting with the police chief but it didn't matter, the things Poe thought mattered did not matter anymore. He would not be able to afford a lawyer, he lived in a trailer. If she got him a lawyer and Simon ever happened to look at the returned checks, that was unlikely but still, if Simon or Simon's father ever discovered she'd written a check for some exboyfriend's lawyer, her lover who was accused of killing someone, it would be over. As simple as that. Poe had stopped talking. He was sitting in his own world, looking out over the river. She couldn't believe how dark it was here.

"I'm not going to rat him out," he said, misinterpreting her silence. "I hope you know that. I'd never do that to him or to you."

"Don't worry about me." She rubbed his shoulder.

"I think he went to Berkeley, that's what he always used to talk about."

"Berkeley, California?"

"Yeah," he said. "The college there."

She shook her head—none of it made any sense. She tried to figure the probability that Poe was simply lying to her. She didn't think so but everything was different now, she probably shouldn't trust half of what he said.

"Is there anyone else who would know?"

"There was one of the old-timers at the library he used to talk to, but that's about it."

"So what happened the other night was he figured out the one person he really needed to trust has been fucking his sister and lying to him about it."

"Lee."

"I guess I'm just confused about why we went out drinking when you guys had just nearly gotten arrested. If you wanted to call me, you could have just done it."

"How could I fucking call you? I didn't even know you were in town."

"We shouldn't have done that," she said. "That was so stupid I can't even believe it. We're supposed to be the ones protecting him."

He looked at her, incredulous. "You don't know anything about him."

"He's my brother."

"You've been gone a long time, Lee."

"Well, now I'm back." She stood up. "I'm going to take you home now."

Poe didn't move. "About two months ago he went for a dive in the river. You probably didn't know that because he would never tell you and because when I called to talk to you about it, you never called me back. But basically I had to jump in after him and pull him out. It was about twenty degrees and I don't know how either of us even made it."

She didn't say anything. She vaguely remembered getting a message from Poe, of course she hadn't called him back, she'd had no idea what it was about.

"It isn't some mystery, Lee. You just pretend everything will turn out fine until you're ready to deal with it."

"Please stop."

"What happened with that man is on me," he said. "I know that. But I'm not the only reason."

He looked at her for a long time and then he stood up.

"A couple years dicking me around and then you get married and don't tell me. Tomorrow I'm going to get locked up for your brother."

"I don't think you really understand everything."

"I understand you pretty well. You're not any different from anyone else."

She was quiet. Her mind seemed to have shut down.

"Your brother was right," he said. "About you, I mean. I don't know how I ever thought otherwise."

He began walking toward the road. She watched him go and then she got up and ran after him.

"Do you have a lawyer?" she said, catching up.

"Harris said he knows a good public defender."

"Stop. Please stop walking a second. Please?"

He did.

"Let's go back to the car," she said. She took his hand and he looked at her but he didn't pull away. When they got in the car she turned it on and turned on the heater but left the lights off. She went to kiss him and he stopped her, he looked hurt, but then he kissed her back. Her mind was working on ten different levels, it was statistics, expected value: you had three people and one choice protected one of them and the other choice protected two of them, another part of her felt Poe's hand between her legs, it was obvious the choice she would make. She pushed against him harder and felt herself go blank, then something else happened and she seemed to surface and was thinking again. Poe would need a lawyer, it felt like there was a flood of words building, she would need to hold them back, you did not get the public defender in these cases, you got Johnnie Cochran. The public defender would fall asleep at your trial, the public defender was just so the state could claim you'd had a fair chance, after they'd put you away for life.

"What's wrong," Poe said.

"Nothing."

"Do you want to just lay here?"

"No." She put his hand back.

* * *

Afterward she laid her head in his lap, smelled herself on him, and tucked her legs up. He traced his hand along her legs to her hips and back down again. The hot air from the heater was on her face. She had a brief feeling of lightness, of weightlessness, like the instant you're above the diving board when gravity hasn't caught you. She thought: I will do anything to keep feeling like this.

Poe was asleep, the warm air blowing on them, the faint light from the dashboard, she ran her hands across his legs, her fingers through the hair between them, then she touched the car window, the cold glass, outside it was very cold. She knew her decision. It was not like Romeo and Juliet. The floating feeling was gone and there was only the sensation of falling, she had to sit up, put her head against the window for the coldness, she couldn't get a clear thought into her head. She had to call Simon. Simon was her anchor. Poe stirred and she rubbed his arm automatically, she felt sick again, she had to get out of the car, she dressed quickly, things were inside out, she took her purse and got out of the car and shut the door quietly.

Her phone had service. She looked back at the car, at Poe sleeping inside, then back at her phone, then pressed Simon's number. There was the famous line: *Granted, I am an inmate at a mental institution.* It was ringing and then Simon answered. She walked a good distance away from the car, under the trees, she could hear the river.

"My love," he said, "are you on your way home?"

"Not yet."

"Did you find your brother?"

"Sort of," she said, "but then I lost him again."

"Well I hope you find him soon," he said. "I'm miserable without you."

"I have to stay. I'm interviewing the nurses tomorrow."

"Fine fine fine. You know I should have offered to come with you. I'm sorry I was being a baby. I should be there with you."

She felt herself choke up, she could hear people talking in the background, she didn't know, she was on the verge of telling him everything.

"Listen," he said, "the boys and girls are all over, up from the city, can I call you later tonight or tomorrow?"

"Okay."

"Everyone says hi. Say hi, everyone."

She could hear all their voices chime in the background, the voices of her friends, nonsensical and distant.

"Our friend Mr. Bolton brought a case of Veuve Clicquot."

"Simon, listen for a second. I may need some money. My brother might need a lawyer."

"Is it serious?"

"I don't know." A pause. "It's not really clear yet."

"Lee," he said. "I'm really sorry. I'm really sorry, I should have come out there with you."

"It's alright, I'm glad you answered. I'm going a little crazy out here."

"I'll fly in tomorrow."

She had to swallow again. "No," she said. "I think it'll be fine. I'm just being neurotic."

"I can be there tomorrow. What the hell, I'll get Bolton to drive me there now, we'll be there by three A.M.

"No, it's okay," she said. "I just needed to hear your voice. I think I already feel a lot better."

"Call me later. Or call tomorrow morning, whatever you want. Do you have the checkbook?"

"Yes," she said.

"Use it. If it's bad trouble I'll ask my father to look someone up."

"Don't ask your father."

"You don't have to worry about him."

"I know. I'd just rather you not ask him."

"Alright," he said. "I love you."

"I love you, too," she said.

After they hung up she stood there in the cold, it was very dark and the air was very clear, there were bright cold spots of light in the sky above her. She began walking back to the car. She would have to keep this inside her forever, there would not be any person she could ever talk to. Well, she thought, at least you know you'll make a good lawyer.

6. Isaac

When he woke up it was morning and he was lying in tall grass behind the warehouse. He could hear several motorboats on the river. Why won't that eye open? He touched it. Dirt and dried blood. Stay here till I'm better, he thought. Root and hibernate. Come out when the weather's better. The locals friendly. He looked around him. It's fine now, he thought. Get up.

It was a warm windy day and above him the sky was dry and deep blue and the clouds were blowing south, a V of geese flying against them. Original itinerants. As for the kid he's not worried. Thinks back to his days in Vietnam—Special Forces—this is nothing. Back from the dead like Easter. Feel of a spear in his busted ribs, bone bruises, a nice day of walking ahead of him.

With the pain in his side and legs it took him half a minute to get to his feet. The ground was wet, his sleeping bag covered in mud; his clothes were filthy. He made his way back, the tall grass moving in the wind, flattening and standing up again, the warehouse was not nearly as remote as it had seemed in the dark—maybe two hundred yards from the main road. The dirt lot strewn with trash and beer cans, an occasional condom. Mark of communion. Wishing to repay his blood debt to Swede Otto, the kid visits the hideout of local delinquents, submits his holy vessel for redemption Milk of his human kindness draws them in like blood, gets baptized in his own there's the church of it. He looked up at the brick warehouse with its scarred facade, the high arched windows. Only see—still his hands are filthy—the debt still owed.

In the dirt lot he came on his own pile of scat from the previous night, stopped to kick dirt over it, thought possibly the kid should not compare himself to Jesus. Then he thought: least of my worries. If there's Hell it's so thick I'll be standing on shoulders—hypocrites at the bottom, plenty of churchgoers. Special compartment for popes.

He limped across the field toward Route 906. There was a good deal of traffic and he could see it wouldn't be a pleasant walk—the road was barely wide enough to hold the cars. He was moving very slowly. Pretty sure you broke a rib—hurts to inhale. Arms, legs, and back all bruised. He touched his face and could tell it was encrusted with a mixture of dirt and blood, his lips and cheeks and eyes swollen. It seemed like a miracle he hadn't lost any teeth. You aren't cut out for this, he thought. But as soon as he thought that he got a picture in his mind of the Swede standing there looking at something, his bulky army coat and his tan cargo pants nearly black from soot. Believe what you want but the evidence shows something different The empirical data supports a different hypothesis. The kid seems to be quite capable—making mistakes but learning quickly. A certain amount of hard-wiring in evidence. Rusty, is all.

Route 906 sat along the edge of the floodplain that ran to Monessen. The side of the valley rose behind it, just woods, but along the riverflat there were old buildings, warehouses, factories. The traffic was heavy, all subcompact American cars and old pickups. There was barely enough pavement for the cars and not much space even in the weeds—the air shook even as the smaller cars passed. A half dozen people were walking at various intervals in the same direction as him—toward Monessen, which had once been one of the most prosperous towns in the Valley but was now one of the poorest. The remnants of a U.S. Steel coking operation still limping along, employing a few hundred people. Otherwise, plenty of Section Eight.

Half an hour later he reached Monessen, the main part of town looked like Buell, a riverflat blending into a steep hillside, neighborhoods terraced along the heights, stone churches, wooden churches, three Eastern Orthodox churches with gilded domes. Trees everywhere. From a distance it looked peaceful. Up close it looked abandoned—most of the buildings in complete disrepair, vandalism and neglect. He passed through the downtown, there were a few cars parked, but mostly it was empty buildings, old signs on old storefronts, ancient For Lease signs in most of the windows. The only hints of life came from the coke plant by the river, long corrugated buildings, a tall ventstack burning off wastegas, occasional billows of steam from the coke quenching. A scooploader big enough to pick up a semitrailer was taking coal from a barge and dumping it onto a conveyor toward the main plant. The train tracks were jammed with open railcars full of dusty black coke but other than Isaac, there was not another actual person in sight.

In the middle of town, he found an open restaurant. The waitress sat alone at a table by the front window, staring at something outside in the distance and smiling until she saw him come in. The sunlight was on her and she didn't want to get up. He guessed she was about fifty, her hair was dyed blond.

"Hon," she said. "I can't have you looking like that."

"I'll get cleaned up," he told her. "I got jumped." He looked around the diner, restaurant, whatever it was, there was only one other patron.

She shook her head. "There's a hospital across the bridge over in Charleroi," she told him.

"I can pay." He opened his wallet to show her. He could smell the food, frying potatoes and meat, he was not going anywhere. He was surprised to be standing up to her—in the old days he would have walked out immediately, gone looking for another place. "Put yourself in my shoes," he said.

For a moment he wondered if he'd said too much, but then she sighed and pointed him toward the back of the diner, toward the bathroom. The other patron, a middle-aged black man with his lunch pail, looked up from his magazine at Isaac and then quickly back to his magazine. He sipped his coffee and didn't look at Isaac again.

To get to the men's washroom he had to edge by stacked boxes of paper towels and cooking oil, and once inside he locked the door and stood in front of the mirror. A corpse mucked up from the riverbed. Or a mass grave. His pants and coat were covered with mud and grass and his face was smeared with ashy dirt He would not have let himself into a diner, or anywhere. One eye was badly swollen and his lip was split and it was hard to tell where the dried blood ended and the dirt began. After using the toilet he stripped and stood in front of the sink and mirror; his filthy brown face didn't belong to his pale white body, pink scrapes along his ribs, the faint purple of developing bruises. He washed his hair and face in the sink, splashing dirt everywhere, thinking man the most fragile creation—them more than you. Now the cold towelwash, way to clean a corpse. Body's last bath. Special attention to crevices—probably they use a hose now, drip dry, automatic wash for bulk processing. Who knows who touches you after you're dead? He took another handful of paper towels and wet them and continued to bathe himself. Shivering already, water cools quickly. A tub a warm womb we take for granted—the nature of wombs. My mother bathed herself. Wonder if they cleaned her after. Like the bogmen—preserved in peat. Not Swede Otto—no baths at taxpayer expense. Pauper's grave too expensive. Incinerator his final warmth. Clear out your head, he thought. You're not there yet.

When he was finished he took out his knife and carefully soaped down the blade, rinsed it and dried it, then dried himself with the last of the wadded paper towel, he had used two entire rolls. The place had been very clean before he came in and he carefully wiped off the floor and sink before going back out into the dining room. He examined himself in the mirror. From the waist up, it was okay. The coat had kept most of the dirt off his shirt and sweater. Don't wear the coat into places, he thought. Take it off first.

When he came out of the bathroom the waitress was watching for him and she raised her bulk up slowly like her knees were going and brought him a menu and a cup of coffee. Sitting there in his booth, the entire back corner of the restaurant to himself, he was warm and clean and dry, it was a comfortable feeling. He added cream and lots of sugar and sipped his coffee and felt his head begin to clear. He would take his time. He would enjoy himself. He ordered country fried steak and hash browns, three eggs over easy, a slice of peach pie. She took the order and refilled his coffee and he adjusted it to his exact preference, sweet and creamy, almost like dessert. He looked around the diner, it was a nice place, it was really more of a restaurant, a few dozen tables with checkered tablecloths, they probably never filled it anymore but it was very clean and pleasantly dim, knotty pine paneling, a high ornate tin ceiling. The walls were covered with team photos of the Monessen Greyhounds football team, photos of Dan Marino and Joe Montana, the Valley's biggest NFL stars, and a few framed posters from bullfights in Spain, souvenirs of a trip someone had made twenty years before. The waitress came back with his food.

"Get any licks in?" She indicated his face.

"Not really."

"That bad, huh?"

"There was a bunch of them."

"You ought to just go home," she said. "It won't get any better."

"You always this nice to your customers?"

She smiled at him and he found himself smiling back. She had braces on her teeth.

"There you go. Don't take that crap off me." She went slowly back to her table, leaving two plates of food in front of him. "I'll bring the pie in a minute," she said.

He cut his steak into small pieces, the crispy fried outside and the meat inside rich and dripping juice, it was the best food he'd ever eaten. He forked some hash browns, fried hard with onion, mixed one of the eggs into it, it felt like he'd never eaten before in his life, he wanted to take small bites and make it last forever but couldn't help shoveling huge forkfuls, she brought his pie and refilled his coffee and the sharpness of the coffee was good with the rich food. When the plate was finally empty he went for the pie.

He sat back with his eyes closed, though he knew he couldn't fall asleep. It is a good life, he thought. It is a good life to walk into someplace and eat food. The waitress appeared again with a bowl of ice cream.

"On the house," she said. "You clean up pretty good."

After sitting for a while he could feel himself drifting off, it was so warm, he decided not to push his luck. He looked at the bill. She'd only charged him for the eggs and coffee, two dollars and eight cents. He looked up to thank her but she was already back at her table, daydreaming.

He thought about a tip, he needed his money to last, but left her ten dollars. Poor to the poor. He was going to spend it anyway.

Back on the street his bruises hurt less and he hadn't felt so good in years, he wanted to lie in the sun and take a nap. Once past the town he left the road and crossed the field to the train tracks again and then found a grassy secluded spot on the riverbank. It was sunny and he took off his shirt and shoes and sat out in just his pants. You need to keep moving. He shook his head. I might be dead tonight. Enjoy the nice things as they come.

He lay there and felt the sun on him. Simple pleasures we're wired for. A million years of evolution—appreciate a sunny day.

You are being tested, he thought. What's going to happen with the Swede? I can't think about that now, he decided. I'll get to Berkeley and I'll see. If something happens, at least I'll have done that. Eventually they'll find out what you did. Poe will talk. It's just the way he is. He can't help it. Even so, he thought. He's the best of them.

He closed his eyes. He wondered if his sister was still in Buell. What if she just drove by right now? I'd go with her. Have everything I need right here. He tried to will it, get into the car, Lee, and drive. Meet you by the side of the 906. But of course it was ridiculous. She couldn't hear him.

At her graduation he remembered how he'd felt sitting next to her. The principal had gone on for ten minutes, National Merit scholar, perfect SATs, got into Yale, Stanford, Cornell, and Duke. All four of you were there. That felt like the moment that everything seemed to make complete sense. You could see the exact moment you would be standing up yourself, felt like seeing through time. Very clear picture in your mind—watching her you imagined yourself. Remember that well. Then Mom was dead and Lee was leaving, you hoped she might stay, but of course. Who would—new life waiting—it became even more important to get out. Can't blame her.

He saw a large hawk, no it was an eagle, they were coming back. Things were always changing. Sometimes good and sometimes bad.

Your only job was to wake up until you were stopped. He would. His sister had had it easier but there was no point in worrying about it. He would make his own way. He would be living in the mountains in northern California, green and much taller than the hills around here, they were actual mountains. Near an observatory. An observatory in the house, look at the stars anytime, the house would have a long porch that stuck way out over a cliff so it felt like you were floating in space. Like Lee you won't be on your own. Remember that visit to New Haven—everyone, in their way, was like you and Lee. It was difficult to imagine but his sister had done it and in most ways she had far less idea of what she wanted. He had always known what he wanted to do. Of course she'd still beaten him on the SATs. Forty points. Within the statistical error. In fact that was the first thing she'd said when he'd told her his score—*well, it's within the margin of error.* Sympathetic human person that she is. Except there was the thing with Poe. That was what screwed it all up. It would not have been a big deal, he knew everyone else she'd slept with in the Valley, there were two others, it hadn't bothered him, or not much, anyway. The thing with Poe somehow seemed like an indication of something much bigger. He couldn't think of exactly why, but he was sure of it.

Change of subject, he thought. Feel that sun. In California it will be like this most of the year. Dose of the ultraviolet. Heals bruises and kills bacteria. Ultra means you can't see it. No, it means *very*. Fuckin retard. He sat up and looked around. There were grass and trees all around and the river right in front of him. To the south was a big intermodal terminal, long piles of coal and cinders and other bulk materials, just to the south of that the three big bridges to Charleroi, and beyond the bridges he could still make out the cranes of the lock. There were barges logjammed, waiting to pass through the lock chamber.

I'm past all that, he thought, to the north it's just woods. The sun was bright, he could feel it on his skin, prickling like fingers running over him, he didn't want to let himself fall asleep, it felt so good. There were four men fishing on the opposite bank and there was something about them sitting there, even across the river, he dozed off. Fishers of men. He woke up in the shade, the sun had crossed over the river and was low over the western hills, the fishermen were gone. Second day you slept through. You could just get a bus ticket, he thought, sleep and be moving at the same time. Right—leave a trail saying just where you're headed. But in a railyard he would need to ask someone anyway, figure what lines ran south or west. It was better than buying a ticket. He checked his wallet and he still had twenty-two dollars, plus the nearly four thousand in the envelope in his cargo pants pocket.

Walking again, his legs had gotten stiff while he slept and he made slow progress. It was long after dark that he passed under the Mon City bridge, the train tracks ran through a long industrial zone with brightly lit warehouses and he walked the treeline, at the edge of the light, passing dozens of old shipping containers, a house sagging into the water, tractor trailers sitting with their tires flattened and their paint weathered away. Across the river were the towns of Mon City and New Eagle, brightly lit, he was happy to not be on that side of the river. Ahead of him was a long dark stretch through high forest, the polished railtops caught what little light there was from the stars, glowing faintly. As soon as he was in the darkness he felt safe again. A few owls hooted but otherwise it was silent except for his footsteps and the drumming of a passing towboat and its barges. He thought he should feel thirsty but for some reason he was not. He would have to get a container for water.

On the other side of the river an enormous plume of smoke and steam rose from the West Penn Power station, its stacks several hundred feet high and the steam plume bright against the night sky. Dark piles of coal next to it, they might have been minor pyramids, several dozen barges coming and going in the river next to the plant. A few miles later, again on the opposite side of the river, he passed the Elrama power plant, even larger, well lit by yellow sodium lights, the main stack maybe five hundred feet tall, the billow of steam blotting out an entire section of the sky, clean and white-looking. Except it's burning coal, he thought. It is definitely not clean. Shortly after that he passed through a dark mine complex with a railyard and big coal tipple, the ground was black with it, the coal crunched underfoot. There were endless railcars loaded with it sitting motionless on the tracks, empty barges tied to their landing cells. Later he came to a brightly lit industrial park and to avoid being seen he cut up the hill into the woods away from the river until he reached a dark road that ran parallel.

There was a small dark hamlet, a fire station, empty and closed for the night. A few houses with aboveground pools, a porch light here or there but otherwise it was pitch black. The road was quiet and he could make out the stars well. Farther along he came to a bonfire in a yard next to one of the houses, two dozen or so people, probably half the town, standing around drinking. Someone was about to jump into a swimming pool, he could see by how white they looked that they weren't wearing any clothes, though it was cold out. He kept his head down and tried to pass quickly but they noticed him.

"Hey," someone shouted from near the fire. "Come on down and have a beer."

He ignored them but they called out again. He waved and put his head down, hoping he would quickly be out of sight.

"Who the hell is that," he heard someone shout to him. "Is that Brian Foote?"

Isaac waved again and kept walking.

Two blocks later at the edge of town he heard a bottle break in the street and turned to see a group of figures following him, silhouetted against the light. There were four of them. Instead of waiting to see what happened he began running immediately, holding his backpack tight against him, ignoring his ankle and the bruises in his thighs and the sharp pain in his ribs, he could hear people yelling things and his legs ached with each step and the pack slapped but he didn't slow down.

When the road curved he jumped off into the woods and waited in the pitch black to see if he'd been followed. No one came. Many explanations—they thought you were someone skipping out on their party. Or they wanted to give you a repeat of last night's treatment. Still . . . He relaxed. Chased by bandits the kid perseveres—this time without injury. Yet, knowing he is the most interesting part of their evening, he fears they'll come after him with a car. There was a drainage that led up the side of the valley away from the river and he followed it. The stream was rushing with a good amount of force and he had to spend a lot of time finding dry footing in the dark. It wound up between steep hills and he quickly lost all sense of direction, felt a sense of panic and then relaxed again. Figure it out in the morning. Be able to see when the sun comes up. Soon enough he came out into a large clearing where the grass had been recently mowed. No lights or houses in sight. It was very soft and he lay down at the edge of it under a few overhanging branches to catch the dew.

Tucked into his sleeping bag he closed his eyes and saw afterimages, of what he didn't know. It looked like people walking. He saw the road he'd walked on that morning and the people on it. He opened his eyes. His face was cool but the rest of him was warm. It was a cold clear night. He saw the Swede again, standing there by the stove, his face half in shadow now. This is normal, he thought. Lying in his sleeping bag he reached out to touch the soft grass again, it was cool and damp and soft. He watched the stars and tried to forget about the Swede.

Knew you shouldn't stay here this long. Knew something bad would come of it. Told yourself you were biding your time but you knew. I had nowhere to go. Neither did Lee—she made a place for herself. Mr. Painter offers to introduce you to his father, professor at Cornell. A pretty sure thing, he told you.

I was not ready to leave yet, he thought. Different for Lee—easy for people to like her. Her mother dies and she leaves the place, the scar erased. Tells you she only thinks about home *the way it used to be*. Never occurred to her that you did not have that luxury. Beginning of sophomore year, suddenly you're alone in the house with the old man. Meanwhile Lee had the whole family waiting on her. Our Daisy Flower. Quiet in the house if she was studying, a big deal over her report cards. Leave yours out for him but he never says a word.

If he were in your shoes he would have put you in a home. Asked him that once, what if I got hurt same as you. Wouldn't answer. Still you stayed. Because that is not how I am, even to people like him. No, he thought, that is not the only thing. You wanted his approval. Because you wanted him to admit he needed you. No, I stayed because it would have been wrong to leave him on his own. But still you left. After five years, he thought. That was not a rational decision. That was not a decision that made any sense.

He closed his eyes. I am doing fine for myself, he thought. Better than yesterday. Tomorrow will be better than today. It was dark and peaceful and after watching the stars for a minute he found the ones he knew and fell into a fitful sleep.

7. Grace

She called Harris four times that day from Steiner's shop, but each time got his voicemail. She was working faster than normal, forcing herself to concentrate; she could not let her mind wander. At one point, Steiner came by her bench, took note of her progress, and smiled at her. She nodded back grimly and put her head down. Billy had killed someone. It was obvious—the way he'd come home Friday, now Harris taking him in for questioning, holding him overnight. She had barely slept. Harris had decided he wouldn't take her calls. She could try him from the office line, he wouldn't recognize that number, but then someone might overhear. She would have to wait until she got home.

Sometime later she was aware of a touch at her shoulder—Steiner again.

"Closing time," he said. "You look like you're in another world."

He seemed concerned but she couldn't bring herself to look at him. It was Steiner. You never knew. He'd slept with Barb and Lindsay Werner, she knew that much. But if somehow he could lend her money for a lawyer, save Billy—of course she would. Between her son and her dignity, it was no contest. It occurred to her suddenly that it was a luxury to not have to do those things.

"I'm alright," she said. "Trying to get us caught up." She smiled at him.

He smiled back at her and squeezed her shoulder and she got an uncomfortable feeling, disgusted with herself.

"See you tomorrow then," she said.

Getting her things together, taking the freight elevator downstairs, walking up the hill to where she'd parked the car, she felt sick. It was not possible anyway that Billy had done that. And if he had—she would have to scrape herself together, keep her chin up. Once you lost your dignity, that was it. Dignity is life.

On the drive home her cellphone rang and it was Harris.

"I just let him go," he said.

"This isn't about that thing from last year, is it?"

"Come on, Grace."

"Will you come over?"

"I'm not sure that's a good idea."

"We'll be alone."

"Grace," he said. "Grace Grace Grace."

"I didn't mean it that way."

"Okay," he said.

She drove quickly, she wanted to take a shower before he got there. Maybe she did mean it that way. Except they couldn't—it would be a dirty thing now. She felt herself tear up and blinked her eyes to clear them. Come on, nothing is fair. Don't get in a wreck. Eyes on the prize.

* * *

Twenty minutes later she was home, but no Billy. She undressed and tried to coax the shower into the position where it wasn't scalding and wasn't cold. Two years working at a hardware store, but Billy hadn't learned, or hadn't cared, to fix the faucet. Don't be mad at him now, she thought. But she was. She couldn't help it. Father's son, she thought. Your old mistakes setting up shop. Always knew it would be this way.

She soaped and rinsed quickly with no special attention. She appreciated her life, all the little things. Went out of her way to help others. That was all you were supposed to do—God was supposed to look after the rest. It had all seemed like it would work, Billy had been so close to leaving, so close to being away at college, a new life it would be hard to screw up too badly, but he had chosen to stay. Maybe that meant he had never been close at all. But still it had never made sense to her, he had loved the game, had a chance to keep playing it. Because he wouldn't have been the star, she thought. Because he knew he wouldn't be the big fish. It had to be more complicated than that. Football had given him a direction, something she'd never seen in him, it had made him question and push himself, but as soon as high school ended he was content to return to the way things had been since he was a child. Satisfied with things, satisfied with being taken care of. The same at twenty as he'd been at thirteen. Maybe she had always known.

Even as a toddler he'd been too brave, she could tell the difference between him and the other kids, by the time he was eleven or twelve she was sure of it, she'd come around the side of the house just in time to see him on his bike, barreling full speed down the hill in their yard, going faster and faster heading for the berm by the stream. At first she thought he was out of control but it quickly became clear he was doing it on purpose—the speed carried him up and over the berm and then high into the air over the stream, impossibly high, he let go of the bike midair and she closed her eyes. When she opened them, Billy was on his feet on the opposite side of the water, taking note of his torn shirt, collecting his bike and carefully straightening the handlebars. He crossed back over the stream, carrying the bike now, looking pleased with himself. Please God, she remembered thinking. Please God, look after my son. Meanwhile, Virgil didn't even want to take Billy's bike away. He wanted Billy to like him.

Now she managed to change into a skirt and put her hair up and get a little makeup on. A deep breath and she looked herself over carefully, deciding that with the fading light she looked more like herself. Had she really thought for a second about George Steiner? She took a deep breath. There was no point in giving up yet. Not on her son, anyway.

*   *   *

When Harris pulled up next to the house she watched him, the way he jumped down from the tall truck, he was over fifty but he moved like a much younger man, the sight of him was comforting.

She went out to the porch.

"Hi," she said.

She was hoping he might come up and kiss her but he made no move to. He stood at the bottom of the steps. He seemed preoccupied.

"I was hoping to save you some worry," he said, "getting Billy before the DA got to him."

"And . . ."

"It's not good news, Grace, though something tells me you already know it."

"He came home the other night hurt pretty bad."

He shook his head. "The other guy got it a lot worse."

"The homeless man." She knew it didn't matter if the man was homeless or not, but somehow it felt like it might.

He nodded, looked beyond the trailer at something far in the distance.

"I've always tried to protect him. You know that."

"Well you can tell them I did it. They can take me instead."

"Grace. Poor Grace." He seemed to want to come up the stairs, but didn't.

She crossed her arms, she could feel herself choking up. "I'm serious," she said.

He finally came up onto the porch; unsure how to comfort her, he stood there. After a short time he opened his arms to hug her but she pushed him in the chest, suddenly she was very angry at him, his awkwardness, she didn't know why but she was.

"I've always done what I can," he repeated.

"What about Isaac English? He was there with Billy."

"He's not a suspect and it's better for now if the DA doesn't know about him. I'm going over tomorrow to talk to him."

"Is Billy being charged?"

"They don't have his name yet, but they will."

She felt herself fading away from him, like she was receding inside herself, like she was a stranger looking out through her own eyes.

"Like I said—"

"This isn't about you," she told him.

"Alright, Grace."

It felt like a pressure building up, she knew she shouldn't say anything but she had to let it out: "Putting in a word with the judge, your fishing buddy, isn't exactly bending over backwards—"

Suddenly he was angry as well. "It was a lot more than a goddamn word. He could have gone up for six, eight years for what he did to that other boy."

"That boy had a goddamn bayonet, Bud. Off an M16."

"That boy was on his knees, Grace."

She glared at him, still didn't know if she was angry or just wanted to seem angry, but he was done with her. He brushed past her and went down the steps and back to his pickup.

"Wait," she called after him. "I'm sorry."

He shook his head and got into the truck.

She ran down after him as he closed the door.

"I'm sorry, Bud. I've been going crazy about this all day."

He seemed not to hear her. After a few seconds he said, "It confuses me sometimes, why I do things for you."

"I'm sorry."

"You really have no idea."

"I'm sorry," she said. "I don't mean to be hard to deal with."

"You know six or seven years ago, right after you and Virgil broke up the umpteenth time, I caught him blowing through a stoplight with Billy in the passenger seat and two big spools of copper wire in the bed that he'd stolen off a job site. Not even under a tarp or anything, just sitting out in the open, four-hundred-pound spools of wire. This is back when they were putting in that industrial park up in Monessen." He shook his head. "Didn't even bother to put a goddamn tarp over it. So you can imagine what kind of position that put me in."

"Bud," she said quietly.

"I'll bet Virgil never told you about that, did he? And of course in hindsight, it might have turned out better for Billy if I'd locked his daddy up right in front of him."

"I know I made a mistake."

"That was when I started making phone calls to try to find you something somewhere else." He looked at her. "That job offer in Philadelphia.

Put my neck out and gave you and Billy a chance and you threw it in my face."

"That wasn't what I was doing."

He was on the verge of saying something more and she stood there, bracing herself. Instead he started the truck. "Well," he said. "That's probably enough for tonight." She stepped up onto the running board and reached through the open window and put her arm over his.

"I didn't want it to go here," she said. "This isn't why I wanted you to come over."

"I know Virgil's back." He seemed frozen in the seat, looking straight ahead out the windshield.

"He's out. He's gone, it didn't even last a day. It's over for good."

Harris was quiet.

"I want us to go back to the way it was."

"Not possible," said Harris.

"We could just try being friends again."

"Grace."

"I know how it looks. I don't care."

"You're definitely right about how it looks."

"I'll call you."

He shook his head and lifted her hand off his arm and she stepped off the running board. He turned his truck around and she watched as he disappeared slowly down the road.

8. Poe

It was daylight the next morning when Lee dropped Poe off at his mother's trailer, they said good-bye but he already felt distracted, he walked quickly to his room and changed into his work boots. After that he went down to the field carrying the sneakers he'd been wearing the night the Swede died, the box they'd come in, a can of gasoline. He doused the shoes and set them on fire. Maybe somewhere there was a receipt for them but no, he didn't save those sorts of things. Not that any of it would make any difference, if they had an eyewitness. He wondered if it was Jesús or the other one. There was no point thinking about it, he'd know soon enough.

He stood in the green field, waist-high in the goldenrod, looking out over things. The falling-down gray barn, way off on the far hill, he'd seen an old man go in it a few times, even glassed him through binocs once, but he'd never found out who the old man was. The man would be dead, probably, by the time Poe got out of prison, he would never see that old man again. He didn't even know the man, but it felt like a loss from his life. He wouldn't see the barn in the distance or these rolling hills either because if he went away any length of time his mother would sell the trailer and move. Things were changing right in front of his eyes, it would all stop existing, as far as he was concerned. He hadn't thought about it that way before. If they gave him the full sentence, he'd be older than his mother when he got out, twenty-five years from now anything could happen, civilizations on the moon, the prime of his life. Only the dregs left over and he had to be honest with himself, from what he'd seen the dregs were not good. No one then or now would want a forty-six-year-old man who'd spent half his life locked up. He would be alone. Of no use to anyone or himself. Not to mention how quickly things happened these days, twenty-five years it would be like coming out of a timewarp, like the movie where they resurrect the caveman. Nothing would make any sense. That was if they didn't get the capital penalty. The injection. He didn't know. He needed to be clear with himself—going in for this, for the killing of the Swede, he was giving up his entire life. Those words, he thought, they sound just like other words, but you cannot even understand what they mean—giving up your life, there should be some other thing besides words that would describe it. A machine that would plug into your mind and give you the feeling. But it would be too much. No one would be able to handle it. You could only handle it little by little, you could not truly understand what that meant.

I am giving up my life, he said out loud. But still the words brought nothing to his mind, no description, only a very faint feeling, he might have been saying I would like a glass of milk.

He was not even the one that had killed the Swede. And the Swede had not even been doing anything, just standing there. If Isaac had killed the Mexican one, sure, maybe Poe could do time for that. But the Swede was just standing doing nothing. Except that was a lie. He was lying to himself. He was lying to himself so as not to go to prison, he knew that if Isaac hadn't killed the Swede then the other one, Jesús, would have cut his throat. There was no point pretending he didn't remember their names. It had come down to him or the Swede. Billy Poe or Otto Carson, a dead rotting body. Otto Carson's end being a necessary factor to his own continuation. Necessary condition, he thought. Meaning it is not on Isaac. It seemed hard to follow but it wasn't. He understood it better than he could say it. The words were no good; if anything, the more he thought about it, the more he talked with himself, the more he'd justify his way out of it. The truth, the truth that mattered, was that he, Poe, was responsible for killing the Swede. There were other truths too, things that were just as true, but this was the one that mattered.

He wanted to sit down awhile, memorize the view from the field, he had never quite seen things well enough, he was not like Isaac, and now time was short. He went back up to the house. He knocked on the door of his mother's bedroom. The room smelled of sleep and whiskey, she was lying on the bed in her nightgown, her thick legs slightly spread, the blankets twisted all around her. He rearranged the sheets to cover her more and then sat down next to her.

"Come here," she mumbled. He lay down in the bed and turned his back to her and she hugged him like that. You're acting like a little kid, he thought. He didn't care. Then he must have fallen asleep because there was an insistent hammering sound that he didn't want to think about and finally someone pushed the bedroom door open. Poe opened his eyes and it was Bud Harris. He was leaning over the bed, he put his hand on Poe's shoulder and Poe flinched away from his touch.

"Come on, buddy," said Harris. "Time to go."

He could see Harris looking at his mother and he sat up immediately, then stood up so Harris had to move back and his view of Poe's mother was blocked.

"I've been knocking out there five minutes," said Harris.

"Alright," Poe told him. "I'll be out."

He heard Harris go outside, the front door slamming, and he sat up and put his boots back on. There was no point in preparing—whatever he brought they would take. Maybe he should have taken a shower, probably be the last time he could shower alone, but there was Lee's smell still on him, he'd heard stories about men in prison, a guy's wife visiting and sticking her fingers down there and then offering the fingers to her husband to smell, or something like that, the closest the husband could get. He'd always thought those stories were exaggerated but now he could imagine that very clearly.

"You need to be getting ready," said his mother. She was sitting up now in her oversize T-shirt. "You need to help him."

"I will," he said to her.

Outside, he found Harris was waiting by the Explorer.

"I'm ready." But they couldn't leave until his mother came out and said good-bye, and he wanted to be gone, in the truck and moving, get it over as quickly as possible. he did not want to look at this place any longer, it would only make things worse, it seemed as if he might start crying at any minute and he didn't want Harris to see him that way. He tried to get into the truck but Harris said:

"Wait for your mother to come and see you off properly."

He stood there, he tried closing his eyes but it didn't make it any better. Finally his mother came out in sweatpants and a coat and hugged him again and he closed his eyes to try to dry them.

"Listen to him," his mother said to Poe. "Do what he says."

Poe nodded and choked something down. Harris fumbled with something inside the truck, pretended not to notice.

"Take care of him," his mother told Harris.

"Call me tonight, Grace," Harris said.

Poe watched his mother look at Harris, something passing between them.

Then Harris motioned him into the front seat. They were nearly to the main road when he pulled the truck over.

"You'll have to ride in the back," he said. "I didn't want her to see you like that but the staties might be waiting when we get to the station so I'll need to cuff you, too."

Poe let himself be handcuffed and put in the passenger area of the truck, behind the partition. Somehow it calmed him down.

"You know how serious this is, right?"

"Yeah."

"Did that English boy have anything to do with what happened? I went over there this morning and his father told me he took off two days ago and they haven't seen him since."

"Nah," said Poe.

Harris shook his head. "This DA is gonna eat you up. Knows what you'll say before the words come out of your mouth."

"I ain't dumb."

"Actually," said Harris. "You are dumb. You need to remember that before this gets any worse, if that's even possible."

"Whatever you say."

"You should have come to me. None of this would be happening."

He could see that Harris was angry. Then he was angry at Harris.

"I see you looking at me," said Harris, "but if this witness gets you out of the lineup, and it sounds like he will, you're up shit's creek. Twenty-five years if you're lucky but like I said this DA is hot for a capital case to get his career moving and he's betting you might be his ticket. I'm not saying he'll get it, it'll be a hard sell to a jury but he'll push for it. Just so you know, this is a very smart man who's going to be working his ass off to get you into the death chamber." He paused a minute. "You," he said again. "Not someone else, but you. Billy Poe."

"What's the witness saying?"

"That the little guy, who I presume is Isaac English, saw a fight brewing and took off. That you stuck around and started a fight and smashed the witness in the head and when he woke up you'd smashed his friend Otto Carson in the head, too, only a lot harder. His friend who is now dead."

"What about the third one, who was holding the knife to me?"

"There wasn't any talk about a knife. And if there's a third one, he's probably in Kansas by now because there's not many people dumb enough to get mixed up in this."

"His name was Jesús. Like I said, he put a knife to my neck."

"Well that ain't what the witness saw."

"Well what the witness is saying isn't what happened but I guess it's settled then."

"For your mother's sake you need to talk to me, because that's the only way we're going to have a chance."

Poe was quiet and he thought all you'd be telling him is the truth but then he reminded himself that it would not be the truth.

They went along the river road, the glare coming off the water made it too much to look at, greenness everywhere there was so much growing, there was a person out trawling, a small boat, a retired person in his years of ease.

Harris continued: "You know I got her a job in Philadelphia. Senior executive assistant at the State's Attorney's Office. Which is kind of ironic, given your situation, but either way she would have gotten thirty-four thousand a year, pension, I got the job lined up for her but you were doing good playing ball and she wasn't ready to separate you from your father. I tried to use logic on her, point out you could play ball anywhere and as for your father he's made about two child support payments in his life. That was six years ago, when you were a freshman. She'd said she'd leave when you went to college but then you were still living at home, sponging off her, couldn't even keep your hours as a stockboy."

"The owner laid everyone off," Poe said. He was numb to Harris. They were coming into town. He didn't want to be getting a lecture now, he wanted Harris to tell him what to say to the state police.

"Your mother is a good woman," said Harris. "You got no idea how many chances you've gotten because of her."

"My mother is married.'

"Please," said Harris. "Your father's diddled half the girls in town. Miracle you don't have twenty brothers and sisters."

"You're a real piece of shit, you know that?"

They pulled into the police station parking lot but Harris didn't move to get out. He said, "Billy, do you remember all those times you and your football buddies got arrested for public consumption?"

Poe snorted. "I never got busted for that," he said.

"Huh. I wonder. What about the time one of my guys pulled you over doing seventy in a thirty, too drunk to even remember to throw your empties out the window? Or even, let me see if I remember this correctly—you hit a young man in the head with a baseball bat, after he'd already gone down and was no longer a threat to you or anyone else, but still you got off with probation."

Poe didn't say anything.

"Thought you were just that lucky, huh?"

"I don't need to hear this right now."

"You aren't lucky. You're spoiled and you're stupid and I've been bending over backwards the last seven or eight years to keep you in one piece."

"You're just trying to make yourself feel better."

"You got too much of your father in you. And that is a goddamn shame for all of us, especially your mother."

"You're lucky I'm back here," said Poe. "You're lucky there's a fuckin wall right now."

"Save that shit for the lockup," Harris told him. "I'll pretty much guarantee you'll need it."

Harris got out of the truck and opened Poe's door and led him into the building. The fat cop, Ho, was sitting at the same desk, as if he hadn't moved in the last twenty-four hours.

"The staties here?"

"No," Ho said. "Their chief dickhead called and they want us to drive him to Uniontown."

"Get his picture and prints," said Harris, motioning to Poe.

Harris disappeared and the other cop led Poe into a small white room with a waist-high shelf. Poe expected the short Chinese cop to be rough but he wasn't.

"Make your hands loose and let me roll your fingers. If you smear them I'll just have to do it again."

"I ain't smearing them."

Harris stuck his head in.

"Before you get this asshole's picture send him to the bathroom to shave and get cleaned up. The other asshole's gonna plaster it all over the newspapers, guaranteed."

Harris looked at Poe: "From here on out if anyone tries to ask you anything, you say 'Lawyer.' They ask you if the sky is blue, you don't say yes, you say lawyer. They ask you who the president is, you know what you say?"

"Lawyer."

The deputy stood outside the bathroom while Poe shaved and then they took four sets of mugshots until Harris was satisfied with the picture. There's the schoolboy look, he said. Then they got back into Harris's truck and headed to Uniontown, the county seat. At least this time Harris didn't make him wear handcuffs. They didn't talk; he guessed Harris was doing him a favor now, taking the long way because he wouldn't see any of it again. The valley got a little flatter as they got south of Brownsville, when they got to the ferry in Fredericktown the river was nearly clear instead of brown, it was strange seeing the Mon that color. Usually the ferry driver made you wait until there was a full boat, six cars, but they just drove Harris across, there was only one other car on the boat and the ferry driver looked Poe over, ignorant fucking hick he was just staring at him, he looked about seventeen or so Poe wanted to get out and beat his skull in but he noticed the people in the other car staring at him too it was a father and some little kid, Poe could tell that the kid was probably getting a lecture from his old man about what happens if you don't follow the rules. Poe being the example. He just looked at the floor of the truck, it was lined with rubber for easy cleanup. There was a bump as the ferry touched the other bank, and then they were driving again.

"Why are we going this way," Poe asked. "Uniontown is on the other side of the river." He said it and got a faint hope that maybe Harris was going to help him escape, let him out at the West Virginia border.

"I figured taking the scenic route might give us more time to talk," said Harris. "Not to mention this might be your final chance to see this stuff before you turn fifty. Or at all."

Poe felt his stomach sink.

"I already told you everything," he said.

Harris shrugged.

Heading west away from the Mon it was more rolling hills, ancient barns and silos, it was farming and not industry. They were really taking the long way to Uniontown—they would have to cross back over the river again. The land changed quickly as you got away from the river, the old stone farmhouses, it reminded you people had been living here two, three hundred years, there were houses that old. His father claimed that was how long their people had been in the Valley, three hundred years, original founders, but it was more like the original drunkards. In the armpit of history there was always a horse thief. Those were the Poes. He wished they had taken the shorter route. Then it occurred to him: this really is your last chance to see all this. That's how serious this is.

Maybe the bum, it occurred to him now it must be Murray, the one who'd recognized him from the football team. Maybe he wouldn't pick Poe out of the lineup but Christ what were the odds of that, he'd known him on a chance meeting and now that he thought Poe had killed his buddy he'd recognize him for sure. Not to mention Poe had given him a good ass-kicking—there was nothing like payback. Murray was going to pay him back that was for goddamn sure and when Poe thought about it that way he was in no hurry to get there at all, he was glad Harris had taken the long drive. He tried to look at every tree, memorize it all. He wondered what the bail would be, it would be steep, he was sure of that, they'd make sure it was too high to pay. They passed a yard where some-one had a collection of tractors, forty or fifty of them on a big lawn in front of a little house, he would remember that, and then they came into a town. They must have crossed the river again without him noticing. How long had he been in the back of the truck? They were in Union-town already, it was about to be over, his final ride.

A few people in the street stared until they saw him staring back. There was a man, clearly crazy, walking down the street talking to some-one who wasn't there. Let me switch places with him, he'll get three meals a day and a place to sleep. I'll fend for myself, wear animal skins. He wondered where Isaac was. On the road somewhere. He thought maybe Isaac should be here for a while, too, not the whole time, just share a few minutes. Maybe they were even. He had saved Isaac and then Isaac had saved him. Were he and Isaac even or not? Harris opened the partition and passed back the bracelets.

"Make em tight so it looks like I did it," he said.

A few minutes later they stopped behind a big brick building like the old police station in Buell. Harris led him inside.

There was a tall desk and a cop behind it and some other cops loiter-ing, talking to a man in a suit, a short good-looking young man with a full head of blond hair, he carried himself like a politician. He looked Poe over carefully, as if Poe was a car he was thinking of buying. Poe nodded but if the man noticed he didn't react at all.

Poe was put in a holding cell with two benches; there was a middle-aged man lying on one of them, his hair mussed, wearing khakis and a golf shirt. He smelled like he'd been sweating booze for a long time, he had circles under his eyes and he'd thrown up on himself at some point in the recent past and he smelled of that, too. He glanced briefly at Poe and must have decided Poe wasn't a threat because he closed his eyes again. Poe felt slightly insulted.

After a time Poe was taken out and stood in a room against a wall with five other men who were approximately his age and height. One of the other men standing with Poe was a cop who'd been in the lobby when Poe came in; now he wore streetclothes. They all faced a mirrored window. After a few minutes, Poe was led back to the cell. Eventually Harris came to the cell and knocked on the bars so Poe would look up.

"Well," said Poe.

Harris shook his head. "Didn't take him long."

"I guess that's it, then." He shrugged.

"There's one good public defender around here. I'm trying to get her to take your case."

"I appreciate it," said Poe.

"I'll be seeing you."

"Wait," said Poe. "Where are they sending me?"

"Fayette."

"Not the jail?"

"Bail's too high for the regular jail. Least that's what our friend the district attorney is saying."

"That's great."

"I'll keep your mother informed."

Poe shrugged.

"Stay out of trouble if you can," said Harris. "If you can't, just make sure the other guy gets it worse. First day's always the hardest."

After Harris left, the man in the golf shirt sat up and looked at Poe.

"Who do you have to blow to get that kind of treatment," he said. "None of those fuckers has said a single goddamn word to me."

"I doubt it's the kind of treatment you want," said Poe.

"I'm on my second DUI," the man said.

"Well, I'm sure they'll let you go again."

"I dunno. I said some dumb things to the cop."

"They got bigger things to worry about than you."

The man sat back down on the bench.

"Christ," he said. "I've got tenure committee next week."

"What does that mean?"

The man looked at Poe. "I'm a professor. Actually I'm a poet."

"At CU?"

The man shook his head.

"I don't give a fuck," Poe said. "It ain't like I'm going there."

"Why are you here anyway," the man said.

"Don't worry yourself."

"C'mon, man. I don't care."

"Supposedly I killed someone," said Poe. "Except I didn't."

"Really?"

"Really."

"Jesus," said the man. But his mood seemed to brighten after that. He went to the sink and washed his face and lay down on the bench and closed his eyes.

Poe felt himself getting angry, he thought you should belt this guy in the face, consoling himself on your situation. Except he was done with that behavior. No that wasn't true. Where he was going, most likely he was not done with that behavior at all. He watched the professor, smelling like puke but resting easily.

Finally a cop came and took Poe to a garage where they put him in a van with a cage in the back of it. He waited there a long time, the cage was like a cage for large animals, bear dogs or something, he closed his eyes. He doubted it was past two in the afternoon but it felt like a long time since he'd been home. He didn't know how long he'd been in the van when he heard the driver's door open and close and then the garage opened and they drove out into the light. The driver didn't say a word and Poe didn't feel like waking up anyway, he was thinking about Lee, the last night, it was hard to figure her out. They'd gone to a motel and done it until morning, but there was something off about her. A married woman, what did you expect? He could see it clearly in his mind, her face in the dark, it was as clear as looking at a picture, that was how you remembered things, by thinking about them over and over, only sometimes you'd begin to remember them differently. He began to feel carsick with all the narrow swooping roads; it was an old van. He had no idea where they were, woods and fields, fields and woods, a never-ending succession, country roads, dipping and turning all the time, he would be sick. When they finally stopped they were at a large compound with low buildings at the top of a hill, it looked brand-new, could have been a

school except for the forty-foot chainlink and razor wire. There was a
good view of the river, four squat gun towers, and a man driving a white
pickup truck down the space between the fences, patrolling. Inside the
inner fence, in what was clearly the prisoners yard, there was no grass,
only dirt, prisoners standing around in blue shirts and tan pants, there
were two separate areas, it looked like weightlifting benches.

The paint was fresh and bright white and the steel razors at the tops
of the fences reflected the sun and the big windows on the guard towers
were spotless. Someone came out to open the gate. Poe watched it close
behind him and get farther and farther away. Inside one of the buildings
they took the big manila envelope with his wallet and watch and counted
the money again in front of him and made him strip. He stood naked facing the wall. There were two guards; both had their batons out. Here it
comes, he thought.

"Open your mouth and lift up your tongue. Run your fingers through
your hair, all of your hair now. Turn around and pull your ears forward."

Poe complied.

"Bend all the way over and spread your cheeks wide."

The men stood at a safe distance. Poe did everything they said.

"You got anything in them boots?"

"In what?"

"Your shoes, boy. You got anything in em?"

"No."

"Do I have to cut them open to look inside them?"

"Please don't cut up my shoes."

Poe turned around. One of the guards was feeling around inside his
shoes with blue latex gloves. Both guards wore gray uniform shirts and
black pants, cheap material; their shirts were pilled from being washed.

"Turn the fuck back around," said the short guard. "I won't ask you
again."

Poe did.

"Alright. Now bend over three times quickly. All the way down to
your toes."

Poe did.

One of them rapped the baton against the wall.

"Do it quick," he said. "Doubletime."

Poe did.

"Nice form," said one of them.

"What was that for?"

"In case you had a shank up your ass. You put something up there and you bend over too quick it'll cut your guts open from the inside."

"I don't have anything," said Poe.

"So keep it in mind for the future. That's a regular part of the drill."

They gave him his boots back and tossed him an orange jumpsuit that smelled like someone else's sweat.

"I don't have any socks or underwear," Poe said. The men ignored him. They led him to another room where he was directed to stand in front of a large desk behind which sat a heavy-set black woman. He greeted her and she ignored him. She verified his name.

"Do you feel suicidal?" she said.

"No," he said.

"Are you a homosexual?"

"No."

"Do you have any medical conditions or allergies?"

"No."

"Have you ever thought about hurting yourself?"

"I just told you that," he said.

She gave him an exasperated look.

"Whatever," he said. "What about my lawyer?"

She acted like she hadn't heard him. He sat there watching her write. He could feel the anger building up inside him but he kept his head on, it would not help him to let his fire get built up.

The woman put his file aside and began looking at other papers that seemed to have nothing to do with him, then she was writing something in her day planner. He stood in front of her desk with his arms behind his back. He stood for a long time. He shifted from foot to foot; his leg fell asleep. Finally she motioned to one of the guards and Poe was taken into another room where an inmate trustee, a short gray-haired black man in his sixties, handed him a pile of sheets, a towel, and a pillow, and asked his clothing sizes.

When the guards had gone back into the other room, the trustee said, "How much you want for those boots, my man. Timberlands?"

"Red Wings."

"Well tell me what you want for them."

"They ain't for sale."

"Don't test my motherfuckin patience, dawg."

Poe didn't say anything. The man left and came back and tossed Poe a pair of polyester khaki pants, two pairs of socks and underwear, and a blue denim button-down shirt.

"None of this is the right size," Poe said.

"You are one stupid-ass fuckin fish, you know that?"

He could have picked the little man up and crushed his skull but for some reason the inmate was not afraid of him. He changed out of the orange jumpsuit and into the new clothes and one of the guards came back and Poe picked up his bundle of sheets and followed him down a long narrow hallway. They passed a guard station with inch-thick Plexiglas, were buzzed through a steel door and into a broad corridor as long as a football field. The corridor was empty except for a pair of guards patrolling and an inmate pushing a mop. The floor was highly polished and the smell of floor wax and solvent overpowering. Following the guard, Poe passed several doors and could see into the cellblocks, he could see men sitting around on chairs and tables, he could hear music blaring. Poe expected the guard to explain where they were going but he didn't.

Finally they reached a door and the guard turned and the door clicked and they entered the cellblock. It was a long wide space with two tiers of cells on each side and a large common area in the center. Several televisions were turned up to maximum volume, blaring *Jerry Springer* and rap videos. There were tables on which men were playing games of some sort, checkers or maybe chess, some wore the same khakis and blue denim shirts as Poe did but most wore sweatshirts or pants that didn't look state-issued. Immediately the noise died down in the room as people sized him up.

"I like them shoes," called one of them.

"Look at that pretty-ass motherfuckin fish."

"Some tight-ass Britney Spears booty down there. I be grabbin on that shit and . . ." Out of the corner of his eye, Poe could see one of the inmates making an exaggerated humping motion.

"Bullshit nigga," said another. He called to Poe: "I'ma take care of you, baby. Don't let these other motherfuckers worry you. You too pretty for them."

There was loud laughter and competing catcalls about what they would do to him.

Poe looked to the guard to say something to quiet the inmates down but he didn't.

"Don't you worry, fish," said someone, "that punk-ass CO won't say shit to us. Will he. Cause that nigga is next in line after you."

The corrections officer was staring rigidly ahead. He waved his arm at a group of inmates blocking the stairs but they only stepped out of the way at the very last second. The CO, who was not much older than Poe, didn't make eye contact with any of them.

All the cell doors were open and finally they got to one that wasn't. The guard checked his keyring and found the correct key and turned it. They stood there until Poe figured he was supposed to slide the door open.

The cell was maybe six feet wide and ten long. Two steel bunkbeds were bolted to the wall and took up half the width; opposite the door was a stainless steel toilet without a seat, a sink with a pushbutton faucet. Only one person would be able to stand up at a time inside the cell.

"This like the place you stick new guys or something?"

"What'd you expect?" said the guard.

"Be a little bit bigger for having two beds."

"You think this is bad," he said, "most of the time the fish get stuck in the hole a couple weeks for processing. Least you're going right in the general population. Plus your cellmate's in the hole right now so you got it to yourself a few days."

"Which bunk," said Poe.

"The one where there isn't anything on it, shitbird."

Poe took the top one, set his bundle on it.

"Lockdown's in five minutes," said the guard. "Don't fuckin go nowhere."

"What about dinner," said Poe.

"You missed it," said the man. He shrugged and walked away.

Poe made his bed, looked for things to occupy himself. There was nothing. He drank water from the faucet. He lay down. There was a pressure inside his head, like the motor up there was spinning too fast, the bolts and screws holding him together were about to let go and he'd end up torn to pieces, he'd choke himself, there would be no stopping him. It was a mistake, is what it was. That was it. It was a mistake. He was not supposed to be here. There was no way he was ever supposed to be put in a place like this.

9. Isaac

The faint light of dawn woke him and he opened his eyes quickly. He thought he might be back in his bed. No. In the sleeping bag at the edge of a lawn. He turned his head. Goes on a ways, out of sight. Fairway of a golf course. Soft bed. Easy on the bruises. He checked the air with his breath, watched the vapor drift up. Cold and not a sound anywhere, could be the only one alive on earth. Used to like being up this early. Back to sleep.

He closed his eyes again and waited until the sky brightened enough to wake all the birds, a single chirp and then a spreading chorus, twitters and warbles, cooing pop pop pop piit piit piit sreeeel sreeel sreeel. Something fluttered just over his face, a gray-and-white flash: kingbird. Bee eater. He put his arms behind his head and lay there for another ten minutes, listening to birdcalls and watching the sky change color as the sun rose.

He sat up quickly and the pain startled him—rib cage. Did I get jumped again yesterday? No. Sunday leftovers. Internal pain, turns the stomach. Better to break an arm. Depends. Good rib-break better than bad arm-break. Leg-break the worst—can't move—done for. Plus lose a quart of blood per femur. Reason they break your legs on the cross—act of mercy.

It took him a long time to get his bag packed, there was no way to move that didn't hurt. Worse than yesterday, he thought. The second day after you get beaten is worse than the first. Body won't let you know you're hurt until you're out of danger—waits till you can handle the news. Preserves your mental outlook.

Finally he stood feeling the sun on him, head down, getting the light directly to the brain, cheering, pineal gland. Also the feeling of danger—they can all see you. See how hurt you are. Sleep by day, move by night. Oldie but goodie—reason animals see in the dark. Night eyes reflect light but also absorb it. Think on that a while, Watson.

Shouldering his pack he made his way back into the forest, down the rocky hill along the drainage, his legs hurting more than yesterday. He walked hunched and with small steps as if carrying an enormous load. He wanted badly to lighten the pack but there was nothing inside it he wouldn't need. There were strange, brightly colored flowers along the stream, but even his slow movement took all his effort; he passed without looking. What's on the day's menu. Broken back, maybe. Fight the old man for his wheelchair. He'd win—special tactics. Wheelchair warfare. What he'd say if he saw you now: ungrateful shit, the strong survive. Send your poor your tired and your hungry. Stick em in a grinder, sausage for the king. Dirt for dinner. How far to the next town.

He reached the ridgetop and looked down over the river flowing in its valley, green and winding, thick with trees. The Elrama plant dominated the skyline on the other side, the stack was bright orange and maybe fifty feet in diameter, five hundred feet tall. The steam plume a mile long. It's only three or four miles to Elizabeth. Only, he thought. Take all day at this pace.

He picked his way slowly down the steep hillside. He could see the road he'd left the previous night and just beyond it the train tracks and the river. Each downhill step hurt his legs. Except the kid is not worried. Knowing how easy the journey will be with two good legs, he prefers to get gimped up. Empty stomachs make for clear heads. Bored with walking he grows gills, swims upriver, comes out downtown. Crowd swoons. Mermaids revere the defeater of Swedes.

*   *   *

Every few hundred steps or so he would stop and rest. He was hungry again. He passed a few small clusters of houses and then a shipping facility of some sort. There was a vending machine outside one of the buildings so he limped around the fence and he found a dollar bill and put it in and got a Dr Pepper. He drank it quickly, standing in front of the machine, and immediately felt better. He spent another dollar on a second can for later.

Out of the corner of his eye he saw someone in uniform crossing the parking lot toward him and made his way quickly back into the woods. That's right, keep moving. Good—he's not following you. A short while later he felt sufficiently alone to rest by a small stream that ran down toward the river. There was no one around. He sat against his pack, dozed for a while, then got up and kept walking until he was back on the train tracks.

Eventually he could see a bridge over the Mon and he knew he was getting close to Elizabeth. The kid perseveres. Chased by man and beast alike, he worries he'll finish his journey with no sense of accomplishment. Complains his legs are only bruised, not broken. The Atlas of his country he's the new Paul Bunyan. A moral emperor—his people renounce popes priests and presidents. He's five foot five and rising. Walking on feet while he's got em.

Approaching Elizabeth the terrain was hilly and wooded though there was a long riverflat with yet another power plant with a tall orange-and-white smokestack, a mountain of coal piled nearby, itself at least a hundred feet tall, barges tied up, unloading more coal. Farther downriver he passed a chemical refinery, another river lock. There were many houses noticeable along the hillside. At the Elizabeth bridge there was a small pier and two kids about his age were sitting on it.

"Spare a cigarette?" the boy called.

Isaac shook his head and went slowly past.

"You sure?" the girl asked.

"I don't smoke," Isaac replied, louder than he'd meant.

"I believe you," said the boy, grinning.

There was a gas station near the bridge with a food mart. The kid strikes gold, he thought. He does fine alone.

Inside the counterman stared at him. Feeling superior. Indian or Pakistani—own all the hotels and gas stations. Wonder why. He ignored the man's stares and filled a basket with Slim Jims, several tins of Vienna sausage, a carton of milk, a half dozen candy bars, two large bottles of water. Just holding all the food in his hands his mouth got very moist, it was all he could do to not tear open the packages. He put it on the counter and the clerk scanned his items. On the map rack he found a road atlas and put it on the counter as well.

"What's up ahead?" Isaac said.

The clerk stared at him.

"What town? Clairton?"

"Clairton is across river. Glassport is next town on this side. Eighteen and seventy."

He paid the clerk and noticed he had only a dollar left in his wallet. Plenty in the pants pocket though. He put the food into his pack and stuffed the atlas in as well and then had a thought, went to the napkin dispenser by the hot dog rack and took a thick handful of napkins. The clerk watched him, making a mental tally of the napkins, but didn't say anything.

A little over thirty dollars now he'd spent, coming twenty miles. He had to get onto the trains. He drank the milk immediately for the vitamins, the entire quart, and began to feel much better. You could actually live off this stuff, he thought. The only liquid that satisfies hunger. Where had he read that? A hangover from infancy.

Elizabeth was as run-down as any other place in the Valley, unpainted houses dotted the hillside, a steel-frame bridge crossed the river, the only for ten miles. Just to the north was Glassport, one of the wealthier towns. He would stand out there and there would be police. He went back toward the bridge. Traffic was heavy—he was getting closer to Pittsburgh. Downriver, toward Pittsburgh, he could make out the long barns of the Clairton coke works, building after building as far as the eye could see, dozens of smokestacks. The plant itself was several miles long—bigger than the town. He passed the first parking lot, newer model cars, men milling about in dark blue mechanic's coats. It was a good job—seventeen an hour to start. Along the river maybe forty or fifty barges in various states of unloading, a huge trainyard. Still, the city was run-down, abandoned houses on the main boulevard. Biggest coke works in the country couldn't stop the city from going to shit. Niggerton the old man calls it now. Don't even repeat that, he thought. Don't be like him. Resting on a grassy hillside, he watched the river and the coke works, the Valley was steep here, on both sides the land rising sharply above the river. Careful you don't get jumped—lots of heroin comes from Clairton. Nursery rhyme. He watched the barges unload their coal for processing. From darkness we pull light—black oil and coal. Carbon the reason—burn your ancestors.

He drifted off and it was near midnight when he woke, he was very cold, he'd left his coat unzipped. It was dark. The only light came from the coke works, small dim safety lights outlining every building and smokestack, as far as the eye could see. In the dark it looks like connect the dots. Several miles long. How many feet of pipe—millions, easily. Hundreds of buildings. Coke ovens, cranes, conveyors, who knew what all those buildings did, steam rose from every pipe and building. Heat and steam and blackness of coal. Underworld.

Walking down a dark street he passed a man wrapped in a blanket sitting against a fence. The man looked at him, then looked away. Isaac passed but then stopped and reached into his pants pocket and tried to fumble a bill out of the envelope in his pocket. It was hard to get just one out. Just give him the entire wad, he thought. If you give it to him you can just go home. He stood there thinking. No. Have to keep going.

He walked back and handed the man a twenty, and looking up at him, the man hesitated before accepting it. He was a young man, Isaac saw. A dirty face, maybe a junkie. "Appreciate you," he said to Isaac.

"No problem," Isaac told him. He continued down the road. Time to catch the train, the great escape. Collecting himself he made his way toward the coke works, the wind shifted and the smell was intense. CITY OF PRAYER the sign called it, more nice old buildings boarded up, dark streets, detritus of an older way. What was the joke? *A boy and girl are making out in his car, and finally she can't take it anymore. Kiss me, she whispers. Kiss me right where it stinks. So he drives her to Clairton.*

Ahead of him along the hillside he could hear a murmuring he knew must be a gathering of people, there was light coming from behind an old building, a school, maybe. There weren't any houses around it. Probably not locals. Maybe someone to tell you a train schedule.

Two enormous fires in trash cans behind the school, nearly two dozen people sitting or standing in groups against the walls, around different fires, a few shelters made of salvaged plywood or corrugated tin. Sitting against one wall, a dreadlocked teenager was beating on two white sheetrock buckets, a stick in each hand, the rhythms syncopated, he was not an amateur, a school band dropout. A drum major gone native.

Isaac stood behind some overgrown bushes, watching. The people were a mix, half local wino types and half younger people, kids in their teens and twenties. It was chilly but a large-breasted girl took her shirt off and danced around the courtyard in her bra and a few whoops went up. Eventually she went and sat down again. A few people were doing something over a candle and he realized they were shooting up.

Just go in there, he thought. You're no different than any of them. But he couldn't bring himself to. A fight broke out suddenly, a big man and small man swinging wildly but neither connecting and finally a few people went and separated them. The big one with the shaved head was younger and he went and stood with his group. The older smaller man went and stood by himself. A few more people came around the end of the building and Isaac saw it was the boy and the girl he'd seen earlier under the bridge. The boy was carrying a case of beer in each hand; the girl carried a grocery bag.

Isaac had just gotten up the nerve to join the group when the skinhead and the older man were fighting again, but this time the skinhead tripped and the older man hit him in the head with a stick and the skinhead fell over and was hit several more times as he rolled around on the ground. The small man who'd done the hitting picked up his backpack and walked immediately out of the area of the loading dock and people watched him, he nearly walked straight into Isaac.

"I can't see you," the man said, crashing through the dark brush, "but I ain't who you want to be worrying about." He was about Isaac's size and Isaac relaxed slightly.

"This ain't a good spot," he continued. "There's a couple of bad seeds in there, dopeheads, and when they take a look at the big bald bastard I was hitting they're gonna be out for serious."

The man was wearing a backpack with a sleeping bag strapped to the bottom of it and he headed downhill toward the train tracks. Isaac hesitated, then decided to follow him.

After a hundred yards or so the man slowed to let Isaac catch up.

"We might as well either fight it out or not."

"I'm not fighting," said Isaac.

"Okay then, so walk together and stop making me nervous."

He started down the dark street again and Isaac kept up with him.

"Some real troublemakers in there," said the man. "Sometimes it goes like that." He had a good deal of blood on the side of his face. He saw Isaac looking. "Christ," he said. "Got me good, didn't he?"

"Looks like it."

"It'll heal, they always do. You know it around here at all?"

"I'm from here."

"You headed out?"

"Somewhere south."

"That's bass-ackwards. Summer be here before you know it—time to head north."

"I'll be alright."

"A rebel, huh?"

Isaac shrugged.

"After my own heart," the man said.

They walked toward the coke plant. When the man stopped to piss in the middle of the tracks, Isaac adjusted his knife and the sheath. You're just being paranoid now, he thought.

"What's your actual destination?"

"California."

"How you getting there?"

"No idea," said Isaac, and then he realized why the question had been asked, was immediately sorry he'd answered it.

"Ah shit, I'll point you the way. Head that way myself for a while."

Isaac didn't say anything.

"Be good for you. Always good to have a mentor around. I don't mind doing it."

"I'm doing fine on my own."

"Well just give me the word and I'll take off then," he said. "If you're one of those loner types that can be a pain in the ass."

Isaac shook his head and grinned. "I got no problems."

They were coming up the north end of the coke plant. Isaac still couldn't get over the size of it, it was bigger even than the mill in Buell had been, but the man seemed not to notice and they stood in the brush at the riverbend, looking at the trainyard. There were at least a dozen different tracks. There were several long trains loaded with coke.

"You wanna go find a rail and ask which is which."

"What do I say to them?" said Isaac.

"Same as anyone else."

Isaac shrugged.

"You don't even know what to ask, do you?"

Screw this guy, he thought. He met his eyes in the dark.

"Alright, I'll do it for us. Sit tight."

The man started to walk off, then stopped.

"My name's Winston, by the way. But most people call me the Baron."

Isaac told him his name, then wondered if he should have made one up. No, he thought, this is what you've wanted. You can give this guy the slip if you need to. At the moment you need his help.

Shortly after that the Baron was back. "It's the big one there with the four units. The one on the end is just going upriver a little ways, but the big one is going to a place near Detroit. All kinds of shit comes and goes from there—it'll be easy for you to find something."

"When's it due to get rolling."

"Any minute is what he said. Usually that means a couple hours."

Just then the triangle of lights came on at the front of the train and there was the sound of diesel engines turning over and then running at high idle.

The man grinned. "Christ, you're bringing luck to me. I'd been wanting to bash that boy in the head for three days. And now we got our taxi coming. You just watch what I do."

"I know how to get on a train," said Isaac.

"Suit yourself then, tough guy. I've been doing it thirty-seven years but I'm sure you can't learn a damn thing from me."

"I'll pay attention."

"Good man."

The train began to move slowly and the headlights swept over them, blinding, and as soon as the engines passed they ran across the other tracks until they were alongside it, Isaac's footing was loose in the gravel, the Baron was running ahead of him and threw his backpack up onto the platform and grabbed the ladder and disappeared between two cars. Isaac tossed his pack up onto the rear platform of a different hopper car and pulled himself up the ladder.

He sat on the small metal platform facing the car behind him. It was still dark but by the grit on his hands he could tell the small platform of the coke car was filthy. He didn't care—you're moving and not lifting a foot to do it. Feels like a miracle after all that walking. See why people make lives out of doing this.

He sat with his legs outstretched, feeling the train gradually pick up speed, the noise from the train doubled then doubled again.

He watched the scenery pass, lights on the other side of the river. They were going faster and faster and it was getting cold in the wind. Get even colder once we get out of the Valley, once the tracks aren't bending around a river. He started to take his sleeping bag out, then he stopped himself—it would get sucked away. You're pretty much just gonna freeze your ass off. No, crawl in that hole. He felt around with his hands, there was a tall slot, a sort of porthole in the back of the car but he couldn't imagine the space inside was very large. At least it was more protected. He decided to wait.

After several minutes he could see Pittsburgh, the skyscrapers, the power plant on the island, and then the train slowed and began to turn left, west, he grabbed onto the railing and grabbed his pack with the other hand so it wouldn't slide off under the wheels. Then the city was receding as well, the tall buildings, the bridges and the river, gone.

Book
Three

1. Grace

Harris had arrested Billy that morning and when Grace came home from work all the lights were off in the trailer, everything was just as she'd left it. Billy was not home, was not coming home. Maybe not ever again. She ought to get a fire going in case it got colder that night but she couldn't bring herself. Couldn't bring herself to get up from the chair. At first she'd been sure nothing would happen to him—blind mother hope all that was. An inability to face the truth. She would have to get used to this new feeling. Thought you were making big compromises but that was nothing compared to what's coming.

She had always thought—she didn't know why but her whole life she had thought that eventually someone would come along and look after her the way she had looked after other people: her own mother, Virgil, Billy. So far that had not happened. It did not look to be happening anytime soon. Seemed that she had made this one bad decision out of love, she had been unwilling to give up Virgil, been unwilling to move away from him, to a place her son might have become a different person, and the consequence was that she had now lost Billy.

All for Virgil. Billy ending up this way, her bad choices all around. Your three semesters of college—how long was it before you stopped reminding people of that? That was dropped for him as well—Virgil—he couldn't make the bills on his own. And resented you for going to school, always asking when it would pay off. Even that early sign you ignored. I was twenty-two, she thought. With a young child and the Valley in a depression. It was a miracle I was able to do any of that at all. Looking back she thought she had been a braver person then. Another thing that had been chipped away. All the things you needed to know in life—you didn't learn them until you'd already made your decisions. For better and worse you were shaped by the people around you. Virgil had undercut her, a gradual erosion, the way the river undercut its banks. He had convinced her to stop educating herself, he'd convinced her to take a job she hated, because at some point he had realized that his wife might be manipulated into supporting his life of ease. A minor miracle given their surroundings, but he had pulled it off, at the cost of his wife and now his son. All it took was lying nearly daily about looking for work and, in the periods in which he did work, cashing his paycheck himself rather than bringing the entire thing home. She always remembered being stunned at tax time by how much money Virgil made on paper—very little of it ever seemed to come back to the family.

It made her sick now to think about it. The fault rested squarely on her shoulders, she couldn't push it off on Virgil. She should have seen through him. It just hadn't occurred to her that anyone could be so manipulative.

And there was Harris. He had offered himself numerous times and she had lost interest and, now that he wasn't interested, she was sick over Harris again. She didn't want to admit those things but they were true, it was some rule of human nature—you want most whatever you can't have. Virgil had always kept her unsure about his feelings, always inserting some sliver of doubt, she had always been the one chasing. Bud Harris had simply made his feelings clear.

She felt sick to her stomach thinking about it. She had done this to herself, to Billy. Deep breath. Of course it wasn't fair. Your entire life's work, that child. But she was not that old. She could expect another thirty, thirty-five years. It was all your outlook. She needed to have her own goals again. She would have to stop living for others. Since Billy making his choice to stick around Buell she'd spent most of her free time worried sick about him and in those years she'd forgotten to look after herself. It really had been her downfall. Other mothers had sons as well, they managed. Maybe it was just the rollercoaster Billy had put her on. Up and down and up again. Now down. But he didn't do it on purpose. It was just who he was.

She needed to collect herself. You could not live for other people. Christ, she thought, I shouldn't be thinking these things right now. But there was no choice. Billy had done what he'd done, and nothing could change it. She would have to go on living.

There was orange juice and a bottle of vodka and she made a tall screwdriver. She could not afford a lawyer, not any of the good ones. If she stopped making payments on the house it was possible but it would take her several months to save the money. By then it would be too late. She would have to trust Harris. The public defender. She shook her head. She would stop making payments anyway. Bank the money. Lose the place if she had to but you couldn't leave your son to the public defender. You might as well just skip the trial if you did that.

Don't make decisions before you have to, she thought. She went out to the back porch, taking the bottle of vodka and the orange juice with her, watched the sky get darker and sipped her drink. How long had it been—three years—it seemed like yesterday, she'd been talking to Harriet, the director of the shelter, about what you had to do to get a job as a counselor. Or social worker, she wasn't sure. They'd sat down, the two of them, and written it all down. School, that was what it came down to. It was a hurdle and you had to jump it. *It's simple,* Harriet told her, *you get some letters after your name BA, MA, whatever. Until then, you'll be scratching in the dirt. A master's especially.* She must have seen the look on Grace's face because she smiled and shrugged. *Hey, we get old whether we do these things or not. Either way, we get old.*

Time for a refill. The sky was dark and the stars were coming out, one by one. She remembered Virgil turning to her, it was Billy's senior year during a football game, Billy had just scored for the Eagles. *We did a good job raising him, didn't we?* That was what Virgil had said. That was when her eyes began to be opened—there had been no *we* involved in raising Billy. She had borne the burden from day one and until that moment at the football stadium, she had presumed that Virgil understood that—throwing a football to your kid an hour a week did not count as raising him. At any rate, that moment in the bleachers, that was when she'd begun to fall out of love with Virgil, though it had taken three more years to fully resolve. It gave her some satisfaction that Billy now hated his father. You can be a small person sometimes, she thought.

Where would you be if you'd taken Bud Harris up on his offer—six years into a government job, guaranteed retirement, health, pension. Billy would have grown up in the city, away from all this. No, she thought, you couldn't. Not when it was handed to you like that, you couldn't take it.

You got your hopes too high. Not for yourself, but for Billy. Thought he could be something he is not. But of course it was always like that. Love always blocked your view of the truth. And now . . .

Whatever happens, she thought. You are going to do your best and that's all. She sat there like that and cried for a while. Enough, she finally thought. Get up. No more drinking. She pitched the vodka bottle over the porch railing and into the yard.

A truck came up the road then, she saw the headlights and then it pulled into the driveway, wondered who it was and stumbled over the step going back into the house. Harris was standing there out front, in his uniform.

He saw she'd been crying and he opened his arms and she leaned into him.

"You want to come inside?"

"I thought I better tell you some things first."

She closed her eyes and knew it would be bad.

"It's standard procedure in big cases like this but they took him to Fayette. Also I made him shave and get cleaned up for the mugshot but most likely his picture will be in the paper tomorrow."

"How does it look?"

"It's not in our favor. Not unless he starts telling us what happened."

"Fayette is the new one," she said. She forced herself to say it: "The one where all those guards got stabbed."

"Billy knows how to take care of himself. He's a big boy and they won't mess with him much, even in a place like that."

"Can we get him out of there?"

"The DA has all the say in where he goes, given the charge."

"I wish I'd voted for Cecil Small now."

"Me, too," said Harris.

"It's all a big game to them, isn't it? They've got no idea what they really do to people."

"No," said Harris. "I don't think any of them do."

She'd set her drink down on the porch rail and she picked it up and finished it.

"This isn't your fault. You did more than anyone could."

She shrugged. "I made one bad decision but I made it every day."

"Some people go their whole lives like that."

"I guess."

"What are you drinking," he said.

"Screwdriver."

It was quiet for a second.

"Do you want one?" she said.

"Do you have anything for grownups?"

"Not really."

"In that case I'll have one."

"I have to find the bottle. I just tossed it into the yard."

"I'll get it," he said, laughing. They went into the house and Harris took out his flashlight and went out back and returned a few seconds later with the bottle. Then he stood looking out the back window, or maybe just looking at their reflections, as she made the drinks.

"Get your tomatoes in yet?"

She nodded.

"I'll get mine in soon, I hope."

She nodded and looked at him. He took a sip of his drink and smiled at her. He was average height, average everything, he looked small standing there in the kitchen in his uniform. But that was not the impression he gave to others, in a room full of people everyone gave him a berth, it was a way he'd learned to act. But right now, even wearing his gunbelt, he was just himself. That was the thing about Harris—he was happy to drop his act. It was the difference between him and Virgil, who was always judging things, sizing you up, even when he was smiling. That was another thing which had never occurred to her before.

"I feel like an idiot for all those things I said yesterday," she said. "I was upset but I know it doesn't excuse them."

"I feel like that every morning." He grinned. "We can sit down." They went into the living room to the couch, she sat down on one end and he sat somewhere near the middle.

"You can slide over here if you want."

He did and they sat quietly for a while and held hands. He adjusted his gunbelt so it wasn't pressing into her and closed his eyes and laid his head on her shoulder. His body went slack as if they had just made love. It was dark but they didn't turn on the lights. She had looked at him. A good-looking man in his way, his long face that changed expressions so easily. He might have made a good clown, he could exaggerate the shape of his face that way, he was a funny person. She ran her hand over the smooth top of his head, the short soft hair on the sides and back. Plenty of men his age would have grown it long, combed it over to hide their bald spot. He trimmed it himself once a week with clippers. As if he had nothing to hide. She'd once suggested he shave it all off, like the cop on that cable show, but he'd dismissed that as vanity.

Maybe it's just your body telling you to do this, knowing you need someone to take care of you. Just the body being practical. Not the heart. But that was not the way it felt. Her neck was tingling where his breath touched it and the feeling was running down her body. She put her hand on his belt but he lifted it away.

"Because you're on the clock?" she said.

"I'm still waiting to be convinced why it should work now when it's never worked before."

"You came over, though."

"I seem to be here."

"We can try again."

She put her hand on his lap a second time.

"I wonder sometimes if you know you're not being fair."

"I don't mean it."

"I know. That doesn't make it any better."

He gently slid away from her, then stood up in the dark trailer. She found herself looking at his pants, just beneath his belt, and he noticed her looking.

"Christ, Grace," he said. He started laughing.

"I'm unstoppable."

"Maybe." He looked around at things, but mostly out the windows. He cleared his throat. "Let's just give it a couple days or something. Let you take it easy awhile."

"Alright," she said.

"I'll see you." He leaned and kissed her forehead and then walked out.

She listened to him go, his light steps across the porch, then the sound of him driving away. She knew she should turn on the light but she didn't want to, she was content just lying there like that in the dark, she could still smell his aftershave lotion in the room, feel where he'd touched her. It seemed the first time in weeks, no months, that she'd really felt hope.

2. Poe

His cell it was a very small place, a narrow rectangle, the front side was open but there were bars. Like a dog cage. A horizontal slit for a window, too small to squeeze through, he tried to figure out what direction it was, where he was facing in relation to the river and his mother's trailer, to Lee's bed or the couch on her porch. Except no. It would only depress him further, those things—they did not really exist for him anymore. He wondered if Lee would come to his trial, even that he couldn't be sure of and Christ this thin mattress he couldn't sleep, he didn't even have a magazine, eventually his mind would turn in on itself. Inevitable as tides. A turning in. A padded cell, smearing himself with excrement.

He would make a belt for his pants. He sat up and after a minute he was able to tear a long strip from his bedsheet, thread it through the loops of his pants, it would be serviceable, a good belt, like a pirate. Then he was done and once more there was nothing to do.

It was noisy in the cellblock, the televisions were off but there was music playing from every direction, little radios, people banging on metal, conversations shouted across the cellblock, he listened to them they were completely pointless such as *Yo Dee what up?*, the reply inevitable: *Coolin* or *A'ight*. Things that did not need to be said. Talk for the sake of talk. He had always hated that, there could be silence it was golden. Or had he? He didn't know. But he hated it now it was under his skin he was very irritated, physically, by the noise. Only it gave him something to focus on, the noise, it was good, annoying but good, he crushed his thin pillow onto his face to make it quieter. He would mind his business. He would suffocate himself. He took the pillow off his face. That would be his rule he would mind his own business, there could be a murder going on and he would mind his business. He was a big man and they would leave him alone.

It began to die down around midnight, though it might have been ten at night or three in the morning, he didn't know. They'd taken his watch. Finally a small amount of morning light came in and he heard footsteps and keys jangling and then his door clicked open. He saw the face of another young CO, a young face with a sparse mustache, trying to look hard.

"They serve breakfast for an hour," the guard told him. "If you wanna eat you better get your ass moving."

He had forgotten he had been hungry all night and now he realized he had no idea where breakfast would be served. He knew better than to ask, he would have to find it himself. He got up and dressed quickly. That was good making the belt last night, he thought, that was good preparation, from the cell next to him came the sound of a person noisily moving his bowels, it did not sound healthy. Everyone crapped basically in plain view, there was a small curtain you could draw but that was it.

Get to breakfast, he thought.

His cell was on the second floor, along a cement catwalk that ran down the length of the tier. There were steps at the end. It was high enough on the tier, fifteen or twenty feet maybe, you would not want to get thrown off. He wondered why they hadn't put a bigger railing up. But then it was probably a help if they got rid of a convict that way, it was all about numbers, available spaces, for instance they had reopened the old prison near Pittsburgh, the one they had closed after they opened this one. They'd decided they wanted to lock up more people so they reopened the old prison and started to use it again, and now they had two.

Down on the main floor of the cellblock he followed the general direction of traffic. They were all looking at him but no one said anything, maybe it was too early for comments. In the wide main corridor the people poured in from the different cellblocks and there was a traffic jam of bodies, a backup. He stared straight ahead, up at the glaring fluorescent lights, he stared at the brightly polished linoleum, anywhere there was not a pair of eyes staring back. There was the smell of food and it was not good, it smelled like school lunches only worse.

He reached the cafeteria where it sounded like a riot had broken out, pandemonium was the word for it, whoever wasn't shouting was talking in their loudest voice, hundreds of inmates, thousands maybe, and not a single guard. But there was no riot. It was business as usual. It was not a good place. It was a place you could get away with anything. He would have to find another spot to eat only it was not like that, there was not a prison restaurant where you could order a steak and have your booth.

There were long institutional tables with the benches attached, most likely so they could not be used as weapons. As for the room itself it was segregated by race, blacks in one area of the room, Hispanics in another, the voices of young men shouting over each other. The whites were visibly a minority, a quieter group, they appeared to be older as well.

In the white area three men were sitting alone at one end of a long table, they were clearly running things, they varied in size but they were all big men and equally sleeved with tattoos. One had a shaved head but a sort of open friendly look about him, another had a black watch cap pulled down to his eyes, the third had a blond pompadour he must have gotten up early to work on. Making a general survey, Poe figured fewer than half the people appeared unusually strong, the others were skinny or pudgy with stringy hair and unhealthy looks, meth-heads, your standard trailer trash. There were plenty of old men as well, just regular-looking old men, men of every age, really. Technically he was trailer trash himself, only he wasn't. He guessed he would naturally fit in with the better half, the only problem being he had only a football tattoo on one pectoral, over his heart, and another tattoo of his player number on his calf, he wondered about that now, how that would look to the others, he had not known he was going to prison when he'd gotten them. A picture of a knife would have been a better choice, a smoking gun. Or, judging from the tattoos the shotcallers had, something that indicated white power, an eagle, the Nazi SS sign was popular, there was one of Adolf Hitler but you could only tell by the mustache, other than that it could have been anyone, it was one of the stupidest-looking tattoos he had ever seen and the guy would have it the rest of his life.

He picked up a tray and got in line, feeling at ease. He held out his tray and was served two pieces of white bread, eggs from a powder mix, sausage, and green Jell-O, he tried to move the tray to the side but they put the Jell-O right on top of his other food. He took a cup of orange Kool-Aid to wash it down.

Carrying his tray he worried someone might try to trip him but no one did, he found a seat in the white area, at the end of a table by himself. A thin shaggy-haired man smiled and made eye contact with him several times, one of the speed freaks, half his teeth were missing. Poe didn't acknowledge him. A few others were sitting at the other end of the table, he nodded to the toughest-looking of the group but was ignored.

A black man about Poe's age came and sat down next to him, he had short dreadlocks, sweatpants flip-flops, and a torn T-shirt, he might have just come from a workout, he looked like someone you'd see in the gym. He didn't seem worried about anything. He had crossed the invisible line that denoted the white area of the room so maybe there were exceptions, the three white shotcallers took note but continued their conversation as before.

" 'Sup," he said.

"What's up," said Poe.

"First day's a bitch, huh?"

"It's alright."

"Dion," he said. He held his fist out and Poe bumped it and introduced himself.

"They probably got a freeze on your account so you won't be able to get no commissary today, no deodorant, shampoo, toothpaste, anything like that."

Poe immediately got the sense he was about to be hustled. "I don't need that shit," he said.

"You like being dirty, huh?"

Poe didn't say anything.

"Alright, Dirty. You look me up you need anything." He smiled and held out his fist to be bumped again but Poe knew he'd just been insulted, he went back to his eggs. The whites at the other end of the table looked at Poe as if they expected him to respond and the man looked back as he walked away but Poe didn't say anything. He began to shovel the food into his mouth, he was getting a feeling, he began to eat as quickly as he could. Everyone smirked and went back to whatever they were doing, and Poe knew that what had happened was very bad, he had just been marked, quick as that.

Another black man came up, crossed the invisible barrier, he was tall and very thick with a scar across his nose and forehead like a pink caterpillar, tattoos all over his arms though Poe could not make them out against his dark skin.

" 'Sup, Dirty."

Poe didn't say anything. There were still no guards in the room. More people were beginning to pay attention.

"Yo, Dirty, gimme one of them sausages."

Poe moved the tray so the newcomer couldn't reach it.

"Why thank you," said the man.

He stood up and reached for Poe's food tray but Poe slid it farther away. Then he put his face in Poe's and laughed loud so his spit went all over Poe's skin.

"You got a problem, Wood? Don't want no niggas touchin your food?"

He was talking in a voice so the other side of the room could hear him, the din was quieting down some.

"I got no problem," said Poe.

It was definitely much quieter, the atmosphere in the room had changed, he was the center of attention. He would have to do something. He was not feeling strong.

"I hope you came up to join your homies in here, baby."

Poe stared at his plate.

"Oh you don't know no one, huh? Not a single motherfuckin soul up in this place?"

Poe knew he should hit him but there was a definite racial feeling, the other blacks would jump him there was no question about it. But he had no choice. He didn't want to fight, he could feel how scared he was, he had never wanted to fight less in his entire life.

"You know I'll take care of you," the man was saying, he softly stroked Poe's arm and the other side of the room erupted in laughter, even some of the whites were laughing and grinning, the man looked toward his friends to bask in his glory and Poe grabbed him in a headlock and rolled them both to the floor, rolled them so the back of the man's head hit the cement with the weight of their two bodies behind it.

The man was limp long enough for Poe to lock an arm around him and start punching him with his free hand, he didn't know how many times he hit him, he wasn't getting good leverage but it was enough, people were shouting a general encouragement, not for Poe but for the fight itself, he was leaning back and bending the man's head back with him, the man was punching awkwardly at Poe's face but it was too late, he had a very strong grip. He had a feeling he could break the neck if he wanted, he smelled sweat and hair oil, he was warm and he felt his strength coming back, the man was completely limp, maybe he'd been limp for a long time, and then someone kicked Poe in the ribs.

It was one of the white guys.

"Get up," he said.

Poe stood up. There was a crowd of men standing around, black and white only there were more of the black. He thought he'd get rushed but that wasn't their purpose.

"Fair fight," one of the white shotcallers was saying.

"Fuck that sucker-punch-ass bullshit," someone from the black side said. Poe started to get the shakes. It was just from adrenaline and he put his hands in his pockets so no one would see. There was a long awkward moment standing there. All of the white men in that area of the cafeteria were on their feet and finally one of the shotcallers seemed to make a decision, he nodded his head slightly in Poe's direction and Poe knew he was supposed to follow him. He felt the relief washing over him, it was like a bucket of warm water pouring down him. About a half dozen of the whites, the ones in charge, were headed toward the exit and he fell in step behind them. Then they were heading down the broad corridor between the cellblocks, they went to the end and turned, there was a metal detector ahead of them and metal doors, the men he was following gave a hand signal to some guards behind a Plexiglas window and the doors popped and they were all suddenly outside, in the rec yard in the bright sunshine, and he heard the doors slam shut behind them.

It was warm outside, the sky was very blue and his eyes hurt. There was dirt under his feet. He continued to follow the tall skinhead until they were near the weight pile. The others from the table had followed them. It was very bright and his eyes were still adjusting, through the fences he could see the greenness of the Valley rolling away from him and, in the distance, not quite the river itself but the far bank of it rising up.

They stopped when they reached the weight pile.

"For a second we thought you were gonna get turned out," said one of them, the one with the shaved head and broad open face, he winked at Poe, the first friendly gesture Poe had felt in days.

The man with the blond pompadour, the leader, added: "You sure took your fuckin time thinking about it."

The others laughed and Poe wasn't sure what to do.

"You'll be alright," said the blond one. "You got it taken care of." He grinned. "I'm Larry," he said, "known also as Black Larry. Call me Black Larry, Larry, I don't give a fuck, really."

The other two introduced themselves. Dwayne, the friendly-looking one with the shaved head, and Clovis, who had the hat pulled down over his eyes. Clovis was substantially wider than Poe, he probably weighed three hundred pounds.

Poe looked back to see if they were being followed. The doors to the main building were still closed and there was no one else in the rec yard.

"Do those guys back there run the place?" Poe said.

"Clovis," said Black Larry, "did our young friend just ask if our black brethren ran this place?"

Clovis made an imperceptible adjustment to his watch cap and said, "Believe he did."

Black Larry sighed loudly.

"In the first place," said Clovis, "do you see those little punks anymore, or are they still locked in behind that fuckin door there? In the second place, don't ask any more stupid fuckin fish questions."

"Sorry," said Poe. "I just got here."

"We fuckin know that," said Clovis.

"I haven't even had my trial yet."

"Listen to this guy," said Clovis.

"That isn't something you want to go around telling people," said Dwayne. "Other than us."

"Sorry," Poe said again. He felt like he was screwing up, he was not sure what he should say. He would be quiet.

"It's fine," Black Larry said. "You're among friends."

"But you need to buck the hell up," said Clovis. "Everyone's gonna be heart-checkin you until you get rid of that mopey-dope fuckin face. It doesn't matter how you fight if you walk around looking like a goddamn clown."

The other two nodded.

"Alright," said Poe. "I hear you."

"He hears us," said Clovis.

"He does," said Poe. "Loud and clear." He grinned and the others smiled, except for Clovis, who shook his head.

"Me and him need to take a walk," said Dwayne, "so he can get his hands washed. That one's got the fuckin ninja."

"Little Man does?" said Black Larry.

"For sure."

"Who's Little Man?"

"The one you hit. He's got the bug."

Poe must have had a look.

"AIDS," said Dwayne. He motioned for Poe to hold his hands out and he held them almost tenderly and looked at them, they were cut and there was blood drying but he couldn't tell whose it was.

"You got any soap," said Dwayne.

"No."

"I'll give you some from my cell."

Black Larry said: "After that he needs to keep his head down a while. Least till we get this worked out with the DCs."

Dwayne nodded. He started walking but Poe was standing rigidly, he was not going to follow an enormous tattooed skinhead back to a prison cell and all the men burst out laughing.

"Don't fuckin worry," Dwayne said. "I ain't tryin to stick anything up yer butt."

* * *

Dwayne had a cell to himself, three rugs on the floor, and a blue curtain with a design of the Virgin Mary. It was on the end of the block so there was light from the window in the cell and light from the big window in the corridor.

"Got that out of the hospice," he said about the curtain.

As Poe washed his hands he smelled lavender. It was not prison soap. It smelled like a soap Lee might use and he washed his hands a second time. "How's all this shit get in here."

"About ten million ways," said Dwayne. "Visitors, COs, they leave and come back at least once a day."

Poe must have made a face because Dwayne continued:

"They make eighteen grand a year. Offer them a couple thousand to bring something in, there ain't many that's gonna turn that down."

"Except if they get caught it comes back on you."

"I'm doing life three times," Dwayne said. "What are they gonna do to me?"

* * *

Later that afternoon he was back in his own cell. They had told him to stay in it until they came and got him the next morning, so he would sleep with his feet to the bars and head by the toilet where it was safe, where no one could reach and put a cord around his neck. A meager light came into the cell, the window was made of the same cheap plastic as the one in the police station, clouded yellow by the sun, the parts ordered and built by the same contractor, probably, getting rich hand over fist. Somewhere there were barons of prisons as there had once been barons of steel.

Down on the main floor of the cellblock it was *Jerry Springer* on the televisions again, aunts who screw nephews, something like that, maybe not exactly but that's why people watched those shows, for the hope of it, he'd watched them himself but now they seemed distasteful. The inmates were shouting encouragement. He noticed he'd started not to hear it, the noise. His stomach was torn up, he was probably hungry again, even the little bit of breakfast he'd eaten had disagreed with him violently. He was glad he'd been alone when it happened. Even eating the food he'd known it would happen, it would make him sick, come out before its time at one end or the other. But what choice did he have—he had to eat. That was his problem he had pampered himself. His whole life he had taken it easy, it was his problem and downfall, the opportunities he'd had, he always took the easy way, and now this, even his pickiness over food, even this was going to hurt him, he needed energy he would have to eat. He would need a shower soon as well, he was not looking forward to it, the shower room. It was not possible that it could be a good place. Except he still smelled like Lee, he would be washing that off as well, he wondered if he could save it somehow but there was no way, smells they came and went you could not save them, it was not like a picture you could make in your mind that you could refer to over and over.

Dwayne had said someone would bring him food from the commissary, he knew it cost money. They had not asked him for money but he was not stupid, it would not be free whatever they gave him. He did not have any choice about it. As far as he knew he had every gang in the prison after him. Dwayne and Black Larry said they would settle things up for him, they would make peace, they just needed him out of the way while they did it. Backdoor agreements, he couldn't tell, he would have to trust them. The week he'd done in the county jail, it was not the same, it was guys in for DUI, small things, it was people going back to their regular lives but not here, these people lived here, it was their world.

But that attitude did not help anything. It was not how you won games or fights, it was not how you won anything. It was another problem of his, his outlook. He was doing just fine. Thriving, practically. It would all work out, there was no reason to be pessimistic, he was not even here for good, he would get out, this was only the prosecutor trying to break him, he was not here for good, he was sure of it. It would be an interlude, a story he would tell in the bars. He was not the same as these people, it would all be figured out, there was no point in thinking otherwise.

3. Isaac

He had no idea how long he'd been on the train, he'd watched the power-lines hurdling up and down until the motion made him sick. Several times they'd pulled over, sat waiting on stub lines as other trains passed, hours, it seemed, he was restless and bored but there was no point to getting off—it was days trying to get on.

Later they were alongside a highway and going fast, the train passing cars. There were so many noises he couldn't separate them, the hammering of the tracks and banging of the couplers and the rushing wind and then the brakes were grating, deafening, the car behind him lurched forward, it would crush him, then all the cars were bouncing and recoiling and the shock nearly jolted him off the platform, under the wheels.

Pay attention. Nearly got lulled to pieces. The ride's either pleasant or miserable. No, it's mostly boring. Nice in the wide open, see a long way out over the hills, other times just a cut through the trees, wall of green in front of your face, claustrophobic. Tunnels the worst.

Think about Poe, what's he doing now? Probably screwing your sister. Or passed out drunk somewhere. Still, he came into the river after you—you can't change that. And he came along on your little caper. Right, and then he started that fight. Would have been better off alone.

He shifted positions again, the platform was very small and not long enough for his legs, it seemed there wasn't any part of him that wasn't cramped or bruised. He climbed the ladder and sat on top of the mound of coal, it was a good view, highest point on the train, he could see the Baron up there as well, seven or eight cars ahead, sitting on a coal pile and watching the scenery. A good feeling. Cold though. Be better in summer. After a time he went back down the ladder and crawled into the narrow slot in the back of the car, where there was no wind. It was a small triangular space between the inside angle of the hopper and the outside shell of the car. It was filthy and he could feel the grit everywhere but he was warm again. Look like a coal miner, probably. Wrap the sleeping bag around you. Safest sleep there is—can't get you on a moving train. Last time your head was clear? Months. Eat some. He opened a tin of Vienna sausages and ate them, spitting the grit that stuck to his fingers. He wasn't sure if he felt better or not and he drank more water.

He woke up sometime later. Sore. No room to stretch. Getting dark now, been on this train an entire day. Could be anywhere, just trees going by. England France or Germany. Imagine it's that instead of . . . Ohio probably. Unless we're to Michigan by now. No way to know until we get there—everything you're seeing is new. Appreciate that while it lasts.

Sleeping or awake, no difference. Gray area between them. Dull blue light from the porthole and the view of the car behind you. Noise of the train, vibration, you're a part of it, rattling. Meat tenderizing. Forgive us our daily softness. Pitch black again—another tunnel. Make you deaf— plug your ears. Pray it ends soon—the fumes. Long enough tunnel you'll suffocate. Short tunnel, please. The fumes got worse and worse yet and his eyes began to burn. He put his head outside the porthole, over the platform—worst yet. Pass out here and you don't wake up. Suicide gas breather. Make sure if you fall asleep you stay away from the wheels. Safer in here.

Then, suddenly, it was bright again and quiet. Get outside before . . . He hung his head out the portal, the wall of green passing next to the train, breathed the clean air and vomited. What is that? A dollar fifty in sausage. Dog food. And you ate that on purpose.

Curling up with his head at the edge of the porthole, he rested on his pack so he could see the trees going by outside. Much darker now, ten minutes till night. The life they all live. Alternative must not be good. What the Swede came from, reason they were so angry when they found you in that old building. Their simple pleasures being taken away.

That's right, he thought, more guilt. Take a lesson from the old man: don't admit you might have been wrong. Lie to yourself and discover true happiness. Lee and Poe the same. An addiction, really, needs its own hotline. No, he thought, the kid should take note. There's gold in them hills. The original business model. Offer forgiveness. Lie cheat and steal and the kid will forgive you. All welcome at the Church of the Kid. Follow his instructions to get to the afterlife. Sixteen virgins and a harpsichord. Your felonies pardoned whether man woman or child. Faith the only requirement—believers go forth and commit. Find forgiveness in reflection. Shine of the collection plate.

He thought about the Swede again. I'm not worried about that anymore, he told himself. Give me water and light and I'll knock down a temple. Jesus Christ? No, a hayseed. Light life and love. The old man who said he never liked my name—sounded Jewish. My mother the one who insisted. I am the Truth and the Light. I am the truth in a knife. Trajectory of a thrown object across level ground: y-axis 9.8 meters per second squared, x-axis zero, initial velocity twenty-five meters per second, release angle fifteen degrees. Presuming no air resistance. Presuming flight uninterrupted by a man's head.

You are going crazy, he thought. *Young man you have plugged Science into the hole left by God.* Your mother had the opposite problem: plugged God into a hole left by . . . Except she took the secret with her. Chose the next world over this one. A slight flaw in her plan—where is she now? Just darkness. If that is what nonexistence is.

He stayed like that for a long time, looking out at the trees rushing past, afraid to touch his eyes and get dirt into them. Keep going, he thought, wash your eyes out. Outside now it was fully dark.

4. Harris

He'd gotten the call from Glen Patacki at lunchtime. *Bud, Glen Patacki here, long time no see. Why don't we have a drink on my boat this afternoon?*

Glen was twenty years older than Harris, the local justice of the peace, the one who'd put in a word for Billy Poe last time. He'd been chief for much of the time Harris was a sergeant, one of the first people Harris met when he moved to Buell. This was the first social call in eight or nine months. The timing is no accident, thought Harris.

Driving up and down the steep hills, all woods and farmers' fields, the sudden ravines and valleys, so much hidden away, you could get to the highest promenade around and still not be able to see half of what was in front of you, the land was so tucked in on itself. Everything green, swamps in the lowlands.

Ho had dropped the morning paper on his desk, Billy Poe's picture on the front page, a story made for newspapers, football star turns murderer. It was the sort of story people couldn't help wanting to read. By tonight, he guessed, there would be few people in Buell, or maybe the entire Mon Valley, who hadn't seen or heard about it.

He downshifted into third gear coming down the long hill so as not to overheat his brakes. He could remember clearly when he'd had ten years left till his pension kicked in but now he was down to eighteen months.

Counting down the end of your life. Hoping things will go by faster. He wondered if everyone was like that, he wondered if, say, doctors or lawyers thought the same things. He was fifty-four now, forty when he'd made chief, the youngest in the history of the town, the youngest in the whole Valley, it was Don Cunko who got him voted in, along with a big push from folks such as Glen Patacki. At the time they'd had fourteen full-time guys and maybe six part-timers. Now those numbers were reversed.

Harris was nineteen when he'd joined the marines, put down law enforcement as his preferred MOS and now, thirty-five years later, here he was, riding out a decision he'd made as a kid. I enjoy my life, he thought. It is work to be happy about things. She is the one who taught you that. Maybe the fact that you had to work at being happy meant it wasn't the natural condition. But he had no excuse. If you had a certain level of comfort, which he did, you just had to decide every morning. Will today be a happy day or a sad day? Listen to that shit, he thought. The only one you'd ever say that to is Fur.

He could imagine himself following Grace until he was old with wandering, he knew he would be comfortable with that. Never close enough to get really burned, or to lose anything. Keeping her just over the next hill. The feeling for her preventing him from finding anyone else. In her own way, she was his even keel.

It was not her fault, to have someone like Billy Poe dependent on her; it had really taken a toll. Don't get too sympathetic, he thought. But it was true. He got worried sick about Fur if the dog was gone too long on one of his runs.

He saw the sign for the marina and went down a long green road under a tunnel of trees. How long had he lived here? Twenty-three years. Before that it was six years with the Philadelphia PD and four as an MP in the marines. He had not planned any of it, he'd enlisted because it was better than getting drafted and the number he pulled made being drafted a certainty. Someone told him MPs were less likely to get sent out on suicide missions by shitbag second lieutenants, not to mention you'd end up coming out, if indeed you came out, with a skill you could actually use.

Coming into the parking lot there was Glen Patacki's black Lincoln, a judge's car, freshly waxed. There were those who waxed their cars and those who didn't. Below that, there were those who washed their cars and those who didn't. Harris being the latter.

Glen was waiting on his boat, he waved from a distance as soon as he saw Harris come out onto the green by the water. A thirty-eight-foot Carver, twin 454 Crusaders. A yacht, as river boats went. Harris had his own slot but his boat, a nineteen-foot Valiant, had been out of the water three years now. One of these days he would sell it. Owning a boat was like having a second dog, except a boat didn't love you for sinking half your paycheck into it.

"Christ what a day, isn't it?" said Glen. He waved his arm, indicating their surroundings. "Couple miles upriver, you'd never know it."

It was a different world. As wooded as Buell was, the southern Mon Valley was beyond the reach of industry. Just trees, branches hanging low over the water and the slow muddy river itself. Quiet, the occasional passing boat, sometimes a tow of barges.

Harris climbed onto the boat. Glen motioned him to sit.

"Bud, to cut the bullshit, the reason I asked you out here is I got the guy from the *Valley Independent* sniffing around, asking about any warrants."

"On what?"

"Anything we might have forgotten to file the seal order on. He's sniffing around, is the point, on anything that might look even worse on this Billy Poe murder."

"There isn't anything to find. If that's the only reason you dragged me all the way out to Millsboro."

"I missed you, baby," said Glen. "You know that's the real reason."

"I know."

"The other thing that's been crossing my mind recently is that I'm not much longer for this job. I thought we might discuss that."

Harris looked at him.

"I'm fine," said Patacki. "It's only that I've made my nut and I was thinking that when I retire, you might consider running for my spot. It'd be a good thing for you."

"Never thought about it."

"Never?"

"Not really."

"That's the beautiful thing about you, Bud. I could have told ten different people that same thing and all of them would be sucking my dick right now."

"I better have a drink first."

"Sure. You know where they're kept."

Harris reached next to him into the cooler and found a High Life.

"From a professional advice standpoint, and, in having a few years on you, I wonder if it might be better if you stayed clear of Billy Poe vis-à-vis this thing in the newspaper," said Patacki. "Which includes his mother as well."

"You don't have to worry about me, you fat prick."

"The only thing that gives me any hope is I hear that the case against him is airtight."

"I did those things for his mother, not him. I always knew he was a lost cause."

Patacki grinned. "You know you made it harder on yourself, not marrying. People want their public servants to act normal. Not have any vices. Like me."

"I hear you," said Harris. "You know I appreciate you going out of your way for me last year. Sorry it's coming back to bite you."

"No, Bud, you're doing alright, I'm just an old drunk and I got worried, not to mention I had a martini powwow with that pussy Huck Cramer and he got me all in a lather."

Huck Cramer was the mayor of Buell, and, like Don Cunko, he was caught up in the town's sewer-bidding problem. "Cramer might have other things he ought to be worrying about."

"Keep in mind that your job is an appointed position, Bud. You end up taking your pension down there in Daniel Boone County, I give you a year before you eat your gun. You're a social animal same as the rest of us."

Harris shrugged.

"I don't envy you, I know that. I heard about the goddamn budget, which I know means more of these part-time fucks."

"It's the benefits," said Harris.

"I can't even get your guys to write tickets anymore, half of them are working twenty-four hours straight, they pull a shift in Charleroi, head down to Buell, then finish up in Brownsville. Meanwhile they live in Greene County. No clue as far as the communities they're policing."

"They're not supposed to work more than twelve straight."

"To be honest I don't care what they do," said Patacki. "As long as they write goddamn tickets. Even ten years ago I did six thousand cases a year, now I'm down to forty-three hundred. My office takes in four hundred and fifty thousand dollars where it used to take in over eight hundred. There's your budget cut right there. Hell, we used to take in one hundred thousand a year just from parking tickets, but now the girl we got working the meters, she's hardly ever out there."

"It's all just symptoms anyway."

Patacki nodded and checked his watch. "Late for my shot," he said. "You mind?" He pulled his briefcase over and opened it and found a small syringe, then lifted his shirt and gave himself an injection into the pale skin on his belly. He smiled at Harris, slightly embarrassed. "They told me all this booze is probably what brought on the diabetes, but . . ."

"How's a man supposed to live?"

"My sentiments exactly." He took another sip of his drink. "Let me give you a scenario I've been turning over in my head. What if, before all those properties got bought up and turned into HUD, we'd just burned them down, say around 1985, every vacant house in the city had been razed before all those people moved in. If you think about it, by now half the city would be all back to woods. The tax base would be exactly the same but with half as many people and none of the new problems."

"Those HUD properties bought Danny Carroll his condos in Colorado and Miami. Without him . . ." Harris shrugged. "There's your problem right there."

Patacki nodded. "A fact I find convenient to ignore, obviously."

"Which is not how I meant it."

"No offense taken." He put up his hand. "Everyone knows you're a good man, Bud. Most of the guys running things are like John Dietz, skimming quarters off the video poker machines. But you," he said.

"That's not my angle."

"Your angle is Grace Poe. That's your slippery slope."

"Not this again."

"Do you still see her?"

Harris looked away, out over the river. It suddenly occurred to him that the Fayette prison, where they were holding Billy Poe, was in La Belle, just on the other side of the water. Less than a mile, probably.

"You should have been here for the seventies, Bud. The department was buying new cruisers with Corvette engines maybe every three years. And then came the eighties, and then it wasn't just that we lost all those jobs, it was that people didn't have anything to be good at anymore." He shrugged. "There's only so good you can be about pushing a mop or emptying a bedpan. We're trending backwards as a nation, probably for the first time in history, and it's not the kids with the green hair and the bones through their noses. Personally I don't care for it, but those things are inevitable. The real problem is the average citizen does not have a job he can be good at. You lose that, you lose the country."

"Did the wife stop talking to you or something?"

"I'm old and fat," said Patacki. "I speculate and theorize."

"You ought to drink more," said Harris. "Or get an intern."

"I do. And I should."

It was quiet for a minute. There were other people sitting on their boats, watching the quiet scene, the shorelines and the sun coming off the water, drinking like Patacki and Harris. Many of the boats never left the dock—gas was too expensive. People drove to the marina to sit and drink on their boats, then went home without ever starting them up.

"Who's getting the axe?" said Patacki.

"Haggerton. Also Miller and Borkowski."

"The new guy?"

"He does more policework than the rest of the department put together."

"Except Miller and Borkowski are lieutenants."

"Just Miller," said Harris. "Borkowski keeps failing the exam. Not to mention the new guy does half his work off the clock."

"You'll have problems with the union."

"I'll handle it."

"This the Chinese guy?"

Harris nodded.

"I can tell you like him," said Patacki. "That's a good thing."

"I guess."

"Permit me a final indulgence, Bud."

"How final?"

"I would like to tell you about the best job I ever worked."

"Why do I suspect that it's Magisterial District Eight?"

"Not even close. It was the Sealtest Dairy making ice cream. Sixty-four to sixty-seven, before I became a cop. This big building, it could have been a mill or something, only you would punch in and change into fresh clothes, then walk under a blue light before you were allowed to touch anything. You were never allowed to get dirty. Big buckets of pistachios and fresh fruit, peaches, cherries, anything you could imagine, mixing it up in the machines. You've probably never seen ice cream before it gets frozen, but I promise you there isn't anything like it." Patacki sipped his drink. "It really was like heaven, just being in there. You'd finish each batch and then take the barrels into the hardener to stack and some-times, because of the humidity from the door always opening and clos-ing, it would be snowing in the hardening room, ice cream stacked to the ceiling and it would be snowing down on you in the middle of the sum-mer. You're making ice cream, it's snowing on you, and you look outside and it's ninety degrees and sunny. I'd take that job again right now if they offered it. It really was like heaven."

Patacki reached into the cooler and took a handful of ice and re-freshed his glass. Then he splashed more gin into it. "Have you seen that lime?"

"I never would have known," said Harris. He handed Patacki a lime quarter.

"I'm worried that you're going down a road, was my point, where maybe you better think if you got one of those jobs you wouldn't mind going back to. Unless it's already worse than I've heard."

"It's not worse," said Harris.

"No?"

But he knew. Patacki could see right through him. He nodded but it was only kindness.

"It will always get worse, old friend. Good deeds will not go unpun-ished."

5. Poe

On his third day he walked out to the yard following Dwayne, it was full of convicts, alone, in small and large groups, pacing in circles, all with something different on their minds, planning how to improve their positions in life, all that could be gotten had to be taken from another. Nonetheless the DC Blacks stuck to their side and Poe was happy to stay on his. The sun was high and the guards looked down from their towers, M16s against their hips or some other rifle, he wasn't sure, no it was M16s, it would be a massacre if they ever wanted it, they could turn it on like water. Beyond the double forty-foot fences and razor wire the Valley was still there in all its greenness but he no longer knew what to make of it, it was a different place to him now.

There was a hierarchy at the weight pile, the shotcallers and their lieutenants pumping out squats and dips and hanging out against the fences while a few dozen yard rats, the meth-heads and assorted trailer folk, they maintained a sort of perimeter, ran errands, occasionally stood close together so as to block a happening from the view of the guards. Poe was in the inner circle with Black Larry and the others, there were maybe seven or eight other men. But his position was tenuous, he could tell he was on a trial run, that was all, he was careful to laugh along with the others and get angry when they did. Once in a while a person who was not part of the group would come in to use the weight pile and one of the lieutenants would take their name down on a piece of paper.

"Nonmembers pay ten a day," said Clovis.

Poe looked at him.

"Least they got an option," Clovis said. "The ones over there—" He pointed to the weight pile run by the DC Blacks. "You go anywhere near there they'll start tossing weights at you, they brained a fuckin fish a few months back, a thirty-pouncer right in the temple."

"Bunch of Olympians," said Poe.

"That's about all they are," said Clovis. He tapped his head.

They worked out on and off the entire day, they worked out more than Poe ever had when he played football. With the exception of Poe, everyone in the inner circle was covered with tattoos, full sleeves on both arms and assorted larger tattoos across backs and chests, vultures or eagles or some imaginary bird Poe couldn't make out. Clovis's triceps said WHITE on one arm and POWER on the other. Dwayne had an eagle like many of the others, the wings spanning his shoulderblades. Black Larry had a pair of jokers on his chest and there was a good deal of writing on his abdomen that Poe didn't feel comfortable looking at closely enough to make out. Most had thick ropy scars scattered randomly. Most of the men were ten or fifteen years older than he was but he was not going to ask, it was not a place where asking questions was rewarded.

One of the yard rats gave him a handrolled cigarette, he smoked it and it was disgusting, it was salvaged half-smoked tobacco. Dwayne saw him smoking it and shook his head and offered him a cigarette from a package. Poe gave the rollie back to the peckerwood, who brushed at it carefully and then finished smoking it. There was a general flow of people paying respects, a group of Latinos who seemed aligned with the Brotherhood, their leader and Black Larry went off and talked alone for a long time. Occasionally, a visitor would surreptitiously let something fall to the dirt. Later, the item would be retrieved.

Black Larry turned to Poe, who had just finished another set of curls and was sitting on the bench eating a candy bar and drinking a soda.

"We need to get you out of those state-issued trousers," said Black

Larry. He sized Poe up. "Look at them curly locks. One handsome, David Hasselhoff–lookin motherfucker, ain't he?"

The others nodded their agreement though a few of the younger lieutenants were clearly only doing so out of respect for Black Larry, they were not particularly happy about Poe's existence.

"Him and Dwayne can fight it out for king stud."

Dwayne grinned.

"Dwayne there got caught banging one of the English teachers, a cute little college girl. They wouldn't let her come back."

"But she still writes me," said Dwayne.

"Anyway, young Poe, you got a lot of catching up to do. Though we have confidence."

In the afternoon a new pair of Dickies work pants appeared for Poe, he gave his old ones to one of the yard rats. It was hot and people were sitting on the benches or against the wall, sweating in the sun and watching the yard. Poe stood with his shirt off like the rest of them, they looked like a bunch of construction workers on lunch break, or firemen, regular guys they were not monsters or supermen, it was no different than anyplace else, no different than outside, that was what he had to focus on. A few hours later they were still in the same spot, he was hot and dehydrated and sunburned, the others didn't seem to notice it, just sitting in the low sun getting burned like that, he was very thirsty but he hadn't wanted to drink any more sodas, it seemed he'd had more than his share already. He was tired but he fought to keep his eyes open, a few of the lieutenants had wandered off but it was not an option for him, he had to stay near Dwayne and Black Larry. Dinnertime came but no one thought it was a good idea to bring Poe back to the messhall yet.

"You need anything?" said Black Larry. "Skittles, cigarettes? Pruno?"

"I could use some real food," said Poe, "but I don't have any money."

"They got smoked packaged salmon at the commissary. Someone'll bring you some. Couple bags of Fritos, too."

*   *   *

Dwayne walked him back to the cell. There was a laundry bag on top of Poe's bunk, full of items from the commissary, deodorant, Snickers bars, four packages of vacuum-sealed salmon, and some saltine crackers.

"You makin out?" said Dwayne. They bumped and tapped fists.

"I'm good," Poe said.

"Your cellie is getting back tonight. He's been locked down six months so when he gets back give him a little elbow room."

"No problem," said Poe.

"He'll be alright. He'll want to talk your ear off is all."

* * *

After he was alone he ate two of the packages of salmon and the crackers, the first good food he'd had in he didn't know, days. He settled back on the bed, the sleepy full feeling, he was going to be fine. At first he couldn't help grinning to himself and then there was the other feeling, they would be wanting something for this. That was fine. He would take it day by day.

Downstairs on the floor of the cellblock they were listening to rap videos on television, cheering along. He closed his eyes and lay on the bunk awhile, couldn't sleep, his hands were sore and he looked at them, they were healing slowly. His blood had definitely mixed with the other one's, with Little Man's. He got up and washed his hands again, he knew it wouldn't do any good, he would have to be more careful, he didn't know, he would have to get something, a lock or some batteries to put in a sock. He was not going to worry about it. AIDS was probably the least of his worries. What would kill him was a knife in the neck, he'd be eating a grilled cheese sandwich in the messhall. Clovis had shown him a nine-inch shank, a bone-crusher he'd called it, and if Clovis had one then the other side did as well. So at the moment worrying about AIDS was like worrying the world would be struck by a comet. He wondered if he was fighting a fight he'd already lost, completely lost only somehow he was still standing. When he was a kid he'd watched Virgil shoot a small buck with his compound bow, the buck jumped a little and then had gone back to eating ryegrass like nothing happened. A few seconds later he toppled over, the arrow had cut right through both sides, severed the aorta, his fatal blow he had barely felt it. And here Poe was congratulating himself when there was nothing good happening, the only thing he could be sure of was the situation was getting worse, it was a trend in his life.

He had not asked for it. He had not asked to go to that machine shop in a rainstorm, a place guaranteed to be a squatter haven. It was because of Isaac they had gone there, because of Isaac that they were sitting in a leaky building in a rainstorm instead of back on Poe's porch looking out over the fields and drinking beer. Poe, he could not afford to be in those situations but that did not bother Isaac, it was a different kind of judgment Poe had, his mind moved differently, he could not just get up and move when a few dripping wet bums came and insulted him, he had pride, he had human dignity, whereas you could say anything to Isaac and he would get up and walk away. And Isaac had gotten them into just that situation and had then wanted to get up and disappear. But Poe was not like that. It was a thing called self-respect and he possessed it and Isaac did not.

He sat up. Nothing had changed, he was in a cell with a yellow window he could not see through, cement and iron bars, downstairs a commercial for car insurance blared on the television, they didn't even bother to turn it down, a thing none of them had any use for. He opened the third package of salmon and ate it, it was greasy and salty, he licked his fingers, a beer would be perfect, it was not bad being here, in this cell, it was safe. But he could not stay in the cell all day and night. The black man he'd choked out was a higher-up, a captain. Poe had gotten lucky, taking him down like that. But it was not some movie where you beat the biggest guy and they left you alone. That was not how things worked. They would have to pay him back and it could not be a beating, payback meant you had to escalate, he knew that from personal experience. You had to get the guy worse than he got you.

He noticed he was breathing hard and his entire body was rigid. His neck was sore from tension and he tried to relax. I'll be fine, he thought. Sort it out. Sort it out fine only you didn't do anything to get here. That dead one Otto was not killed by you. All you did was get your balls crushed and your head nearly cut off from your body. Why are you here for that, he thought. You are here and it is only getting worse, tomorrow you may turn a corner and wham, five guys are on you and that's your end but Isaac is still out there. Walking around free.

6. Isaac

All through the night the train kept pulling over, hours would pass waiting on secondary tracks, he'd sit out on the platform, go back into the porthole, climb the ladder and sit with his feet in the mound of coal, looking at the stars. He guessed it was two A.M. If you'd thought to bring your star chart, you'd know. Or put a new battery in your watch. He shuffled his feet in the bed of coke, felt the cold metal wall of the hopper car in his hands. Close your eyes and sense the rotation of the earth. Stars always moving. Change every hour. Big Dipper starting to turn over—springtime. Ursa Major, technically. Makes more sense as the Dipper. Polaris, temporary as all polestars. Used to be Thuban. Eventually it'll be Alderamin. Then Deneb. Ptolemy's full catalog A.D. 150. Namer of stars—a good legacy. Even if no one knows. Learned it from the Babylonians, but all the records lost, burned at Alexandria. Julius Caesar the culprit. More knowledge lost than you'll ever know.

He scanned the rest of the sky. Cancer and Leo. Probably Gemini disappearing. Should have brought something to read. No, should have brought penlight batteries. Stupid to have forgotten. He looked at the ground below him. The temptation was strong to climb down, the train would not start moving immediately. No—in the dark you'll never be able to find this car again, you'll lose your pack. Not to mention you've got no idea where you are. By next week you'll be in Berkeley and you won't remember any of this.

He climbed down and back into the porthole, into his sleeping bag, his head outside where he got a small view of the sky. Try to sleep.

*   *   *

Morning came, hours passed, he rode on the platform as much as possible, up in the air on top until it got too cold. Your clothes all filthy. Probably your face as well.

They were going along a big river, much wider than the Mon, in the distance he could see a factory that resolved itself into an enormous steelmill, dozens of long buildings, blast furnaces, steam rising everywhere. The place had a modern look, the buildings were being repaired. There was a sign: U.S. STEEL, GREAT LAKES WORKS. That is Michigan, he thought. One of the mills they kept open. Parking lot of cars, the way Buell used to look, there's the town behind it. Never seen land so flat.

The brakes grated as they wound through an enormous trainyard, plug your ears, time to get off. They'll dump the coke here and you'll get seen. Get packed. Cramming his things into the bag again he was back out on the platform, crouching down thinking don't wait for full stop. They were near the end of the trainyard and the train was crawling along, he was hanging his head off the side and he saw the Baron climb down a few cars ahead of him. He swung himself down to the ground and the Baron caught up to him.

It was the first time he'd seen the Baron in daylight, his face was red and swollen and deeply creased and his skin looked hard and thick, his nose was bent and one eye hung much lower than the other, bones that had broken and never been fixed properly. The whole structure of his face was crooked and he was covered in coal dust; he gave off the impression of something pulled from a fire.

"Goddamn," said the Baron, staring at him equally, "someone had their way with you, didn't they?"

Isaac just looked at him.

"Your face got whomped on pretty good, is what I mean. You got a matched pair of shiners."

"It was four guys," said Isaac.

They began crossing the other tracks toward the town, dodging quickly to get out of the way of a blue locomotive coming toward them.

"Keep your eye out," said the Baron. "Won't believe how quiet they roll, I had a partner get cut in half once. Nothing you can do when that happens."

They crossed more tracks and then climbed down and up through a drainage ditch. They were standing on a small road.

"We in the right spot?"

"Yeah," said the Baron. "It's called Ekkers. There's your unloading spot for the coke up there."

"Thought you said we'd be in Detroit."

"Don't get picky on me. It's only ten goddamn miles up the road."

As they walked the industrial buildings gradually gave way to a town, they passed a field of tall white storage tanks with the grass around them neatly clipped, then they were on a residential street. There was a big sign that said ECORSE. *Ekkers.* The name of the town. The houses were larger than the typical millhouse in Buell but most looked just as run-down. This is progress, he reminded himself. You just got six, seven hundred miles closer to California. Won't be wine and roses the whole way.

"Spot me dinner if I find us a place?" said the Baron.

Need to get rid of him first thing, he thought, but he said: "Sure. I've got to get going south soon, though."

"You will. We passed another yard back there. All we gotta do is follow those tracks back to where we split from the main line. Then you'll find your train."

They continued down the street, the houses getting better, then worse, then better again. A group of black men were sitting on a porch playing dice in puffy down jackets. They stared at the Baron and Isaac as they passed.

"Get a fuckin shower," one of them said, and the others burst out laughing. Isaac prepared to take off running, but the men went back to their dice.

"We do have to find a Laundromat," said the Baron. "Stash our packs and get cleaned up. We can get cleaned up where we get food, though."

"I want to find that yard soon."

"Rushin around don't help anything. We eat, we get cleaned up, find a place to sack out. I can tell you're tired, and running around trainyards zonked out of your head don't lead to nothing but getting run over. I seen it happen, too, those trains roll right over you without noticing, same way you'd step on an ant."

You already said that, Isaac thought, but didn't say anything. After walking a while longer, they found a fried chicken place. They took turns washing in the bathroom. The Baron went first and took forever and when Isaac went in the place reeked of feces and the sink was splashed with black grit. Isaac used the toilet and cleaned up as well, his face and hands and coat were filthy. When he came out he looked more respectable but still. These clothes ought to be thrown out.

Back at the counter the Baron ordered a bucket of fried chicken with several sides and Isaac was immediately sorry they'd come, the bill was over twenty dollars and he got out his wallet to pay but only had a single dollar bill. The Baron was looking at him.

"You got this or no?" he said.

The people at the counter stared at them and waited. Isaac turned away and unzipped his pocket with the money and tried to carefully slip a bill from the envelope, but it wouldn't come, it was awkward getting at the envelope and he had to lift it slightly out of his pocket to get at it. The Baron saw it and then looked the other way. It was a fifty-dollar bill that Isaac handed the clerk, and she held it up to the light and checked it with a felt-tip pen.

"Glad you had something else," said the Baron. He picked up the food and carried it out as Isaac zipped his pocket back up.

"Tells you we're near Detroit," said the Baron. "They love fried chicken."

They sat on the curb and ate. Isaac bit into a drumstick, there was a hard thin crust, it was peppery and salty and the juice from the meat dripped down to the curb. He ate it as quickly as he could, the crunchiness of the skin and the tenderness of the meat underneath, stuffing it into his mouth, it tasted like the best food he'd ever eaten, there was an entire bucket. He was beginning to get an easy feeling about everything.

Every time you eat, now. The kid is a simple animal. World's Best Fried Chicken. The kid agrees with that claim, gives his highest endorsement. Diddy Curtin's chicken. He will remember.

They ate until they couldn't force any more food down, then wrapped the remaining pieces in napkins and put them in their packs. Isaac lay back on the sidewalk, he looked around, he didn't think anyone would bother them for a minute. He closed his eyes. For the first time in several days he didn't notice the bruises on his hips and shoulders, the aches from sleeping in hard places.

"We lie here like this we're going to catch trouble," the Baron said. "What we ought to do is get a motel, sleep in a real bed, do our laundry, maybe watch some movies even."

"Nah," Isaac said, without opening his eyes. It occurred to him: you can ditch this guy easily. The next time they were separated, used the bathroom, anything, he would take off. He began to feel even better about things.

"I been riding rails all my life. You got to take the little luxuries when you can afford em. Keeps you sane. You can always make more money."

"Well, you can pay for it if you want."

"At least how bout we get something to drink," he said. "Can you spare that?"

"Fine. Gimme a minute to rest here."

When Isaac noticed someone watching them through the window of the fried chicken place they sat up and got walking. There were houses and then businesses and then houses again, the road passed over a broad canal, then under a freeway, then dead-ended into a large boulevard. Everything was so flat, you didn't know if you were coming or going. Isaac realized he'd been expecting the houses to end and give way to woods but they just continued, the town went on forever. It had been gray all day and they'd been out of sight of the river for a long time, it was the same low buildings everwhere, he had no idea what direction they were headed, he guessed they'd come two miles since the steelmill. People would know where that was, if he had to ask someone. On the other side of the street they saw a Laundromat, it had a handwritten sign stating WE NOW HAVE HOT WATER, but it was closed. "Our luck," said the Baron. "But look."

Farther down there was a liquor store. "You old enough to buy," said the Baron.

"No."

"Then give me ten and I'll make sure we're well taken care of."

Isaac thought for a second. He gave the Baron a bill. "Here's twenty," he said. "Take your time."

The Baron went in and Isaac was already walking down the street when the Baron caught up to him. He was carrying a handle of whiskey.

"Keep going," he said. "The clerk was in the back."

"What?"

"Go go go."

They began to walk more quickly down the street. When it was safe, the Baron held up his trophy again. "Goddamn Jack Daniel's. Just saved us thirty-four bucks."

Isaac nodded.

"Let's find our spot for the night," the Baron continued. "Now that I think about it we should have either rode that train longer or not as long. We got no resources around here."

"I just want to get back to that other trainyard."

"One thing I been thinking about," he said, "is that with sixty, eighty bucks, I could get to see my sister in Canada. They got free clinics up there."

"You got twenty already."

"I'll get our next meal," said the Baron. "You know I had to ask. I've never been good at saving money myself. I respect that about you."

"It's fine."

"In a lot of ways I have a million-dollar mind, which basically runs in my family. My father had his own business. Only I saw what happened to him and all these people, too." He waved his arms around. "They're trapped by all this shit. We own it as much as them. It'll be around after they're all gone—what does that tell you? You build a cage for yourself. You don't ever own anything, really, that thing just owns you."

Isaac nodded. They continued to walk.

★   ★   ★

He guessed they were close when they came to another small canal with a park alongside it. There were trees and mown grass. On one side of the canal there was an upscale trailer park and a small office complex, on the other side a nicer neighborhood, single-family homes with fenced yards.

"There's our spot," said the Baron. "We don't gotta spend a nickel."

Walking the edge of the canal they found a suitably large cluster of bushes and trees and made their way to the center of it. Isaac could hear cars passing on the road a hundred yards away and it was comforting. Tomorrow you get a train south, wake up before him.

He was at the end of one thing and the beginning of another. Tomorrow you will head south. He wondered if a warrant from Pennsylvania would transfer to Michigan, or if there was a warrant yet, and he could feel himself getting depressed. Best not to think about it, he decided.

In a small clearing they both unrolled their sleeping bags. There was music coming from the trailer park and people laughing. Isaac was extremely tired but he did not want to fall asleep.

"Well, good night," said the Baron.

"Night to you."

He tried to zip his sleeping bag up but something was wrong with the zipper, it had come apart and it was too dark to fix. Better this way anyway, he thought. Keep my boots on. He pulled the sleeping bag around him like a comforter and found a position where his hand could stay close to his knife as he slept. Then he thought about the dew settling overnight and got up again in the dark and crawled partway under a fallen tree. He took the knife out of the sheath.

After a few hours he woke up, he could still see the Baron sleeping twenty feet away, he hadn't moved. You should get up and get going now, he thought, but he was too tired, he couldn't move his legs. He woke up again later, heard leaves rustling, looked for a long time in the darkness before deciding it was just an animal. The Baron was still right where he'd gone to sleep.

He knew he ought to get up but he couldn't. It seemed like he could sleep forever.

7. Lee

She made lunch for her father, risotto with a starter of *insalata caprese*, French bread she'd bought at the Keystone Bakery in Monessen. She rarely got time to cook at home, as Simon preferred to eat out. Which was fine. Another reason to enjoy coming back. Afterward they sat at the dining-room table quietly drinking coffee, Henry reading his paper while she sat there, chin in hand, staring out over the long sloping lawn, the low brick walls around the property. The walls were ornamental, an un-believable indulgence now, enough brick to build another large house. Like everything else, they were crumbling.

Her father was making his way through the *Post-Gazette*, the sun was coming strongly into the window, she let her mind wander, decided to cancel the interviews with the nurses that afternoon. She wondered if maybe Poe had made everything up, the reasons being obvious. That would be the easy thing to believe. But she was sure that Poe was telling the truth. She wasn't sure how, but she knew.

Poe's picture had been on the front page of the *Valley Independent*, un-der the headline FOOTBALL STAR CHARGED IN KILLING. She'd hidden the pa-per before her father had a chance to see it. It hadn't mattered. Last night, the chief of police had come around looking for Isaac. A thin, balding, pleasant-looking man, obviously thoughtful. She had liked him right away and wanted to hear what he thought but he only wanted to speak to her father. She realized it was out of respect, but still. She was able to get the gist of it—Poe was being charged with the killing of the man in the factory, Isaac was most likely a witness but, at this point, not a suspect.

This morning, her father had looked haggard. He was sliding. In fact he'd gotten worse since she'd gotten here. How long? She counted: Saturday through today, Thursday. Six days. It felt much longer than that. Her father hadn't shaved in two days now and his white hair was tangled and flat on his scalp, his shoulders dusted with dandruff. The look of a heavy drinker—cheeks and nose mottled with burst capillaries—though he barely touched the stuff. Watery eyes. His clock running down.

They ate in the dining room, the old walnut furniture, an antique china cabinet and credenza, the waterstained wallpaper around the windows. A large room with a tall ceiling and a glass chandelier. It occurred to her that maybe her father had bought this house because of her mother, because he'd wanted to impress her. It was difficult to know.

They still hadn't talked about the visit from the police officer. There was something extraordinary about their desire to avoid conflict. But it would have to be discussed. She got up and decided to do the dishes.

"You finished?" she said to him.

"I got a couple years yet."

She smiled but couldn't bring herself to laugh. She took his plate to the kitchen and ran the water until it was steaming hot, found the rubber gloves and began to scrub the dishes. When she was done she wiped down the stove and countertop, though they weren't dirty; she'd cleaned them that morning as well. At the apartment in New Haven of course they had a dishwasher, they also had a maid service once a week, she'd protested against that at first but Simon had looked at her like she was crazy. Normal people had maid service.

A feeling of loneliness came over her, this place wasn't home and neither was the other, she stood with the hot water running over her hands and then she thought: you don't deserve to feel sorry for yourself. You have to go in and talk to him.

Instead she looked for something else to clean. She would sweep the back porch. It was one in the afternoon and the deer had come out to graze in the yard among the old apple trees. The porch was filthy and she saw the stain on the couch where she'd slept with Poe. She swept. It was pleasant, sunny and green with the deer and the trees and distant hills but that was all there was, all this place had to offer. She didn't understand why her mother had come here. She didn't understand why her mother had married Henry English.

Of course she herself was making compromises but it wasn't the same as her mother. Married rich and early. When she thought of it that way it was like being punched in the stomach. She didn't want to go to law school, either, she was probably more the art school type, more the comp lit type, but she'd never let herself run with those crowds, it was out of the question given the family situation. It would have been equally nice to join the Peace Corps and just see where she landed, let the wind take her instead of having such a trajectory. Like Siddhartha— the stone falling through water. In a few years she'd have a law degree, an insurance policy—even if things went bad with Simon, her father and Isaac would be taken care of. She had a good plan and a good backup. Nothing was perfect but she went to bed happy.

Given that, how she'd arranged her life, it was baffling what had happened to her mother. Somehow she'd decided that Henry English was her best option. You are a bitch for thinking that, she decided, you are a terrible person. But the fact remained. It had been much harder for her, Lee thought. Thirty-one, unmarried, no family in the country. Henry English sits down next to her in a dive bar, a stable, predictable, honest man. A man who is proud of her, who would never leave her, who knows she's more than he deserves. Then everything in the Valley falls apart and he loses his job and there goes the stability and on top of it there are two kids. He's out of work for two years and then lives in Indiana for three years, sending money back until his accident.

Then you get into college and things begin to change. Her moods get deeper—higher highs and lower lows. Sunday after graduation, everyone goes to church and that afternoon she disappears. Two months later you leave for New Haven.

Before her father, she knew, her mother had been engaged to another man, a student in the music department at CMU, but he'd broken off the engagement at the last minute. Long before that, her mother had split from her family in Mexico, she'd come from money but been too proud to return to it, and by the time she died she hadn't spoken to them in twenty-five years. Lee wondered about this side of her family occasionally, but her interest was only theoretical. Meeting them would not unlock any secrets that she needed unlocked. She suspected it would only depress her.

In the end it was impossible to know. Her mother must have felt some sense of desperation, or loneliness, or time creeping in on her, if she had married Henry English. A beautiful woman with a master's degree in music composition. But she was also thirty-one, living in a country that was not her own, no family to speak of, little support structure, and here was a man who would never leave her, a man with a good job, a man who wanted to take care of her. Knowing how her position might be worse if she married a wealthy man. Or maybe Mary English, née María Salinas, had the same notions as Lee's Marxist friends at Yale— solidarity, noble workers, an impending revolution. She had wanted to marry a worker, a final rejection of her family. There were certainly people like that in the Valley, Mr. Painter, the history teacher at Buell High who'd written Lee's letter of recommendation, he told Lee he'd moved to the Valley to bring socialism to the mills, he'd been a steelworker for ten years, lost his job and become a teacher. Graduated from Cornell and became a steelworker. *There were lots of us,* he'd told her. *Reds working right alongside the good old boys.* But there had never been any revolution, not anything close, a hundred and fifty thousand people lost their jobs but they had all gone quietly. It was obvious there were people responsible, there were living breathing men who'd made those decisions to put the entire Valley out of work, they had vacation homes in Aspen, they sent their kids to Yale, their portfolios went up when the mills shut down. But, aside from a few ministers who'd famously snuck into a white-glove church and thrown skunk oil on the wealthy pastor, no one lifted a hand in protest. There was something particularly American about it—blaming yourself for bad luck—that resistance to seeing your life as affected by social forces, a tendency to attribute larger problems to individual behavior. The ugly reverse of the American Dream. In France, she thought, they would have shut down the country. They would have stopped the mills from closing. But of course you couldn't say that in public, especially not to her father.

The porch was swept. There was no point in putting it off further. Lee went back into the house, through the kitchen, and into the dining room, where her father was still sitting.

"Dad?" she said.

"That's me." He looked up reluctantly. He knew what was coming.

"What did the police chief talk to you about?"

"Isaac's friend Billy," he said. "They locked him up for killing some-one."

He went back to his paper and she could tell he was uncomfortable. She wondered how much he knew. It seemed much warmer in the room all of a sudden.

"I don't think he did it."

"I guess that's possible, but it's not worth speculating over. They'll get it figured out in court."

"Maybe what I'm getting at is I'm pretty sure he didn't do it."

"Maybe your view of him is skewed."

It was quiet for a few seconds; she felt her face get hot. Her father wanted to drop the conversation and she did also but she forced herself to keep talking: "He told me that Isaac is the one who killed that guy."

"Lee," he said, without missing a beat, "Billy Poe nearly killed some-one last year, beat the guy's head in with a baseball bat, and the only rea-son he didn't get locked up for that is that Bud Harris, the police officer who came by yesterday, is friends with Billy's mother. *Friends,* if you know what I mean. Which is something that now they're all going to have to deal with, now that he's done this other thing."

"I know all that," she said. But she hadn't known it—that was not ex-actly how she'd heard the story.

"I didn't mean to snap at you. What Bud Harris told me is that he thinks Isaac was there, but that it's better if Isaac stays out of it. He doesn't think Isaac should get involved unless it's absolutely necessary, which is fine with me."

"If there's a trial, you can be sure Isaac will get involved."

"I know that. I've been up all night thinking about who I know who's a lawyer around here."

"It doesn't bother you that Isaac saw those things?"

"I feel guilty about it, if that's what you mean."

"That wasn't what I was getting at." She didn't know, though. Maybe it was. She went and stood next to him and he reached up to squeeze her hand.

"I already told Simon. He said we can use the family checkbook."

"We'll be fine on our own," he said. He squeezed her hand again. "That was smart, though. That was good thinking."

She was struck by the absurdity of what was happening: you've both just admitted you've been hiding something from each other, that the police chief thinks Isaac witnessed a murder, that Poe thinks that Isaac was involved in the murder, but you're going to keep on acting like everything's normal.

"What else should we be doing?"

He shrugged. "It sounds like you already took care of it. In any case, I think it's pretty safe not to trust what Billy Poe tells you." He looked up briefly from the newspaper. "Goes without saying that you're married now."

She could feel her face flushing even more and she looked around the room, she knew if she said anything else she would start crying. Henry rattled the paper and cleared his throat and made a show of being interested in something.

"Your friend Hillary Clinton is making more speeches."

She nodded. Let him change the subject. She looked out the window and then she felt him take her hand again.

"You're a good kid," he said.

"I'm not sure."

"I mean it. You're a good kid and I'm proud as hell of you."

She nodded and cleared her throat again and smiled at him and he smiled back sympathetically.

"I think I need some air."

"Alright."

Outside, she sat against the brick wall that wrapped down around the lawn, field, whatever it was, down toward the ravine, out over the empty woods and hills, the long high ridge in the distance. The old man knew about her and Poe, it wasn't that surprising. He forgave her—she was surprised by that, of course she was. But maybe those were the things her mother had seen in him.

She wondered what he really thought about Simon, and her new life, and the fact that she never came home. He was not a simple man, he only acted that way when it was convenient. He wanted peace with her at all costs. Only he was wrong about Poe. She thought about that. She thought about Simon's accident, the feeling had begun to nag her—what if he hadn't been trapped in the car? What if he could have walked away, left that girl pinned there?

That was the thing about Simon and all the others, so pleasant on the surface, always knowing what to say, but underneath there was something else, they were not the kind to sacrifice themselves—they'd all been taught they had too much to lose. No more verdicts, she told herself. But there was John Bolton, caught in Manhattan with all that cocaine—charges dropped—and later you find out there was another man with Bolton when he was arrested, but everyone knows better than to ask what happened to him. Meanwhile Poe goes to jail for something he didn't do. For your brother.

She wondered where Isaac was now. California, Poe had said. It didn't make any sense. She could hire a private investigator or something to follow him, he would have left a trail, airline tickets, bus tickets, something—four thousand dollars is what her father said he'd taken—that would be more than enough to pay for his trip and leave plenty of seed money to settle down, Isaac was happy to live on macaroni and cheese. How had he reached this level of desperation? But she knew it was simple. Not hard to understand at all. You simply chose not to. Always knew his life wouldn't be easy, he didn't know how to relate to people. No ability to conduct small talk, thinks he should speak his mind honestly at all times, expects others should do the same. Nothing he ever said was tied up in *what are they going to think of me?* It made her both admire him more than anyone else she knew and feel enormously sad for him. To her, that seemed like the smallest part of human communication.

Maybe all people with minds like Isaac's were the same. She knew he would make a much larger contribution than she ever would—he cared only about things much bigger than his own life. Ideas, truths, the reasons things were. As if he himself, his own existence, was somehow incidental. At Yale, her friends had accepted him immediately—there Isaac was a personality type everyone was familiar with. But not here.

And now he'd killed that man. She squeezed her forehead. She knew he'd done it. He'd gone back in there to rescue his friend, he hadn't hesitated. There couldn't be anyone less suited for a task like that, but that had not stopped him, he'd done the only thing he could do, if those men had been strong enough to overpower Poe, the risk to Isaac would have been enormous, he would have been scared. And of course he'd gone back in there anyway. It was the right thing to do and he'd done it.

And you? She felt weak and she let herself ease farther into the tall grass, the sun and wind would cut through her, wear her to nothing, she would sink into the earth. I'm not supposed to feel guilty, she thought. I'm supposed to be proud of myself. But even thinking that brought on an incredible isolation, a suspicion she'd always had that she didn't belong anywhere, she was going to outlive everyone she knew. She was going to be alone, the same as her mother. Her mother who had tried to reinvent herself and it had killed her. Lee tried again to figure the probabilities that she herself was free from blame. There was Dad's accident and Mom dying and now this, there was no logic, there was only the most important piece of evidence: you're the only one still in one piece.

She would have to find him. She couldn't wait anymore. Hire the lawyer, a private investigator, this is not going to take care of itself. She stood up and brushed the grass off her, looking out over the trees and rolling fields, the ravine where she and Isaac had played, lain on their backs on the warm rocks and looked up at the narrow corridor of sky above them, Isaac watching for birds, he loved birds and hawks, he loved knowing the names of things, she was content just to watch, most memories she had of being happy in childhood involved only her and Isaac; the rest of the time she was just waiting to get older.

Lawyer and a private investigator. She would have to tell Simon the entire story, his parents would have to know as well. Easy to make a case for Isaac—1560 on his SATs, something they'll understand. But she did not want to have to say that. They would decide to help Isaac because he was her brother. They either would or they wouldn't, and she would know. Alright, she thought, it's better to know. You've got plenty of credit cards, with or without them you'll figure something out. Start by calling Simon and asking him to figure out the lawyer. He'll be happy to have a mission.

8. Harris

After work he cleaned up and took a quick shower and called the dog in. Fur came back slowly and reluctantly, knowing what it meant. He came over to Harris and leaned against his leg.

"Sorry, buddy," said Harris. "Company calling."

He thought about leaving Fur out to run, but the coyotes were getting bigger, they'd nearly doubled in size in the last twenty years, and there were more of them. Plenty of the neighbors took potshots at them and Harris had a .22-250 that would reach four hundred yards, but he would not shoot a coyote. They were noble animals, is why. They had a will—they made other animals take them into consideration. Mountain lions, wolves, it was all the same. You could not kill an animal like that unless you were very sure of your motives.

"Your pick, meathead. Stay in or fend for yourself."

But of course he would not really give his dog that choice Maybe that was contradictory. Still. He nudged Fur gently inside, away from the door, and closed it.

Ten minutes later he was on a paved road, heading toward Grace's house, and not exactly sure why he was doing it. As he'd gotten dressed he'd looked at himself in the mirror and thought *the next time you get undressed it will be with her* but now, headed toward her house, he was not sure. Amazing coincidence, calling you right when her son gets pinched. He shook his head. It was fine. He presumed those things about people, forgave the ones he liked in advance. Grace was forgiven. Her son, though, doing wrong ever since he was old enough. Harris had done all that was possible. He had talked Glen Patacki and Cecil Small into a lenient plea agreement. He had talked Cecil Small into a slap on the wrist and then Billy had gone out and murdered someone.

It was protection, she expected him to work magic but it was too late now, the wheels were turning and Billy was caught. He felt himself getting angry, he nearly stabbed the brake pedal and wheeled the truck around, it was a fine life he'd made for himself, a levelness he worked hard at, he could feel it being upset. He made himself keep driving and the anger passed quickly. Most everything you feel passes quickly. What the hell, he told the steering wheel. I'm bored.

Then there was the Virgil question. He felt his anger coming on again, anger and hurt, but it was no mark of shame, it was just the way things went. Virgil Poe couldn't keep a job, was as mean and dumb as they made them, a born liar. Still Grace had chased after him nearly twenty years. Twice Harris had helped the game warden arrest Virgil's father, it ran in the family. And the incident with the stolen copper. Everyone understood Virgil. Except Grace. But look whose son you've been protecting. Yes, he thought, he's got you beat. Why didn't you lock him up? Once he'd run Virgil in the computer, two outstanding warrants, all it would have taken was a phone call. But that was not the kind of person Bud Harris was.

Passing through the town, past the old police station and the new one, he'd seen the Fall, the shuttering of the mills, and the Great Migration that followed. Migration to nowhere—thousands of people moved to Texas, tens of thousands, probably, hoping for jobs on oil rigs, but there weren't many of those jobs to be had. So those people had ended up worse off than they started, broke and jobless in a place they didn't know anyone. The rest had just disappeared. And you would never know it. He'd watched guys go from making thirty dollars an hour to four-fifteen, a big steelworker bagging his groceries, stone-faced, there was no easy way for anyone to deal with it. He'd moved out here to have an easy life, be a small-town cop instead of cracking heads in Philadelphia, but the job had changed quickly once the mills went under—it was head-cracking time all over again. It wasn't naturally in him but he'd learned, made it a science, learned to watch a man's face as he did it. It had been a mistake to spare Virgil. He had done that out of pride.

It felt different with Grace this time, he didn't know why, it really seemed the hillbilly was no longer in the picture. The spare tire comes out. The spare tire is you. He was not sure about any of it. There were people who were meant to die alone, maybe he was one of them. You're getting a little ahead of yourself, he thought.

He turned up the clay road that led to her trailer. There was still time to turn around—it would be a clear cold night, he had a humidor full of cigars, a nice bottle of scotch, the dog would be happy to see him. The deck chairs were set up, he could sit out tonight, he'd splurged at Christmas and replaced his old sleeping bag with a pricey down model made by a company in Colorado, all winter he had sat out looking over the mountains at night, no matter how cold it got, he'd sat out after ice storms, nothing moving for miles, total silence except the ice cracking in the cold, the warmth in the sleeping bag. A feeling of being the only one on earth. One of these days he needed to buy a telescope. Next Christmas, maybe.

Ahead of him the road ended in a dirt bank and he pulled in next to Grace's trailer. She was already on the porch waiting for him and he handed her the bottle of wine he'd brought and kissed her lightly on the lips, she was made up, a faint perfume smell.

As he followed her inside he felt as if he was looking at himself from a height, the different parts of him coming out, competing with each other, he decided he would watch and see which one ended up on top—Even Keel or horny old cop. It was warm and he could smell fresh fish cooking, sautéed garlic, bread. Instead of commenting on it, he said:

"I don't know anything more about Billy." He wasn't sure why he said it. Self-preservation. Even Keel.

She frowned. "I thought we didn't have to talk about that."

"Well, I'm sure it's on your mind."

"It is, but . . ." She smiled at him, forgiving. "Glass of wine?"

In the kitchen he watched her move around, took a piece of Italian bread she'd heated up, buttered it. The outside was crisp and the inside soft and he sat there chewing and happy, feeling himself relax. Then Even Keel started in again:

"I went to visit Isaac English last night, just in case the DA somehow figures out he was with Billy. He's gone, though."

She looked at him and cocked her head a little. She wasn't sure what to say, she looked like she really didn't want to talk about it.

"He took off Sunday morning and his family hasn't heard from him since."

"Bud," she said. "Please?"

"Alright. I'm sorry."

"Eat some more bread."

He took another piece and felt guilty, playing games with her, he thought, a game for you but it's not for her. Another part of him said no, she's the one playing games, but he ignored it. He stared at her rear end when she turned around to look for the corkscrew, it was shapely, she'd put on weight but she carried it well, her freckles and delicate skin and gray-blond hair, she looked younger than she was, he decided.

"I can't find the opener," she said. "Do you want some bourbon?"

He nodded and sat down at the small table and she poured them each two fingers. Doomed. Even Keel takes a torpedo.

"Let's sip at this," he said.

She put it down in a gulp. "You turning into some kind of pussy, Bud Harris?"

"She's sassy for not even being drunk yet."

"She is." But then she sat looking at the empty glass and he knew he'd ruined it. Six minutes. About par, he thought.

"Who is it," she said.

"Who's what?"

"The one who got him arrested."

Telling her wouldn't make it any better and he thought about saying he didn't know. Maybe he could still save it. Then he thought no it's better now than later. Go home and start a fire and cuddle up with the dog.

"He's no one, really, unemployed car mechanic. In and out of jail. He gave two addresses in Brownsville."

She put her head in her hands. "Jesus, Bud. I don't know why that matters, but it does."

"I'm sorry," he said.

"I'll have another," she said "You can pour it a little heavier."

He pushed the bottle away from both of them.

"They cut his throat, Bud. They were trying to kill him and he was defending himself."

"He's not talking, Grace, that's the problem."

"It was Isaac English," she said. "That's the only reason Billy wouldn't be saying anything."

"Billy's never walked away from a fight in his life and the English kid is a hundred ten pounds. The man who died was six foot eight."

"That's what they all think, isn't it?"

"People are worried about what this place is turning into. They're worried we'll get as bad as Donora or Republic." He stopped himself. "Until he talks to a lawyer we're just speculating, anyway. We can start worrying about it then."

It was quiet for a time. He heard the oven ticking, wondered if the fish was burning, wondered if he would end up eating any of it. Grace was staring at the Formica table like he wasn't there.

"There's no point to caring about it because he's basically gone already. It's pointless even worrying about it, right? That's what you're telling me."

"No," he said. "That's not what I'm telling you at all."

He watched her start crying and he touched her but she didn't respond, she just sat there and cried, Harris looked at her across the table for a long time and couldn't figure out what to do with his hands, he had a sense of something lurking close and then his ears started ringing and he felt shaky. Part of him was trying to make the other part stand up and walk out of the house. Instead he reached and took her face in both hands.

"I'm sorry," she said. "I can't help it."

"It's early in the game."

"This is going to wreck me."

"You shouldn't be thinking those things yet, he hasn't even talked to a lawyer."

"Please don't."

"I'm not just trying to get your hopes up."

"It's too late for us, too, I know that."

He kissed her and she pulled back for a second.

"Don't just do it to make me feel better."

"I'm not," he said.

She let herself be kissed again.

"Be patient for a couple of days. It'll all change with a lawyer."

"Okay," she said.

She took his hands across the table and then came over and sat on his lap and hugged him around the waist and kissed him on the neck. He didn't move, let himself sit there just feeling it. She kissed him more. He touched her hair. He felt her heart speed up or it might have been his, he had a prickly rushing feeling in his throat that spread all over.

"I should powder my nose," she told him.

She went into the bathroom and he made no move to leave. When she came back she sat on his lap again, she grabbed his belt loops as a child might grab her father and pulled herself tight against his chest, he kissed the top of her head and they sat like that. When she looked up her face was shining for him.

"I'm sorry," she said, "I made a promise to myself I wouldn't think about it when you were here."

She smiled and squirmed purposefully in his lap.

"Christ I feel like a teenager. Horny and then crying and then horny again."

"I think you should make me a nice dinner first. So I don't feel like a slut." Then he said: "That was a joke."

"Ha-ha."

"Ha."

He got up and slid his pistol and holster from their spot in the small of his back, stood up and put it on top of the refrigerator.

"You bring that in for a reason?"

"I live alone, I guess."

"You used to leave it in the car."

He shrugged. "Times are changing. What's for dinner?"

"Trout."

"From the river?"

"I might live in a trailer," she said, "but . . ."

"I didn't think so."

"Sit."

"I'll work on the wine." After a minute of trying he got the cork out with a knife and a pair of pliers. He decided to do the other bottle while he was at it.

They ate, the fish was tender and the skin crispy with salt and she'd made a sweet cream sauce to go with it, something French. He wiped the sauce up with the bread and they ate the fish down to the bones. He thought about eating the cheeks, as Ho had shown him, but decided to leave it.

"That's probably the best fish I ever ate."

"Food Network," she said. "God's gift to men, indirectly."

When they'd finished wiping up the sauce and put down the second bottle of wine she said: "Can I ask one more question?"

He nodded.

"Who's the public defender you were talking about?"

"She's good and I think I can get her to take the case instead of one of the idiots. She's probably got a real career waiting for her somewhere, but for now she's putting her time in, serve the community type of thing. Hopefully she'll embarrass the lifers into working a little harder."

"She's a woman."

He nodded.

"I like that," she said.

"Thought you might."

They looked at each other for a long time.

"I'm sorry I brought that up."

"You're his mother. We can talk about it all you want."

"Do you want to open that third bottle?"

"I shouldn't," he said. But he did.

*　　*　　*

They sat on the edge of the bed and they were kissing again, touching each other everywhere and his body felt very light and he felt the heaviness between his legs. There was no trouble. Not that it was a surprise. A slight surprise. Once in a while with the pills he wasn't sure. He would throw the pills away, he thought, and grinned.

"Happy?" she said.

He nodded.

"Me too."

She knelt down in front of him, he stroked her hair and thought look at you old man, your life is not so bad. Then he rolled on top of her, sped up quickly, they still knew each other's timing. The sounds she made— same noises you hear in your own head and you could keep to yourself but she shares them, lets you know how good you're making her feel.

An hour later they lay on top of the covers and she ran her fingernails up and down his back. She got up to refill their wine glasses and they sat next to each other against the headboard, he looked down at himself, getting thinner and his hair gone gray but still he had muscle on his chest and stomach, a few years back he'd developed a beer gut but quickly gotten rid of it. Why, he hadn't been sure. Now he knew.

"Have you been with other people?" she asked.

"Sure," he said, shrugging. But the truth was he hadn't.

*   *   *

In the night he woke up and she was watching him. She ran her hands along the soft hair at the sides of his head.

"Shhhhhhh," she said.

He opened his eyes all the way.

"I like looking at you."

"I like looking at you, too."

She pulled the covers down. She had beautiful shoulders, the lines of the bones around her neck, the softness of her just right. She was a beautiful woman, he could barely bring himself to touch her. He felt full and happy, it seemed amazing his skin could hold it all, it seemed he had never felt this way in his life. No, he thought, it's only that this is something you can't store away, you can only feel in the minute.

He didn't know how much longer he looked at her like that, touching her lightly with his fingertips. He could feel her skin getting warmer. She parted her legs. He put his finger there and she opened them farther and looked at him.

"I thought it might have been the wine before."

She shook her head. Then she smiled and said, "So you're saying you got me drunk on purpose?"

"Basically."

"Next time I'll be a cheaper date."

They rolled on their sides and she wrapped one leg around him, moving very slowly with their eyes focused. It was right what they said about sex, it did just keep getting better, all of this, his supposedly worn-out body. He'd nearly turned it down. He felt light, no awareness of lying on the bed, they could have been anywhere, the feeling he usually had of things passing quickly, of fading, why had he ever felt that? I can feel this, touching her, and then his thoughts turned into something else and didn't make any sense at all.

9. Isaac

In the dream he was with his mother and sister in the backyard, looking out at the distant hills behind the house. They were all waiting for Isaac's father—he was coming home for Easter, driving from Indiana. Something felt wrong about the dream; he and his sister were too old— high school age. By then his father had already had the accident. His mother and sister were sitting on the porch rocker, kicking their feet, laughing about something, and Isaac was in the garden, digging a hole. *Isaac keep away from the roses,* said his mother. But his sister stuck up for him. Then they were in the kitchen, his mother was putting dinner back into the refrigerator because his father was still not home yet, he was hungry and everyone was feeling let down, but Lee kept goosing his neck. Then she was joking around with his clothes, untucking his shirt. *Very funny,* he said.

Something was wrong. Wake up. Where am I? In the clearing. Morning now. What is he doing? The Baron was squatting over him. He was removing his hand from the pocket of Isaac's cargo pants, very gentle, he had the envelope with Isaac's money.

Isaac had the knife in one hand, he had slept like that all night, he could feel himself tensing his grip, getting ready to use the knife. *No,* he thought, *there is no way.* He let go of the knife and grabbed at the Baron's coat with both hands and tried to roll on top of him. But the Baron easily shook loose and then he was up and running.

Isaac seemed to float up and onto his feet and then he was moving as well. He could not believe how fast the Baron was covering the ground, the white envelope flashing in his hand, Isaac was running as fast as he could, the trees were a blur. The knife was in his left hand and he switched it to his right. You need to catch him, he thought. The woods ended and they passed the trailer park, they were in the open now, a parking lot, they reached a four-lane road with traffic going both directions.

The Baron turned onto the sidewalk and kept running, past a line of stopped traffic, startled faces. After a block Isaac began to gain on him. What if I catch him? *Use the knife.* He's stronger than you and you'll have to use it. I can't do that, he thought. Then catch him anyway. He'll be tired and you might have a chance. He was only a few steps behind the Baron now. They were right out in the open, he had a feeling everyone was watching them, they had passed several dozen cars now. There were spots in his vision and his lungs were burning but it didn't matter. He'd never run this fast in his life. He could run forever. There was a tall chain-link fence to the left and the sidewalk they were running on and then the road to the right. When you tackle him drop the knife. You'll cut yourself. A white car passed in the other direction and out of the corner of his eye Isaac saw blue lights flashing as the car pulled a U-turn, he was nearly close enough to touch the Baron and then there was a siren and the blue lights again. No, he thought, he could see the envelope pumping up and down in the Baron's hand, you can almost touch him, then the cop car jerked across three lanes of traffic and jumped up the curb thirty feet in front of them, the cop was out quickly, he was behind the door, Isaac couldn't see his hand but he knew: drawing his gun.

Stop stop stop he heard, it's the knife, he thought, get rid of the knife, there was the tall fence to his left and before he could think he'd leapt up and rolled over it, pivoting on his chest over the top, ripping his coat open and landing on his hands and knees. *Stay down stay down* the cop was screaming, the knife had flown off somewhere into the dirt. Everything was in slow motion now, he wanted to stand up but the cop had his gun trained on him, does he see you dropped the knife? Get up. Get up get up get up. He might shoot me. No get up. Focus on your legs. He was running again. Do not shoot if he shoots you will feel it before you hear it, it won't feel like anything, he glanced back again, he had a quick impression of the cop, an older black man, talking into the radio on his collar, the Baron must have stopped running because now the cop was pointing the gun in a different direction, away from Isaac.

Entire areas of his vision were blurred out but he forced himself to keep running, across a parking lot between two small office buildings, he plunged through a row of bushes, going back in the direction he'd come.

10. Poe

The next morning, he waited in his cell for several hours to get an escort out to the yard. His cellmate had still not come back. A guard came by to tell him that his lawyer would be visiting tomorrow, but Poe did not want to think about the lawyer. Finally Clovis banged on the bars.

"Dwayne busy?" Poe said.

Clovis didn't answer, so Poe followed behind him, down to the end of the tier, down the stairs, through the cellblock, there was dust floating in the light from the windows, close your eyes and you'd think it was any locker room, stinking like socks and toilet stalls and moldy cement, people talking too loud, everyone saying stupid shit. He followed Clovis into the main corridor and then out through the metal detectors into the yard, open air, sand and sunshine, blue sky. Practically like the beach in summertime. Pretend the towers are lifeguards.

Clovis still hadn't said a word and everyone took notice when Poe arrived at the weight pile, either smiling in a way he didn't like or turning so they didn't have to talk to him. He got nervous immediately but he found a place against the fence and acted like he didn't notice. Black Larry came over.

"Young Poe," he said, "we've been having some discussions about your future."

Poe nodded.

"I'll give you the straight dope. The consensus is we need to have a little papers party. Take a look at your charge sheets. Satisfy our own curiosity, if you're amenable."

"Whatever y'all want. I don't give a fuck." Poe shrugged.

"I wouldn't be so fuckin smug if I were you," said Clovis. "Half the people in here are after you."

"Well, I know for a fact there's one of them who ain't after me, at least until he gets out of the fuckin infirmary."

"Little Man ain't shit and I guaran-fuckin-tee you the minute you're out of our circle they'll find your fuckin corpse in a laundry tub. You're part of the minority in here, if you ain't noticed, and every single one of them niggers been lacin up since the minute they fuckin saw you."

"Clovis," said Dwayne.

"Young Poe understands," Black Larry said to Dwayne. He looked at Poe. "Sunshine, Young Poe. The best disinfectant."

"Alright," said Poe.

"Go with him, Dwayne."

"Yo Dwayne," Clovis said.

Dwayne turned back to look.

"Bring em all back so the rest of us can get a look."

"No fuckin shit," Dwayne said.

They passed through the metal detectors. The detector went off but Dwayne nodded to the guard and kept walking.

"You worried, bud?" said Dwayne. " 'Cause if you are, you might as well catch it from me as opposed to them."

"I'm cool," said Poe. "I ain't causin no problems."

"That's good to hear, bud. There was a racketeering case against Black Larry, so he's got good reason to be suspicious. They charged me, too."

"What about Clovis?"

Dwayne was silent and they continued down the cellblock. When they were out of earshot of anyone, he said: "At the moment, Clovis has his own reasons."

After retrieving the folder, Poe and Dwayne went back to the yard. Black Larry took the folder and looked through it carefully, then passed it around.

"Francis."

"Yeah," said Poe.

"What's that?" Clovis said.

"William Francis Poe," said Black Larry. "That's his name."

"This is still bullshit," said Clovis. "A charge is just a fuckin charge."

"Murder One," said Dwayne.

"Is there anyone to roll over on, Young Poe?"

"No," Poe said quickly. "It's on me."

"Well that still don't mean shit."

"It'll do for now," said Black Larry. He reached behind him and pulled out a jug of pruno and they all drank from it. The mood lightened, they drank the rest of the pruno, Poe sat against the bench and everyone relaxed. The rest of the day went like normal, there were the usual comings and goings only Poe got drunk, he sat quietly with the sun in his face, he was feeling good, there was a strong breeze, he was feeling easy about things and then he was thinking of Lee, it was the last time he'd been drunk. He thought about calling her. It was too embarrassing. He'd called his mother and she wasn't home, they would have to work out a schedule, the phones only worked collect. His lawyer would be coming, sometime tomorrow, the lawyer would only want one thing from him.

He was thinking about that, there was a hawk high up over the yard, hovering, it was hovering in the breeze like someone had it on a string, he watched it there for a long time.

"Wake up," said Dwayne.

The only others left at the weight pile were Black Larry, Dwayne, and Clovis. Everyone else was gone.

"I'm awake."

"Need you to pay attention to something," said Black Larry.

Poe got up from the bench and Black Larry sat down, ran his fingers through his blond pompadour, picked up a dumbbell and began curling it, he might have been a surfer lifting weights on the beach in California, the one they always showed on television. A good-looking guy, Black Larry, he had an easy way about him, a juror had once fallen in love with him. Dwayne and Clovis looked relaxed, they could have been talking about football, but with the faintest nod of his chin, Dwayne indicated a guard on the other side of the yard, pacing near the fence.

"See that toad? The skinny little fucker that's been avoiding looking over here?"

"Him?"

"Don't fuckin point," said Clovis. He slapped Poe's hand down. "Jesus fuckin Christ this guy."

"Clovis," said Black Larry. "Why don't we just stay on message?" He looked up from his bench and dropped the dumbbell into the sand.

Clovis said: "That guy over there is gonna be lookin for Black Larry tomorrow morning, the hallway between the showers and the laundry room. It's a quiet place where people can have a talk. In case you can't see him from here, he's a skinny fucker with a goatee, looks like a fuckin tweaker because he is one."

Poe knew what they were about to ask and he got cold all over, the hair on his neck and arms stood up. He hoped it didn't show.

"His name is Fisher," said Dwayne quietly. "He's got kind of a rat face. But his name will be on the shirt."

"Fisher," said Poe distantly.

"There won't be anyone else there. You just do what you do, that's all."

"Why?"

"The fuckin questions," said Clovis.

Black Larry raised a hand as if in surrender. "Reasonable enough, Young Poe. The answer is that Mr. Fisher over there owes us, there being some items we paid him to procure that he claims were confiscated. Mr. Fisher being a fresh hand at this game, he believes that his position allows him to rip us off."

"I'm still waitin for my trial," said Poe. "I don't want to be hitting a fuckin guard."

"Mr. Fisher isn't one of these straight-and-narrow types who's working this job to feed his family. He's a drug dealer. And even worse," Black Larry said, "he's a drug dealer who steals from his business partners. If that makes you feel better."

Poe shook his head and looked down the fence, wondered what would happen if he just started climbing. They would shoot him. That was the whole point of this place.

"Young Poe." Black Larry walked over close to him and lifted his face up, the way a father would, or a coach. "There are people on the outside who really do not like you. If you are here already, it means this is your new home, and will be, most likely, for a very long time. Do you follow what I'm telling you?"

"Still," Poe said. Black Larry kept holding Poe's face and Poe didn't know what to do with his hands, he let them hang limply by his sides. He could smell Black Larry's breath, sweet from pruno, the sunburned smell of his skin, he had heavy blond eyebrows and stubble. He had soft blue eyes, he was a fair man, he wanted the best for everyone, that was the feeling he gave off.

"You've caused some trouble with our black brothers over there, but at the moment they know that if they lay a finger on you, every single one of us goes into full combat mode. Doesn't matter whether it's twenty niggers or twenty toads. Usually there's a much longer probationary period, but you've been put on the fast track." Black Larry was looking for something in Poe's face but it seemed he didn't find it. He let go suddenly and Poe just stood there.

Clovis said, "You ain't even getting asked that much. Reason your cellmate's been on lockdown six months is for putting a knife in a toad's back, maybe you read about it in the paper, three guards and twelve inmates went to the hospital."

"No," said Poe.

"He doesn't read the newspaper," said Clovis.

Dwayne held up his hand. "Bud, you got lucky and you didn't. You got one of their upper guys you embarrassed the shit out of in front of the whole fuckin place and a lot of them would put a knife in you to get on his good side, not to mention you kicked open some old scabs between us and the DC Blacks. Causing us a good deal of hassle over matters we'd worked hard to settle."

"So I got to hit this guard."

"Not too many times," Black Larry told him. "We want him to be alive to pay us." He grinned.

"I understand the situation," said Poe. "I just need to think about it some."

Black Larry looked down at the ground and Clovis was shaking his head. "I told you guys the first fuckin time I laid eyes on this douchebag, when he first walked in the fuckin messhall."

"There's a spot for you right here," said Black Larry. He indicated the weight bench. "Or there's a spot for you out there." He jabbed his thumb at the yard, at the men on the other side, at everything. "Band of brothers, Young Poe. It's all pretty simple."

He nodded to Clovis and the two of them turned away. They walked, ambled really, slowly toward the other end of the yard. Black Larry stretched and yawned. He and Clovis approached a large group of black men who parted for them as they passed, nodded to the DC Blacks at their weight pile, then joined a group of Hispanic prisoners standing in the shade of the building; Poe could see the men gathering around to pay respect.

"This ain't the kind of thing that gets asked twice, bud. To be honest, you're kind of fucking up more than you realize right now."

It was just him and Dwayne. Poe looked across the yard at the black men gathered on the far side, by the other weight pile, there might have been two hundred of them. There was nothing he could say. He would agree to do it and then he would figure something out. He would agree to it and get himself a few hours to think. No, he thought. You will agree to it and you will do it.

"Alright," he said to Dwayne. "I'm in."

Dwayne's face had no expression.

"Whatever else, too. You want me to stab the guy, whatever. Sometimes it just takes me a while to think."

"I was the same way," Dwayne said. "Took me a while to accept what was happening."

"You think Larry'll be good with me."

"He knows," said Dwayne. "Don't think for a second he doesn't. We were all in the same spot as you when we came in. Especially bigmouth Clovis." He walked over to the dirt by the fence and kicked his foot into it.

There was something there and Poe picked it up, a sock full of D-cell batteries.

"Separate it out," said Dwayne. "Put the batteries in your pocket. When the detector goes off you show them what you have and they'll let you pass."

Book
Four

1. Isaac

The cop hadn't pursued him and he could hear the sirens of a second and then a third car and he guessed they had caught the Baron. Back to the canal. Get the pack. Minute or two at most—he'll be trying to explain what he's doing with all that cash.

He crossed a few residential streets without seeing anyone. It was quiet, early morning, the sun wasn't quite up. There's the park—the canal is in those trees. But where's that clearing? When he reached the treeline he hunkered down in the brush, trying to figure out where he was in relation to where he'd left his backpack. Sirens still coming. At least four cars now. Shouldn't have chased him in the open like that.

You could have gotten him with the knife when you sat up but you grabbed his coat instead. That's stupid to think about. No, it was a choice. Don't pretend it wasn't. There was a car coming and he crouched lower in the brush, watching a police cruiser race up the road he'd just crossed, lights flashing. Closer than you thought. They do this for a living. Forget the pack.

He didn't want to move. I'm well hidden, I can stay here until they leave. No, he thought, get up. Get further into those trees and get away from here. Stand up. Alright. I'm doing it. He stood up. Through the trees it was twenty yards to the canal and once he reached it, he began walking through the thin woods, away from the north end of the park, away from the road where he'd chased the Baron. Where did you leave the pack? Where is that clearing?

On the other side of the canal was a broad public lawn, and up ahead, on his side, he could now see where the trees ended—a grassy common area behind a row of houses. The pack is behind you. Know where it is now. There were other sirens in the distance and the closest sirens had already stopped. How many cars is that, he thought. Six. Maybe seven. A man armed with a knife—that's you. You need to keep going, you don't have time for the pack.

He felt a despair wash over him. Need to think a minute. No one can see me here. Alright, the pack is gone—accept that. Change the way you look, they saw a coat and black watch cap. Fine, he thought, it's progress. He stripped off his coat and hat and tossed them into the canal, along with the sheath for the knife. Better—brown sweater with a blue flannel shirt. Tuck in the shirt and pull the collar above the sweater. Schoolkid look. Christ it's even colder. Twenty-five degrees, maybe. Better that than arrested.

He stood numbly for a few seconds, glancing at the houses up ahead and the blue lights flashing behind him at the edge of the park. Forget the pack, he told himself again. Best-case scenario is you get out of here without handcuffs. Get your head straight. Don't walk too fast.

He crossed from the woods into the open area, fifty yards behind the row of single-family houses. Looking casual. Out for a stroll. Morning air clears the head. Hope no one's looking out a window. Christ you couldn't have done worse—big park on the other side. Half-mile visibility. Don't look nervous. Pray for late risers. He'll tell them you chased him with a knife, attempted murder. Who'll believe you? Shouldn't have brought it in the first place.

You are stupid. He could feel tears welling up in him. You could have gotten away the first time you woke up, then you'd have the money and the notebooks and everything else. I was so tired, he thought. No, you were stupid. This is the second time. No more mistakes.

On the other side there was a large public gazebo and two women jogging. Witnesses. Except the kid will make it. He refuses to do anything the easy way. Too far to see your face. More blue lights coming from the trailer park now—they're on your scent.

He was near a large storage building, there were blue lights reflecting on the wall, he looked around behind him and on the other side of the park, a few hundred yards away, a cop car was driving slowly across the lawn, approaching the two joggers. Does he see you? No. Run or walk? Just keep going.

He ducked behind the building and kept going along the canal but there were more houses on the other side, he could clearly see a man in his kitchen, standing at his counter drinking coffee in his boxer shorts. These early risers are going to fuck you. No he doesn't see you. Lost in his own worries.

A few hundred yards later he crossed a train trestle over the canal, it was a broad railroad cut with half a dozen sets of tracks. Now you're south of the steelmill. You are going to be fine. Stick to the smaller streets and you'll be fine. See them before they see you.

* * *

He'd been walking maybe an hour when he came to a wide boulevard, there was a shopping mall ahead of him and heavy traffic, rush hour, it was an overcast day. Even worse than the Mon Valley. Middle of April and just like winter. Meanwhile here comes a bus. Crowd of people. That is your bus. Get across this street and you'll make it, where's your wallet?

Jogging across the road, he arrived behind the idling bus and got in line with the others. A few people turned to look at him. No coat and the bruises on your face, up to no good, they can smell it. Shirt and sweater wrinkled and your pants filthy. Not to mention you're white. He made himself fixate on a stain on the curb and soon enough people stopped looking at him. In through the nose and out through the mouth. The Homicide Kid is headed south. The entire precinct after him, he gives them the slip. Day of the Jackal. Walks casually onto a bus.

There were no seats left and he found a place in the middle and stood. Warm in here. Where do I get off? How much money do I have? He tried to think. Nine bucks after the bus fare. A few meals' worth. Ride this till the end—put as much distance as possible. The bus went on forever, traffic was slow, he was drowsy. People got off and he found a seat. After a while he realized the bus hadn't moved for a long time. He opened his eyes and it was empty and the driver was looking at him in the big mirror. Isaac nodded and got off and looked around.

How far did you come? Ten miles maybe. Different world here. It was very green and the houses were large with hedges or stone walls in front of their yards. He passed athletic fields, stone buildings, a school of some kind. A handful of boys, fourteen or sixteen years old and wearing blue blazers, were smoking between classes. He nodded to them and all but the oldest boy looked away. Prefer you didn't exist. That is their desire—stop making me uncomfortable.

A block later he slowed to inspect himself in a car window. Surprise, you aren't any cleaner. Look like a street kid. Which you are.

He kept his eye out for cops but nothing happened. Hungry again. Doesn't matter. He walked aimlessly, turning down streets at random, trying to guess the position of the sun in the overcast sky, always moving.

*   *   *

When night came he was on a large road, a state highway, it was near the end of the evening rush hour and there were no lights except for the cars, taillights and headlights, he could see all the people. Warm and happy. Picking their noses and singing to the radio. Don't see you. Cheap sweater you're wearing, wind cuts right through. He was numb with cold. If even one of them would switch with you . . . Inside and out, seems like a simple difference.

This wind, he thought. Should have hung on to the coat and hat. Maybe I'm not really that cold, just hungry and tired. But you ate last night, that's enough calories. One day is nothing. Figure out your bearings. I am having trouble thinking. That is my problem. Should have stopped to eat but didn't feel safe. This highway—ought to have boxes with food and blankets for people, like emergency call boxes. Flag one of these people down. *Sir, I would like to rent your jacket. Or the backseat of your car—you've got the heater on anyway. Just until tomorrow.* This is what it feels like to be crazy. Simple things don't make sense.

Here by choice—you could have stopped him. When his hand was in your pocket you could have gotten him with the knife but instead you grabbed his coat. You'd still have the money and all your things, no loss to anyone. Fatal mistake, choose the hand over the knife. Nine dollars and no coat. Other guy's sleeping at the Hyatt. More money than he's seen in his life.

Here is the truth: you are going to freeze to death. You've always been precocious, ahead of schedule on this as well, makes perfect sense. Universe wants equality. Let no man be warmer than the air. Let no man hoard his heat. Stole it from someone to begin with—no change in energy since the Big Bang. Temporary borrower. The heat of my expiring body will raise the temperature of the earth one-trillionth of one degree. Detectable with the finest instruments. Mildest way to go. They say drowning but that's impossible—choking on water—ask your mother. How long? You'll know when you start to feel warm. From warmth and back to it.

He passed a strip mall but it was abandoned and empty. It would be out of the wind at least. No, keep moving. Lights up ahead. You're just hungry. Get some food and you'll see I'm right. Forty percent of calories transformed to waste heat. Fine, you talked me into it. I'll get some food and we'll see if you're right. Cold enough to snow but the air's too dry, small blessings. Won't matter. Plenty of lights up there, a mile, maybe. One foot forward. Judge your speed. Soon you'll have to make some decisions.

2. Grace

Billy had only been gone three days but everyone in town knew. At work they were polite but she heard them talking, Lynn Booth and Kyla Evans being the worst, though Grace's friend Jenna Herrin was no better, all three were from Buell and they'd all seen Billy play football. How hard he'd hit the other kids during the games—*You could tell he liked it a little too much . . . You know if he'd just shot that guy or something, but . . . Busting someone's head in like that, it's like you'd have to put some thought into it . . .* Grace kept her eyes down, trying not to listen, pushing the fabric through the machine, making very even stitches.

In the Giant Eagle on the way back from work she'd run into Nessie Campbell, even fat old Nessie had pretended to be interested in frozen fish until Grace took her basket to the checkout, Nessie Campbell who'd chase you down in the street and sell you Amway products every chance she got.

It was not any better at home. The day had been overcast and the house was cold. It would be fine, she would get under the covers. It was April 15 it should not be so cold. Taxes due, she thought. She hadn't finished them, started last week but then everything had happened. Still, how had she forgotten? She went to the table and opened the folder and began to look over the forms, but there was no chance. She couldn't think straight. Taxes were the least of her worries.

Billy would be fine, he was a big man. He was a big man but that was not how she thought of him, she could see him compared to others that way but still, it was not how she saw him. Then for some reason she was thinking about her father, she hadn't spoken to him in eighteen years, he still called every Christmas and Easter. He'd left her mother twenty years ago. Her mother did not have a flexible personality, hadn't been able to bear what was happening to the Valley, her daughter and son-in-law living in the basement apartment, no one was making any money, the town seemed to change overnight, cars were getting broken into, empty houses with their lawns grown up into brush.

It had changed her, she was constantly riding everyone, it had gone on until 1987 and then her father announced to everyone at dinner that he was leaving, that he needed a break from things. At first Grace hadn't blamed him and then she had, and then had forgiven him, and then she blamed him again. But in a way it had been a brave act. His children were all grown up, he'd left her mother plenty of money. She couldn't imagine anyone being happy with her mother. Her father had moved to East Texas and she had not returned his calls. He still called at Christmas and Easter but she wouldn't pick up. She felt all of that like a weight around her neck now. Most of her good memories involved her father, and all he had done was rescue himself. But he'd thrown a wrench into Grace's life, because the burden of looking after her mother's sanity had shifted onto her. That was the real reason she hadn't returned his phone calls, probably. Selfishness, she thought. Now that you need people, too, you can see that.

There was Bud. She reminded herself of that, don't get your hopes up yet, but it seemed to be going somewhere. She would not be alone, she had someone to love her, someone she could love. The high she had felt last night and this morning, waking up to him and making love again, had faded, there was only this worry about Billy.

She had a brother she could call, Roy, he was a good man in his way, done a stint in Albion—and then she hadn't wanted him coming around, he was a likable guy same as Virgil and she was worried about Billy, her whole life she'd been surrounded by them, men who were good in their way. They'd caught Roy coming in from the woods with a bale of mari-juana plants, harvesttime, claimed he'd been doing someone a favor. For a while his phones had been tapped. Now he was living outside Houston, he claimed he was on the straight and narrow, driving for a freight company, had moved in with an older woman who helped him keep his head clear. Virgil had never liked her brother and her brother had never liked Virgil, they were the same person is why. Each thought the other wasn't good enough for her. But they were the same, one thing on the surface but underneath entirely different. All his money gone on booze and girls and then—light bulb, Virgil remembers he has a wife who has a place he can live, a wife who would take care of him. At least she'd finally stood up to him. That, she could feel good about.

She didn't want to be inside the house. She put on her coat and went and stood in the backyard, looking out over the rolling hills, the big barn in the distance, it was very green, cool and dry, it was not like summer, stifling and humid, it was still fresh. If Buddy Harris had a son, he would not be in jail right now. That is the one it should have been. Looked out for Billy more than Virgil ever did. Owed you nothing but still he helped you. She wondered if that was why she'd always taken him for granted. Virgil always had the eye for tail and women had the eye for him and it kept you scared, the fear of losing him owned you. For fifteen years. It was amazing how an idea could hold you like that, for that long.

And now Billy is locked up and Virgil, well, who knew where he was. But Buddy Harris's son would not be in prison. One way or the other. They said Harris had killed people but she had always doubted it, she had been positive, really, that it wasn't true. Dopers, they said. It was just a rumor that Harris had let fly around for his own purposes, it made his job easier, but looking at him you knew it wasn't true, couldn't be. But what if it was? She wondered why she was thinking about these things. She wondered if it could be true that Harris had killed someone.

She felt shaken and went back inside, sat in front of the TV. She flipped through all the channels, nothing worth watching, she would have to get more channels, she would have to remind herself to do that. It didn't help—she couldn't stop thinking about it. At first it seemed possible and then she was sure of it. Something in Bud Harris could kill a person if he thought it was best. He'd been in Vietnam.

You have to get out of this house, she thought. Harris had said he wouldn't come over tonight, that they should take it slow. She would have to be optimistic. It was just getting started, like Harris said. There was no way of knowing what would happen. And part of her *was* optimistic. Part of her thought it really was going to turn out fine. It was Friday night, a week now since Billy had come home half-frozen and all cut up. She would go to Rego's and have dinner. She called Ray and Rosalyn Parker but there was no answer, so she called Danny Welsh, who didn't answer either. She left messages for both—going to Rego's. She didn't know if she should be showing her face in public. But there was not much else to be done.

When she got there, the place was busy but she spotted an empty stool at the end of the bar and made her way to it. There was a pause as she walked in, people taking note of her, extremely brief but she noticed it.

Bessie Sheetz, the bartender, came over.

"Beer and a shot, I bet."

"Just the shot," said Grace.

Bessie poured her drink.

"How you holding up these days?"

"I'm fine."

"You know you're among friends, don't you?" The woman slid the shot over and leaned on the bar. "I doubt you remember but I lost my son a ways back. You know I never stop thinking about him."

"How old was he?"

"Forty-six."

"Young."

"It was so quick. It might have been a year but it felt like bing bang boom. Of course he'd smoked since he was twelve years old, plus being in the war and all, that didn't help either."

"This one?"

"No, the first one they had over there, in '91."

"I'm sorry," said Grace.

"Wheel of life, that's what I tell myself."

"Ma'am, we're interested in some counter service as well," called a man from the other end of the bar. He was joking. He winked at Grace.

"You don't tip," Bessie called back to him.

"Wait till she gets to know you. She'll start tipping less, too."

"Yeah yeah, you spend five dollars in here. A dollar an hour."

"Don't let me keep you," said Grace.

"Screw them," said Bessie. She stood up straight and shook her head. *"Ma'am.* You believe that crap?"

*   *   *

Half an hour later, Ray and Rosalyn still hadn't shown up, one of the women at the bar had caught her eye and smiled at her a few times, a bottle blonde, the wife of Howard Peele of Peele Supply, a company that sold pipes and tubes to the coal mines and one of the two biggest employers in town. She was a few years younger than Grace and maybe twenty years younger than her husband, tight black pants and a tight pink top, always wore heels. Grace tried to remember her name. Caught Virgil making eyes at her at someone's barbecue, that's why you never liked her. Heather. Realistically, of course, someone like Heather wouldn't risk that for someone like Virgil. Hard to admit that at the time. Right now, at the bar, two men were laughing at something Heather had said but Grace could tell they didn't really think it was funny.

She was getting up the nerve to leave when Ray and Rosalyn came in. Ray smiled guiltily. "Sorry we're late—Pirates against the Cubs."

"We're sorry," said Rosalyn. "This asshole." She pointed to her husband. "I'll get us some drinks. You guys want to get that table?"

Ray kissed her on the cheek and sat down across from her. "So how you doin, princess?"

"I guess I'm doing good," she said.

"Well, I could understand that."

Grace looked into her drink.

"What I mean is you know you got my sympathies, Grace. You know . . . Christ." He shook his head. "I'm a bad talker."

"Thank you, Ray," she said. She patted his hand.

"Waiting on anyone else?"

"Not really."

"I'm sorry I made us late." Someone came up behind him and Grace looked up. The bottle blonde had come over.

"You two met?" said Ray.

"About ten times. I'm Heather, she's Grace."

"I remember," Grace said.

"I'm gonna sit down, you two mind? Need to get away from those numbskulls."

Ray swept his arm toward the seat just as Rosalyn came back with three glasses of wine.

"Oh hi sweetheart," said Heather.

"You need another," said Rosalyn.

"Hell no. I need someone to put a stop to me."

"Ray, why don't you get your ass up and help me carry the food."

Ray followed Rosalyn back to the bar.

Heather smiled at Grace. "Your poor son. I was so sorry to hear that."

"Thank you."

"You know, if there's anything you ever need . . ."

"We're fine."

"I understand what you're going through, I really do."

There was an awkward silence and Grace looked over toward Ray and Rosalyn, who were still at the bar, caught up talking to people.

"Remind me how you and Howard met," said Grace.

"He hired me as his secretary. I was tending bar in New Martinsville and he came in and offered me a job. Which was pretty obvious but, well . . ." She shrugged. "I made him work for it."

"You miss your hometown ever?"

"Hell, no. Howard had to spend ten grand just getting my teeth fixed. See?" She grinned. "I used to be bucktoothed, you should have seen me."

"I doubt that."

"Sad but true. But . . ."

Grace looked at her.

"I really mean that about your son. I just always thought there was something about you and I was so sad to see that paper the other day."

"It's not over yet. Just getting started, really."

"Probably the last thing you want to think about right now."

"It's alright."

"I'm always apologizing," said Heather. "It's my special talent."

"Manicotti," said Ray. "Plates for everyone."

"How'd you get that so fast?"

"Called from the road."

"I can't even look," said Heather. "I ought to use the restroom."

Rosalyn checked to see that Heather was out of earshot, then leaned over toward Grace. "You ought to see their goddamn house. Every single piece of furniture is black. They got a big exercise room and there's art on every wall."

Ray said, "You mean those pictures that look like a retard drew them?"

Grace rolled her eyes.

"I'm not kidding you," said Ray. "Looks like someone drew them with their eyes closed. Then you hear what they paid for them."

"Like you would even know." She turned back to Grace. "She told me they've spent two hundred thousand dollars on those paintings. Said it's all doubled in price just in the past year."

Ray snorted.

Heather was back, sniffling. She didn't sit down. "I'm sorry y'all, I really ought to get going."

"Good to see you again," Grace said.

"You too, sweetheart." She squeezed Grace's shoulder then walked out, tottering slightly on three-inch heels, the men at the bar watching her tight pants as she left, the door banging behind her.

"Moneyman must be calling," announced someone at the bar, after the door had swung shut. A few people chuckled.

Ray tapped his nose. "Thirty thousand a year goes up there, from what I hear."

Grace was surprised at this slight cruelty. But then she was guilty of it herself.

"Anyway . . ." said Rosalyn.

The front door banged open again and Heather reappeared, heading back toward their table. When she reached it she leaned over to Grace. "You let us know if you need anything, hon." She pressed a scrap of paper into Grace's hand. "Just in case, whatever, you call me." She noticed everyone staring at her and walked quickly out of the bar before Grace had time to respond.

"What was that about?" said Rosalyn, once she'd left again.

"Everybody loves Grace, especially women who—"

"Stop it," said Rosalyn. She punched her husband on the shoulder, hard. "What the hell is wrong with you today?"

"My piehole needs manicotti." He spooned a large portion onto his dish. "I'm just hungry, is all, it's just my sugar."

"I'm sorry we've been away," said Rosalyn. "How're you holding up?"

"I'm making it," Grace told her. "Staying optimistic." ·

"You really think it'll be okay," said Ray.

"Yeah," said Grace. "Somehow."

3. Poe

He was lying in his bunk, thinking about what he would have to do to the guard, thinking about his lawyer coming and what he would have to say to the lawyer, when the cell door clattered open and a young inmate appeared, escorted by a CO. The inmate was about twenty, a sandy-haired country-boy type, a hucklebuck, despite being in the hole six months the kid still had freckles around his nose. He was much smaller than Poe, thin and good-looking in an almost girlish way but his arms were covered with tattoos the same as the others, a green shamrock prominent on one arm, the letters AB on the other, spiderwebs around each elbow. The CO closed the cell door and walked off down the tier.

Poe sat up in his bunk.

"I'm Tucker," said the inmate. "They told me about you."

Poe introduced himself and they bumped fists.

"Heard you're gonna take care of that piece of shit Fisher tomorrow."

Poe didn't say anything.

"You got something to get him with?"

"Yeah, but I'm not sure about any of it, to be honest."

Tucker got a confused look.

"I'm still waitin for my trial."

"Well did you tell them that? 'Cause they told me you was a definite."

Poe shrugged.

Tucker said, "I know you just got in and all, but these ain't a bunch of people you want to fuck with. You gotta put your mind to this shit. I'll go along and keep lookout if you want, but you got to be the one doing the hitting."

"I want to get out of here," said Poe.

"Well you fuckin won't," said his cellmate. "If they even overheard us having this conversation they'd cut you into fuckin pieces. Larry and Dwayne got about a half dozen life sentences between them."

"I'm more worried about Clovis."

"Clovis is just muscle. Fuck Clovis."

"I dunno," said Poe.

"I'm telling you don't go back on your word. I'll fuckin forget we had this talk. Knowin how they work they'll stick me on the other end of the knife that goes in your fuckin neck."

"Whatever."

"You don't do it," said his cellmate. "You might as well just fuckin hang-yourself. This is a bad place for a young white man to go walkin around without friends."

Poe went back to staring at the ceiling and Tucker took out his footlocker and began to arrange his things.

"You touch any of this shit?"

"I didn't even see it. They must have just brought it today."

"I'll know if you did."

"Don't worry yourself," Poe said.

That night when all the lights were shut off there was a tapping at the bars and Poe woke up. He looked out and saw a guard standing there. The guard looked up and down the cellblock, then unbuttoned the front of her pants so her pubic hair was visible. He heard a rustling in the bunk underneath. That fuckin pervert is jerkin off, Poe thought. To that fat fuckin guard. He watched the guard for a time, out of curiosity more than anything else, and then lay back on the bed until it was over.

After some time he heard: "Don't look at her again. I been down six fuckin months and I paid for that shit."

"I wasn't looking," said Poe.

"I heard you looking. I know you were looking."

"I got no interest in your friend," he said. "I didn't know what was happening."

Tucker grunted and didn't say anything further. Poe tried to fall back asleep but he was thinking about the guard. It was maybe a setup. They jerk off to one guard but want me to flatback the other one. He couldn't make sense of it. He wondered if they were all working for the DA, trying to trap him further. Except he doubted the DA had any idea what went on here, he doubted anyone did, they wouldn't allow it, it was gladiators every day. It was Roman times. Except maybe he had been sent here on purpose. They acted one way, they wanted the law served, but they didn't mind if you got raped in the shower or your skull cracked by a combination lock. Really, there was no such thing as the law. There was only what people wanted to do to you.

He lay still for a while and he was shaking, fear or anger he didn't know. He thought if I don't beat that guard I got all of them after me, the whites and the blacks both, and the guards won't care. If I do hit the guard I got the guards and the blacks after me. Except certain guards had side deals. Invisible webs. There were deals going down everywhere, only not with him.

He thought about it more and more and he wanted to punch something, he slammed his palm into the wall and rocked the bed, the wall didn't move it would never move, his cellmate punched his mattress from the bottom. He would ignore the cellmate. But still he had just been punched. Though no one had seen it he would let it pass.

He wished Isaac was in front of him, he would knock the shit out of Isaac. All he'd done was get his throat cut and his balls nearly yanked off. He'd paid enough. He'd paid enough that night for anything he'd done. Isaac hadn't paid at all, not a fucking thing.

There was the same din going on outside, the same pointless shouting and music, underneath him his cellmate moving around on his mattress, trying to get comfortable. Isaac would get massacred. The whole hundred ten pounds of him. He would be a snack for these people. That was why he, Poe, was here. He was doing the right thing. He was being a hero. He would act like other people were watching—it would keep his thoughts and actions pure. That was the key to anything: pretend others are watching. It was just like the field, a bunch of big guys wanting to knock the shit out of you, it was your choice. Wolf or sheep, if you didn't choose it was chosen for you. Hunter or hunted, predator or prey, everyone knew it was the ancient relationship.

But it was not just that. It was not just pure nobility. In simple truth this place had been waiting for him. There were those who had capabilities and those who didn't and even in his glory days he had known it, known they would figure it out one day, a bullet he would never dodge. His mother she'd had her hopes but he had known. It was his own insides. He'd run out his luck and was living his fate and things considered, he'd been lucky.

He would knock the shit out of the guard. And whoever else. He would treat it like a game he had to play. He would go down to the hallway early and run it through his head, visualize the other guy already on the ground. He would take the guard from behind so his face wouldn't be seen. All that mattered here was your deeds, your acts as others saw them, he hadn't known it that morning in the cafeteria but now he did. Then he thought: no. He could not do it. He could not hit the guard. His legs were shaking again and he had to piss and he got down from the bunk and afterward he ran the water in the sink and washed his face.

He heard Tucker say, "You're wakin me up when you do that. Once you're up there you need to stay there for the night."

"You woke me up jerkin off and now you're telling me when I can piss."

"That's right," said Tucker. "I ain't gonna tell you again, neither."

"You can talk all you want," said Poe. "I don't give a fuck what you say."

He was about to get back into his bunk when he heard Tucker's weight shift, he swung hard and hit Tucker in the face just as he was standing up, Tucker fell back to his bunk but then seemed to rebound off it, he was on top of Poe, he was very fast. They throttled around like that, they were rolling around in the tiny space between the wall and the bunkbeds, grunting, it was a slow fight it was a wrestle for leverage, to get a chokehold, only Poe was much stronger. He got a few hits in and soon enough he had Tucker's head in both hands and was knocking it against the floor.

Then he realized that Tucker had stopped hitting back and that the lights had come on. The guards were already outside the cage. He put his hands up but they peppersprayed him anyway and cracked him in the back and legs with their batons, it wasn't like getting hit with a fist, he could feel the damage it was doing. He covered up and finally they stopped hitting, he couldn't see a thing, his eyes were burning, he was shouting for water. He let himself be cuffed and lifted to his feet, he was dragged down the tier, the inmates were all shouting things, everyone was awake and watching, he was blind, he was choking and crying, wet everywhere, he couldn't tell if it was water or spit or tears or blood. He stumbled into someone, a guard, they thought he was trying to break loose and they were hitting him again, he went down. Then they were dragging him again, it must have been a lot of them. They dragged him down a flight of stairs, he pulled his head up so it wouldn't hit the cement, they threw a bucket of water into his face, his eyes felt better, they hoisted him up and bent him over something, this is where it comes, he thought, this is where they take that from you. But then there was more water on his face, a hose, they were squirting it right into his eyes. It was just a sink. They were washing his face. He was taken to another part of the prison, it was the basement, he was in a cell the same size as his old one only there was one bunk. He was on his back on the thin mattress, feeling the relief of his eyes not burning anymore.

Poe could hear that one of the guards was still there. He heard the guard light a cigarette and he smelled it.

"You got any money," he said.

"No," Poe said. His nose was still running profusely from the pepperspray and he had to sit up to blow it on the floor.

"Must have someone you can call."

"Not really."

"Well," said the guard. He looked thoughtful. He offered Poe the remainder of the cigarette and Poe got up from his bed to take it.

"For reasons you may or may not know," said the guard, "we're all glad to see that particular white nigger get beat. But that was real dumb on your part. They ain't gonna let you walk away from that."

4. Harris

Of course he wanted to see Grace tonight but Even Keel knew it was better to wait. Take things a little easy. He was halfway to the compound when the idea of being home all night with the dog seemed more lonely than he could handle. He pulled over and went through his cellphone and found Riley Coyle s number.

"I'm out with the regular crowd of pricks," said Riley. "If you want to meet us at the Dead End."

Harris went home and changed out of his uniform and headed back toward town. Of course half the reason, no, not half, maybe slightly less, twenty percent, was that if he had a few drinks he would call Grace. And she would answer, and then . . .

The Dead End was one of the few bars that had remained open the entire time since the mill had closed, and the joke was it hadn't been cleaned since before the mill had opened. It was a long wood-paneled room, dim and comfortable, with a view from the back deck over the water. Riley, Chester, and Frank had worked at the mill before it closed. Eventually Frank had gotten rehired at U.S. Steel in Irvin, Riley had opened a small machine shop, and Chester had gotten an MBA. He now ran with a slightly different crowd, consulting work for drug companies. When Harris got to the bar, all three of them were sitting at a table, flirting with the owner's wife.

"Boys."

"Mr. Johnny Law," said Riley. He turned to the owner's wife, a pretty brunette about Grace's age. She'd stiffened noticeably since Harris's arrival. "He says he's thirsty."

"I'm fine," said Harris.

"He's thirsty," Riley insisted. The woman smiled at Harris and went back to the bar. It was hard to believe she was married to Fat Stan, the owner. Pickins in the Valley must be slim. Obviously, he thought. Look at you. A woman like Grace . . . He decided to sit down.

"How's everyone?"

"Doing great," said Frank. "Best day of my life."

"Frankie just got a new toy," said Chester. "Would have driven it here if the wife let him."

"You finally get that 'Vette?"

"Nah," said Frank. "It's just a four-wheeler. But a 660 Yamaha, four-wheel drive, automatic, snowplow, winch, the works. Cart that hooks up behind it."

"Probably cost more than your truck," Riley added.

"There's skateboards that cost more than my truck," said Harris. He nodded to Frank. "Company looking after you?"

"Yep. Got us on this profit-sharing plan, stock's up a hundred percent. We just hired Benny Garnic's son, matter of fact."

"I thought he was a computer programmer."

"Shipped his job to India," said Riley. "Kid goes to school so he wouldn't get laid off like his dad did, but then . . ."

Harris shook his head.

"It does make you feel better about things," said Frank, "in a purely cynical way. Those kinds of people didn't have much sympathy for us twenty years ago, I can remember it was asshole after asshole going on TV and saying it was our faults not going to college."

"Benny Garnic's son probably doesn't feel better."

"I got him started at nineteen-sixty an hour," said Frank. "He won't lose his house the way we all did."

The owner's wife reappeared with a tray of drinks. "These are from Fat Stan. On the house." From the other side of the bar, Fat Stan waved and Harris waved back. Fat Stan's wife set a glass of beer and a shot of whiskey in front of each of them but only glanced briefly at Harris. "Pleased to make your acquaintance, Sheriff."

"I'm just a policeman," said Harris. "And I'm off the clock."

"Well, nice to meet you anyway." She smiled but then walked away quickly.

"Mista Sheriff," said Riley, "you're not going to use those handcuffs on me, are you? I been so bad . . ."

Harris looked into his whiskey and tried to remember. Had he ever arrested her? It could have been a brother or something. Or her father, or her boyfriend, really, it could have been anything. Some people were just nervous around cops.

"Careful if you drink that. Fat boy over there probably needs help collecting money."

"Or he's got a growroom in the basement."

Harris sipped the drink. "Least he knows I don't come cheap."

"Quality costs."

"Tell by his wife."

"Word is she came mail-order."

"No. Serious?" The woman was dark-haired but Harris hadn't noticed an accent. She might have been eastern European, but so was half the Valley.

Riley burst out laughing.

"She's from goddamn Uniontown," Chester said, "she used to dance at that place he had over there."

"Speaking of," said Riley, "how's your squeeze, Johnny Law?"

"Which one?"

"Grace Poe. Or just plain Grace, if that's now how she goes."

"No idea," said Harris. "That fizzled out a long time ago."

The table was quiet for a few seconds and all four men looked in different directions.

Chester turned his glass in his hands. "Well, you know we all sympathize with what happened to her son."

"Get your waders on. It's about to rain horseshit."

"Be serious a minute, Riley," said Frank.

"I am being serious. If we brought all those boys back from the sand-box, gave them blue uniforms and let them keep their M16's, pretty soon we'd have a crime-free society. Stop wasting money on Arabs and put it to work right here."

"What are you talking about," said Chester.

"We could walk three blocks in any direction and score whatever we wanted. That's what I'm talking about. No offense to Johnny Law, he'd need about three hundred guys to get this place under control. So you can't expect kids to grow up here and not do dumb-ass shit."

"We aren't quite there yet. It isn't quite anarchy yet, is it, Bud?" said Chester.

"No," said Harris. "Far from."

"Well, there's a lot of loose talk about what it would mean if a person was literally allowed to get away with murder."

"I have no idea about that." But he was thinking about the jacket.

"The rumor mill is in high gear right now, is what Chester's get-ting at."

"I don't give a fuck, Bud," said Riley. "Just for the record."

"This could still be a good place. It's just that the laws have to be en-forced and people are worried about that you know, crime stats get up too high, no one wants to move here, gets hard to attract business, et cetera."

"Chester," said Riley, "that kid isn't even a goddamn blip on the kind of radar you're talking about. It was a goddamn derelict, even if he did do it and it wasn't self-defense or something. Probably the same piece of shit that stole the camper shell off my truck."

"I don't know about that," said Chester.

"Well you do know there was ten, fifteen smaller plants that closed around here just in the past year or so. I mean, you can't smell it from your place in Seven Springs, but it's still happening. Our time might have been the big bloodbath, but they're still shooting the survivors. There's gonna be fallout to it, just like there was in our time and hangin some kid out to dry doesn't do shit for anyone."

"Aside from all the HUD people," said Chester, "this is still a good place to live."

"I need a drink," said Riley.

Harris pushed his untouched beer over.

"Listen, Bud, we all know it seemed like the right thing to do when you got Billy a slap on the wrist last year."

"Only now," said Frank, "from certain people's point of view, I'm not saying my own, but from certain people's viewpoint, Billy Poe should have been locked up and then this other thing wouldn't have happened."

"None of us knows what happened there," said Harris. "There's no one who knows."

"Well, we all hear he's not talking. Which might make him smart, but it doesn't make him innocent."

"I'm not involved."

Riley was halfway through Harris's beer. Fat Stan and his wife were both watching from the bar. Harris wondered how much they could hear.

"There's people out there who want you to be involved," said Chester. "It would make them happier than pigs in shit if they were to hear you're still messing around in Billy Poe's business."

"That's right."

"There are people who think that boy is a bad seed, and that the reason he was on the loose is you.'

Harris shifted in his chair. He could feel that his ears were warm. Well, he thought, what did you expect. Better to know it.

"Keep your sails trimmed," said Chester, "that's all we're saying."

"Yeah, right," said Riley. He glanced at Harris. "What I hear, they're looking to hang you on the cross along with Cunko." He tossed down the rest of the beer. "Think of it as a reward for a lifetime of service."

"Who is it?" said Harris. Then he said: "Actually, you guys don't have to answer that."

"It's a lot of people, Bud."

Riley smirked. "It ain't that many. It's Howard Peele of Peele Supply and Tony DiPietro. And Joey Roskins along with them. Basically your whole cocaine-snorting, wife-swapping chamber of commerce."

Chester gave Riley a look.

"Fuck those people," said Riley.

"It's not just them."

"Buddy," said Riley. He leaned in close to Harris. "I know for a fact that Howie Peele gets his nose powder dropped off once a week by a guy from Clairton. You get in a jam, you got that in your back pocket."

Chester's face had become very stiff and Harris was feeling worse and worse. He'd let Howie Peele off for a DUI a year ago, made him call his wife for a ride home. Wrong message, he thought. It had seemed like a mistake at the time, but he hadn't known why. No, he thought, that's the wrong way to think about things. He wondered if he should talk to Glen Patacki again. He needed to get somewhere he could think about this.

Riley interrupted: "I can see you too, Chester. I ain't afraid of that prick and I don't care who you tell."

"Settle down," said Harris.

"A murder is a serious thing," Frank said quietly. "No one would deny that."

"That depends," said Riley, coming back to the conversation.

"People are worried it might be time for new blood."

"Well," said Harris. "They're probably right."

5. Isaac

A head of him were the lights and signs of a Wal-Mart. He was walking very slowly; it took forever just to cross the parking lot and when he got inside he stood in the doorway in the blast of hot air until the greeter motioned him forward. Salvation Army type—looking you over. Probably call security.

Bright in here, he thought. I just want to sleep. Find a quiet corner. No, eat first. Do not leave without eating. Taco Bell right there and a Pizza Hut, you can spend two dollars. He made his way to the line for the Taco Bell and looked at the menu overhead. What has the most calories? Two bean burritos and a taco. Balanced meal. The body a temple.

After his food came he took a glass of water and sat slowly eating. Almost too tired to eat. Give it a few minutes. No, your head is clearing already—coming up from under water. Blood sugar rising. Close the eyes, just a minute.

"Young man? Young man?"

He opened his eyes. An old lady at the next table was looking to him.

"You fell asleep," she said.

He nodded. Alright wake up. Look at her—satisfied—acting like she saved you from something. Find another place to rest. No that is not a real option; the store will close eventually, you'll be right back where you started. I could find a shelter, he thought. Except that is the first place they'll come looking for you. A vagrant felon. Anyone else would have skipped town. Except I don't have a coat and I don't know where I am, he thought. He looked out over the store. Fine. Fine, I'll do it.

There was music playing in the store, easy listening, as he pushed his shopping cart down the aisle. The other customers stared intently at their merchandise until he passed. Embarrassed to look at you. Who wouldn't be? Except the kid does not care. Possessed of a higher mission—self-improvement. Resource gathering. Like the original man—starts from scratch. A new society. Beginning in Men's Outerwear. All those coats. Never know how much you value a coat. Took months to make in the old days. Now you just go to a store. Don't be nervous, she's looking at you.

An employee in a smock passed by, giving him a long look. Isaac detoured around to the other side of the store, the pharmacy aisles, found a razor and a travel-sized soap and shaving cream. Perhaps some deodorant. Plan for the future. In another section of the store he picked up a handful of energy bars. Same ones Lee eats. Kid gives his highest endorsement. Don't take more than you can carry, though. Now sporting goods—wall full of hunting knives. Put one in the cart. Four inches. The kid knows the truth: man without a knife is not a man.

Back in clothing he found a clean pair of pants, button-down shirt, socks, underwear, a pack of T-shirts. Fresh new smell. A few aisles away he took the thickest coat they sold, blanket-lined heavy canvas. Practically a sleeping bag, this coat. Get another fleece as well. The kid appreciates quality. Now a hat and maybe a second one. Sleep like a king in two hats. The kid, he is concerned with his future. A maker of preparations. Here comes a meddler.

A different employee, a short thin woman in her late sixties, came over and asked if he wanted to try anything on.

"No ma'am," he said. "I know my sizes." He smiled at her.

"Yes, sir," she said. She stood there. Thinks she sees through the kid. Suspects him of plans. Meanwhile he could be her grandson, but she doesn't care—her loyalty is to the company. Company over humanity. Head to the checkout. Act like you're buying.

He waited at the cash register, listening to a man ahead of him talking on a cellphone. The store is busy, he thought, and the kid is small and unthreatening. He sends out vibrations—a hundred ten pounds of love. No reason for suspicion. Plenty else to look at.

The queue was moving slowly and finally the employee watching him went and did something else. Isaac broke out of line and pushed his cart toward the dressing rooms. Hope they're unlocked. Get in quick. There's one.

Piling all the loose items onto the coat, he carried everything into the small room, locked the door, then stripped off all his clothes. He began to put on the new pants. Hold on, change your underwear. Small dignities. He undressed fully and paused in front of the mirror—the sickly kid, his hair filthy, a week's scraggle on his face. Your standard refugee. Any skinnier and the wind will take him to Kansas.

He dressed himself in the new clothes, then put his old clothes back on overtop of them. Look about the same. Maybe lumpier. Knife in your belt, soap and razor in your pants pocket, energy bars in your jacket. Ready for combat. Handsome Charlie. Hang the coat on your shoulder like you own it. The kid can be slowed but not stopped. Those above would prefer he froze—their money, his life. But they have not walked in his shoes and he holds no hard feelings. Truly a generous kid.

He checked both ways as he left the dressing room, then walked quickly toward the exit, already beginning to sweat from the extra clothing. Beating them at their own game, he stares at the linoleum, not nervous. Long lines of people wasting money. Exit right. Thirty seconds. Uh-oh. Here's trouble. Time to put on the coat.

"Sir," a woman's voice was calling. "Sir you need to pay for that."

Don't turn around. Act like you don't hear. Get that coat on. He felt a surge of adrenaline as he approached the doors, keep walking, he thought, keep walking you are nearly there *Sir,* he heard, *sir we need to speak to you,* and then people were yelling and something came over the loudspeaker, *all employees report for a code seventy-six.*

Out of the corner of his eye he saw someone running and then he started to run himself. The only thing between him and the door was the old man in his blue vest, the store greeter, they locked eyes, Isaac was running at him full speed and finally the man stepped out of his way.

He stumbled against the doors and lost ground but then he was out into the parking lot, it was wide open, what is the shortest distance go right. They're behind you. Pull that cart to slow them. No, don't. He was running all-out toward the wooded area at the edge of the lot. Past idling cars, past people with shopping carts, he heard footsteps just behind him. He felt his muscles burning and he saw every step he would take. Reach the woods and you're safe. Just get to the woods. Something brushed against his coat, a person's hand, but he heard them stumble and fall behind. Still there's someone else.

At the very edge of the parking lot he heard the footfalls slow and cease and he jumped the high curb without slowing, plunging into the grass and running downhill, you're going to fall, he thought, but he kept his footing. Then he was into the woods, safely into the darkness, still running.

6. Henry English

His daughter had gone to sleep and Henry was sitting in the wheelchair in his bedroom, trying to get the nerve to get into bed. It had been the den, a spare bedroom, maybe the nanny's or the maid's.

There was a handrail at the head of the bed but still. Usually the boy gave him a boost. Now it was a gap he had to make, grab the rail with one arm and try to heave himself over, legs dragging along behind him. He'd made it the last five nights but only barely. If he fell, he'd spend the night on the floor. Freeze to death, probably. He had not wanted Lee to help him. Better to manage on his own. It would cost.

He was worse off than he thought, the boy being gone forced him to admit that. Even if he made it onto the bed it would take him forty-five minutes to get undressed, planning his strategy and levering himself, move the first leg a few degrees, then the other leg, bend the knee so much, then the other knee, hope the first knee doesn't pop back while you're doing the second. He was weaker and stiffer, like having rigor mortis. I'll sleep in the chair, he thought. But that was not a real option.

He wouldn't be able to keep it from her much longer, the truth of his condition. He needed a bath, he hadn't had one since the boy left, he knew she could tell. The way she looked at him when she said good night, like kissing a baby. That was bad enough. Put you in a home. Isaac wouldn't, it had never crossed Isaac's mind, but his daughter was practical. Her heart ran a couple degrees colder.

It is the boy distracting you. Gone six days. Bums must have got him. Then he thought: No, he's tougher than he looks. Not to mention your four thousand dollars in his pocket, slim motivation to come home. Christ, he thought. He felt the pressure come up inside him, he needed to hit something, he punched the arm of the chair, he punched the mattress, he squeezed his jaw as tight as he could make it, he would break his teeth. Then he caught a look at himself in the mirror, face twisted and red, a tantrum.

Calm down. Read some. He rolled his chair to the other side of the room, under the lamp where he couldn't see the mirror. He picked up the *TV Guide*. It was his own fault, the mattress was too soft and he couldn't get a purchase, the bed was older than both his children. Wedding bed. He could feel the springs in his back as he slept but he would never get rid of it. It was Mary's last bed, it would be his too, there were times she still came to him in the night.

Truth was he was close. He was stealing his days. An old pine, weak in the roots, its own weight pulls it over. Everything inside him was going on strike, kidneys, liver, and pancreas, they were yanking out parts of his guts, appendix, gall bladder, there was nothing he was allowed to eat. No alcohols or fats. No salts. Lee's lunch yesterday, all the cheese and dairy, he'd spent half the day on the throne. Shitting your guts out. She'd wanted to take him to the movies, but he'd had to pretend to be tired. Didn't tell her the real reason. Got her out of the house to make your movements in peace.

You could go on forever if they ate you in small enough bites—he used to think that was beautiful, triumph of human spirit, wanting to go on no matter what. It was Shackleton going up mountains, a normal person could not endure it. Reason to hold the head up. The problem being it was only an outlook, a way of thinking that did not change reality. Reality being he was meat in a slow rot. A head hooked up to old meat, barely get your own pants off. Any other animal they'd put you down, lying in your own slops.

You're just talking, he thought. Full of bullshit. There's a nine-millimeter in the drawer for any time you get too tired, you can always talk to Mr. Browning, he's got good advice when you're ready to listen. But he's been quiet thirteen years. Because you yourself are just talk.

He put down his *TV Guide*, there was no point. He rolled to his desk, he had caused the whole thing, it was the small slips of the mind that did you in. He'd gotten sloppy, left the money where the boy could find it. He should have locked the money up, hidden it somewhere else. There were bills all over, the hospital, he had another appointment, they wouldn't schedule anything together, it was a bunch of shithead tailchasers, they wanted to get their twenty-five a visit. It was the bush leagues, you didn't get good doctors at a little hospital like that, they were practically veterinarians. When they'd found that lump on his prostate, he could practically see their hands rubbing together, more tests and operations. He'd made another appointment with a specialist in the city, Indian guy, Ramesh, Ramid, barely understood what he was saying but he was good, a likable guy. Ramesh checked and checked but the lump was gone, probably never there to begin with. Told him: Doc, I never been so happy to have a man stick his finger up my ass. Took you the wrong way. Small careful man. Said *I didn't like it any more than you did, Mr. English*. After that he wouldn't look at you. Liked him except now you can't go back.

He rolled himself to the window, there was a quarter moon, he could see everything, the skeleton of the neighbor's house, Pappy Cross, gone twelve years. Moves to Nevada to be with his sons, within two weeks someone came and stole his gutters, security door, doublepane windows. Called him in Nevada to tell him, never got a call back. Whole house rotting to nothing.

There was a noise from upstairs but it was just Lee walking around. Soon she would have to go back, she would not wait around here forever as Isaac had. Admit it, he thought. A man would not have done that. What you did to that boy, it is sacrifice yourself for your children, not the other way around. The boy was technically a genius, they'd had him tested but he had never told the boy, 167, that was the number he'd scored, it was higher than his sister. But, he didn't know, there'd always been something about the boy, he was smart and stupid at the same time. As if he was meant to do everything the wrong way. Junior league ball, the boy was twelve, they subbed him in for the pitcher, good arm but he chokes, eight runs straight, loses the game. Afterward acting like nothing happened. It made no sense. The feeling that gave you, watching your son lose the game, but he just shrugged it off, didn't care.

No, he thought, you never had any choice, Lee Anne left first and there was nothing more to it. And the boy could take it, he's stronger than she is. She talks one way but inside she's another. Would've killed her staying here.

Henry thought about it, he would have wheeled himself in front of a train for either of them. Went without saying. The boy was his son. It was normal to have a preference, his own father had preferred him to his brother, it was just the way life went. He did not have enough to give to both of them. No, he thought, that is a lie. You did not want to be alone and you made choices.

Either way it would have been time to let the boy go, make your final journey. Into the home with the old folks, men in diapers, cleaned by strangers. Last about two weeks. Life for a life. He watched the deer browsing around Pappy Cross's old house, wondered if Pappy was even still alive, the house had been on the market twelve years and one of the sons had come back, stayed in a hotel, contracted someone to cut all the trees down, even the young pines, forty-dollar trees, sold them to the mill and got the money out that way. He wondered if Pappy knew about it. Rotting house in a stump field, soon enough there'd be no trace, a million places just like this, right now and throughout time. Earth is made of bones. From wood and back to wood and you'll never know what came before you.

7. Poe

The new cell didn't have a window and they never turned out the lights but at least it was his alone. He knew it was late morning sometime; they had brought him breakfast, that had been a few hours ago though he wasn't sure even of that. It didn't matter, though. They would all be after him now, everyone in the prison, black gangs and white, a coalition of the willing, he had gone back on his word and taken another man down to boot, he had taken men from both sides. He wondered how he had done that, a basic rule, choose your enemies. He had chosen everyone. He wondered if he had killed Tucker. It didn't seem to matter much, it was the least of his worries, it was not a game of sums. No matter what you did in life, there was still your own death at the end of it. There was no question they would kill him, they would take their first chance.

He felt a shiver go through him and the sweat was coming fast now, he was drenched and cold where a second ago he had been warm. He was up on his feet and pacing around the cell, he was testing the walls with his hands, the bars, it was no use, the natural laws, he was going to scream, there were things inside that needed to escape. Only he would not. He would be a man. He would lie on the bed and calm his mind. He did. He was wet everywhere and his scalp was tingling, it felt like a heart attack, he would die there in his bed. After a few minutes the wave passed and there was a feeling of weakness and being emptied of everything.

And yet there was a way out. It was right in front of him, staring him in the face. He could tell the truth and change everything, his lawyer would want the same thing as all of them. That was the purpose of the lawyer. To get him out of here. To save his actual life.

Except it was not saving as much as trading. Isaac and Lee. But his life. Versus a promise he had made. Versus what he knew, there were good ones and bad ones and Isaac was one of the rare good ones. Him, Poe, from the natural standpoint he was where he was supposed to be, he belonged here and Isaac didn't. Maybe not this exact place, maybe this was not exactly where he belonged, but he admitted it, he was not surprised, not really. He had nearly made a vacation here last year, and his mother and Harris had gotten him out of it. It was not some unfair twist of fate, he had not been born a refugee, it was his own choices, he could be a man about it. He could accept the consequences.

And yet—if a lawyer asked what happened, it would be difficult to withhold a description of the events, it would not be human thoughts but another part of him. If someone asked him, he would tell. He would have no choice. But if they didn't ask him he wouldn't tell. It was a fair chance, it gave equal weights to both sides. Except he knew they would ask him. It was an obvious question: who killed the man in the machine shop? Christ it seemed so long ago, ancient times, part of the past. But it was the reason he was here. They would ask it and he would tell them. It was the truth, was all it was. It was nothing more than the truth.

He was up and pacing again, three steps to the back wall and turn and come back. Before lunch, they had said, that was when the lawyer was coming it had been some time now since breakfast. Yes, he thought, that is who you are. If there is any bad luck you will find it only it was not just luck, there had been many ways to avoid it, he hadn't taken any of them. It was hopeless, a lost cause. He had slept through life, let the currents take him. He had let the currents take him faster and faster and he had not noticed. He was at the end now, the big drop. It was not only college there had been other choices as well, choices that had revealed him to others, choices that half the town would have jumped at but he, Poe, had chosen another way. It was Orn Seidel calling him right after graduation, there was an opening at a company that did the plastic seals for landfills. Traveling all over the country. At new landfills they would lay down the plastic liners in preparation for garbage to be dumped there, to prevent leakage into nearby streams and such. At the old landfills they would seal them up, it was like a giant ziplock, a heavy layer of plastic overtop the garbage and then they blew them up with air to test them, just before they dumped the soil on top you could run across the acres of plastic, bouncing, it was like running on the moon, Orn said, it was fourteen dollars an hour to start. But it was not really running on the moon. It was working with other people's trash. Technicians, they called themselves, but it was not really that. It was laying plastic overtop of trash heaps, it was hanging around city dumps. Your country is supposed to do better than that for you, he thought.

And from Mike DeLuca's uncle, Poe's last big chance, strike three is what it was, dismantling work, taking apart mills and old factories, they had taken down old steelmills all over the country, locally and nationally. But another traveling job, Poe had applied and gotten the interview but there was so much traveling, it was living out of a suitcase the entire year, and the man giving the interview must have seen something in Poe's face. The work was all in the Midwest now, taking down the auto plants in Michigan and Indiana. And one day even that work would end, and there would be no record, nothing left standing, to show that anything had ever been built in America. It was going to cause big problems, he didn't know how but he felt it. You could not have a country, not this big, that didn't make things for itself. There would be ramifications eventually.

As for Mike DeLuca's uncle, he'd spent twenty years working in steelmills and then twenty years taking them apart, scrapping them, it was like his revenge against the steelmills, against getting laid off, but it was not really revenge, it was not a job anyone would want, the lies he had to tell when he visited the small towns and some waitress asked him *so what're you in town for?*

It was not all bad. He had lived a good life, the leader of the pack, a local hero, it was more than most. Slept with fourteen girls, it was more than most. Maybe one of them had a baby he didn't know about, life after death. Except it did not have to go that way. He could tell the simple truth. Truth and nothing but. He had not killed the man Otto, they would let him go and these men, Clovis and these men who would kill him here, he would never see them again.

It was the old saying, the truth will set you free. He could breathe outside and sit and feel the river air on him as he fished in the shade and ate egg sandwiches, jump a rabbit with a .22. Christ a .22 what he could do in here with that, a .22, the weakest of calibers, he could run the entire place. He could leave here, lie under the covers warm with Lee with her legs holding them up like a tent, smell of her smooth skin the slight rough patch between her legs. It was countless the pleasures of life there were millions, you could spend your entire life listing them, they were different for every person the feel of oak bark, light in a room, watching a big buck and deciding not to shoot it. It was a privilege you could lose at any time, he had taken it for granted, but he would change his life. He would make his life mean something. You could not go with the current and expect it to turn out fine, he had not known it before but he knew it now, he would change everything.

He lay down on the cold cement floor. He put his head under the bunk and lay there with his face in darkness. He could not tell the truth because it was not really the truth. Lee would not forgive him. She would see him for what he was. She would never think of him again, she would hate him more than she had ever hated anyone, it did not take a genius to figure that out. She already knew the story. It had been a mistake telling her. But he could not go back now, there was no way around it, she would not forgive him it was her brother, she would not be able to turn a blind eye to it.

He thought about that and felt even sicker, he was sweating again. No he could not allow that. He had closed the door on himself when he told her. But he could not lie anyway. He would not have done it anyway, ratted out his best friend, it was not in him to do that, he could think it but not do it. It was like look but don't touch.

Except he would just see. It was life. It was comparing ideas to actual life, it was not a valid comparison, it was words versus blood. He would see. When the lawyer came he would sign the papers and that would be all. He would not offer but if they asked him he would tell. He would have no choice. But if they didn't ask he wouldn't tell. Except they would ask. It would be the first question, most likely.

He could not talk to the lawyer. He would stay angry, he would think about getting Clovis or even Black Larry, he would take them down with him. He would go down a legend it was as simple as that, you could change your destiny that quickly. He heard a noise coming from somewhere. He was still lying under his rack. He looked out and saw a guard rapping on the bars.

"Cuff up," he said. "Your lawyer's here." He opened the slot in the door for Poe to stick his hands through.

Poe shook his head. He got to his feet and stood over the toilet and tried to urinate but he was too nervous, nothing would come out.

"Get the fuck over here and cuff up," said the guard. He was a short fat man with thinning hair and a jovial face, a plump fat face, he could not help but look happy.

"I ain't goin anywhere," said Poe.

"Stop being a fuckin hard-ass. Get the fuck out of that cell before I call the fuckin SORT team on your ass."

"Fuckin call em. They can drag me out but I ain't going."

"You are one stupid-ass motherfucker, aren't you?"

"Open that door and you'll see how stupid I am."

The fat man stared at him with an amused expression. "Alright then," he finally said. He rapped on the cell and began to walk away.

"Hey," Poe said.

"Change your mind already?"

"What happened to that boy? My cellmate."

"They took him to the hospital in Pittsburgh."

"He comin back?"

"If he does I don't think he'll be much trouble to you or anyone else."

"I don't give a shit about him."

"No one else does, either. If they hadn't gotten him out of the infirmary so quick, there's about fifty guys who would have sat on his chest."

"Is that gonna help me?"

"You aren't getting any new charges pressed, I can guarantee you that. Now get your ass over here and cuff up and see your lawyer."

"No," said Poe.

"Whatever your reason," the guard said. "You might think your good buddies back home would do the same for you, but I can promise you they wouldn't, and if you don't believe me you can look around inside that cell there and tell me if you see them anywhere. So cuff up. Least give yourself a chance."

"Don't trouble yourself," Poe said.

The guard gave him a final look. Then he disappeared from view, and Poe heard him shuffling back down the hall.

8. Lee

She'd spent most of the day driving around, finding places to read and then driving, past the houses of old friends, teachers, but it was all the same. The place held nothing for her. Maybe one day it would, but not now. She had a few nostalgic memories, but not many. Mostly they involved being with Isaac. Or maybe she was just telling herself that now.

She'd always known it wouldn't be easy for him, his awkwardness around people, around her high school friends. No one knew what to make of him. He didn't know what to make of himself. With the exception of his sister, he didn't know anyone like him. And people his age tended to mistake his generosity for condescension, presuming that Isaac held them to the same impossible standard to which he held himself. Eventually, she thought, he must have decided to stop trying.

She could feel herself getting angry, at herself mostly but also at her former classmates. Her sophomore year, everyone was sitting around Gretchen Mills's room and someone, it might have been Bunny Sachs, said, "You guys do realize this is the hardest thing we'll ever do. Getting in here is basically the hardest thing there is in the world and we've already done it."

But of course they hadn't done anything. They'd all been born to the right parents, in the right neighborhoods, they went to the right schools, had all the right social instructions, had taken all the right tests. There was simply not a chance they would fail. They'd worked hard but always with the expectation they would get what they wanted—the world had never shown them anything different. Very few of them had earned their places. Everyone admitted how spoiled they were but underneath, there was always the presumption that they deserved it.

Of course, she hadn't said a word. She wished she had but she hadn't. It was easy now to look back and think these things, but at the time she'd wanted to fit in and go along with Bunny and think yes I deserve this happy life I'm living.

Isaac's friendship with Poe still baffled her. But of course her friendship with Poe must have baffled him as well. Maybe it was that people had always set them, Poe and Isaac, so far apart—Poe because of his talent for everything physical, Isaac because of his mind. The truth was they were both the best at what they did in that school. It was a special sort of small-town bitterness that must have thrived on seeing them both fail.

After Isaac's first visit to New Haven, she'd thought maybe he'd come back, a month during the summer, she would scrape together money for a full-time caretaker for her father, just for the month. By then she already had two credit cards—she would find a way to pay for it somehow.

But Isaac had not responded to her offers to come. He was already changing. No, she thought, he might just have cared about his father too much. Henry would have seen it as Isaac going on vacation in Connecticut, and Isaac cared too much about what Henry thought of him to risk it. You had it easy, she thought. You got let off the hook.

The truth was that Isaac was not as ready to leave as he claimed. He had had a longer time to think about their mother, whereas she was already being pulled into another orbit—she'd left for New Haven almost immediately. What kind of people Isaac and her father could have become in the intervening years, she had no idea. Anything could have happened. You got lucky, she thought. You were too selfish to even consider staying.

Isaac: you could give him two random numbers, tell him to multiply them in his head: 439 times 892. He could tell you the answer in a few seconds. He just saw the answer, he didn't even do the calculation. Divide them—it was the same. Once she'd sat with a calculator, testing him, certain he must have memorized certain combinations of numbers, certain there was some trick. But there was no trick. There's parts of me I don't understand, he said, and shrugged.

Her boyfriend from freshman year, Todd Hughes, the physics major, had loved Isaac, seen his brilliance, offered to help with the applications. Isaac had sat next to Todd for most of the weekend. But she'd gotten bored with Todd. Or maybe he had just come too soon, she had been too young. You should have stayed with him just for Isaac, she thought. You're the only one in this family who isn't making any sacrifices. Simon, who had met Isaac that same weekend, had formed no real impression of him, and Isaac had formed no impression of Simon.

There had been a time once, through most of high school, when it had seemed to her that if she closed her eyes and thought about it long enough, she could see exactly where Isaac was. Because you knew his routine, she thought. There was no magic in it. She continued to drive along the high road that followed the river.

Alright, she thought. She pulled over at the place by the river and turned off the car and looked out over the grass and the gorge rising steeply out of the water and the way the river bent quickly out of sight, unknowable. She put her head on the steering wheel and closed her eyes and thought about her brother.

9. Isaac

From the dark woods, through the screen of leaves, he could see two people standing at the edge of the Wal-Mart parking lot, where it was well lit. They were young men, around his age, wearing their blue vests. Happy for the diversion—chase the shoplifter. Tell all their friends they nearly caught you. But following you into the dark . . .

He turned and continued farther into the woods, reaching a stream after a few hundred yards, the water shining in the faint moonlight that came through the canopy. Old tires and mattresses, beer bottles. No one coming down here after you. There's a path on the other side.

He wasn't sure of the direction but he followed the flowing water. That was easy, he thought. You knew you needed that coat, didn't have to think about it. Allow things to happen and they work out fine. Overthink, get self-conscious, that's when your mistakes happen. Staying in that old factory when the Swede showed up, then going back to move the body. Deciding to sleep in that clearing near a person you didn't trust. Letting go of your knife while he robs you of everything, instead you grab his coat, then chase him down the street. What would you have done if you'd caught him—used your powers of rhetoric?

If Poe were here he wouldn't have let you do that, keep sleeping near the Baron. No, if Poe were here I wouldn't have even met the Baron. Except Poe is not here. You will probably never see him again. Think about that, Watson—all those people are gone to you. There was a hollow feeling that started in his stomach and quickly spread through the rest of his body. Keep walking, he thought. It'll pass.

A mile or so later it felt safe enough to stop. He'd crossed under several bridges, it was a different neighborhood, less trash along the stream. Time to get cleaned up. One last look around. See—you're alone. He stripped off his old clothes. There were lights from distant houses but it was very dark along the stream, comforting. Everything changing. Used to be afraid of the dark, now it makes you feel safe. Remember being a kid, sleeping out in the yard and leaving the tent fly open so you could see the house. Different story these days.

Alright, stop dawdling. Get that scraggle off your face. He set the stolen toiletries on a rock by the water and stripped down until he was just wearing his new pants, then splashed the streamwater on his face and hair, lathered and rinsed, rubbed the shaving gel onto his cheeks and neck and shaved by feel. Picked a cheap razor like you were paying for it. Make another pass to be sure. He relathered his face and shaved a second time. Dry off quick—tainted water, a trillion bacteria per gallon. Smells like fuel oil. *E. coli*. A new man, washed clean by filth. Where's your undershirt?

He dressed carefully, tucking his new clean shirt into his clean pants, pulling the fleece on top and then the jacket. All the energy bars had fallen out of his pockets, probably while he was running. Forgot to close the zippers, he thought. An entire day's worth of food. He shook his head. Doesn't matter. Focus on the good—clean hair, clean face, clean clothes. In a minute you'll be warm again.

Still following the stream, he passed behind a long apartment complex and under another busy roadway, then a second development, townhomes with backyards that came down to the water. Suburban dreamland, creek in your backyard. Meanwhile there's a dark side—a conduit for wanted men.

He stopped to look at the houses just up the hill, the people oblivious in their good lighting. Woodsmoke in the air, cozy fires. A teenager on her back porch talking on a cellphone; a dozen or so people in the house next door, some sort of party, all oblivious to Isaac walking through the darkness, fifty yards away.

Theoretical situation: let's say you had to choose between you and them—those people there, total strangers. Press the red button, drop a nuke. That's not a useful question, he thought. Okay so imagine *they* had to answer—if they had to choose between themselves and you? No mystery there, especially now. Strange body means nothing. Call the police, half minute of angst and back to your chardonnay. Worry more about your Labrador. Alright Watson, keep moving. No rest for the weary.

Up on someone's porch, a dog began to bark. Speaking of—thinks you'll steal his kibble. The people at the party looked through the window toward Isaac, but didn't see him. Meanwhile pooch knows you're here—the supposedly dumb animal.

He kept walking. Don't think about these people, your day has been bad enough. Spared the rod spoiled the Baron. Seemed like the only choice but maybe it was not—six dollars in your pocket and the police have seen your face. He felt a shiver go through him. Ended up in gunsights. Cop could have shot you dead. Would have been legal, a fleeing felon. His compassion made the trigger too heavy—you reminded him of his son. Only luck you've had in years.

Two days and you'll be out of food and money, presuming something doesn't happen before then. Can't beg on streetcorners—they know your description. Most likely they have your pack as well, your name. Not to mention any fallout from the Swede. Interstate warrant.

Keep on like this and they'll find your body in the bushes. To them just another mystery, to you *no please,* then a whispered *sorry kid,* feel your life fading out. Maybe not tomorrow but eventually. Don't pretend it's one way when it's another. You need to start doing things differently.

He kept walking, glanced around him in the darkness. No one is watching, just you. Might be too late anyway. You might have already traded yourself for the Baron.

∗   ∗   ∗

Much later the stream teed into a broad clearing for a powerline. It was clear and flat and with the starlight and faint moon he could see a long way in both directions, the land stretching out on either side of him.

Polaris behind you—going south. Sit a minute. He found a place in the tall grass and relaxed, looking into the distance, down the long swath cut for the powerlines. He closed his eyes and the afterimages quickly resolved into faces. He opened them again and looked around in the darkness. There was nothing. Big deal, he thought. He put his head on his bony knees. He could see men sitting around a fire. You're just tired, he thought. But the faces wouldn't go away, it was the Swede and the others and something else as well, a dim shape just outside the light. Then the Swede was standing there, fully lit in the glow from the stove, saying *he must have already took off.* Last words. Small choices—you came in a different door than you went out. *Knew* not to go back in the same way.

Only reason you and Poe are alive, that small choice. Your own body trying to keep you breathing—*go in the other door.* Hard-wiring. Old as gravity. Look what you did to the Swede: no premeditation, no knife, gun, or club. A found object. A natural part of you, the lower level. Built into every man woman child, you tell yourself you don't need it but look around you. Your friend over the stranger. Yourself over the friend. Highest stakes and you are still here and the other guy is not.

Then what is the point? He took a deep breath. Need to get moving again. He was exhausted, his legs had stiffened and cramped in the few minutes he'd been sitting, but he stood up and began to walk.

Here is the point: keep setting one foot in front of the other. Stay warm. What you did in that store you'll have to do again, maybe not tomorrow but the next day. Pretend you're different but you're not. Still have to eat.

You need to admit this. Stop walking. No, I would rather not. Put my faith in the kid, he'll figure something out.

He continued to push through the tall grass. Above him the sky was broad and dark and he could no longer see lights from any houses.

There is no kid, he thought. There is only you.

10. Grace

She'd barely slept and the light had been coming in the window awhile now, morning again, there was no point. She called in sick to work. She had to think. She found herself standing by Billy's door; the hole he'd punched and covered with masking tape, some tantrum or other, she didn't remember the reason, she pushed the door open and went into his room. There was a stillness, sunlight and old dustmotes. Feel of a tomb. She eased herself into his bed, the smell of him still strong, her boy and the man he'd become.

The childish feel of the place, old posters sagging, piles of things clumped together, clothes and shoes and hunting magazines, school papers he'd labored over, a curtain rod that had fallen down months ago but he hadn't bothered to put back up. She should eat but she wasn't hungry. She had done the best she could, it had not been enough. She would never know the reasons but she had not been good enough, she would never understand it. He had made her life simple, she saw now— how many times did you keep going *just for him*. A reason for living the same as a reason for dying. The heaviness she felt, she could not imagine herself getting up.

His hunting bow leaning in one corner, his rifle next to the bed, the only two things he religiously took care of, he always waxed the bowstring and oiled the rifle and kept them both on their respective mounts on the wall, wooden pegs he had made himself. She got up and lifted the Winchester, cocked the hammer, she didn't know if it was loaded or not. She didn't check the chamber, just held it in her hands and felt the weight. It was a game she could play, loaded or not. If it turned out to be loaded it would not be her fault.

After a time she put the gun down and her hands began to shake. She needed to leave the room, leave Billy's room, but she didn't want to. She sat back down on the bed.

She would have to get rid of the gun, give it to Harris. But maybe it was too late, the thought had entered her mind, a slow undermining, like water along a river, or the way an old mineshaft could suddenly collapse a house. It took the earth out from under you and then . . .

Except there was still Harris. She wouldn't be alone. But without Billy she wondered if she would get quieter and quieter, shrink until there was nothing, it had always been borrowed time, it was all built on hope. Underneath all the bullshit about choosing to be happy, there was hope. Meaning doubt. The heart doing its skip jump that everything was about to change.

It was faith she was talking about, always thinking better things were waiting when really it was a rat's nest, one of those knots you couldn't untie.

She stood up and opened Billy's closet, nothing was on shelves, it was all a tall pile that was barely held back by the closet door. It would all have to be thrown away, he was never coming back.

Except I didn't hurt anyone, she said out loud. Why should I be the one to pay for it. That was true—she hadn't hurt anyone. The work she did at the women's shelter—she had helped a lot of people. On Billy's dresser there were a few old beer bottles, she didn't know how long they'd been sitting there, she picked up one by the neck, hefted it, she wanted to throw it through the window, she wanted to scream and smash everything in the room. But there was no one there to see it, or hear her. If no one heard your sounds then you did not really make them.

I am a good person, she said out loud, I have always done the right thing. She was the kind of person who went out of her way for people. And Billy, it was self-defense, she could not stop thinking that. Self-defense, she had seen his neck. One of those people, probably the man who'd died, had been trying to cut her son's throat. It was self-defense but no one was saying that. He would go to prison, lose his life for nothing. And the ones who put him there . . .

Say it, she thought. Say what you're thinking. Say what you're meaning now. She went into the bathroom and looked at herself in the mirror, washed her hands and face. I am a good person but it is not fair what is happening to my son. And Harris can find that man. Good person or a good mother, there was not supposed to be a difference. But there was. It was not the same thing. Except it was. It was self-defense, it was this man, this homeless man, a *no one*, Harris said, or Billy. There was no question about it, it was not how you were supposed to think but there it was, it was the other man for Billy.

★   ★   ★

She took a long bath and used the sandalwood bubble soap she'd been saving for a year now, a present from the women at the shelter. What would they say? But they would all do the same thing, any mother would, there wasn't a choice about it. She called Harris and he promised to come over.

11. Harris

There was something wrong with Grace, she was sitting on the couch as if surprised to see him there, for a second he wondered if Virgil had come back but his truck wasn't outside. Then he thought no, she must be drunk.

"I didn't hear you come up," she said. She patted the couch next to her.

"Bad day?"

She nodded.

"Anything I can do?"

She shook her head. "I guess I just got to thinking it was a sign, Billy and all. Like I gave it my best and . . ." She shrugged.

"It's not a sign. It's still early."

"You don't have to lie about it anymore."

"He's a good boy," he said. "Things will start going better for him." He said it and it didn't even feel like a lie, Billy being a good kid, it was just something he wished were true.

"Thanks," she said.

"I mean it."

They kissed a little but there wasn't any heat in it. He had a moment of panic, he wanted to shake her, he had the feeling he was going to lose her again. They were both just sitting there on the couch staring at different things like an old couple.

"Let's go out somewhere," he said. "I'll take you to Speers Street."

"Nah," she said. She lifted her hand and brought it down hard on his, almost a slap. She squeezed it.

"There's still a lot that has to happen."

"I know what's going to happen to him, Bud."

He started to contradict her but there was no point, Billy was not going to be saved, in fact he was going to drag her under as well, he was going to drag all three of them under. There was a sudden rush of anger and he crossed his arms over his chest as if to squeeze it out of himself. The looks she used to give Billy, it had always made him jealous, he was embarrassed to admit it but it was true, he had been jealous of her son. A guilty thought came to him: it would have been better if the boy had died—she'd be able to move on, believe what she wanted. Now the boy both existed and didn't exist, he was there but being kept from her, she would never be able to stop thinking about him. The only torch she could carry.

She interrupted his thoughts: "You're lucky you're alone."

"Grace," he said. "Poor Grace."

"I'm serious, it's not worth it."

"Let's get out of here. We could go up to the city, even. We could go to Vincent's, we haven't been there in years."

She leaned over, hugging herself. "I just want my stomach to stop hurting."

"Have you eaten anything?"

"I can't."

"You need to."

She shook her head.

He rubbed her back, then ran his fingers up and down it, gentle, and closed his eyes and felt the fabric of her blouse.

"I know I'm lucky," she said. "I'm sorry I'm being so dramatic."

"No, come here," he said. She leaned into him, put her head on his shoulder, and he closed his eyes again.

"Maybe I need to make love," she said. "I think that's what I need."

They kissed some more and it was awkward and he half-wanted to stop but she wouldn't let him. It was a long time before they were both ready and then it took a long time to finish. He felt drained and she got up and she went to the bedroom and came back wearing a bathrobe; he sat awkwardly on the couch without his clothes. After a while he put his undershirt over his lap.

"Not to beat a dead horse," he said. "You should try to eat."

"I just want to lie down."

"Okay."

"I need to give you these things before I forget."

She got up again and came back with the lever-action rifle, he recognized the old .30-30 that was Billy's, and an old single-barrel shotgun.

"It's probably better if you take these."

He stood up naked and looked into her eyes but there was nothing in them. She handed the guns over impassively. He set them in the corner by the door.

*   *   *

After lying in the bed awhile they slept together again, not awkwardly but as if by routine, she was responding to his touch but it was not the same, she had retreated to some place the signals barely reached. When they were done they lay there holding hands. She would never get over this. He would have to make a decision.

Except it was already made. Possibly he'd made it when he'd first hidden Billy's jacket. He was not going to leave her like this. He smoothed the blankets on top of him, it seemed that if he pushed hard enough he could break through his own skin like a drum. He had done this to himself, let the dark times catch up. It was an old feeling. The last time it had come was on a hunting trip in Wyoming, lost and trapped two nights in a snowcave, out of food and the snow kept collapsing on him. He knew he would die, there was no question about it, he had earned it, gone out with weather coming in, known it might turn bad and walked out into it anyway, he had flown all the way out to Wyoming and had not wanted to waste his big trip.

It was no different than this. He'd walked into it. At dawn the third morning he'd left the cave and started to walk, set out postholing through the snow, too weak to carry his rifle or daypack, and ten hours later, in the last few minutes of daylight, he'd found a road. He had never told a soul what happened, not Grace, not Ho, not his doctor, he'd checked into a motel and caught his flight the next day. A piece of him had stayed out there. This will make sense also, he told himself. This is the only thing you can give her.

He started to pull the covers up but he made himself stand and walk around the room. Maybe he had always known it. He stood by the window and waited to see what he would say.

"Come back to bed." She patted the place next to her.

"I will." Out the window there was a faint light, a few stars, he was looking for something but he didn't know what.

"I'll be alright, it's just that it all hit me today. I promise I'll be better. Just come back a minute."

Later that night he opened his eyes and realized he hadn't really been sleeping. It would be no different than anything else he'd done before, getting rid of a bad element. A talking to. There wasn't any point in thinking about it. It had always been Billy over everyone else, there were people who lived for their children and she was one of them. She would be a different person otherwise. Plenty of other people didn't, it was good there were people like her in the world. It was lucky he knew one of those people.

"What did you say?" she whispered.

"I'll take care of Billy. I'll make sure nothing happens to him."

They looked at each other for a long time across the dark. She doesn't know, he thought. She doesn't know what this is going to mean.

"Just in case, it's better if you don't say a word about this to anyone. Not a word."

He could see that her eyes got wet but she wiped them and that was all.

"I'm a bad person," she said. "Aren't I?"

He reached and stroked the hair from her face. "You're his mother."

12. Isaac

He slept in the undergrowth at the edge of a field and was awakened by the sound of an approaching truck, its headlights bearing down on him. Get up, he thought, here they come. He tried to remember where he was, and where he was going to run, and the noise got louder and the headlights swept to a different part of the woods and Isaac jumped to his feet.

It was a green farm tractor. Isaac sat down again and the farmer shot past, not noticing him, a large John Deere planter trailing a plume of bright yellow seeds. Christ these early risers. His blood was rushing and part of him wished he was still asleep but he couldn't help grinning. The old man's driving that thing like a racecar. Except very straight rows. He stayed where he was and watched the farmer work and then watched the sun come up over the long flat field before collecting himself and slipping the back way out of the hedgerow. There was a road on the other side.

The land was very flat, mostly agricultural. A few scattered housing developments, but mostly broad rectangles of tilled soil, separated by narrow treelines or old fences. Everything in neat grids. Stick to the roads. Planting time, don't get caught trespassing. Course you might get a meal out of it. Or at least a drink of water out of someone's hose.

Around noon he came to a large river that stretched on forever in three directions, as far as he could see. Or it might be Lake Erie. That would be close to here. Wonder if it's safe, just to wet the mouth. No don't try it. End up even worse off. To his left there were houses along the water, a large gated community, to his right, farther away, was a small marina, just open land beyond it. He made his way toward the marina. As he approached he saw an overflowing trashcan by the gate.

Will you? But there was no question. He looked around for witnesses, then picked through the trash as quickly as possible. There was uneaten and unspoiled food, he could smell it intensely, more strongly even than the rot of the trashcan. No he thought I'm not there yet. He dug through paper bags of fast food, wine bottles, empty beer cans, water bottles. That one is heavy. Nearly full. Water or something else? Make sure it isn't someone's piss. He was up to his shoulders in the trashcan and he retrieved the bottle and held it up to the light. Clear and cold. Hope they didn't have anything. Better than lake water—share with one stranger instead of a few million. He drank half the bottle, which had a faint taste of cigarettes, then capped it and put it into his pocket. There you go. Feel better already. Hope no one saw.

He continued to walk, following the contour of the shoreline. There was a nuclear plant in the distance, the tall cooling towers by the lake. Where are you headed? I don't know. Just walking now. What is Poe doing? Probably not eating out of trashcans. Probably taking a nap. Drunk and asleep in his hammock. Except that is not the only possibility. There is still a dead body they found and his coat. He will not be able to get away from that.

When do I stop being the same person? In other people's minds or your own? Mine, he thought. I don't know. Something's wrong, you're getting farther from the lake—on some sort of tributary. Keep following this and it'll get you all turned around. Pick a direction and stick to it. Alright, west. But he knew that it didn't matter. There was nowhere he was going, and no one waiting for him, and it no longer mattered where he'd been.

★   ★   ★

A few hours later he passed under an interstate and the land became more open, woods and fields. He allowed himself one small swallow from the water bottle every so often. Sooner or later you'll come on something else. Bucket of fried chicken. Steak and eggs. The road dead-ended in a patch of woods so he went into the woods. Still going west. This makes no sense. It doesn't make sense to be here and it doesn't make sense to be on the road. Just keep walking.

It was alternately a forest, the edges wide enough so he could not see the end of the trees, and a narrower boundary between farmland. By late in the afternoon he was getting the sensation of being followed. Stupid to come here, you are not going to be able to find anything to eat. The ground was wet and riddled with deer tracks. His pulse was beginning to speed up. Paranoid is all. Ignore it or you'll go crazy. Mental health your only health. He continued to walk but the feeling didn't abate. When he got to a natural choke point in the trail he crouched down behind a rock outcropping and waited.

Three dogs soon appeared, strays, trotting quickly along the path, and then the lead dog stopped suddenly to sniff the air. The dogs were thin and filthy, missing patches of fur, mixtures of various farm dogs—border collies, shepherds, it was impossible to tell.

A shiver passed through him as he watched. A fourth dog soon caught up to the others, and as he got Isaac's scent he stiffened and turned toward the rocks where Isaac was hiding. Can they see you? Probably not. But that is not a friendly interest. He glanced around him and found several large rocks. You moved—now they see you. The lead dog started forward, hesitantly and slightly crouched, ears back, and Isaac stood up and hit it in the chest with a rock. He had not thrown the rock very hard and the dog only skittered slightly before resuming its approach. The second rock Isaac threw much harder, clipping the dog in the nose, and then hit it a third time as it bolted and ran. The other dogs looked unsure until the rocks began raining down on them as well. He continued to pelt them as they ran.

Was that cruel? Don't know. Get going, he thought. Cross that field and find a road. Sorry, pooches. Except they knew you had nothing to eat. They weren't coming looking for a handout—they were testing. Strays worse than coyotes—less fear of people. Reason farmers shoot them. Still.

Near sundown he stopped to rest under a wooden bridge. The sun was large in the sky and low over the fields and lines of trees. Pretty. He took a sip of water but the bottle was nearly empty and his stomach ached from hunger. If you had more water you'd be fine. Should have kept looking in that trashcan, found a second bottle. No you should have gone along that interstate. Need to stay near food and people. This was stupid.

I am trying to get away from people, he thought. He felt tears of frustration coming to his face. Need to get back to that interstate. Probably five or six miles. Get up. Soon as it's dark you won't be able to navigate. There's a state highway back there somewhere. That will intersect the interstate at some point.

By dark he'd reached the state highway, trekking across the fields. His feet felt heavy with mud, he'd been making slow progress. Far enough, he thought. This is far enough for today. If I see a stream I'll drink out of it. How long did I walk? Twenty miles? Your headache is dehydration. Won't kill you. Need a meal and a bed, another sip of water. Save the rest for later. An ounce or two left. Pines over there—should be soft underneath.

In the far distance he could hear dogs barking. Need a good stick. No, need a sleeping bag. Cold coming up through the ground. Let me sleep. When he closed his eyes he could see the figures standing around the fire but when he opened his eyes the figures were still there, up in the trees. The Swede smiling, his face lit orange from the fire and all the shadows behind him. Poe was standing next to the Swede. Tired people hallucinate, he thought. So do hungry people. Just let me sleep.

No, tomorrow you will have to do something. Steal again, probably. Fine. Nature of nature, take what it needs. Feed off others. Like old Otto—down for good, a dirt sack. Scarecrow bones. Wonder where he is now. Any family to claim him. Empty as any other dead thing only he's a man, name and a story, child of two others, a girl who loved him. Human nature to come in for the dead ones and the weak ones. Animal nature the opposite. Comes out when you're alone. Your higher values lose their color.

His mouth was dry. Get up you can find a faucet at one of those

barns, a garden hose or something. Do it now while it's dark. Think—if
your mother could see you. Stake through her broken heart. The family
disease, her quiet moments. Lee didn't catch it. Old man thinks you did,
but he doesn't know better. Wanted a different kind of family, himself at
the head of the table.

How long ago was that? A month. Feels like a year. That was when
you decided to leave, seems pointless now. Sitting with him out back,
wearing your coats and grilling, listening to the radio—spring training
highlights. Reds over the Pirates. *Zach Duke*, he said. *Get him up to the ma-
jors—that's the guy who's gonna bring us out of this slump.* What did you say
back to him? Can't remember. *You wonder what it'd be like to be someone like
that. A guy who's gonna matter, basically.* He looked at you. *You know what I
mean?* Then he goes on: *Course, for a person your size, you always had a hell
of an arm.*

Isaac looked up at the dark sky, then rolled onto his side and curled up
for warmth. Was that what started all this? Of course not—just another
on the pile. It could have been something else, anything—this whole
time you were staying to get his approval. Admit that. It was not out of
charity that you were staying. You were staying to get him to realize
things about you. Meanwhile you only made it worse. One day he thanks
you for dinner, the next he says how you've been living off his pension.
Testing you. Same as he did to Mom. Neither one of you ever pushed
back. She must have known she made a mistake. Wasn't sure how to get
out of it. Tried to bear up but couldn't. Finally made a choice.

She was not a saint herself. Decided her duty was done once Lee got
into Yale, same as him. Time to check out. Except you don't know that,
anything could have happened. No note, spur of the moment. You look
off a high bridge and get a strange feeling. You don't know what happened.

*   *   *

He woke up several times during the night, it was very cold and finally he
was so cold and stiff he couldn't fall back asleep. Start walking or you'll
freeze. He took another sip from the water bottle, stumbled to his feet
and dusted himself off, then began to walk again, half conscious, toward

the sound of the freeway, until the sun was up and he knew he didn't need to move any longer to stay warm.

An hour or it might have been three hours after reaching the interstate he found a McDonald's, where he got three egg sandwiches off the dollar menu and drank several cups of water for his headache before refilling his water bottle. People were alternately staring at him and trying to pretend he wasn't there. With tax he had two dollars and eighty cents left. The third egg sandwich he wrapped carefully in a white bag and put in his big coat pocket. He used the washroom to clean up. His clothes were getting wrinkled and filthy again, but nothing like before. He wondered if people were really watching him. Something about your face, he thought. Not just the bruises.

Walking again he stayed parallel to the highway, on the private property side of the fenceline so no cops would pull over. Need to find a train, he thought. Now I can think again. Get a train and get south so I don't freeze. Why, he thought. Where are you going? Someplace warm, I don't know.

I'm fine. Adjusting. Need to scrounge a little today. You mean like rob something? I don't know. Still feel hungry somehow. Need to ration, though. Two dollars and change left—have to eat tomorrow as well. And every day after. Save the other sandwich. I will eat half tonight, he thought.

He continued to parallel the interstate, making slow progress because of all the fences he needed to cross, all the brush, taking his time, staying out of sight. Then there was an open area ahead of him, a reststop with a bathroom and cars pulling in and out, he refilled his water bottle and drank for a long time from the fountain. He sat outside the main building, resting at one of the picnic tables. Soon enough a Camry pulled up directly in front of him and a man got out and jogged quickly toward the bathrooms. Isaac stood up and walked past the car, the man's wallet was sitting in front of the gearshift, the doors were plainly unlocked, it was fifty yards to the treeline.

He stood for a half minute with his back to the car, then walked away from it, continued walking, out of the reststop. That was stupid, he thought. You won't have that luxury again. No, I am not going to do that to someone. Yes you will. That or you will starve. I don't have to eat to-day, he thought. I still have money.

*   *   *

Even as the sun went down he could feel the temperature dropping quickly so he spent an hour collecting brush, laying piles of branches against a downed log, leaving a small space underneath, then piling old leaves and pine branches and anything else he could to add on top until the pile was several feet high. There was barely enough space to wriggle in. Tight but very warm. Blanket of leaves. Badge of honor.

He must have fallen asleep because he woke up in the pitch black with a sense that he'd been buried alive and started to knock apart the shelter before he looked out the end of it and remembered where he was. There was moonlight on the leaves and an animal moving outside, long legs, a deer. *Step step step. Step.* It jumped when it got his scent, cracking branches as it fled. He closed his eyes again. His mother was walking in the sunlight down the driveway, the light on her dark hair, by then streaked with gray, her head was up and she was smiling about something. Then he could no longer see her face. They were with his father in the hospital, *climb on up,* he said, and Isaac was boosted up onto the bed, his father's face was swollen from burns, nearly hairless, and he stroked Isaac's head. *My young man,* he said. *How's my son?* Looked nothing like your father. Not even the eyes. Hospital mix-up. Hamlet story, replaced by another man. Beginning of the end, that was then. When he got laid off it was one thing and when that happened it was another. Wore everyone down—you're the only one who stayed. Remember wishing Mom would have an affair, leave him. But of course you couldn't leave him yourself.

Your one time visiting Lee, she was so happy to see you, she could not stop kissing you. God it is so good to see you. Quit it or they'll think it's incest, you told her. She shrugged and mouthed the banjo sound from *Deliverance.* You're going to be here soon. The tall stone towers, the buildings like castles. Don't worry about Dad, she said.

Expected everyone to be superior but they didn't act it. It's beautiful where you come from, isn't it? *I guess. Not like here, though.* People thought that was funny: you mean not like New Haven? No, he's right. It is beautiful here, we all take it for granted. That was the physics major, boyfriend of the moment.

I am burying these things, he thought. I am never going to think about them again.

*   *   *

In the morning he kicked the shelter apart and dug a hole for his scat and kicked dirt over it when he was finished. Erase your traces. Still have that last sandwich. He walked a little until he could see the interstate and the cars rushing on it and the sun was on him. Then he ate his last bit of food and drank the rest of his water.

He continued the same way along the interstate. No idea where you are. Up in Michigan. What would Poe do if he were here? No idea. Make a bow and arrow or something. Don't need it. Wonder what's happened with Otto the Swede. Can't guess. No point. Sooner or later I'll cross some tracks. Need to get some money first or something to eat. Find a reststop and wait long enough, something will turn up. Except I don't want to do that. As you prefer. Starve then. There's an overpass, take a survey.

From the overpass he could see far down the highway, how flat the land was, the cars and trucks rushing underneath, the noise deafening. The sun bright you tore your new pants. Wonder when. Thorns and all that barbed wire fencing. Lucky you don't have lockjaw. Don't lean too far over that rail now. Feel the air pushing up at you. You could float, just for a second. Kinetic energy of a Mack truck: one-half mass velocity squared. Eighty thousand pounds times eighty miles per hour square it over two. Except you need feet per second. Alright a hundred fifteen, then. Five hundred twenty-nine million foot-pounds. Your weight, one hundred ten pounds. Would not slow the truck. No, technically I would. Just not enough to notice.

Get off the bridge she would have done it no matter what she wasn't a tough person. If she had married someone different, though. Then you would not exist. You existing means on one specific second they did that and it was you. You existing means she married him. You existing means she did that. Two weeks missing you all knew what she'd done none of you would admit it. Hoping she left the family, started a new life, knew the alternative. Burying her he refused to leave, wouldn't move his chair from next to the hole. You and Lee had to push him. Telling people at the funeral, all his friends, anyone who would listen he told them she'd been murdered. Except people knew. They always know after someone does something—put two and two together. You blamed him and you didn't. He blamed himself, though. If there's one thing you can be sure of it's that. Meanwhile he kept testing you—*will you leave me, too?*

Now he is alone, knowing what he did to her, that you don't forgive him. Alone, his daughter forgave him so she could leave. No I forgive him for that it's the act he puts on. Because he has to. What his insides must look like. Same as what you did to the Swede, part of you will die so as not to understand it. Cold white hollow at your center. Kept warm by others or it leaks out into the world. What makes a man: love honor morals. Someone to protect. Man alone the rational animal. A man alone is a rational animal. Strip away what's decent. Hang on to your knife. Keep on until you're stopped.

You keep going like this or you can lean here, lean a little farther, hurt for a half second and then nothing. I am not afraid of that, he thought. It is the unfinished business. Leaving plenty of it. It is only Poe. *Only Poe* that is not what you thought when he pulled you out of the water.

I am lucky he thought I am lucky they cannot see me like this. Walk then. Start walking. Alright. I will get off this bridge. I will get off this bridge I will choose something.

Book
Five

1. Poe

On his third day in the hole, the same short pudgy guard came back again and rapped on the bars and told him to cuff up.

"I ain't gonna talk to him," said Poe. "Today or ever."

"You got to sign your papers. Until you sign your papers, you don't even got a fuckin lawyer."

"I ain't signing nothing."

"Christ," said the guard. "And I wondered why you were in here."

The guard stood waiting, just in case. Poe decided he would ask the question. He would let himself ask it. Finally he said, "Can he come down here?"

"Fuck no your lawyer can't come down to no fuckin SHU. They got a fuckin room upstairs all laid out for it."

"Well I ain't moving. He can come and see me."

"You are one stupid-ass convict, you know that."

"I ain't convicted yet."

"Well something tells me you will be."

"Tell him to mail me those papers."

"Suit yourself," said the guard. "But anyway, it's a woman, you should probably know that about your own goddamn lawyer. She's not bad-looking, either."

"How long am I gonna be down here, anyway?"

"Not too long," said the guard. "Not too long."

He listened to the man's shuffling footsteps disappear. The other in-mates on the block called out to him but the guard passed them by as if both deaf and blind. Poe decided he had not done badly. He had not caved in, his second chance he had not taken it. But he didn't know the third time, he was not sure he could say no again. He sat back in his bunk. He could hear one of the J-8s, the loonytoons, shouting for help that would never come, he had been shouting for two days straight.

There was no good answer. It was him or Isaac. There was no way they could both come out of it. The day they took him out of isolation was the day Clovis and the others would be waiting for him. One way or the other he was spilling his guts—shank or lawyer it was his decision. As soon as the lawyer knew who really killed old Otto, from there it would go to the DA and then it would be Isaac in these shoes and not him. But maybe Isaac would have some way of coping with it better than he himself did. It was a distinct possibility. Though smaller, he might be better equipped. Mentally stronger. You're just scared, he thought. If you stay scared you know what you'll pick.

He closed his eyes and ate the last section of orange he'd saved from breakfast, the eating would distract him. He lay and chewed and waited for the empty feeling to be interrupted, he was either empty or full, over-full, there was no in-between. The truth was people died every minute. Were dying. The only real miracle was the human perception that it would not be him. But it would be. It was the only certainty. It was back to the darkness, a cycle. It was back to the darkness, a cycle, a comfort. There was no point to the putting off. It was a spiral of shame, shame of being wrong, of being wrong that you were the source of all existence, when really, when you were born, you were the same as a name on a gravestone. A gravestone of the future. A born destiny. Only now his name would be put upon the list of men. There was a list kept some-where and his name would be recorded it was an honor.

Except it wasn't. It was only dying. It was dying and being afraid. No matter how many sums in your favor, hero or coward it did not matter, it would not change the truth of your own death.

He was a good person. His choices had done some good. If he had

gone away to Colgate, if he had not been living in Buell, he would not
have been home the day Isaac decided to walk out on the thin ice over
the Mon. That was the one brave thing he had done. Isaac had gone
maybe ten feet, it was obvious the ice wouldn't hold him, then he just
dropped through and Poe had run out after him and dropped through as
well, felt the ice give way and had his moment of panic and stayed on
course. He had saved Isaac English. It was the best thing he had done.
Isaac had not had it easy but he was a good man—rarity, that combination—you were not supposed to say it, it was not the American Way to
admit it, but generally the harder you had it the more of a piece of shit
you were. Except the rich were even worse, they didn't understand life,
the stories Lee told her rich friends looked at the world the same as a re-
tarded person, as a person with actual brain damage, that was how they
understood life, it was no wonder that the world was such a fucked-up
place. It was nearly all of them, it was all people, really, that were pieces
of shit. He himself was lucky that way, not rich and not poor. And Isaac,
when he'd changed his mind about taking his own life, he had come to
Poe. Poe had gotten him warmed up and then given him an ear and listened to him, they had sat there talking all night. If that wasn't a sign, he
didn't know. It showed you there was a reason for all of it, despite nearly
killing that boy from Donora, he had saved Isaac English. It was a sign
and fuck all the rest of them, Harris, the DA, and all the rest who were
coming after him that he hadn't even met yet, he wouldn't tell them a
fucking thing, this was the one thing in his life he was not going to
fuck up.

He was at the end of his rope it had not been a long one. He didn't
know what he expected. More warning, like a cancer, only there had
been warning, there had been many warnings, it was only that he had
not been capable of seeing them. And so here he was, it was inevitable, it
could not have gone another way.

There was nothing in the hole he could use for a weapon and besides
they would search him anyway. He would figure something out when he
got back to the general population, find a piece of metal, sharpen his
toothbrush handle, make a razor out of a Coke can, it was better than
nothing. He would take as many of them with him as he could.

2. Lee

Sunday night and she was going slightly crazy, she'd already talked to Simon, she didn't think she could read a single word of another book, she needed to get out of the house. She searched her planner for phone numbers, found Joelle Caruso and Christy Hanam. She called them both and they agreed to meet at Joelle's uncle's bar.

The bar was busy for a Sunday, nearly all faces she knew from high school, or at least the older and younger siblings of people she'd known. She was struck by how big all the men were, more than weight-room big, it was steroid big, sitting in overlarge T-shirts with the sleeves cut off, their arms crossed, muscles on display. But what else was there to do? Many of the women, it seemed, were starting to soften, barely into their twenties, maybe they weren't welcome at the gym. Lee was glad she'd worn a sweatshirt and no makeup.

"Good to see you again, hon. I can't believe you're back so soon. That was Christmas, right?"

Lee looked at her. "I think it might have been last Christmas."

"God," Joelle said, "you serious?"

"I think," said Lee. She pretended to consider it. "Yeah, it was last Christmas, a year and a half ago."

"Well, I guess that tells you all you really need to know then, doesn't it." Joelle shook her head.

"You got married," said Christy, touching her ring.

Lee held it out. She was glad she hadn't worn the engagement ring.

"Congratulations, girl. A guy from school?"

"His name's Simon."

"Church wedding or one of those modern ones?"

"We didn't really have one," said Lee. "We went to the JP."

"Holy shit, she's having a kid."

"No. It was just a spur-of-the-moment thing."

"Listen to us," said Christy. "What a bunch of bitches."

"How are you guys, anyway?"

"Oh, fat, everyone's fat. The men lift weights, shoot steroids in their butts, we just get fat."

"They get fat too," said Christy.

There must have been some agreement in Lee's face, because Christy said:

"No, we're all doing pretty good. I got my own house now, I pay my own mortgage. We're not all doing bad."

"Christy wrangles retards for a living."

"Special ed," said Christy. "I teach speds." She shoved Joelle playfully. "You are such a little bitch."

"What do you do?"

Lee wondered why she hadn't come up with an answer to this question. "Well," she stammered, "I guess I've been applying to schools again, and I dunno, helping my mother-in-law with her business."

"So did he at least give you an engagement ring or anything? I don't see one."

"No, it didn't fit right." The truth being she'd been embarrassed to wear it.

"They're all the same, aren't they? You want another drink?"

Joelle could have gone behind the bar herself, but instead they all waited for her uncle to come over.

"This is a weird question," Lee said, "but you guys haven't seen or heard anything about my brother, have you?"

"I thought he was off in school."

"No," said Christy, "he's still here. You see him around sometimes."

"What's he doing, then?"

"Looking after our father," said Lee.

"That's weird. Even between the two of you, he always seemed to be the one who would get out of here."

Lee felt her ears getting warm.

"All I mean is, you always knew how to get along with people. He just seemed like the type that was so smart he didn't know how to talk. You could tell he probably belonged somewhere else."

"I dunno. There was my dad to look after, I guess."

"Your dad?" Joelle shook her head. "It ain't like there's a shortage of places for your dad around here, not with a steelworker's pension. I mean right now, just put your head out the door and look. They're building towers for old people all up and down this valley. Home health is about the only kind of job you can get now, teaching's out, home health is in. If Christy hadn't gotten that job with the kids, she'd be swapping out bedpans."

Christy nodded. "She's right, unfortunately."

"It was probably your mother," said Joelle. "A kid like that is going to be tight with his mother. Something like that happens, it's gonna hurt him pretty bad."

There was silence as they all looked into their drinks.

"On worse news that might cheer you up," said Christy, "you remember Billy Poe? From the football team, freshman when we were seniors?"

"Sure."

"Killed a bum in one of the old factories. Beat him to death."

"Why the hell would you even be in one of those places," said Joelle. "Nothing good could come of it."

"Everyone's got secrets."

"What does that mean?"

"Maybe he was gay or something. They meet up in strange places, it's not exactly like they could come in here and have a date or something."

"I can tell you for sure that he wasn't gay," said Joelle.

"You cannot."

"As a matter of fact, I can." She held her two fingers a good distance apart. "Course the asshole never called me once he got it."

Lee felt her face getting hot.

"Well, I'm sure now he'd be happy to have any of us. He isn't gonna see a woman for a long time."

"I feel sorry for him," said Joelle.

"Do you think he did it?" said Lee. She felt guilty for asking and had to look away, but neither of the two caught it.

"Who knows?"

"He did beat the absolute shit out of Rich Welker once, who entirely deserved it, but everyone noticed that it went on longer than it could have."

"And that kid he got arrested for last year."

"That one too," said Joelle.

Lee nodded and sipped her white wine, it was very sweet.

"So you ever think you'd move back here or anything?"

"I don't think so," Lee said. "Or not anytime soon."

"Thank God," said Joelle. "I'd never get laid if you did."

"You really are a whore," said Christy.

Lee smiled and raised her eyebrows.

"Nah, it's just a joke, it's nothing around here but the same old faces since the third grade. Do a boy once in school, know it's a mistake but five years later there's no one else and the bar is closing so you do it again. Ten years later you're married to him. Look at our mothers and it's even worse today. All the smart ones leave."

"You guys think you'd ever do that?" Lee immediately regretted asking it but both Joelle and Christy shrugged it off.

"Doubt it. I'll probably work here until I die." Joelle waved her hand around, encompassing the bar. "And she'll take care of the retards."

"From the fetal alcohol."

"We're practically a team."

They both laughed.

"But really, it's not bad. Your car breaks down along the road, you know you only gotta wait two minutes before someone you know comes by. There just isn't that far you can fall."

"You two ought to come visit me," said Lee. "We could go to New York."

"I'd like to do that," said Joelle.

"Please," said Christy.

"No," Joelle said. "I'm serious. Me and Jon-Jon went on that cruise to Jamaica, I'm not like you. I'm practically an adventurer."

3. Harris

He left Grace's house and made his way directly to the police station, thinking maybe this is what she wanted from you the whole time. Only if this went bad it would be both him and Billy Poe hanging around in that prison. He wondered if it was better for everyone to just let Billy stand trial—Murray Clark was a drunk, he was not going to come off well in front of a jury. Not to mention if anything happens to old Murray the DA will tear up the earth trying to figure it out.

Murray Clark had given two addresses in Brownsville—Harris had glanced at the papers in the Uniontown police station, then gone into the bathroom to write them down. At the time he didn't know why he'd done it, collecting information, the old instinct. I'm bored, he thought. His head felt numb, he tried to focus on his driving. He was justifying.

This will be the worst thing you have ever done, he thought. I am just going to talk to him, he repeated to himself. Back in ancient history, his marine days, there was the man he'd shot in Da Nang. If this was a sin, so was that. At least this would mean something. He had a feeling he had generally done right but there was a way in which that was not true at all. He had lied to put people in prison, he had lied many times in court. Never about what the person had done, he had never said the person had committed a crime they had not actually committed. He had lied only to justify his instincts, why he'd stopped a certain car, why he'd searched the car or decided to frisk someone. He'd lied to explain things he knew, but could not explain why he knew.

As for the man in Da Nang, there had been no point. Another rocket barrage and not quite sunup and Harris was eating Dexedrine, bored and high. He was a year out of high school, it was insane they'd even brought him over there. He was posted in one of the outer bunkers near the helipad. The man was carrying a package, possibly a satchel charge—Harris never found out, he watched him walk a small dyke that edged the perimeter, no one was supposed to be out there, the flat-baked clay no-man's-land on Harris's side and the fertile green rice paddy beyond. He waited to see if the man would go another direction but he didn't and at two hundred meters Harris had led his target slightly and pressed the trigger of the M60, held it down for a long second. Every fifth round was a tracer and Harris watched them meet the body and then continue across the brilliant green paddy. The sapper didn't fall, he stood still for a long time as if not willing to accept what was happening and Harris, confused, offended for some reason, he pulled the trigger and held it long after the man went down, he played the tracers above the area where the man had fallen, arcing them back and forth as if trying to erase the evidence. He used up a belt of ammunition and the floor of the bunker was covered with sooty brass cases.

Later they found the man next to the dyke, human only by the shredded remnants of clothing. It could have been the result of a farming accident. The package was gone. No one else thought about it twice—a dead Vietnamese was a dead VC—but Harris had the feeling that he was owed punishment, killing someone, it seemed he should not get off so easily. He was debriefed, explained what he'd done to a bored lieutenant who made a notation in the file. One confirmed kill. Five months later, May 1971, they handed over their post to the South Vietnamese and Harris was on his way home. All the dead men of the world—they had once been alive. That was what people forgot.

He pulled into the station and thought about Grace again. She had been sleeping when he left the house and he'd kissed her and she hadn't woken up and he knew then, knew because she was sleeping deeply, he knew that she didn't really understand what she wanted him to do.

It would not be hard, it would not take long to find Murray, Carzano wanted to keep his witness around so he was giving him a hundred dollars a week in state funds, calling it witness protection though there was no protection. It was just money that Murray Clark needed and he would stick around the area to keep collecting it unless someone, Harris, made it clear it wasn't safe for him. But he would have to really make an impression.

Murray Clark wasn't a bad type. It might not be hard to get him to run off. Or it might be. You're trading yourself for Billy Poe, thought Harris. I know that.

He parked his truck, nearly forgot to turn it off, he went inside the station then downstairs to the evidence room, he felt like he was running on autopilot, there were all the old boxes of crap stacked up from their move from the old station, there were boxes that dated back to the 1950s and no one would ever go through it, at the time he'd thought about destroying it all but now he knew why he hadn't. It took him several minutes of rummaging but he found a five-shot revolver someone had turned in years ago, the date on the tag was 1974. He looked at it. He thought about Grace. Then he thought: if you're just going to talk to him, why bring it . . .

He checked the timing and cylinder lockup and squeezed the trigger to make sure the firing pin fell all the way. Then he went back upstairs to his office. There was a box of .38 plus-P hollowpoints and he used a tissue to pick up the rounds and load them in the gun. Looking around the office he could feel his inertia starting to build, looking at the old paintings, it was only a year and a half to retirement. You aren't going to use this thing anyway. Just give him the Talk.

His jacket pocket was sagging with the weight of the small revolver but he knew he ought to bring backup. His duty Sig didn't seem right. He went back to the safe in his office and got his .45, a Gold Cup he'd bought himself when he got back from the marines, he tucked a spare magazine in his pocket and the gun in a rear waistband holster. A final thought occurred to him and he stripped down to his undershirt, put his ballistic vest on, and then got dressed again. You're scared, he thought. When was the last time you were this scared, you're dressing up for combat.

Haven't worn this thing in years. Where's your light. He took the small xenon flashlight from his duty belt and put that into his pocket as well. He could tell he was not thinking clearly. He was going to forget something. Usually, the mistake that killed people—soldiers, pilots, racecar drivers—was the second one. You lived through the first one and then realized it had happened and you were so distracted by it that you made another one. The second one got you. His father had been a Corsair pilot and told Harris that if you were in a dogfight and you screwed up you were supposed to peel off immediately and put some space around you, get your head clear before you got back into the fight. Which was this? He wasn't sure. Walking out he called to Ho:

"I might be taking the next day off. Call up Miller or Borkowski or whoever else you need if you don't hear from me by seven."

"Where you going?" said Ho.

"Fishing. You just hold the fort. Better call those two now, actually. Just tell one of them to be here when you get off."

He got into his old Silverado and drove home. While Fur was out running, Harris put a change of clothes and a pair of running shoes into a backpack, then refilled the dog's food and water, setting the entire bag of food on the floor where the dog could get to it, then a second large pot of cold water on the floor next to it. The dog came back in and immediately sensed something was wrong and Harris had to knee him firmly out of the way to get out of the house. He made his way down the rutted road, eyes focused straight ahead, he thought you better get food and coffee, might be out there all night and all day tomorrow maybe.

In Brownsville he parked at the top of the hill near the old stone houses and sat looking at his map book. He found the addresses and memorized them without making a note on the map and got breakfast and filled up both of the truck's fuel tanks in case he had to drive a long way. There were two houses Murray Clark had given as addresses, and Harris began driving toward the first one.

4. Isaac

After staring out over the rushing traffic for a long time, he finally left the overpass and made his way toward the on-ramp for southbound Interstate 75. He took off his coat and brushed the dirt off as best as possible and retucked and smoothed his collared shirt and ran his fingers through his hair to get the burrs and tangles out. Student on a nine-day bender, that's all you are. Pure coincidence he looks like a bum. What about the knife? Put the coat on over it.

A purple semi pulling a tanker was pulling out of the gas station and Isaac put out his thumb and stood waiting and the truck stopped. Isaac jogged over and climbed up onto the truck, pulling the heavy door open.

"Where you headed?"

"Pennsylvania, I think."

"You think?"

The truck driver was a short thin man in his late forties, clean-shaven. He winked at Isaac. "I can drop you at Interstate 70 if you pay for gas. There's probably shorter ways to get there, though."

"I don't have any money."

"I'm just kidding you," said the man. "The company pays gas and I'm going that way anyway."

The truck was big inside, dark and comfortable. Wizard of Oz, he thought, looks like a huge beast but inside it, perched way up high, this tiny man. They were high off the ground and moving fast. About eighty.

It took a minute before he could focus on the objects they passed, just watching them made his vertigo even worse. Someone made this, he thought. He looked over at the driver, sitting behind the wheel, listening to AM radio. Noises came occasionally from the CB. Mind can adjust to anything—voices coming out of a metal box. Two different metal boxes. Meanwhile you look over the road and the body knows it's going too fast. But it adjusts as well. He watched things appear and disappear, trucks, metal signs, houses, roads, and overpasses. Made all of it. Even the air, radio waves and satellites. Feels like that should all mean something. Doesn't—it's just what we do. What has it gotten us, our difference from animals. Better rifles and antibiotics—they come together. Smart bombs and cancer surgery. Don't get one without the other, even our own nature keeps itself in balance. Colonize Mars, it won't matter—babies and cheatin' hearts. Democracy and hemorrhoids. Preachers with syphilis. A kid jerking off in his moonsuit, thinking about his older sister. He began to giggle. The kid's on fire, he thought.

"You mind sharing," said the driver.

"Been by myself for a while," said Isaac. "Plus it's the first time I've been in a truck."

"Playin hooky or something? Or you in college—I can't tell, no offense."

"Neither. I ought to be in college, probably."

"You're kind of a sight. At first I thought you were one of those Christ lovers, going around converting people in truck stops and whatnot, and then I saw you closer and thought maybe you were one of those people, only you'd gone off the rails. Then I wasn't sure. That's probably why I stopped."

"Mystery of the day."

"Basically."

"Well, I appreciate it."

"Never know," said the man. "You might have been Christ himself and I would have been well rewarded."

"Might still be."

"Now you sound like a proper crazy hitchhiker."

"Busted," said Isaac.

The driver chuckled. "I'm just joking you. Actually, you mind listening to the radio at all? They're saying those nuts in Korea just built a rocket big enough to tie a nuke on."

"You mean North Korea?"

"But I can tell already you're not into that sort of thing."

"A little."

"Myself personally I think we ought to hit them right now, just flatten them. Next thing you know they'll have a nuke in Toledo."

"They probably think the same thing about us."

"Well," said the driver. He was quiet for a few seconds. "You give yourself twenty years and see if you don't start appreciating everything just a little bit more, you follow me? Maybe that's what I'm trying to describe here." He looked at Isaac. "You don't follow me."

"No, I do."

"Wait twenty years, you'll know then. Course you're young so I'm sure there's plenty I'm missing out on as well. I wasn't old enough in the sixties and now I'm missing all this. Sometimes you get it coming and going."

"I doubt you're missing much," said Isaac.

"Nah, I watch all the shows, I know. Only thing I feel bad for you is all the girls you can fantasize about, you've already seen them all naked. Britney Spears, Paris Hilton, all the rest, there's penetration shots of all of them. For me, Bambi Woods was big news. That was all you could hope for. But it was probably better like that."

"Maybe."

"Well, we sure got to the heavy stuff quick, didn't we." The driver winked at him again. "You mind holding on a second? You ought to listen to this guy who's coming on."

"Alright."

"You know him?"

Isaac could hear the voice chattering away. "I think my dad likes this guy."

"G. Gordon Liddy." He shrugged. "I don't always agree with him but he's interesting."

Isaac settled himself while the driver turned the radio up. Then suddenly he turned it down again.

"I realized my point," he said. "There's no mystery for your generation. But back to our programming." He turned up the radio again.

Isaac started to disagree but it was okay. The kid will be fine, he thought. Plenty of mysteries. The universe is fourteen billion years old but a hundred fifty billion light-years across. There's quantum mechanics versus relativity. The kid will have to make new rules—immune to the laws of man beast and fruit, he'll live the fourth way. His mind occupied by higher systems, he'll discover flight. The stratosphere. Cold up here, he'll think. Cold and blue. Nitrogen—makes skies blue and plants green. Building block. Who dreams of flying most—men in wheelchairs. The old men of the world, trapped in their humidity. As for the kid, he returns like Odysseus. A long exile. His only allegiance to the king of the cannibals.

"You alright over there?"

"Doing good," said Isaac.

"You know how to keep yourself amused, don't you?"

"Hope I'm not annoying you."

"No, I'm glad I stopped. I promised my little girl I'd be home so I've only slept about an hour since yesterday morning, and then when I pulled over to refuel I realized I better find someone to talk to or I'd end up asleep in a ditch. Anyway, there you were. So in a way, if you think about it, you're saving my life."

"That's the Jesus in me."

The driver nodded solemnly. "Yup," he said. "That's exactly what it is."

*   *   *

A few hours later he dropped Isaac off at an on-ramp in Dayton. As he got out the driver said, "You wouldn't spend it on drugs or anything would you, buddy?"

"I never have."

"Well, at least get yourself some dinner first." He gave Isaac five dollars.

Isaac walked a mile or so to a truck stop on I-70 and ordered a meatball sandwich. He sat at a table inside but it didn't feel right yet so he went back out again and ate on the curb. There was the hammering of diesel engines and the smell of it and trucks coming and going like a train station. He thought he might have to wait awhile but ten minutes later he was picked up by an eastbound rig with a load of tractor parts. This one asked where he had been and Isaac said Michigan and the driver said you gotta make it a little more interesting than that if you wanna ride free, so Isaac told him he'd been riding the trains and was now going home to his family. The driver was happy to be a part of it and they rode the rest of the way without speaking much.

After dark, the driver turned south on I-79, leaving Isaac a few miles past Little Washington. After walking east for a while, he climbed to the top of a hill and sat looking out over the dark highway, toward the Mon River. How far? Twenty miles, maybe. Probably hitch if you can make it to a gas station. He sat and thought about it. Nah. Go in the same way you came out.

What is Lee doing right now? Used to be you could know it. Still might be able to. The three months between when she got into Yale and Mom dying—think about that. Everything made complete sense. All of us going to the Carnegie Museum, dinosaur bones, looking up at the tyrannosaurus. Old man saying *I don't want to look at anything that can bite me in half. I'm happy they went extinct.* But even he couldn't help staring at it for a long time. *Imagine being the guy who found that thing,* he said. *I mean imagine being him before he'd told anyone else he'd found it.* Think about that, Watson. That was the old man.

He looked out over the hills. He couldn't see the river but of course it was there. If he walked it would probably take two days to get home. No, day and a half. That's okay, he thought. Familiar ground.

5. Poe

The next day instead of sliding his dinner under the cell door, they told him to cuff up.

"My lawyer here again?"

"Don't know what you're talking about," said the guard. "Put your hands through."

"I ain't going."

"If I don't see your hands outside these bars in ten seconds, I'm calling the SORT guys. I don't give a fuck what your problems are."

He was a different guard from the previous day. He was tall and thin with neat gray hair and thick glasses.

"Anyway," he said. "They're letting you back in GP."

"But what I did, it should be a few months."

"Given the victim, if you'd killed the little bastard the warden probably would have commuted your sentence."

Poe looked at him.

"Just kidding," said the guard. "There's no such thing."

"What if I stay here?"

"You can't. They've got mental cases stacked to the ceiling."

"Christ," said Poe.

"Get up now."

"I'm applying for protective custody."

"I hear you," said the guard, "but you need to talk to the people upstairs, I can't do it from down here."

They led him upstairs and back through the cellblock to a different cell on the tier. One of the younger members of the Brotherhood spotted him and took off walking in the other direction.

When the guard left him alone in the cell, Poe drew the privacy curtain and found his toothbrush and rubbed the plastic handle on the cement until it was a sharp point. He tested the bars and windows for any metal he could pry off, make a real weapon with, but there was nothing. He lay on his bunk with his head to the toilet and his feet to the bars. It was a solution, was what it was. It was the way out. Free ticket. He could get up now and make a run for the guard station, demand protective custody. But he would be right back where he was yesterday.

It was him or Isaac there was not a middle ground. He was breathing very quickly and sweating, his clothes were soaked, it felt like he'd taken a shower. Then there were loud footsteps down the tier, he could hear people walking everywhere. He had told the guard he wanted protective custody. That would be his compromise, he had told the guard, if the guard told someone else they would come for him and take him back to the hole, but if the guard didn't tell anyone they would not come. It was a fair chance either way.

He was still breathing but it was temporary, it always had been. Your life was on a fuse, it was set when you were born it was all people and all lives. It was inevitable, he had never thought about it that way, it was inevitable, that was the one thing you could be sure of there was no reason to be afraid of it, it was coming, a sure thing, it was cold in winter. Except he was still afraid. It was just fear. He would make it mean something, that was all he could do. He would save Isaac English. He hoped he would hold out. He would stop thinking about it.

He was hungry again, there was nothing to eat in his new cell, the third in four days. He wondered if they had really needed the space in the SHU or if the Brotherhood had worked something out, got him stuck back in the general population.

What would it have mattered, doing landfills or playing football. Just another guy doing those things. There was no one else who would do this, there was no one else who would give Isaac a helping hand in any way, not even his own family. Even Lee, in the end, she lived only for herself. It would need to happen soon, though. He would not keep a clear mind very long, he knew that about himself. He'd always been fucked he was born that way, it was time to give in to that reality. He would give all he had like the heroes of the past. The higher calling. He was saving Isaac English, that was why he had been put here, there was a design to it, his whole life had led to this moment, he would prove himself the equal. He would be the protector.

He was hungry, he should eat something. Then he heard keys jingling and footsteps, it was definitely a guard coming up the stairs and then onto the tier, they were coming to take him to protective custody, he would be saved. He listened to the jingling keys get closer and there was a feeling of relief. I will be saved. Then he had another feeling, a feeling of being sick, a feeling of change coming over him, a feeling of the rest of his life stretched long in front of him it was despair. He was going to lose—his own legs would betray him, they would not let him die so soon, whatever he thought it didn't matter, his own body would overpower him. He lay there.

But the guard didn't stop at his cell. He kept walking. Poe sat up. The guard walked right past, heading to some other cell, he dropped something off and then turned and went back down the tier and down the stairs, his footsteps disappearing. I am a coward, he thought.

Before he could think about it more he stood up and unlocked the door, he was going to get a quick dinner, that was all, get a quick dinner and save his strength, he was walking quickly down the tier and onto the main floor of the cellblock and then out into the main corridor, he could smell the messhall, he saw the door and walked right through it.

Everyone sitting at the AB tables looked up. Clovis was there with all the younger lieutenants, Dwayne was there, he looked down and he pretended he hadn't seen Poe but Clovis was already standing up, grinning like he'd been expecting him all along and Poe's legs started shaking, he hesitated, then turned around and walked out of the cafeteria. There were only the squares of the hallway tiles in front of him, he made his legs move, the wide empty corridor, he didn't know where he was going. His body felt very light, he thought he passed another inmate but he was no longer sure, he seemed to be moving in slow motion. He turned into his cellblock but then changed his mind, they would trap him there, he went back into the corridor, then turned down the hall toward the rec yard. It was very quiet. There were no other voices behind him. He reached the metal detectors and then the doors. There was no one at the guard station. He tried the doors and they were locked. He shook the doors but they didn't open, then he kicked them as hard as he could. There was no chance.

When he turned behind him it was Clovis and several of the younger men. Clovis was not wearing his hat, and Poe saw for the first time that he had thin red hair that he combed forward, Clovis was very bald.

One of the lieutenants had a knife with a long blade and a handle made of blue tape. Poe tried the doors to the yard again, hit them hard but they wouldn't open. Then he feinted and tried to break past the five men but one of them was too fast, he tackled Poe only Poe wouldn't go down, he was running and dragging the man holding on to him when the others caught up. They were punching him only it hurt much more and then everything was blurry, when he finally went over he saw that his own blood was already all over the floor.

Book
Six

1. Grace

She was sitting on the porch, staring out over the Valley and watching the light change, she could feel the sun burning her skin but didn't move out of the chair. She'd gone two days without eating now. Three times she'd decided to go inside and call Harris, to tell him not to do it, that she would rather face other consequences. Three times she had thought of Billy laid out on the mortuary table or in a drawer and how his face would look. She'd stayed in her chair. She could remember the first time he'd moved inside her, a schedule, every night around eleven. His kicking felt like a very strong heartbeat.

He hadn't wanted to come out. Nearly ten months she had carried him and after that she hadn't been able to get pregnant again. As if he had known he would be all she could handle, known he would need all her attention. Looking around now at the hills and soft pastures and clearness of sky it all seemed hostile and cold, an illusion, the land had always made her feel calm, seemed some inseparable part of her, but she saw now how unreal that feeling was. Those things never changed, they were not loving and suffering.

But she was not doing anything. She could not even be sure of what Bud Harris intended. No, she knew. That man, the former auto mechanic, had tried to kill her son once and now he was trying to do it again. But even that, she thought, that's only a lie you're telling yourself, the truth is you have no idea what that man did, or what your son did, but still you have to make this choice, innocent or guilty it has all stopped mattering. That seems like it can't be true, she thought.

But what she wanted was Bud Harris out there right now, going to kill that man. That was what she wanted. She wanted that man dead who she knew only because he had seen her son do something. Or was lying about her son doing something. She wanted that man dead so her son would live. That was the truth. Any mother would want this, she thought. Anyone in your shoes would want this same thing.

No, I didn't tell him anything, I did not actually come out and say that to Bud Harris. He will make his own decisions. Except it was a lie to think that. She didn't have to say anything. They had both known. They knew right now. If Bud Harris does something to that man it will be the same as if you did it yourself. You cannot put this off on someone else. There is evidence you are choosing to ignore—that man who went to the police when your son did not. But that evidence does not change the truth. What would Billy have to have done for you to not want this?

You're at the end, she said out loud. They'll all know. In the past week, Cultrap, the farmer at the other end of the road, had looked right at her as she drove by but hadn't waved, she had known Ed Cultrap twenty years. It was because of Billy killing that man. People forgave you your children but this was too much.

No, what had passed between her and Bud Harris was just as clear as if they'd spoken. And it would be just as clear to anyone else. They would run her out of town or worse, they had all known when Bud Harris got Billy out of his last scrape, that was supposed to be kept very quiet but, somehow, everyone had found out. Now, this—she could not even imagine. I don't care, she thought. As long as it's me and not him.

2. Isaac

It was long after dark and he'd walked all day from Little Washington to Speers, nearly twenty miles. From Speers it was only eight miles to Buell.

He stood on the I-70 bridge looking out over the Mon River for a few minutes before making his way down to the train tracks. He passed a group of teenagers sitting under the highway and one of them started to say something. But then Isaac must have given them a look because they all got quiet and when he was past them he realized they had seen his hunting knife.

When he was out of sight he undid the knife from his belt and tossed it into the river without ceremony. The kid renounces the old ways. If he doesn't choose it gets chosen for him. Look at him—walking—he decides to put one foot in front of the other; it happens. Think about that. The way Lee's cat used to knock pencils off your desk. Why? To remind itself that it could Because some part of it—oldest part—knew that one day it wouldn't be able to. Take a lesson, he thought. Wake up ignorant every morning. Remind yourself you're in the land of the living.

He continued heading south. The tracks passed through a wide meadow and the night was clear and black and the stars stretched down to the horizon. Billions of them out there, all around us, an ocean of them, you're right in the middle. There's your God—star particles. Come from and go back. Star becomes earth becomes man becomes God. Your mother becomes river becomes ocean. Becomes rain. You can forgive someone who is dead. He had a sense of something draining out of him, down his head and neck and the rest of his body, like stepping out of a skin.

South of Naomi he decided to stop for the night. A few miles left for morning. He went to a flat place by the river and sat to think. Can't go home—they'll just talk you out of it. As you would do for them. Better to wait.

The old man, he tried. He did try. You can say that for him. Tomorrow you will go and tell Harris what you did. That is the right thing.

As he sat there on the ground he could feel the stiffness easing out of him, as if his bruises were healing. The Swede might have sat in this same camp two weeks ago. Old fire rings. Nice to have one now. No matches, though. He looked out at the river, flowing slowly through the trees. Bedtime, he thought. Your last night of freedom, sleep it off.

3. Henry English

They drove to Pittsburgh to talk to the lawyer that day, a big firm at the top of the old Koppers Building near Grant Street. He could tell as Lee wheeled him into the elevator that it was going to be expensive. He couldn't stand the thought of her new husband helping the family with money, but no other arrangement was possible.

The lawyer had a corner office, he was a man nearly Henry's age but tall, thin, and fit with a full head of gray hair, the type that probably played tennis. Most women after a certain age would have found him attractive. Henry took an immediate dislike to him but when he glanced at Lee he could tell she felt comfortable. These were her people now. It gave Henry a sick, jittery feeling, or maybe it was just being in this office, or maybe it was knowing why they were here, or maybe it was all three. He shifted himself in his wheelchair.

"Are you comfortable enough, Mr. English?"

"I'm fine. Used to this by now."

They sat and the man went over the fees and rates and a client's bill of rights, the most important feature of which seemed to be that they could expect their phone calls to be returned promptly. Lee nodded and took out the checkbook. Henry saw her name was on the top along with Simon's. Only it was still Henry's last name. That was a comfort, anyway. All these things he'd never asked her about.

Peter Brown, the lawyer, quizzed them amicably about Isaac's background, where they lived, what Henry had done, even how his accident had occurred. He asked about Isaac's mother and Henry would have protested but Lee told the man everything. She told him too much. Then Lee told the man what Billy Poe said about Isaac having killed the man in the factory. Peter Brown set down his pen for a moment and brought out a small digital recorder from his desk.

"Maybe we shouldn't make a tape of this," said Henry.

"Those are good instincts, Mr. English, but this is for our purposes and not the state's. They'd have to break in here and steal it from us." The man had a quiet voice and you had to sit still to listen to him. Henry looked at Lee again.

"Do you remember exactly what he said?" asked Peter Brown.

"I can try," said Lee.

"My son didn't kill that man. There's no point in making a tape recording."

"Dad."

"Your son was there when this man died. If we don't face up to this now, they'll make us face up to it in court. That's the only reason we're doing it."

"Except that Billy Poe hasn't said a word about this. If he had, they would have already charged my son."

"Billy Poe hasn't even seen his lawyer yet and once he does, things will start changing pretty quickly. The fact that Isaac hasn't been charged yet is more a technicality than anything else." He looked down at his notepad. "I'm sorry," he said.

* * *

It was ten o'clock and Henry was sitting in his bedroom in the wheelchair, looking at his desk, going through his papers. He heard the shower running upstairs for a long time and then Lee knocked on the door and asked if he needed help getting in bed but he said no. She waited for a minute outside the door.

"Anything else?"

"No. Get some sleep."

He heard her moving around the house and then she went upstairs and settled into her room and then it was quiet except for the creaking of the house, cooling. He dozed off in his chair, he dreamed he was still working at Penn Steel, he looked forward to waking up, he was tired at the end of the days and dirty and happy to be home to his wife but in the mornings he was always ready to go to work. Something creaked and he woke up hungry for air.

He was still in his bedroom. With effort he took deep breaths, sometimes when he slept he didn't get enough oxygen. How small your life feels—that was what you couldn't explain to people. If I could have known how it would turn out I would have known what to do. Slow slip down.

Mary had left him alone, he knew that, she had given up. It shouldn't have been her to do that, it made no sense. If they had talked about it they could have come to an arrangement that made sense, she could have taken the kids and gone somewhere else, but she had gone and done it without telling him a thing. His arms were trembling, how many times had he wanted to do that, he should have, but she had gone first. She was weak, that was the truth of her, the truth of all women, it was why he'd laid his bets on Lee. He had to get her out, he couldn't have her ending up like her mother.

Maybe you were the one who was weak, he thought. Maybe her doing that makes her stronger. You know the reason she went to the river and you know the reason your son ended up like this. Still, he didn't see what he could have done. The three years he'd commuted from Indiana, home once a month, that had not been easy for them but it had not been easy for him, either, living in boardinghouses and month-to-month hotels. But Steelcor paid plenty well. They just worked you hard and it was not safe. You looked at the stats, they had more accidents. But you didn't have to look at the stats. They were there to make money. They were trying to squeeze every dollar out of that mill before they'd ironed all the kinks out. What would you give to have called in sick that day.

At first he hadn't minded being nonunion, like Reagan said, the labor costs were out of control, it was a problem with the unions, you voted for him. Except it was not just that. Penn Steel hadn't spent a dime in their factories in fifteen years, most of the other big American mills were the same, the places were all falling apart, plenty of them were single-process right up to the day they closed, whereas the Germans and Japs had all been running basic oxygen since the sixties. That was what you didn't hear till later: they—the Japs and Germans—were always sinking money into their plants. They were always investing in new infrastructure, they were always investing in themselves. Meanwhile Penn Steel never invested a dime in its mills, guaranteed its own downfall. And all those welfare states, Germany and Sweden, they still made plenty of steel. Meanwhile they were the ones supposed to go bankrupt. He looked at his desk and couldn't remember what he was supposed to be doing. He drifted off again.

★   ★   ★

They'd tapped the furnace and filled the crucible and the crane was bringing it over, getting ready to make the pour. Then there was a different sound, he'd heard it over all the other noise. Crane keeps swinging but the ladle gives a little wobble and then it's headed for the ground, fifty tons of liquid steel. See the ladle hit the floor and boom, all that steel comes blooming into the air, blinding light, like the sun rising up out of the crucible, everything else was shadows, Chuck Cunningham and Wayne Davis they were shadows, the steel washed over them like lava from a volcano. Missing you by ten feet. Should not have been able to see that and survive, felt like the last thing you would see. Hiding there waiting to die. Felt the building shake as the back end of the shop blew out. Felt how small you were. Didn't seem fair. Didn't think of Mary, only thought it is not fair this is happening.

Supposed to be a safety brake on the hoisting drum. Company too cheap. Something sheared in the gearbox.

Tower was burning and the whole place was on fire and you decided to jump. Three stories. Scrap metal flying through the air, a five-hundred-pound toolbox goes by your head and hits the shop roof. Things kept exploding, the sound like a dragster running nitrous, too loud to even hear, you just felt it, felt your skin start burning under the silver suit, can't see anything, there's nothing but fire and shadows. Dead anyway—fuck it, take a leap. Come to and that black boy is dragging you out—

came back through the fire for you. Air full of burning steel and he doesn't get a scratch. Ought to play the lottery. Says he saw you jump.

OSHA fines the company thirty grand. Same amount the company makes every minute.

That was it. Chucky Cunningham gone, Wayne Davis, fat old Wayne, Wayne, you always told him, you're too fat Wayne, hot load washed right over them, you'd been standing there a minute before. Took the jump and that was your mistake. Should have stood your ground, family would have been taken care of, nice payout from the pension and the company. First you felt sorry for Wayne and Chuck but they saved themselves and their families and you did not.

The house had been silent a long time. He thought the longer you wait the more scared you'll be. The boy had done it and it wasn't Billy Poe, all of that is on you. He wheeled his chair back and forth. Regardless of what the boy had done, he himself was the one who'd caused it, the boy was never supposed to stay here. They all want you dead anyway, he thought, your own family. You never should have waited this long. Afraid of your own children. Afraid they would leave you alone, you wouldn't be able to stand it. To lose Mary and Lee in the same year. You were not going to lose Isaac as well.

He rolled to the drawer and opened it and there was his pistol but if Lee were to find him . . . there was a half bottle of Dewar's he hadn't touched since they told him not to. There you go, he thought. Look after yourself like a prize racehorse but don't give a second to anyone else. He began to feel calm. He knew what he had to do. He wished he'd eaten more of that steak. In the medicine cabinet he found an old bottle of OxyContin, nearly full, he'd been off it a year, he wrapped a blanket around himself and rolled quietly out into the living room and then out the back door to the porch. He closed the door carefully behind him.

It was cold outside and to brace himself he took a big pull off the Dewar's. Then he jiggered open the pill container and took two or three of them, chewed them, they tasted awful but it would make them hit faster. His hands were shaking and he put the top back on so as not to spill the rest. Look at you, he thought, everything has been trying to take this from you and now you're just going to give it away. Because I should have before, he thought. Isaac would not have been here, he would have been gone just like Lee.

He decided to roll all the way into the backyard, get to the right spot and then he would think about it some more. He eased himself down the ramp into the grass, felt the wheels sinking into the soft earth and he rolled himself quickly to get to where he wanted to be, scattering the deer that had been standing there.

He took the pill bottle and weighed it in his hand, he was beginning to change his mind again, right there it was all you needed, go out with a smile on your face. There's your choice, he thought. One way or the other you will lose them. It seemed so obvious, he had never thought of it that way before. He had been fighting a battle that he would never win. Dragging them all down with you.

He held the bottle in his hand. No, it would just be from shame. That would not be the right way. They would go down much too easy. You can bear the burden yourself for once, that is not too much to ask, bear your own burden. Well? He put the container back into his pocket. How many did I take? Three I think. Not enough to kill me. Except any minute now you'll be feeling pretty good. Wrap that blanket around you so you don't freeze.

He looked out over the dark woods and the river in the distance, it was a good spot he had chosen, you could see all the way down the Valley. Many good years, more than anyone deserved, it was time to do what was best for the others. For his family. As he thought this the land seemed to fall away, he was on a high ledge, there was a wall of stars and sky in front of him. He had never seen anything like it. The air was so clear. With his last bit of energy, before he fell asleep, he pulled the blanket around his shoulders and began to feel warm.

4. Harris

He parked his truck around the corner from the first address. The grass in the small front yard was cut but in the rear of the house the lot was badly overgrown. A large willow tree hung over the yard and there was the shell of an ancient Oldsmobile and a wheelless farm tractor, strangely out of place in the small backyard. A refrigerator sat on the back porch, humming noisily, and the roof of the porch sagged so low it nearly blocked the door to the house. Harris discerned only one person inside and he stayed in the shadows and made his way through the waist-high brush trying to avoid debris that was hidden in the grass. He went through the back door. In the living room an old woman was lying on a narrow bed with an oxygen tank stood up next to her. He put his gun away.

"Where's Murray," he said to her.

"He ain't here," she said. "He don't have any money, neither."

They looked at each other.

"Been laid off three years," she said. "You ain't gonna get nothing from him."

*   *   *

Several hours after dark he was in a different neighborhood, sitting on an empty bucket in an abandoned house. As far as he could tell, the houses on this end of the street were all empty—the grass was tall in all the yards, except for a clear path beaten through that led from the street to the porch of the house he had his eye on. At the far end of the block there were two houses with their porch lights on, but aside from that there was no sign of habitation. At midnight a few deer strolled down the street, it was strange to see them walking on pavement, browsing on bushes, then they filed between the house he was sitting in and the house he was watching. They didn't spook or notice his presence and he took it for a good omen.

He was wearing gloves and a watch cap but he was beginning to get cold and hungry. Around three A.M., a pair of men went into the house he'd been watching and he was pretty sure one of them was Murray. The electricity must have been off because they were lighting candles and building up a fire in a fireplace. Shortly after that, one of the men went into another room and lay down. It wasn't the best situation, two men being there, he wondered if he should wait until he could get Murray alone but there was no telling what would happen, Murray Clark might up and disappear at any minute, come back for the trial.

He watched for another half hour and decided the second man was asleep.

He opened and closed the revolver's cylinder and checked his .45 to make sure there was a round chambered, there was a faint glow from the night sights. At least you can see your sights, he thought, it was comforting, he was happy he'd gotten those sights installed, it was Ho who'd made him do it, *gun's no good if you can't see your sights,* those were not things Harris worried about. It had always seemed like bad luck to think about those things too much, about the particulars of your weapons, it was like looking for an excuse to use the weapon. The best way into this house was from the back, past the bedroom where the second man was sleeping now.

The steps creaked slightly but he froze for a long time and didn't hear anything. He opened the back door very slowly and made his way inside, through a kitchen, there was junk and boxes piled everywhere, construction debris, a long hallway to the front room. As he made his way down the hallway, someone said, "That you, Jesús?"

He took a few quick steps and he was into the living room holding on to the gun in his coat pocket, there were two old couches and candles stuck in beer bottles.

There was a man in his forties sitting on the sofa. There were circles under his eyes and he hadn't shaved in a long time.

"Murray," said Harris.

"You look familiar," said Murray. He peered at Harris's face under the watch cap. "Chief Harris?"

Harris took the revolver from his pocket and pointed it at Murray. Murray put his hands up.

"Whoa," he said. "You got the wrong guy, Chief."

"You need to leave this valley," Harris heard himself say. He had a distant awareness that his finger had come to rest on the trigger.

"Sure," said Murray. "Anything you say."

"If anyone tells me they even saw you in this state they're gonna find you in the river. I find out you've been talking to that DA in Uniontown anymore, same thing."

"I'm gone," said Murray, but then he made a strange gesture and Harris felt someone behind him and he knew it was either turn around or pull the trigger. He pulled the trigger. The gun went off and Murray knuckled over on the couch. Someone tackled Harris from behind, sending them both crashing into the wall. He tried to roll the man off but he was pinned on his stomach with the man on top of him, there was a peculiar feeling, he was being punched in the ribs but it hurt more; the man was stabbing him but having a hard time getting through his vest. Then he dropped his knife and went for Harris's gun. Both of his hands were pinning the revolver to the floor and working it out of Harris's right hand. Harris's other gun was in his rear waistband and he was arching his back trying to get at it left-handed, the grip was facing the wrong way, the man broke something in Harris's hand, Harris heard the noise but barely noticed, he was focusing on getting each finger of his left hand closed around the grip of his automatic, the man got control of the revolver just as Harris got the .45 free and cleared the safety with his index finger and crammed the muzzle into the tangle of hair behind the man's ear. He was faintly aware of the gun going off, saw the shell casing bounce off the wall next to him. Murray stumbled past and Harris shot him through the pelvis; Murray made it through the door and was gone.

The room was dark with only the flickering light from the candle; he rolled out from under the dead man and ran out onto the porch after Murray, half deaf; the .45 had gone off right next to his head. He couldn't hear his own footsteps, it felt like his ears were clogged.

The street was pitch black and his heart sank—there was nothing. He raised the gun in his left hand and scanned closely, fumbling in his pocket for the flashlight, looking for anything moving, there—something there in the brush at twenty or twenty-five yards, he got his light out and worked it with his mostly broken hand and saw Murray, crouched over and limping through the undergrowth; when the light hit him he froze. Harris made a small adjustment to his sights and shot him between the shoulderblades. Then he fired a second careful shot.

When Harris caught up to him Murray was on his hands and knees, as if praying to someone Harris couldn't see. He seemed to have no idea he wasn't alone and after a few seconds he sank slowly into the tall grass, not moving again. Harris's hands were shaking; he tried to reholster his gun, but couldn't.

He stayed in the shadows on the way back to his truck, a two-block walk. He couldn't get his head clear, all he could think was Keep Moving. *Should have gotten their wallets, make this look like something else.* Too late. His right hand was broken and throbbing. There was one shell casing in the house or maybe it was two and then a few more on the porch—he couldn't remember how many shots he'd fired. It was too dark to find the shell casings. The revolver was still in there as well—had his gloves come off? No. Is your hat still on? He checked. Yes.

Before getting into his truck he shucked off his hat, coat, and gloves because of the blood and powder residue, threw them in the bed of the pickup, and pulled out as quietly as he could, driving without headlights until he reached the main road. As he drove he tried to inspect himself but his hands were shaking badly, under his vest he could feel blood trickling down his side but he didn't want to stop to see how bad it was. He was still breathing easily so it couldn't be all that bad, the Kevlar had done its job. Two miles away and counting. He watched the odometer. Three miles.

Shortly after that he killed the lights and stopped at a turnaround next to the river to throw the .45 far out into the water. He pulled out and was driving down the road again when he realized he'd forgotten to get rid of the coat and hat in the back of the truck. Everything else, too, he thought. He stopped at the next pullout and changed into his spare clothes and running shoes and threw everything he'd been wearing, including the Kevlar, into the river.

He got to the office as the sun was coming up. He wondered who would take care of his dog.

5. Poe

The rushing came back to his head, so loud he couldn't stand it but he couldn't make it stop and there was a feeling of motion, I am in the river, he thought, I am going over the falls. Ninety over sixty, he heard. The feeling didn't so much stop as slowly fade and he could see again and it was bright. I fell. I am in the dirt by the house under the tree. The light was very bright. They were trying to cram something in his mouth, they were choking him, he was going to throw up. He's back, someone said. Get the tube out. Mr. Poe stay with us. There were ceiling tiles and bright lights. The rushing was back in his ears and he was seeing things, he was moving again, the falling feeling in his stomach, he was going over, he wanted to get away from the sounds. Stay with us Mr. Poe. They are touching me, he thought. He reached a hand down to cover his nakedness, they had taken his clothes. Squeeze my hand William. William can you hear me?

He tried to sit up, there wasn't enough air.

"No no no," they all said. There were strong hands holding him.

"Mr. Poe do you know where you are?"

He did remember but it seemed like if he didn't answer them he might make it untrue. There were other things he worried he might say, about Isaac. I won't say anything, he thought, they are trying to make me talk.

"You may have hurt your neck. You can't move until we get the pictures back."

Crippled, he thought. He felt tears coming into his eyes. He was having trouble breathing, he couldn't get enough air in.

"Do you know where you are," they said. "William. William can you hear me?"

"You've got holes in your lungs. We're going to get the fluid out so you can breathe. It's going to hurt a little bit."

He tried to speak but nothing came out. He wanted to go back to sleep.

"Hold him," they said.

They stabbed him in the side with something and then it went deeper and then they were putting something so deep in him that the pain was coming right from the center of him, he was rushing again, moving, and then he was awake, he could hear himself screaming.

"Hold him," he heard someone shouting and he knew they were talking about him, don't he told them don't don't don't don't and then he felt himself go down and under.

He came up in a different room. Very bright lights. Someone was right over him. They were doing something to his head. Stop, he said, but no sound came out. Stop, he said, but his lips wouldn't move and there was something over his face. He tried to move it but he couldn't. His arm wouldn't move. They were doing something to him. He could smell something, it was burning hair, they were doing something to him. He's awake, said someone. I see it, someone else said, and then he felt the tingling rush up his arm. I have felt this before, he thought, and then he was under the water again.

*   *   *

When he came up the third time it was dark. He remembered not to sit up. He looked down at himself and tried not to move too much. In a bed. Blankets on me. There was an IV bag hanging on one side of him and a window on the other with yellow light coming through it, he thought there might be houses outside. There was another bed in the room and someone was snoring. Quiet, he said, and then he felt guilty. There were machines beeping and chirping. Quiet, he whispered. He couldn't see the machines. I will sit up. They can't stop me. He moved and the pain came back everywhere and then he slipped under it.

Stay down. Stay down, he thought. Move your toes. He couldn't see his feet. He tried to move his arm but it wouldn't go anywhere, he looked and saw it was handcuffed to the bedrail. There was a deep pain in his chest and sides but he could breathe now. They got my head all wrapped up. He touched it. Something sticking out of my head. There was a tube, a plastic tube coming out of the back of his skull. Stay down. After a minute it occurred to him: I am alive.

6. Isaac

When he walked into the door there was a cop behind the desk, the short Asian one from the night he and Poe had been caught at the machine shop. He was drinking coffee and looked like he'd been up for days.

"I need to talk to Chief Harris," said Isaac.

Ho looked at him. "He isn't available."

There's your excuse, thought Isaac. But then he said, "I see his truck out there. Tell him it's Isaac English."

Ho got up reluctantly and disappeared down a hallway. Isaac watched: *your last chance.* But he knew he was not going to leave. There was not another way to do it.

Then Ho came back. "Door at the end."

Isaac went down the hall alone and knocked on the metal door and then, he didn't know why, opened it before he heard an answer. It was a big room and something was strange about it, the same cinderblock walls and fluorescent lights as the rest of the building, but the furniture was all wood and leather and there were paintings hanging on the walls. Harris was sitting up on a couch, a blanket around his shoulders. He was pale and disheveled and one of his hands was taped with a splint.

"You're back in town."

"I'm turning myself in."

"Whoa," said Harris. He put his hand up to stop Isaac's speech, stood up slowly, clearly in some pain, and walked to the door. He checked outside and then closed and locked it. "Come sit." He motioned to the couch. Isaac sat down on one side, Harris on the other.

"Billy Poe didn't kill that homeless guy," Isaac said.

Harris looked stricken. He sagged back against the cushion and closed his eyes. "Please don't say anything else," he asked quietly.

"I'm telling you the truth."

"No, you're not."

"Billy and I were—"

But Harris leaned over suddenly and took him by the shirt, as an older brother might, and put his hand so as to nearly cover Isaac's mouth. His skin was pale and damp-looking and Isaac could smell his sour breath.

"The district attorney just called to tell me that those two men you were in that factory with were found dead." He let go of Isaac and sat back toward his side of the couch. "All three of those men are gone now, Isaac. The only people from that night who are still here are you and Billy Poe. You understand?"

"What happened to them?"

"It could have been anything," said Harris.

They sat in silence for a long time, it might have been minutes, until Harris got up slowly and went to his desk and opened a wooden box, taking a long time to peer into it before removing a cigar. "You don't smoke these, do you?"

"No."

"I need one." He cut the end off and lit it and stood by the open window. He seemed to be collecting himself.

"I don't know if you know this, because when I went to your house to talk to you, you had already taken off. They charged Billy with killing that man but it now appears they'll have to let him go. And you they've never heard of and I'm guessing that since Billy hasn't given you up yet, he probably won't ever, especially once his lawyer hears about these new developments. Which I'll call her as soon as we're done here."

"When did he get locked up?"

"I don't remember exactly. Last week sometime?"

"What was he charged with?"

"He was charged with killing that man," said Harris. "With murder."

"He didn't say anything?"

Harris shook his head.

Isaac was quiet a minute. "I'm going to leave here," he said. "I should probably go live with my sister in Connecticut." He was surprised to hear himself say it. But it felt right.

"That's a good idea," Harris told him.

"So what happens to Billy?"

"Probably after a month, give or take, they'll have no choice but to release him." He walked away from the window and took a pen and a notepad from his desk. "Listen, you start feeling bad about something, you come see me. I'm going to give you my cell number and my home number, too, just call me and I'll meet you."

"I don't think that'll be necessary," said Isaac. "I think I feel fine."

"You did the right thing, you know that? I wish I could give you something for coming down here, because I don't think I've known many people who would have done it. But now . . ." He shrugged. "Time for you to go home."

*   *   *

Isaac felt himself walk out of the office, down the steps, and onto the road toward town. The clouds were beginning to move. He was halfway through town and nearly to the river when it occurred to him that he'd decided to trust Harris. The others as well. He would try that and see how it turned out.

A few blocks more and he crossed the old railroad and stood on the bank in the reeds. His mind was quiet. He stood watching the sun on the slow river, he knelt and put his hand into it, the ripples growing out, there was light on the dome of the cathedral and the windows of all the houses, a pair of terns headed for open water and soon that would be him, gone.

7. Harris

He watched Isaac leave, shutting the door politely behind him. He wondered if he would be able to keep quiet. It all could have been a disaster. It might still be.

He hadn't told Isaac that Billy Poe had been stabbed and nearly died, after refusing to see his lawyer for several days. A different person than you thought. Grace didn't know yet. He could not be the one to tell her. He could feel his head begin to swim but sooner or later the DA would come around asking and he would have to get himself in order. His fingers ached and the pain was radiating up his arm, the wound on his rib cage refused to close, it ought to be stitched but tape would have to do.

He had to get up. There was a story to get straight about where he had been last night, he needed to go over the truck with a Q-tip. New tires, probably. The tires—that was being too careful. Maybe not. Hell hath no fury like a spurned lawyer. He grinned at his little joke and then felt a lightness come over him. Both of those boys were worth saving, he thought. That is something you wouldn't have known.

Ho hadn't called in relief—he'd stayed the entire night himself. He'd known something was happening. All of them, he thought. All of these people. Harris knew he had to get up but it was two days since he'd really slept, the sun was coming in the window now, he'd been waiting for it, it was easing across the floor, it was moving so slowly he watched it inch across every grain of wood, he would rest another minute and feel it on his face. Then he would start his day.

8. Poe

He knew he'd been in the hospital for a while but it seemed like he was waking up for the first time. It was daylight and hot in the room, there was a parking lot outside his window and on the other side of the parking lot there were houses and an old man watering a planter box.

A woman, a nurse he guessed, opened the curtain.

"Here I am," he said.

"You're lucky," she said. "You lost so much blood your heart stopped. You're lucky you're young."

"I'll trade you anytime you want."

"We were worried you'd have brain damage."

"I probably do, but it ain't from that."

She smiled but went on checking things.

"Did I say anything while I was out?"

She shrugged. She didn't know what he was talking about.

"What's going to happen to me?"

"They want to take you back but we're keeping you a few more days. You can't move around too much, you've got too much stitched up inside you."

"Am I going back to Fayette?"

"You're going back somewhere," she said. "But I doubt they'll take you back there."

"Can I have visitors?"

"No," she said.

"Can I call my mother?"

"Maybe tonight." She started to walk out. "There's a state policeman outside the door. Just so you know."

9. Grace

Later that day there was a knock at the back door. She was lying on the couch. She hadn't eaten in three days and she hadn't heard any car come up the road.

There were footsteps at the back of the trailer and a short sturdy man appeared in the living room, taking note of her on the couch, then making a circuit of the house. She didn't recognize him. He went in and out of all the rooms before returning to stand next to her. Here it comes, she thought. This is the one they sent for you.

"I'm Ho," said the man. "I'm a friend of Chief Harris."

She stared. He wasn't wearing a uniform.

"I hear you have family in Houston."

"Where's Bud Harris?"

Ho shook his head. "He's a busy man."

She felt a wave pass over her and then fade again. She closed her eyes.

"Has anyone else come over here, or tried to contact you?"

"No," she said quietly. "You're the first person I've seen."

"That's good," he said. "That's good news."

"Would you tell me what happened?"

Ho cleared his throat and glanced around the room. "Your son is going to be fine," he told her. "But you can't stay here."

"When do I leave?"

"Tomorrow morning at the latest."

"You know I haven't talked to my brother in years."

Ho shrugged.

"Can't I see Bud?"

"You have to pack now," he said gently.

She nodded. She was beginning to smell food very strongly.

"He said I ought to bring you something to eat."

"He would."

"I used to hear him talk about you."

He knelt next to her and he must have noticed how dirty she was, she was suddenly conscious of it, but he didn't react. He lifted her gently and got a pillow behind her. He took a small container from a bag.

"Here," he said. "Nice and slow."

"I don't know if I can."

But when he brought the food to her lips, she opened her mouth to accept it.

★   ★   ★

She stood looking out the window a long time, there was nothing moving, a quiet cool night. She closed her eyes and she could see her son walking, it was summer and the road was baked and dusty and he reached the end and there was nothing left. He was looking out over things, it was all gone, the trailer was a burned shell, even the trees around it had burned. Poe stood looking for a long time and then he was walking back down the road, toward a new place. Making his way toward her.

Acknowledgments

I am blessed with an extremely supportive family and for that I will always be grateful. All my love and thanks to them: Rita, Eugene, and Jamie Meyer; also Alexandra Seifert and Christine Young. Many other people were crucial to getting this book into its final form: my agents, Esther Newberg and Peter Straus, my editors, Cindy Spiegel and Suzanne Baboneau. Dan McGuiness of Loyola College, who first convinced me I could be a writer. Dan McCall of Cornell University, who has given me moral support and encouragement for over a decade. Jim Magnuson, Steve Harrigan, and everyone else at the Michener Center for Writers in Austin, Texas. Colm Tóíbín, for his counsel on many matters. Wil S. Hylton. For time and a quiet place to write: the Corporation of Yaddo, Blue Mountain Center, Ucross, and the Anderson Center for the Arts.

In Pennsylvania: Diego McGreevy and the Reverends Beckie and Joey Hickock, who opened many doors in the Mon Valley for me. The United Steelworkers, specifically Gary Hubbard, Wayne Donato, Rich Pastore, Ross McClellan, John Borkowski, John Guy, Andy Kahler, and Jan Finnegan. Paul Lodico of the Mon Valley Unemployed Committee. Finally, I'd like to thank the good people of Pittsburgh and the Monongahela River Valley, whose cooperation and kindness were crucial to the completion of this book.

POCKET
BOOKS

Katie Kitamura

The Longshot

'An extraordinary novel from a major new talent' Hari Kunzru

*Cal was the one. The kid had everything a fighter needed and
if he didn't become a champion then Riley would have no one
to blame but himself...*

Cal and his long-standing friend and trainer Riley are on their
way to Mexico for a make-or-break rematch with the legendary
Rivera, who has never been beaten. Four years ago, Cal
became the only fighter to ever take Rivera the distance, even
though it nearly ended him. Only Riley, who has been at his
side for the last ten years, knows how much that fight changed
everything for Cal. And only Riley really knows what's now at
stake, for both of them...

'Reads the way we imagine the best fighters to be: quiet,
measured, self-assured, always thinking ahead...reeks of
authenticity' *The Daily Beast*

'Hemingway's returned to life – and this time, he's a woman'
Tom McCarthy

ISBN: 978-1-84739-521-4
PRICE £7.99

POCKET
BOOKS

Anita Diamant

Day After Night

Day After Night is based on the extraordinary true story of the
October 1945 rescue of more than 200 prisoners from the Atlit
internment camp - a prison for 'illegal' immigrants run by the
British military near the Mediterranean coast north of Haifa.
The story is told through the eyes of four young women at the
camp, all of whom survived the Holocaust: Shayndel, a Polish
Zionist; Leonie, a Parisian beauty; Tedi, a hidden Dutch Jew;
and Zorah, a concentration camp survivor. Haunted by
unspeakable memories and losses, afraid to begin to hope, the
women find salvation in the bonds of friendship even as they
confront the challenge of recreating themselves in a strange
new country.

'Offers all the satisfactions found in *The Red Tent* . . . rich
portraits of female friendship, unflinching acknowledgment of
life's cruelty and resolute assertion of hope, enfolded in a
strong story line developed in lucid prose' *Washington Post*

ISBN: 978-1-84739-861-1
PRICE £7.99

SIMON &
SCHUSTER

Jeannette Walls

Half Broke Horses

Lily Casey Smith is a sassy, straight-talking heroine for whom saving lives, taming wild horses and beating ranch hands at poker are all in a day's work. Born in 1901, in a dirt house in the rolling gritty grassland of Texas, at age six she is helping her father break horses. At fifteen she leaves home to teach in a town five hundred miles away, riding there on her pony, all alone. Lily handles everything that life throws at her – flash floods and tornadoes, the Great Depression, the most heartbreaking personal tragedy – with immense courage and determination and a wide smile.

The story of Lily's life has been passed down from one generation of her family to another. Now, in the words of her granddaughter Jeannette Walls, who draws on her own vivid imagination and compelling narrative powers, Lily's indomitable passion and spirit will shine through to readers everywhere, in this extraordinary novel.

ISBN 978-1-84737-675-6
PRICE £12.99

POCKET
BOOKS

This book and other **Pocket Books** and **Simon and Schuster** titles are available from your local bookshop or can be ordered direct from the publisher.

978-1-84739-521-4	The Longshot	£7.99
978-1-84739-861-1	Day After Night	£7.99
978-1-84737-675-6	Half Broke Horses	£12.99